LA MORDIDA

LA MORDIDA

JIM SANDERSON

UNIVERSITY OF NEW MEXICO PRESS

ALBUQUERQUE

Acknowledgments

Portions of Chapter 1 appeared as "Above the South Rim," novel excerpt, in *Rosebud,* special edition with guest editor Gordon Weaver, Cambridge, Wis., issue 19, 2000.

Library of Congress Cataloging-in-Publication Data

Sanderson, Jim, 1953–
    La mordida / Jim Sanderson.— 1st ed.
        p. cm.
    ISBN 0-8263-2815-6 (alk. paper)
    1. Mexican American Border Region—Fiction.   2. Border patrols—Fiction.   3. Smuggling—Fiction.   4. Texas—Fiction.   I. Title.

    PS3569.A5146 M67 2002
    813'.54—dc21

                                2001008482

For Sam Gwynn, Renee Smith,
and Jill Patterson for being friends
and giving me good cheer and sound advice,
and for Beth Hadas for being my editor
and giving me a career.

PART I

ABOVE THE SOUTH RIM

ONE

In my rearview mirror were the dark shapes of the Del Norte Mountains. Ahead and to my right, beyond the expanse of mesquite, prickly pear, yucca, sage, and sotol were the more distant dark shapes of the Glass Mountains. I took my eyes from my headlights' beam as best I could to watch a sliver of orange spread over the tops of the distant humps. I glanced in the rearview mirror and saw a shimmer on the dark edges of the closer mountains. I looked again—ahead, behind, and to the right. Then the gleaming orange ball of the sun emerged above the Glass Mountains. They became dull, brown humps at a considerable distance. The sunlight flowed across the flat, thorny expanse, and a half-dozen pronghorn antelopes tried to outrace it. Out early, looking for food, scraggly and hungry, all nerves and fear, they just ran, right up to the barbed wire fence to my right, then up and over it, frozen for a moment in the air, then nearly floating to touch down in front of my car. And I had to tap my brakes to keep from hitting them.

Shifting my eyes from windshield to rearview mirror, I got glimpses of silver purple along the slopes of the closer Del Norte Mountains and of the valleys filling with light and growing gray, then brown, then nearly green. Then the world was filled with light, and I turned off my headlights.

With my aging eyes, if I stared too long, in front of me or behind me, the lines in the distance, the big, panoramic picture, the view that the details made and tourists saw, got fuzzy. Still, despite my oblong cornea, despite my new desk job, despite my white shirt and tie that I now usually wore instead of a green uniform, I hadn't completely lost my ability at tracking the signs. This sunrise was mine; I had caught it. A piece of the world's cosmic time, a moment, was mine—just like those other pieces I had caught out in the Chihuahuan Desert. And I kept them in my mind—just like I kept Sister Quinn's vial of silver-blue liquid in the nightstand drawer next to my bed.

Stretching overhead and before me were the silvery, shimmering power lines quivering slightly in the breeze that had just come up. Behind me, sagging between the outstretched arms of the four-legged steel girders holding them up, the power lines, glistening like silver reins, guided the sunrise down Texas Highway 67, then on down U.S. 90 to my new hometown, Alpine. And besides the sun they brought modernity and its comforts to my new outpost on the edge of civilization. But maybe I wasn't completely modern and comfortable. Maybe I could still squat among the cacti and rocks, squint into the sun, and see tracks emerge in a dusty drag. Maybe I could still catch the flash of a white shirt in a khaki desert and spot the wets. Maybe I could still climb a mesa and get a panorama of the desert a few feet beneath it—"high pointing," we called it. Maybe I wasn't that old. Maybe I could put off bifocals another couple of years.

"Stop this car, you motherfucker," the passenger in the backseat of my Crown Vic screamed. The Thorazine had worn off. I adjusted the rearview mirror to look at him. Lyle Blackwell, his hands cuffed behind him, twisted and stamped his thick-soled boots against the Plexiglas I had installed between my front and back seats. "Hey, you son of a bitch, I ain't done nothing. What the fuck is up with you?" Coming off the drug, he'd be wild, pissed off, and strong. "Stop this fucking car."

"You don't want another shot. Coming back from being brain numb hurts like hell," I said over my shoulder.

"You got no legal rights. What are you doing? I ain't done nothing."

The chipped concrete picnic table came into view. At one time the picnic table had had a corrugated iron roof over it, but a strong wind had curled the iron back so that its curlicue edge looked like the front tread of a sleigh. U.S. 67 wasn't U.S. 90, with its traffic, so the state never fixed the roof over the picnic table. No one ever stopped here. Most motorists never even noticed it. So this was the spot where I would drop my "suspects."

I pulled off the road, and Lyle Blackwell's voice grew high and shrill. He almost sounded like a girl cussing me. I opened my door and could hear my boots crunch the gravel as I stepped out. For a moment I stopped and breathed and looked around me. The scraggly desert was fully lit now—no humidity, no trees, no softness—all distinct edges, shadow and light meeting. My eyes, not the desert, made fuzzy edges. The October air was dry and cool. You could see a long way and breathe deeply and feel the air freshen your lungs. We were above the south rim. It was high desert, mountain pastureland. It wasn't as rough as the true Chihuahuan Desert below the south rim. It wasn't as barren—not as many oblong rocks sticking out of the earth, not as many thorns. Thicker brush and cacti grew out of Trans-Pecos caliche and up the sides of several mountain ranges that tourists and state officials referred to as the Davis Mountains.

I opened the door to the backseat, and immediately Lyle Blackwell swiveled on his butt, his feet flailing in the doorway. His boot heel came straight at me like a fist. I pulled my face to one side just in time. "Lyle, if you kick me, things are just gonna be worse for you."

"Fuck you."

I reached in and caught his boot, but my hand slid down its shank, and I came up empty-handed. I straightened up, and Lyle just kept kicking. "Okay, Lyle, let's suppose you kick me. Then you stomp the shit out of me. What are you going to do? Run handcuffed into the desert? How long you think you'll last?"

"You son of a bitch, I'm innocent."

"Or suppose I do take your handcuffs off and you escape, where are you going to go?"

"I didn't do it."

"Do what, Lyle? I got no idea what you're talking about." I reached in again, and again Lyle swiveled and kicked at me. I jammed myself into the door opening, and Lyle got a knee up under my chin just as I grabbed his belt. I tasted the copper of blood in my mouth, a taste that I got when I anticipated a nine-millimeter bullet slamming into my body. I got ahold of his belt and yanked on it. His cowboy belt buckle gave way, I tugged, the snaps in the fly of his jeans popped, I pulled harder, and his jeans were a wad around his boots.

"You bastard, you bastard," Lyle yelled, and tried to kick, but with his pants around his ankles, binding them together, he had to flail at me with both feet. His western belt snaked through a couple of loops and dangled beneath his rhythmically kicking bound ankles.

"Lyle, Lyle, you're caught. There's nothing you can do. Now you can only hope for a good lawyer. Accept it, Lyle."

"Fuck you, you cocksucker. You pig. You fucking Nazi bastard. You can't just pull me out of a whole 'nother foreign fucking country."

"Jesus, Lyle." My patience was going. I needed to be going. So I exhaled, reached into the door opening, grabbed what I could, and tugged. Lyle plopped out of the car and landed with a hard thud on his butt. He rolled and grunted, his pants still around his ankles, his white Jockey shorts growing dirty. I straightened up and swung the tip of my boot into his gut. Air came up out of him, and he sucked in to get some more. As he gasped like a fish fresh out of water, I dragged him to the picnic table. I swirled him around, pulled another pair of handcuffs out of my back pocket, clamped one end around his wrist, then clamped the other cuff around the steel girder between the concrete legs of the picnic table. I stepped back and raised my hands as though I had just roped and tied a calf.

Lyle got some of his air back. "Look, okay, okay, look. There's no way you can get me. I'm innocent. I'll get off. No one can convict me. Let's just save the trouble."

Lyle writhed and spread dirt over his bear thighs and his Jockey shorts. He looked down at himself. "Jesus, at least pull up my pants."

"What? And risk getting kicked again?"

"I promise. I'll be still. Pull up my pants."

"Like you promised before?"

"Come on. Pull up my pants. I'm innocent."

"Lyle, I've got no idea what you're accused of. I've got no idea why I picked you up. And if you recall, I warned you to stop kicking at me."

"Shit, shit," Lyle said. "Luna. Goddamn Luna."

I knelt in front of Lyle. "Who?"

Lyle squirmed and twisted until he could see me. "I ain't telling you nothing." He now looked as though he was going to cry.

"Luna who?"

Lyle just twisted and moaned. "I'm just talking about the moon."

I straightened and breathed in some air. I was actually at a moderately high altitude, much higher than the Chihuahuan Desert around Presidio, where I used to work. As a result the air seemed clear and clean to me. Where I now lived, in Alpine, I was higher still. That's how it got its name, from the old railroad workers and cattlemen. It would have been a nice morning if I didn't have a half-naked hoodlum squirming in front of me and handcuffed to a concrete picnic table. I walked to the car and reached into the backseat and came out with Lyle's backpack. I twisted to face him. I reached into the backpack and pulled out a small nine-millimeter pistol—the preferred weapon of young, desperate thugs like the young backpacker who shot me. "This doesn't look innocent." I held up the pistol.

"Fuck you." I dug around past clothes and felt a wallet. I pulled it out—the usual: Texas license, $200 in twenties, social security card. I folded the wallet and jammed it back into the backpack. I reached in again and felt some folded papers. I pulled them out, and Lyle rolled his head away from me.

I had picked him up, early in the morning, still dark, as the bars in Ojinaga's boys town were washing the dirt, spilled liquor, piss, and puke off their wooden floors. This was the first time I had accompanied Trujillo on the actual apprehension of a criminal. Before, I just picked up the drugged, handcuffed, or beaten bad guy on the bridge. Trujillo—my informant, my partner, my fellow soldier in the war against drugs—had approached him as an Ojinaga policeman came up beside him. The Ojinaga policeman jabbed the needle into him to make him a slobbering idiot. We stuffed him into a cop car and drove to the Mexican side of the international bridge. I walked to the American side, retrieved my car, and, with a customs agent beside me, drove to the Mexican side. Then Trujillo, the Mexican cop, the customs agent, and I transferred the glassy-eyed, drooling, weak-kneed Lyle to my backseat. Because I knew them, because of my special task force, the customs station agents had let me drop my gun off at the station. They returned it to me when I pulled back up to the station. And then I started for the pickup point.

One of the papers in Lyle's backpack was a notarized form. I read it. It was a marriage "form," notarized but not sanctioned by a county judge. "What's this, Lyle?"

"Fuck you."

"You really ought to try to come up with something better." Lyle Blackwell was notarized to be married to somebody, but the line for the bride's name was blank. The notary's name was Dorothy McFarland.

"Lyle, this isn't legal." I waved the form in front of him. He turned away from me. "How much did you get for this?"

He didn't answer me. I unfolded another paper. The same form, again with the bride's name blank but this one notarized by an Eduardo Suárez. And a third paper, a third copy of the form, again notarized by Eduardo Suárez. I folded two of the forms back up and stuffed them into the backpack. I folded the third and stuffed it in my shirt pocket. "Hey, hey, that's evidence," Lyle yelled.

"Well, then you ought to be glad I took it. I'm hiding evidence for you. You're innocent, remember?"

Lyle started a stream of cussing, so I shut the door to the backseat and stepped in behind the wheel. "Good luck, Lyle," I said, started my car, and pulled away. A few yards down the road I pulled off the road and waited. In about five minutes a Texas Department of Public Safety car passed by me; the officer nodded, and then he pulled off at the picnic table. He got out, looked down at Lyle, then knelt by him to unlock the handcuffs with his key. I didn't know the officer. I didn't know that the DPS would be by to pick up Lyle. But now he was out of my hands. I had done my job.

I eased my Crown Vic back onto the road and pointed it toward the juncture of the Glass and Del Norte Mountains, now my mountains, becoming distinct in the morning light. They weren't as ugly as those squat caved-in domes the Chinatis, as San Antonio Peak, that I gazed at from my cabin at Cleburne Hot Springs Resort, or as the jagged-tooth edges of the old domes that you saw off El Camino del Rio—Texas 170. I now had prettier mountains to look at. They seemed inviting, not mean.

I was pushing fifty and no longer saw the need to stay prepared, fit, or attuned to the desert. I wanted softness, some gentleness. Because of where I came from, I had earned Alpine. I no longer dreamed that I was a puma chasing some prey or that I was a lizard dragging my sagging belly across hot rocks, my cold blood absorbing the desert heat. The dreams that Sister Quinn gave me— when, ten years ago, she dragged me to safety, to life, to a new existence after a hiker with a backpack full of marijuana had gut shot me with his nine-millimeter pistol and left me dying—just went away when I left the desert around Presidio and got beyond Sister Quinn's broadcast frequency.

But my new mountains and the new softness of my life couldn't help me escape everything. Now I woke some nights from a dream that was a replay of a memory—the image of blood and brains spraying out of the side of Vincent Fuentes's head, and then the movement of the Paso Lajitas boys dipping their white handkerchiefs in the pool of his blood draining from the exit wound, and then the sound of Sister Quinn's voice as she begged me and the world for forgiveness, mercy, and grace.

We were in Paso Lajitas, and Vincent Fuentes had raised a tiny pistol to his head and begged me to take him across the river and arrest him on American soil so that he could do American time, not Mexican time. The Mexican government wouldn't execute him, but the gangsters and corrupt officials he had played certainly would. When I refused, he pulled the trigger, and I went a little crazy. But that was several years ago, and I would get better.

Fuentes had known me. He had become a part of my life without my knowing it. He had been a priest, then a professor, then a political activist, then a revolutionary. Youthful, promising, "a pretty boy," he had a future, but somehow he spiraled into becoming a drunk, a cokehead, and a criminal. He had coaxed Pepper to stop smuggling refrigerators and start smuggling guns into Mexico. And then he had gotten Pepper to accept Mexican-made illegal pharmaceuticals as payments. And he had gotten Sister Quinn to believe that his mules were political refugees from Central America so that she would help guide them across the border. Lately I had to guard against thinking about him, because sometimes he talked to me.

The sun was fully up, and I could make out the valley and arroyos in the clear, dry distance. They were scars that seemed to absorb the sunlight until they lightened into every shade of gray, then into brown, and then into a dirty green. From this distance the shrubs and trees on the sides of the mountains—the mesquite, which was replaced by cedar farther up on the slopes, which in turn was replaced by the first barely visible piñon pines—made streaks of richening and darkening color. In those mountains was clear cool air that let you sit out on a porch all year long, not like the sun-baked desert lowlands along El Camino del Rio, Texas Highway 170—the place I had come from.

Because I had "captured" Vincent Fuentes (and because I had busted my best buddy and roommate, Pepper Cleburne, for smuggling drugs to this country and refrigerators and guns to Mexico), I had become a hero in the Border Patrol. So I became the agent-in-charge at the Presidio station. As agent-in-charge I no longer squinted into the sun, looking for signs. I no longer sat up nights. I no longer squatted during daylight under some scraggly plant or ledge to have a little shade. Mostly I made schedules, talked to locals, became a better politician. And when the Marfa sector headquarters decided that it needed a public relations director, my name came up. And my life became softer, gentler. I got one of the most coveted jobs in the Border Patrol, assistant chief patrol agent.

I had a master's degree in history. My reports were well written. I got along with a variety of people on both sides of the border. I was able to clean up real good. So I became a promotions man for the Border Patrol. I wrote news releases, held press conferences, answered questions, wrote narratives about our budget. I wrote speeches for Sector Headquarters Chief Billy Sosa. I moved to Alpine, existed mainly in an air-conditioned office and home, got a dress uniform for formal affairs or public appearances, and mostly wore a tie rather than the green uniform. The only thing to show me off as a Border Patrol agent was the badge and pistol.

U.S. 67 curved into four-lane U.S. 90. Moneyed people lived in Alpine, so the state made sure that 90 into and out of Alpine was well paved. Farther east, toward Del Rio, and farther west, toward I-10 and El Paso, it turned into a desolate, forgotten highway. I turned down 90, felt the rise in the road, and watched as the Davis Mountains came closer to me and became my mountains. Then the ground leveled. I slowed down. The sheriff and the police chief had officers strictly enforcing the quick reduction of speed from seventy to fifty. Alpine was safe. I glanced on either side of me—at the horse barn and dilapidated old ranch house. I raised my eyes to look at the mansions blooming up around my valley. U.S. 90 split into two one-way roads, and off to the right, welcoming me to town, were the old buildings of Sul Ross State University. That's right, I lived in a town with a college, and a McDonald's too.

I wasn't supposed to know what Lyle was wanted for, but it was an easy guess. In Mexico, a notario has almost as much power as a lawyer. So a notarized document is impressive as hell in Mexico. A down-and-out, poor girl's daddy or brother might pay a year's salary to get her married to an American. Instant American, no green card, no visa. Then a coyote would show up and offer to get her across the border to her new husband. Of course the document wasn't legal, the husband wasn't obliged, and no one would prosecute him, so he was off the hook and could "marry" another girl. Of course she owed money, had to pay it off, and so became cheap labor for a booming economy, or a prostitute, or a small-time, street-corner drug dealer.

What I didn't know was who wanted Lyle. Of course no one would want him just for signing a bunch of meaningless notarized forms. He had to be involved in something a little bigger. I had done my job, which was just to pick him up and deliver him.

Of course nothing about picking up Lyle was official. It might not have been legal. I turned right off 90 into the main entrance of Sul Ross State University and drove up the snaky road to the top of the campus. Sul Ross perched on this mountain, and from its top you could see Alpine beneath you. I stepped out of the car and breathed in. During October, the best time of the year, in the mornings you might need a light jacket, but by noon the sun would be up. But because we were high, with low humidity, you could find shade and sip your beer and be happy and cool all day long. Even in midsummer, with just a little shade, you could be cool. Try that down by Presidio. Try that anywhere else along the border, anywhere else in Texas. Lyle was part of the deal that I had made to live here. My job was my mordida. But I had earned Alpine. I deserved the softness.

Looking over Alpine from the top of Sul Ross State University was sort of like the high pointing I used to do off El Camino del Rio. I squinted to pick out the details within the fuzzy big picture. The houses were turning out their lights, cars were pulling out of driveways. Soon kids would be walking to school. I spotted the tall pecan and oak trees that hid the old rancher's house where I lived. I looked off to my left to spot the Southern Pacific line. Beneath me, north of that railroad, the older houses were Anglo-Victorian, forties modern with their casement windows, or fifties and sixties cinder block. Above me perched the environmentally conscious monstrosities of new rich people. South of that railroad line was the old Mexican part of town. The houses were original, crumbling adobe or lumber. The area looked like a poor man's Santa Fe. The town was no longer strictly divided: a few young, newly marrieds lived in the south part of town, and Mexicans and Anglos freely crossed the railroad tracks. Anglos and Mexicans voted different, still had squabbles about property or the school district, and fought over who would control the county, but in Alpine at least we finally all seemed to be getting along. I'm half Mexican. I've been getting along for years. It's where I came from.

In this country's war on drugs, several years ago, we decided to make a real war. As a part of Joint Task Force 6, a specially funded joint military and civilian cooperative effort to patrol for drugs, our government sent a unit of marines commanded by a marine colonel to help the Border Patrol stop marijuana smuggling in this area. The Border Patrol knew about the patrols and officially welcomed the help. Then in Redford, close to Sister Quinn's templo, in the wild, mean slopes just north of the Alamendariz onion and cantaloupe fields, a squad of commandos shot and killed a boy herding his father's sheep on a winter morning. Azul Mendoza was spooking the sheep out of the brush and counting them so that he and his father, Gilbert Mendoza, a Vietnam veteran, could drive them across Texas Highway 170 down its slope to the Rio Grande, where they'd have better grass and water. The boy, on this day, sat down for lunch and cradled his .22 automatic rifle across his lap. He heard a hissing rattle, and pretending to be a commando himself, he whirled around and let off several rounds toward the rattler.

The commandos, in heavy camouflage gear, no doubt blinded by their sweat and the Chihuahuan Desert's sun—not the Mojave sun they were used to—thought that this wet was shooting at one of their own. So, trained as soldiers, not as policemen or Border Patrol agents, unconcerned with a warning shot, unconcerned about firing only at the last moment and only when you or a fellow agent or a wet is in danger, they put the boy down.

There was a public outcry. Everyone caught hell for it. And I, as public relations man with the Marfa sector headquarters of the Border Patrol, was the contact between the Border Patrol and the colonel's special unit. People in the area knew me because I was a hero, because I cleaned up good and could speak well, and so I became the spokesman for everybody. I was quoted in newspapers across the state. I appeared in a clip on the national news—my fifteen seconds of fame. The heat went away. Neither the Border Patrol, the marines, customs, the Drug Enforcement Administration, nor

Joint Task Force 6 suffered much after the apologies I wrote, the spins I spun, the explanations I gave. The poor confused young soldiers got off. The colonel shut up. The case disappeared. And I became more of an asset to the Border Patrol and to the federal government than ever.

But we still had a war on drugs. So, while I worked with public relations, I became a part of a new unit, a special task force, a cooperative venture that was to replace the colonel's task force. Over time I met with the sheriffs of Brewster, Presidio, Pecos, and Terrell counties, several DEA officers, and customs agents. We agreed to jointly investigate crimes or stop new ones. Upon my invitation and suggestion, we brought in Colonel Henri Trujillo, newly appointed to the army garrison in Ojinaga. If one of us was missing a couple of pieces from his big puzzle, he might contact another one of us for the right piece. Basically we traded information—for this piece, I'll trade you two of these. For U.S., Texas, Chihuahuan, Coahuilan, or Ojinagan agencies, I stepped across agency and national lines. I made phone calls. I did favors. I cut through the red tape that wrapped around the fingers of U.S. and Mexican officials. They in turn would help me—if I needed it. I developed my own sources—friends, names, associates, contacts—and sometimes for federal money, sometimes for a favor, sometimes for looking the other way, they would tell me what they could.

Three times now somebody, somewhere, wanted someone out of Mexico for something. So they would find someone in my task force, and then I would get a call from Henri Trujillo. I could get back and forth across the border. No one would check my car. I was a respected Border Patrol agent. So Trujillo would subdue the person somebody somewhere wanted and meet me at the border, and I would leave him handcuffed somewhere deserted for somebody to pick up. An old private eye from Midland who specialized in getting people out of Mexico told me about this trick. My white Crown Vic was just like the Border Patrol's, but it had no green stripe, no official emblem. It was mine. The Plexiglas between the front and back seats was mine too. So what I did on my special trips wasn't an official part of my job with the Border Patrol. I gave the federal, state, and county agencies "deniability."

I felt bad about leaving Lyle without his pants, but he had pissed me off. I hoped that whoever picked him up wanted him because of his notarized marriage licenses.

After one last look at what I had gained—Alpine—I walked back to my car, slid under the wheel, and closed my door behind me. Pepper Cleburne and my mother expected me for breakfast, and then Pepper and I had to descend back into the desert, back to Sister Quinn's templo, for Ignacio's funeral.

TWO

I turned down Sixth Street toward my home, a slowly evolving renovation of a long-dead rich rancher's city house—all Pepper's idea. Since he had gotten out of prison, he figured that Cleburne Hot Springs Resort—a resort in the middle of the desert—was a bad idea but that a bed-and-breakfast in a town like Alpine was a great idea—more people, closer to a real highway, U.S. 90, limited expectations on his part. As I cruised down Sixth Street, I waved in the general direction of my neighbors, the Alpine police station. Yes, I lived across from a police station; no more drugs being stored where I lived. I was a Border Patrol agent living with an ex-con still on parole across from a ten-man police force in a small, isolated town. It was probably the safest place in Texas.

I turned on the corner of D Street and pulled into my huge lot, parked under one of the large pecan trees that marked the border of my property. The renovating of the old carriage house, which the late rancher built just as he bought his first car, was taking shape. The old bricks were being replaced with new ones that looked old. The old tiled roof was mostly replaced with expensive new imitation tile. The new private bathrooms were installed. We had two guest rooms upstairs and another two downstairs.

Behind the carriage house was a tennis court. Pepper had disgraced his family, had shown that he couldn't hold on to a buck, had lost money on two different ranches, had drunk too much, hadn't succeeded in turning an old hot springs resort from the thirties into a tourist trap, and finally had gotten busted for drugs, so his daddy left him just enough to help him get started after he got out of prison. Pepper had seen what this old house in Alpine could become, so he made a down payment and then, first thing, with the help of a few locals, built himself a tennis court. He had taken up tennis in prison.

As I stepped out of my car, I felt the sleepiness that I had been pushing out of my head; I turned slowly to breathe, to feel the high desert's early fall air in my lungs. And I saw Pepper running toward me with the sun behind him and the shadows of the pecan trees stretching in front of him.

I turned my wrist up and over in front of my face to see my watch. "Kind of late for you to just be finishing up."

Pepper panted, "I'm getting like you public officials. I need more sleep." The truth was that Pepper hardly ever slept.

He trotted toward me, stopped, bent over, straightened, and breathed deeply. The chest of his sweatshirt was soaked through with his sweat. "Where were you? I thought you were going to start jogging with me."

"I had a job to do."

"Bullshit, you just like getting fat."

Pepper huffed some more. Since he got out of prison, his short, bandy, horseman's legs had gotten muscular, and he started working out with my junior Olympian weight set. He had lost four inches from his waist in prison and was determined to keep it off. I had gained four inches. Since he had gotten out of prison, he seemed to want to shave his whole body. His cowboy's waxed mustache was gone; he had some clippers, shears really, that he cut his hair with, so what hair he had on his balding head stuck out like the barbs on a prickly pear. He no longer chewed tobacco and sliced open beer cans to spit in. He wouldn't drink more than two beers at a sitting. He had a pair of "dress" boots, but he mostly wore jogging shoes. The only thing left from before I sent Pepper to prison was the diamond stud in his earlobe.

"I was hoping for some breakfast."

Pepper circled his arms. "Your momma is cooking it."

I walked with Pepper toward the back door. "You trust her in that stainless steel industrial-strength kitchen you been spending our money on?"

"She's learning. Someday she'll cook as good as me."

"And I wonder why I'm getting fat."

"I cook healthy now. No more chili and ribs. Low fat. No cholesterol. You're eating what's good for you."

"God save us from health nuts."

"Prison rehabilitated me."

We came in through the back delivery room, where Pepper had installed two deep freezers. If all the grocery stores in Texas were wiped out, we could survive for years. Pepper stomped and slipped one jogging shoe off, then the other. Then we walked into the kitchen, which was filled with the smell of coffee, chopped onions and peppers, toast, frying eggs, and turkey bacon, and for a moment, I stood still, like Pepper, because both of us kind of drifted back to mornings at Cleburne Hot Springs when Pepper and Ignacio (and sometimes two whores), and, there for a while, the last great love of my life, Ariel, would gather in his dining room and eat mounds of fried eggs, bacon, frijoles, warmed tortillas, and sliced tomatoes.

Pepper reached into one of the refrigerators, pulled out a carton of orange juice, and began drinking it right out of the carton. "Save some," I said.

I stepped through the kitchen and into the dining room. My mother had insisted on renovating the dining room first. It was the most important room for a bed-and-breakfast, she said. A wooden table stretched down the length of the long dining room. The wood floors glowed in the light that came in the one large window. Charlie appeared, still in his long pajamas, house shoes, and robe. Charlie was my mother's boyfriend.

Then my mother appeared, and the light caught her golden tan. It had taken me until middle age to figure out that my mother was an attractive Anglo lady. I just then began to figure that at eighteen, my Mexican father must have been attracted to her first because she was so teeth-itching good-looking and second because she was a rich white girl. And it wasn't until my middle age that I regretted that after their breakup, while my mother dedicated long years to running her father's clothing stores and while my father dedicated himself to drinking himself to death, Sandra Beeson neglected men. But she was making up for it. In her sixties, my mother decided to spend my inheritance on making up for lost time.

Charlie sat down and looked up at my mother like a puppy, like a boy, and my mother, teasing him, flowed around the table with her open thin silk robe flowing behind her. It was immodest, especially around Pepper and me, but my mother showed off her best asset to Charlie: her shapely legs. I was looking at fifty sneaking up on me, and my mother was looking at seventy, but I believe she had convinced Charlie that she was no more than ten years older than me. Sandra Beeson was the only child of a rich man, and as such, though she worked hard in her father's and then her own business, and despite her brief marriage to my worthless father, she had the time and the money to pamper herself and preserve her best features. "Beeson" was my mother's maiden name. I kept my worthless, Mexican father's name, "Martinez," with the accent left out so it was easier to type on military and government forms.

"Dolph, Dolph, you're late," my mother said.

"I'm sorry," I said, and sat down, straight, back rigid. Sometimes my mother still called me "pretty boy," just as she did when I was a child.

"I was showing Charlie what we're going to do in the sitting room," my mother said as Pepper came in, still sweating, with a plate of omelettes and another of turkey bacon. The sitting room was the old kids' room. The old rancher and his relatives put all the children in a small room that opened to the dining room on one side and the living room on the other. On each door of the children's parlor was a small, ornate, wooden gate that kept them in their parlor. Even though we had no kids in the house, my mother liked the wooden gates, so she was scrubbing and varnishing them along with all the rest of the ornate wood in the house.

"Chow," Pepper said as he put a plate in front of me and another in front of Charlie.

Charlie let his glance leave my mother to look down at his plate. He turned to me. "Good morning, Dolph." Charlie had been a TV producer. When he retired, he didn't have the money to settle in Santa Fe, and he didn't have the fortitude for a Montana winter, so he found this isolated place in a temperate part of Texas that a few Yankees and Californians had discovered. He built a modest mansion on some property south of town but spent several nights a week with my mother.

My mother came out of the kitchen with a round tray stacked high with plates. She had learned how to balance a serving tray on her palm just like a waitress. She expertly lowered the tray, bent over it, and unloaded it: a coffeepot, plates of biscuits, bowls of jelly, a butter server. As she raised up, she gave Charlie a little peck on the cheek, and he caught himself pulling away from her but checked himself. Pepper emerged with utensils, and then he and my mother served Charlie and me, as they always did, in practice for the guests who would eventually check in. I was like a guest in my own home.

We ate silently, hungrily, greedily, sucking down coffee to wake us up, using biscuits to scoop chunks of my mother's and Pepper's special "Trans-Pecos Omelettes" onto our forks, and we chatted about the weather, the school district raising taxes, the renovations yet to occur. And then I turned to Pepper. "Pepper, you know a Dorothy McFarland or an Eduardo Suárez? They're both notaries." Pepper raised his head. His eyes darted about, he kept some food stuffed in his cheek—just as he used to keep a wad of tobacco. "No, no. They're probably not from around here."

My mother, while raising her fork to her mouth, started to speak, then held the fork poised in front of her mouth. "There's a Dorothy McFarland who works at the courthouse."

Both Pepper and I looked at my mother. She was becoming a local.

When Pepper got out of prison, we never talked about the fact that I sent him there. It was as though the whole incident was inevitable, something chancy, something almost evil that just got ahold of both of us. He had a few dreams left from the days before—like this bed-and-breakfast, like his suggestion that I retire and we form a private detective agency to investigate cattle rustling in the area. I listened, and considered, but gave up on the idea. It sounded good, but given his record, if Pepper suggested it, I just couldn't fully trust it. Since I had sent him to prison and since we never really talked about it, I gave him some of my savings and took out a loan against a chunk of my retirement to help him fix this place up. I was ready for a loss.

When I told my mother about my new investment, she scolded me, and then she came up from the Rio Grande Valley. Since Pepper could always charm women, just as he had charmed all his ex-wives, she listened to his schemes, then put in some of her own money and began to help him. She decorated, shopped, ordered, sanded, painted, and hammered. And the plan was to name it for her, Beeson's Alpine Bed-and-Breakfast.

Four days a week, at ten-thirty, Pepper walked down the street to Reata, the swankiest restaurant in the area, and prepared their lunch menu and then their dinner. Pepper had been rehabilitated in prison. A good reputation, a good lawyer arguing that Vincent Fuentes had led him astray, a couple of names that Pepper had dropped, and a plea bargain got Pepper out of the mandatory maximum sentence that was a part of our "war on drugs." After three years in maximum security, Pepper got into minimum security. There he took up tennis, jogging, and cooking. While still in the minimum-security prison, he became the head cook and managed the menu and the entire kitchen. Pepper came out of prison trim and employable, knowing how to cook cheaply and well for a lot of people. The parole board gave him three years' parole under the watchful eye of a Border Patrol agent and let him reside in a county other than the one where he committed the crime because of me, the better job opportunity, his family, and potential psychological treatment centers. He was, to the state, my responsibility, so he was pegged as low risk. To check up on him, his parole agent sometimes just called me. And if he made it one full year without a violation, which he would, because he was my responsibility, he'd be dismissed from parole. He had just three months to go.

But really, I was Pepper's responsibility. Because of where Pepper and I came from, I moved to Alpine to get soft, find some comfort, to grow fat. Pepper came out of prison lean, watchful, expectant. He would have now made a better agent for the Presidio area than I would ever be again. It was as though Pepper had discovered evil. And evil to him was the unexpected, the accident, your fate waiting for you. *It* might be an accident, but because of what you were, where you had been, its effect on you was all your own. He wanted to be prepared for *it,* for he was sure *it* would come again. In his own way, he had become just as spooky as Sister Quinn.

My mother sat down and reached under the table. I could tell by Charlie's quick smile and glance at her that she had reached under the table to pat his thigh. But she couldn't keep her hands anywhere for long, for even when sitting still, my mother seemed to move. "Upstairs would really look nice in Pergo, but it's so expensive. Tile is cheaper, but not as 'western.' What do you think, Dolph?"

"What's Pergo?"

"It's wood," Pepper said.

I don't know why my mother was asking me. She knew I had no opinions. "Whatever, Mother. Whatever."

"It's your inheritance."

"Hell, spend it all." That sort of talk always pissed her off.

"Dolph, someday you'll find more to your life than this Border Patrol silliness."

Her eyes opened wide, and she mockingly slapped at smiling Charlie. He must have reached under the table to goose her.

This is how I lived. I should have lived alone. Dede told me that eventually I had to live by myself. But I felt that it was my turn to take care of my mother and Pepper. With the renovations, the Pergo floors, the tennis courts, I hoped that my money would hold out longer than their wishes.

THREE

I put on my one suit, and Pepper put on his. I slicked my hair back, and Pepper ran his shears over his head and shaved the rest of his face. We iced down a cooler full of bottles of beer and put it in the backseat of the Crown Vic. We had decided that my Crown Vic was more appropriate for a funeral than Pepper's Ford Bronco. When he went to prison, Pepper had left his '55 orange and white Chevy with a nephew, who had driven it to Ojinaga. The kid went to several bars, then took a taxi out to boys town, then returned to find Pepper's Chevy nearly gutted. It was beyond repair. No one would have harmed it on this side of the river. I heard from Sister Quinn that people out along El Camino del Rio and up toward Candelaria burned candles and prayed for Pepper's car. Some said that it was blessed for Pepper but not for his nephew.

We drove across the flat plain of grazing land to Marfa, then south on 67 toward Presidio. As we dropped out of the high pastures, down off the south rim, the short piñon turning to mesquite, then to yucca and century plants, a world of rock and thorn, I got a little spooked. Since I had come out of this place to live in comfort in Alpine, I always got a little spooked when I descended into the Chihuahuan Desert. I couldn't just plop a wrist over the wheel and steer. My hands squeezed the wheel of my Crown Vic. This mean country, these badlands, made me tense up. And because I hadn't actually patrolled in years, I feared that I had gone soft, that I could no longer make it, that I would just dry up and sizzle out here. The desert would win.

I felt the old relief, though, of being inside a car, a protective bubble of climate control. But I was an old hand and knew that all those thorns could pierce this bubble, and then Pepper and I would be on foot and fighting the desert. It was what this damned placed demanded of you. You could never completely relax.

Pepper had his forehead pressed to the side window of my Crown Vic. When he got into this area, Pepper got surly. We were headed toward the territory where he had his most conspicuous failure: Cleburne Hot Springs Resort. And we were going to the funeral of Pepper's closest companion for most of his life. Ignacio had worked for Pepper's father and was that wayward uncle or illegitimate father (sort of like old Miguel Martinez, my absent father) who you weren't supposed to listen to. Of course Pepper had listened to Ignacio, and when Pepper got to be an adult, then Ignacio unwisely started listening to Pepper. So of course I had busted Ignacio, too. He was in on Pepper's refrigerator, guns, and dope scheme. But I had given him a chance to run to Mexico, a chance Pepper didn't have. Ignacio didn't take that chance. But because I testified as to how much he helped me bust Pepper, because the old ladies and Mexicans in the jury looked at this tiny brown man dried up by the sun so that he looked like a raisin but held himself straight and never flinched, and because they heard him try to shift from Spanish to English to explain himself, they didn't convict him. And the lawyer that Pepper made his daddy hire for Ignacio didn't hurt.

"That Pergo flooring sure would look nice throughout that old house, but goddamn, that stuff is expensive."

"That goddamn house. Remember, you're spending my and my mother's money this time."

"Put together, y'all got more money than God."

Pepper leaned his head against the window and looked out at the scenery again. "You know, there's all sorts of rustling going on up in the Davis Mountains," Pepper said. "The only last by-

God true cattle country left, except for those goddamn icebergs in Wyoming and Montana. And goddamn it, a couple of smart fellas like us could make a small fortune stopping rustling." When he got surly, Pepper started thinking about all the shoulds and shouldn't haves that he normally suppressed. "And from Fort Stockton to Midland, oil field detectives make a good living tracking those laser-embossed parts numbers."

"Pepper, in less than ten years, I can retire and do nothing if I want."

"Well, that's the pussy way out. Just like you government officials. Once you get on that government or state tit, you can't get off again."

"We've had this discussion."

"And you just don't listen. You goddamn bleed green for the fucking Border Patrol. There's money to be made, and you want to chase wetbacks. You ain't ever gonna stop them. You ought to do something useful with your life and chase after brands on cattle or oil field equipment."

This conversation was going nowhere. Pepper and I both knew it. "You're starting to sound like you did when you wanted to build that pool in a hot springs in the middle of a desert where nobody ever came or even knew about."

"That's why I needed that pool. The tourists would have come if they'd had a pool."

"That's why you went to jail."

Pepper turned to look at me, and we both knew that we were approaching a point we might regret going beyond. "Shit, Dolph. Just shit. That's all old-timey history. Just like Ignacio. And he's dead."

I looked up from the road at Pepper. He looked like he might cry. "But you wait. Me and your momma are going to make a bed-and-breakfast that'll rival that goddamn Gage Hotel. And people'll drive in, from all over the world, rock stars and shit, just to stay at our place."

"Just like that place out by Shafter where Mick Jagger stays."

"That guy don't know shit. Your momma and me are smarter." I don't think that Pepper really believed what he said, not since he got out of prison. But he needed something in front of him, some idea, some hope, even if prison taught him that most everybody's grand schemes come to naught. "Course, what you and me really need is some kind of woman."

"That's true, but you're ugly and I'm married to the Border Patrol."

"And poor fucking Ignacio's dead."

"I'm sure we'll get what we deserve."

Pepper turned to look at me and chuckled, "And then some too, if our past records have anything to do with it."

We pulled into Presidio, and I honked at the old cinder block Border Patrol station. No one answered my call, but I just felt like letting them know that I was around. We picked up 170 and drove toward Redford. We turned off a newly bulldozed road and drove between the Alamendarizes' onion and cantaloupe fields. Pepper could tell that I was getting a bit antsy. "Like old times," he said. It was noon, and all the clouds had vanished, so the desert had that clear, intense, midday brightness—all sun and glare, no shadows, all distinct shapes, like the world's spotlight was turned on Sister Quinn's cemetery for Ignacio's funeral. Thank God it wasn't summer.

I pulled up into the gravel-and-dirt parking lot surrounded by mesquite and lechuguilla. Pepper and I stepped out of the air-conditioned bubble of my Crown Vic and followed the trail toward Sister Quinn's templo. Once you drop out of the high grazing land above the south rim, the temperature rises maybe ten or twenty degrees, even in winter. Here on the very edge of the Rio Grande, just downriver from the juncture with the Rio Concho, the air picks up a little bit of humidity from the river, less than a hundred yards away, so you have, sometimes during the year, the worst of all possible worlds. But the river, that humidity, and the relatively flat land in between several mountain ranges make this tiny strip the only irrigable land in the area. People have sweated and dried up in it for centuries, trying to grow a crop. And not so long ago, the Apaches and then the Comanches raided the area to steal what the poor, sweating agricultural people grew.

Pepper stuck his finger between his shirt collar and tie. Because he was lifting weights, his neck was getting bigger. "What the hell would Ignacio care if I didn't wear a tie?" He unbuttoned his collar button and loosened his tie. I noticed that my own summerweight wool suit was biting at my crotch. When I used to live here, I would drive up the south rim and start shivering. My blood had turned cold, like a desert lizard. But now I was used to the pleasant, cooler temperatures in Alpine. I wondered why we hadn't all just shriveled up out here.

We got up to Sister Quinn's templo, and she appeared at the front door. This once big woman had lost a lot of weight, but her midsection formed a swollen pooched-out half dome, like you could poke a fork in her and she'd just fizzle. That poofed-out belly seemed to have caused her cheeks to become ashen, her once enormous breasts to shrivel and droop, her skin to take on a yellow tint. The locals probably took Sister Quinn's jaundice as some sort of sign. They whispered among themselves that sometimes she turned into a tecolote and perched at night on the tombstones of the dead. Sometimes, she had admitted to me, she felt herself fly, and she wished she could still flap her flabby arms and get airborne.

Sister Quinn wrapped her arms around me, and I could smell her rancid sweat and the staleness of her breath. In our last conversation, she had told me that she got chills, then hot flashes. "Hello, Barbara," Pepper said.

"Dolph. My Dolph," she said as she squeezed me. "So good to see you. And you too, Pepper." She turned to Pepper. "It was Ignacio's time."

I twisted out from her grip. She was already working up a good sweat. A few of her red curls were pasted to her forehead, but she didn't have her usual tennis hat pulled way low on her head. She wore a dress that she must have found to fit her when she was fat, but now it flowed around her and sagged. And she must have been cold because she wore a blue jean jacket over the dress. "I'm so glad you're here. Of course you'd come, though, of course." And she clapped as though she were a child, fingers straight up and coming perfectly together. I had busted her umpteen times for leading wets across. The last time, they carried Vincent Fuentes's Mexican-made pharmaceuticals, and then the archbishop in El Paso just got tired of her ass and excommunicated her. "How old was Ignacio, Pepper?"

"I've got no idea. He was born old."

Gilbert Mendoza, with the permanent frown the death of his son had put on his face, stepped up to Pepper and shook his hand. Pepper looked at me as though for guidance. "Another sad day," Gilbert said. "So many sad days." Pepper slapped at Gilbert's shoulder with his other hand and nodded. Gilbert's ill-fitting suit was double-breasted and a mixture of mostly polyester and wool. You could tell because over the past twenty years the polyester had disintegrated to leave a shiny gloss in the thin fabric. I felt a slight breeze lift my hair, and I walked past Gilbert. Sister Quinn was at my side. "He lived a full life, his way," she chattered as Gilbert and Pepper followed us.

We walked silently past Sister Quinn's templo, down a trail that sloped gently toward the river and then opened up into a small cemetery. Through her good works, through the belief or superstition of the locals, Sister Quinn had gotten first a templo, then a cemetery. Gilbert Mendoza had scraped out the area with a bulldozer. The Alamendarizes contributed carpet grass. Long runners of St. Augustine spreading out from a small patch struggled against the desert. No city or county recognized it, but officials looked the other way when the first person was buried. It would soon have its second body.

When we got to the mostly level cemetery, my dress shoes stopped rolling in the gravel. I hunched my shoulders, then relaxed them to feel more room in my own suit. Pepper's expanded chest stretched his suit's jacket. My expanding middle stretched my suit pants.

Father Jesse Guzmán from St. Mary's over in Presidio stood between the tombstone for the only other inhabitant of Sister Quinn's cemetery and Ignacio's freshly dug grave. This time Gilbert Mendoza got ahold of a backhoe and scooped out a site for Ignacio, who was in a cheap pine box kept over the grave by two boards lain across the hole. Sister Quinn looked up at Father Guzmán, and he smiled. He should have nothing to do with her, but nobody in his congregation paid much attention to the fact that this buena curandera was no longer a member of the Catholic Church. When she started to sniffle, I lightly put my arm around her waist. I didn't want to bruise or puncture her swollen torso.

The other grave belonged to Azul, Gilbert Mendoza's boy, the shepherd boy that the marine special unit had killed. Azul had been hers. Because she had saved his life when he was born a blue baby, Gilbert let the boy stay at her templo. I used to feel sorry for Azul because I found out about the strange imaginings that went on in Sister Quinn's mind, and thus in the templo, and thus the strange psychological abuse she put the boy through. Sister Quinn must have made poor Azul unfit for normal people because of her visions, beliefs, weirdness. But he followed her around like a puppy and, even as a teenager, he never lost interest in helping her.

I felt an arm around me, one more slender than Sister Quinn's. I turned to see one of the few Border Patrol agents shorter than me— Dede Pate. Dede was in a knee-length black dress that gave her length and curves that I didn't know she had. And she had on a hat, a woman's hat with a long brim, not a Border Patrol cap or the kind of wide-brimmed straw hat from Ojinaga that I told her to wear. I lowered my head as she raised up on her toes to kiss my cheek.

As I pulled away from her, I noticed that some more wrinkles had worked their way into the corners of her eyes—too much squinting into the desert glare and heat. She kept her arm around me, and I kept my arm around Sister Quinn, and Gilbert and Pepper stepped to the other side of Dede, and from out of the brush a man and a woman emerged.

The man was Socorro. He took off his battered straw hat, and his ponytail fell down over the sport coat that was too small for him. His jeans didn't match the sport coat, and his boots were scuffed and dusty. He hadn't trimmed the thick mustache that hung over his top lip. He spotted me and slowly nodded. The woman who was with him had on a loosely fitting print dress, but unlike Dede, she didn't wear heels but hiking boots, and she had a straw cowboy hat pressed down on her head. As she got closer, Pepper whispered, "Sylvia." I glanced over at him. "She works over at that general store and bookstore in Terlingua. She's Socorro's latest 'old lady.'"

She was a rebound. I had heard about this really classy woman, not Sylvia, some lawyer running away from some disgrace, coming to Lajitas and, miracle of miracles, dating Socorro. And now he had Sylvia.

Then from out of the brush another man emerged. He just kept emerging. His head, big as a basketball, was bald except for tufts of hair above either ear. He wasn't so much fat as just thick, a series of bulges of muscles, sinew, and flesh from his neck to his waist. As he walked, he held his hands at his sides and turned his palms backward. Like Pepper, he seemed to be fighting against his tie.

Sister Quinn had left me and was closing in on the other group. She hugged them all, took the large man's hands, and pulled him toward us, leaving Socorro staring at his boots and grumbling. Then Socorro pulled Sylvia toward us.

When they got to us, I noticed that Sylvia's face had the red-tinted tan that Anglos get after a year or two in the desert. The hat was an attempt to delay the inevitable. If she was one of the few who lasted, then she'd burn her skin into a wrinkled brown. If she was with Socorro and if she got to know him well, she wouldn't be around long. The large man was my age, but his skin was smoother, white, no tan, except his head was sunburned.

Father Guzmán starting speaking, the standard stuff, but it wasn't a Catholic service, some hybrid. And when he finished, Sister Quinn stepped between the two graves and started her usual sermon about the poor of the world and our debt to them. We owe our lives to those who suffer for us. And they do suffer. For everything we are, we have, they suffer. While she spoke, everyone except the new woman dropped their eyes and squirmed, including Father Guzmán. Her voice, though, lost steam. She could no longer bellow at her audiences as she used to. She couldn't finish this tangled thread. It would have to stay in her mind. The big man stepped toward her, and she looked at him and then at me. "In a just world, in a Christian world, grace and mercy just have to trump justice," she said with the last of her strength.

The big man with the tufts of hair over his ears walked up to one side of her, and I walked to the other. The big man and I squinted at each other, and Sister Quinn's head swiveled between him and me. "Boys, boys."

We all eased toward the new grave. And as Father Guzmán stood at the head of the coffin, ready to bless it, the men gathered around it. Sister Quinn turned her back to us and walked to her shack. Where she used to waddle with force and determination, she now took small, delicate steps, as though she might crack a rock if she stepped on it too hard. She gave one last look and then went inside.

Socorro and the big man each grabbed a rope and hoisted, Socorro straining against his, the big man idly pulling with one hand. Not trusting Socorro's strength, kneeling into the dirt and gravel in our good slacks, Pepper, Gilbert, and I worked the wooden slats out from under the coffin. The big man waved me off, but Gilbert and Pepper helped Socorro lower Ignacio into his grave. Then Gilbert left us, we walked back to Dede, and Gilbert Mendoza, in his twenty-year-old twice-a-year church suit, chugged from around Sister Quinn's templo in one of the Alamendarizes' bulldozers.

Dede held my hand as Gilbert Mendoza pushed the mound of dirt back into the hole that now had Ignacio in it. Dede pulled off her wide-brimmed hat, yanked a clamp from her hair, and shook her head. Her hair fell into the short pageboy that I recognized. When I went to Marfa sector headquarters, I recommend Dede as my replacement as agent-in-charge at the Presidio station. Dede, my student, became the youngest agent-in-charge in the Border Patrol and one of the few women agents-in-charge. She was a public relations dream. She was also a good agent.

"How you been, Dede? You found any kind of a man?"

"A part-time one," Dede said, and I pulled away. I had expected her to complain about the crude types she had to choose from in the desert. Because of our slim choices, Dede and I sometimes fell into bed together. Dede smiled, then her smile stretched across her face. She beamed. "It's going nowhere, but . . ." She shrugged.

"Anybody I know?" I asked, thinking that of course I'd know him. There weren't many people down here.

"No," Dede said. I put my arm around her to congratulate her, console her, to hold on to her.

"She won't get away, Dolph. You can let her go," Pepper said, and walked up to us, his forehead beaded with sweat, his suit jacket in a wad up under his arm.

"You're damn right about that," Dede said. "The Border Patrol ain't sending me nowhere."

Gilbert Mendoza backed his two-year-old pickup truck up to the grave site. He had bought the pickup with the money that came his way when Azul was killed. He got out of the cab and lowered the tailgate, and Pepper ran to the truck. The big bald man, moving gracefully and forcefully, ran to the truck too. I moved toward it, but Dede tugged on my arm. "They have enough help." The three of them shimmied a tombstone out onto the tailgate. I watched the material in the big man's suit strain against his bulging back. Then the big man took off his jacket and grabbed either side of the tombstone and, with Pepper and Gilbert guiding him, got the tombstone to the head of Ignacio's grave. The other two men helped him lower it into place.

"Dede," I said in a tone that indicated business, and Dede turned to me, her smile gone, ready for business. "Have you stopped any wets, women, claiming they were married to an American? Maybe they might have had some kind of documentation."

"We had one. About two weeks ago. Shipped her to Marfa, and then I think she went on to Pecos for questioning. She kept yelling 'esposo' and waving this form around."

"A notarized marriage license."

"Yeah."

"I hope you jotted down the name on the form for me, honey."

"Dorothy McFarland." Dede stepped away from me and toed the dirt with her high-heeled shoe. "Dolph, I knew you'd ask. I almost know how you think." She looked at me now with soft eyes. "Can you tell me what you think?"

"I don't know enough to think anything right now."

Socorro walked up to us, pulling Sylvia after him. He stopped in front of me and nodded. He pulled Sylvia up to him, dipped his head toward her, then looked at me "This is Sylvia Walker."

Sylvia looked out of the corner of her eyes at Socorro but mostly sized me up. And I sized her up, a plain woman in her midthirties, something of a free spirit, she was one of those who drifted down looking for some tame adventure.

She let go of his hand and stuck out her hand, and I gently shook it. Sylvia took off her hat, and a tangle of her brown hair fell over her ears.

"I'm Dolph Martinez, and this is Dede Pate." I motioned to Dede.

The woman shook Dede's hand. "We've met," Sylvia said. Socorro stepped up to her and put his arm around her. Socorro liked to show his women off, especially to me. The big man stepped up and towered over Socorro.

"I understand that you are a friend of Sister Quinn's," the big man said.

"We go back a ways."

He smiled and stuck out his hand. "I'm Pooter Elam."

"Sister Quinn's a remarkable woman," Sylvia said.

Pooter squinted and shifted his eyes between me and Sylvia. "Another three or four trips down, and I might understand what she's talking about."

Socorro muttered, "Shit," just loud enough for Pooter to hear.

"I've known her for over ten years. She still makes no sense to me," I said.

"You've got to tilt your head sideways," Pooter Elam said. "She makes her points in sort of Socratic riddles." Socorro scrunched his eyes and took a sideways glance at the man.

Socorro turned his back to all of us and walked away. Sylvia dutifully followed, and then Pooter nodded and walked away.

"What the hell are they doing here?" I asked Dede.

"Sylvia lets Socorro spend the night in her condo at Lajitas once in a while, and Pooter comes down to visit Sister Quinn." Dede smiled as she mentioned Pooter. Dede walked away from me and wobbled in her heels. Whoever invented high heels never saw a desert animal's paw, hoof, or toes. I watched Dede wobble up to Pooter's side. He put an arm around her, and I thought he might just lift her up. He bent from his side for Dede to give him a kiss.

"I'll be damned," Pepper said. He was suddenly at my side. "Things must have been going on while I was doing my time and you were becoming an administrator." Pepper's sleeves were pushed up past his elbows.

"So that's the guy."

"What guy?" I didn't answer Pepper but walked away from the rest toward the templo. Sister Quinn had built the chapel and her shack next to it with help and donations of lumber, furniture, and labor from the locals. I had thought that once she was excommunicated, the locals would stop helping her, stop coming to her "services," which were little more than tirades about the unfairness in the world. But unlike the archbishop, the locals saw no discrepancy between being a nun and a curandera. So when she was excommunicated, the locals simply stopped using her as a nun and starting using her just as a curandera. And I think, in a way that they didn't know, Sister Quinn used the locals.

I stepped into the dark shack (I no longer knocked) and looked around for Sister Quinn. My eyes hurt from trying to adjust to the dark, but then I caught sight of her lying in her queen-size bed. I had bought her that bed. "Here, Dolph. Here."

"Why don't you turn on a light?"

"In the daytime? And waste electricity?"

I walked to the side of the bed and sat down beside her. I reached into my pocket and pulled out the glass vial with the silver-blue metallic liquid in it. She had given it to me when she had hiked high up a canyon and was busting one of our sensors—something she did so that the Border Patrol couldn't catch what she called poor political refugees. Then she had thought she heard shots. And as she waddled down the trail, surprisingly agile for a fat lady, she found me and pressed the vial against the nine-millimeter wounds in my belly. She told me to hold it and pray. She said the vial would save me. Then she pulled me down the trail, out of the dead zone so that she could use my radio, and called for help. It's an old story, a part of her beatification by the locals and my reputation among them.

I held the vial between my thumb and finger, and it caught

some of the light in the dark shack and reflected it. "Do you think this still works, Barbara?"

Sister Quinn raised up on her elbows and chuckled. The bed creaked. "Dolph, it never worked. Only faith works." I palmed the vial and put it back into my pocket. "What about your faith, Dolph?"

"It's getting better," I said. I could smell her sickness, a rich but rotting smell, like peaches going bad.

"I haven't given up on you. Someday you're going to do something great for the world."

"You thought Vincent Fuentes was going to do something great for the world." I was immediately sorry that I had brought up his name.

She giggled and clapped, fingers straight up, like a child claps. "You know, he said you were like him. I always said you were like him."

"He was trying to con me. He was a great con man. He would have said anything to get me to take him to this side of the river."

She smiled. "And save him from sure death in Mexico."

"I know, mercy, grace."

"You should have listened to him." I squirmed when we got into this discussion. Like most of our discussions, the one about Fuentes went in circles, but just like the others, it delighted her. I think that this discussion was what gave me my memories, or dreams, of Fuentes's brains bursting out the side of his head.

"He didn't even believe what he said."

"But if you really listened, if you really paid attention, you could hear what he could have been. He was like you, Dolph. He got confused and then lost. But sometimes, his heart came back and he meant what he said." Sister Quinn smiled at me. "You should try to pay more attention."

I dropped my head, forced a smile, then raised my head to show her my smile. "Who is with Socorro?"

"She's been here about a year. But you should have seen the woman who broke his heart. Joan was her name. No, on second thought, you shouldn't have. She would have broken your heart. She was Pooter's friend, a lawyer, and she got involved in some sort of disgrace or scandal, and when she ran away, Pooter followed her, for a while. She was beautiful, Dolph."

"So what the hell was she doing with Socorro?"

"I guess she was just lonely or needed a man around. She was a real help, though, when Arnie Patton died."

"That old drunk up around Terlingua. The one walked around with that enormous backpack with the American flags on it."

Sister Quinn nodded. "I felt something was wrong." She stopped and smiled at me. "That's right, sometimes, I can still feel others' pain."

I always got uneasy when we talked about her powers. "I thought you quit that."

"You have no choice over something like that. So I felt his suffering, so I drove out there, and Socorro flagged me down. He was stumbling across the desert." Sister Quinn had started to believe what the locals said about her: that she could feel someone's pain and then would turn into an owl and fly to them to help them. Then Sister Quinn giggled. "Socorro was bringing a twelve-pack of beer to Arnie, and he was on a horse, and he found Arnie in the middle of a stroke, and he got on his horse and tried to gallop for help." Sister Quinn laughed hard now and clapped. "And the beers started blowing up, and his horse threw him."

I laughed too. "I wish I had seen that."

Sister Quinn's mouth dropped out of the smile. "But Arnie died, and then the other two, that woman, Joan, and the big man, Pooter, showed up. Socorro had called her, too. We waited with Arnie until he died. He was in a coma, but I think he felt us around him."

"What happened to that woman, the one who was with Socorro?"

Sister Quinn smiled and shrugged. "She ran back. Arnie's death scared her." Sister Quinn shook her finger. "But not Pooter. He keeps coming back. And he stays with me or Socorro . . ." She looked at me. "Or Dede."

"I noticed." I smiled at her. "He's good for Dede."

"You'd be better. But he's good for me and to me. He just got this Ph.D. in philosophy. And he's so full of questions. We have these talks. He's a good man, Dolph. Consider him."

I reached out toward her, but then let my hand fall until it was palm down on the bed. Sister Quinn laid her hand on top of mine. The bed creaked. It was a cheap mattress. I should have mail ordered for a better one. Her red curls were hanging on her forehead. When she smiled, I got a glimpse of that chubby Irish Catholic New Jersey girl who must have been so lively, so smart, and so weird. As I feared, she could read my mind. "Mostly I have bad days now, but once in a while, I have a good one."

I couldn't look at her. "How about today?"

"It started out all right. But then I gave the oration and got tired. Oh, Dolph . . ." She started a laugh that never fully became real, so that it sounded desperate. "I'm in the middle of a desert, and I can't tolerate the light. It's just so bright, it hurts." I looked up. She had lost her laugh and her smile. "So I stay in here in the dark a lot more lately."

"Barbara, I'll fill out the forms. I'll put in the application. You're a prime candidate."

She chuckled. "What kind of a nun would I be if—"

I interrupted. "You're not a nun. Not anymore."

She clicked her tongue as though scolding me. "What good would my faith be if I took some other person's chance for a life?"

"What makes their life better than yours?"

"Nothing—in fact, I am assuming some superiority for myself."

"So let the hospitals and the government decide who gets the liver transplants."

"So someone dies because I live?" She turned her head to one side and smiled at me. "And this way I still have a choice." We didn't get into these arguments as often, but she still was able to prod me into considering some dark voodoo shit if I didn't keep my guard up. When Sister Quinn and I started our discussions, I was the voice of reason, or normalcy, of my mother's Episcopalianism. "Remember, Dolph? Remember about the pain?" She was the voice of voodoo, witchcraft, and paganism.

"Let's not rehash that."

She smiled. "So we whipped each other. And in that pain, didn't you see, maybe just for a moment, more clearly? Didn't you feel the weight of humanity, the suffering of the world?"

"No, I felt stupid, and I felt pain."

"Well, Dolph, then let me have this pain because I do feel more with it."

"I wish you would finally consider my criticism, take my advice, listen to me."

"Oh, Dolph, I do listen to you." She was right. I had finally convinced her to trust my judgment about the evil shit that can go across or come across the border; she had begun to trust me. She was one of my informers. My visit and our mourning for Ignacio were about to turn into business.

"Barbara, there are some people selling poor Mexican girls false marriage licenses. The girls get here and they end up prostitutes or worse."

"See, now I listen to you about such things." She lay back on her pillow, and her mattress whooshed like it had sighed too. Her bed creaked some more.

"Do you know anything? Have you heard anything?"

"Some talk. Gossip. No more than what you said."

"Do you know a Dorothy McFarland?"

"No."

"Eduardo Suárez?"

"He has a little bar between here and Presidio. It's just off 170."

"I know the place," I said, and smiled.

Sister Quinn let the mattress absorb her weight, and she sighed again. I stood so that I could see her. One bead of sweat formed on her forehead. "I sometimes just hurt."

"Like now."

"It's not real bad today."

As I was about to beg her once again to apply for a liver transplant, Father Guzmán stepped into the shack. "Oh, excuse me. Excuse me, I didn't know that you had a guest."

"Come in," I said, but smiled at Sister Quinn instead of looking at him. Her eyes rolled toward him, then back to me. She smiled.

"Barbara," Guzmán said. "How are you doing?"

"Pray for me, Father Guzmán," Sister Quinn said, and because I was used to her, I could hear her sarcasm. Father Guzmán, with his thin mustache with long stringy hair going in odd directions and his flat, bridgeless nose that let his glasses slide to the very tip of his nose, looked and acted like a boy. He had never been a match for her. He had been ordered to shoulder the authority of the Catholic Church and warn her that helping illegal aliens, some of whom had smuggled drugs, was counter to the church's desires. He couldn't convince her. He couldn't argue with her. So even now, this excommunicated nun still ordered him about.

Guzmán smiled, for, like me, he knew her strength and his limitations. He sat down on the bed and patted her hand. He started to massage her forearm. "That feels good," she said. Then she looked sheepishly at him, then me. "But what hurts the worst is my feet." Father Jesse Guzmán, the priest from the new modern church in Presidio, St. Margaret Mary's, began massaging Sister Quinn's feet.

As he kneaded her soles, Father Guzmán begged, "Barbara, I could fill out the form myself. Let the government administer this justice or mercy," he said.

Sister Quinn looked up at me. "See, Dolph? See what I have to put up with?"

"Good luck, Jesse. Good luck, I hope you convince her." I stepped across her shack and through the door into the blinding glare of the sun. She didn't know when, where, or how she got the hepatitis. She didn't even go to a doctor until she started turning yellow and losing weight. Dying like this was sheer nonsense to me but had some kind of logic to her.

I adjusted my eyes to the intense glare of the desert, almost like a sunny day in the snow, and tried to find my friends. Pepper had pulled the ice chest out of his car and was passing out beer bottles. I walked toward them and noticed that Socorro was walking beside me. "You still owe me a hundred dollars."

"It's coming. We have to fill out the right forms."

"You know it's getting harder for me dig up this information. People are beginning to think I'm asking too many questions."

"Soc, I'll try. I'll keep trying to get as much money for you as I can."

"Well, I mean, shit, it's dangerous."

I stopped walking and turned to Socorro. He had shoved his old straw cowboy hat down over his head. He had a cigarette dangling off his lip. His sport coat was in one hand, his beer in the other. The dress shirt that he wore, like nearly all his shirts, had the sleeves cut out, showing his bare, tattooed biceps. "How's Barbara doing?"

Socorro shrugged. "Not good, really. She's a stubborn bitch. Won't listen. What can you do?" I had lied to him and told him that the last money I had given him for information required him to keep an eye on Sister Quinn. I believe that he knew I was lying, but he watched her anyway. Here, in this part of the world, all our histories intertwine.

"What's the deal she mentioned about Arnie Patton?"

"Oh God, it was awful. He died ugly. My former old lady and her bozo buddy and I watched him die. Along with Sister Quinn, that is. Of course, she gets off on that shit." He pulled his cigarette out of his mouth and exhaled smoke. "You should of seen my former old lady. Better looking than that blond bitch broke your heart."

"Did she like it when you called her 'your ol' lady'?"

"You never let up on me, do you, fucker?"

"That's because you never let up."

"So what the fuck am I doing now? I got my heart broke just like you. That's where Sylvia comes in."

I turned away from him, and he grabbed at my bicep. I hung my head. "Socorro, we got a working relationship. That's all. Let's be cordial."

"Okay," he said, slouched, drank out of his beer—his fist wrapped around the neck, his head thrown back. "Sylvia ain't bad, is she?"

"She's a looker. And I hear she lets you sleep in her air-conditioning. What do you know about the other guy?"

"Some ex–football player from UT. Used to follow Joan Phelan, my ex–old lady, the real good-looking one, around. He was like a little goddamn puppy. Kind of like Azul was. Said he was watching over her. Whenever she had the bad political shit fall down around her ears, he was 'there for her.'"

"What bad political shit?"

"Get this. She was gonna be elected senator or governor or mayor or something."

"There's a difference, you know."

"You know I don't pay attention to this goddamn corrupt government. Which of course you work for. And for which of course you hassle private citizens like myself."

"I get my sermons from Sister Quinn."

"So she's found in bed with like the mayor of Austin. And his wife is real pissed. And then come to find out, he donated to her campaign with some kind of funny money. So she's disgraced. Falls into the bottle. Well, the bottle she falls into is in this bar in Austin, and that's where stud boy works, and they're old friends from college, and so now they got this perverse kind of thing going on."

"So you like him, huh?"

"Get this. He's got some kind of Ph.D. in philosophy, yet he works as a bartender. He comes down here on his vacations. He talks all kind of bullshit. Airy, stupid shit. Strange thing is, since he sees her with Arnie Patton, he likes Sister Quinn. He talks to her. They sit around fucking talking about religion or philosophy. Strange shit." Socorro took a long drag off his cigarette and then let the smoke creep out of the side of his mouth.

I was sometimes surprised that Socorro didn't join that crazy-ass Republic of Texas bunch that shot it out with the National Guard up in Fort Davis. He automatically hated everyone in uniform. I couldn't wear mine around him. "You know of anybody selling fake marriage licenses to young Mexican girls?"

Socorro looked me straight in the eye. When he tried to show his sincerity, I knew he would lie. "No," he said.

"You know Eduardo Suárez?"

He sucked in on his cigarette, knelt, and crushed out the orange tip on some rocks. His eyes shifted to the corners of their sockets to look at me. "I've helped you a lot, Dolph. But you and whatever government bullshit don't own me. I still got to make a living. So 'cause you help me out, I'm telling you just stay away from this shit."

"So you know about Suárez?"

"I didn't say that. I don't know shit. Hell, stick all your information up your ass." He stomped away from me. For years I had been paying off Socorro, and I had learned how to interpret his lies. He knew it, so when I got too close, he would leave.

I walked toward the group standing around Pepper's ice chest of beer. I saw him step out of the group and walk toward Ignacio's grave. I veered over to Pepper. He stared at the tombstone. There was no date of birth, no sentiments, just IGNACIO LOPEZ—FRIEND and the date of his death. "Why don't you go ahead and get drunk? I'm the designated driver."

Pepper shook his head. "I'll drink enough. You get fuzzy headed, you can lose control." Pepper sipped from his beer. "You should remember that, Dolph." He sucked at the beer in his bottle to drain it. He raised his forearm to cock it behind his ear, then he threw the beer bottle against Ignacio's tombstone. When the beer bottle splattered, everyone turned to look at us. "So long, Ignacio."

"So have another beer, Pepper. Relax," I said.

"Especially not today," Pepper said, and I turned from Pepper to see Dede kissing Pooter Elam.

FOUR

Socorro, Sylvia, and Pooter piled into his decrepit van and headed back down El Camino del Rio, hugging the Rio Grande, clinging to the side of canyon walls, toward Lajitas and Terlingua. This area around Presidio, the fastest-growing but poorest town in the area, following El Camino del Rio on up to Big Bend, was mostly Mexican. The Anglos taught school in Presidio or scattered around the outskirts of Big Bend. They were either adventurous or running from something—like Socorro. Socorro was probably hiding from some crime. You knew from talking to him that you shouldn't ask. I think that he was an Anglo because he wasn't a native, but you couldn't tell for sure. His dark hair and drooping mustache were turning gray. His skin was burned to a permanent brown, creased with wrinkles. The few natives, Mexican or Anglo, if they got some money, left. The new folks, Anglo or Mexican, were federal employees. Mostly in this area, you were smuggling something, trying to catch smugglers, or dropping out from the normal world.

Dede followed Pepper and me to Presidio, and when we pulled off at the Three Palms Inn for a cup of coffee, Dede pulled in behind us. We stared out the window at orange and purple streaks forming above the Chinati Mountains, a familiar sight to all of us. A little closer to those mountains, on the other side of San Antonio Peak, was Cleburne Hot Springs Resort, Pepper's fantasy and downfall and the last place to ever seem like home to me. Pepper sipped his coffee and growled at the mountains. We had nearly a hundred miles yet to go. "Dede, it's been really nice to see you. Pepper, we ought to get started back."

"Why don't we go look, Dolph?"

"At what?"

"You know I ain't seen it since I got out."

"I've got to go to work."

"Hell, you got seniority. Take a few days off."

"Shit, Pepper."

So Pepper and I drove up El Camino del Rio with the sun setting on the passenger corner of the window and then shifting to the side passenger window, the Chinatis' jagged, mean-looking peaks lighting up for us. For ten years, I had watched the colors of the sunsets on the Chinatis. After so long a time here, people became unfit for life anywhere else. But I had gotten out. And because I had sent him to prison, Pepper had gotten out. Hopefully, we were all saner.

By the time we turned off 170 and bounced over the gravel road to the gate of Cleburne Hot Springs, toward the Chinatis and the far side of San Antonio Peak, the sun had slid behind the mountains and left just a few fine streaks of orange behind it. When I turned onto the gravel road leading to the hot springs, Pepper was out of my car before I skidded to a halt. He walked in front of my headlight beams to the locked gate. I got out of the driver's seat. "It's locked. I've got to go to work in the morning."

"You federal guys always think of your own comfort. Always worried about sleep. You ought to try real work," Pepper said as he felt along the concrete base of the cedar post. "You got a flashlight?" I turned back toward my car. "No, wait." He came out with a key. "My uncle always hid a key or two in the base for the fence post." He slid the key into the lock. "He was trapping coyotes once for their hides. You know, wrap a hunk of bad meat around a big hook and then hang it up in a tree. Coyote eats it, gets hung up, dies, but the coat isn't damaged. Anyway, he skinned and gutted this one coyote, and he punctured the stomach . . ." Pepper pulled the chain from around the post and opened the gate. "And there was the key to the lock on his west gate." I turned back to face my headlights and nodded into Dede's headlights. "My uncle figured that if a coyote would eat a key, he'd swallow a metal hook, so he wondered why he bothered baiting his traps." He hadn't even stepped onto his old property, and he had turned into his old bull-shitting self.

We drove down the grade into the center of the stucco cabins, built in the 1930s when Pepper's uncle got the first idea of a desert resort at these hot springs. The branches of willow trees swished the side of my car. I could tell from the sound of the crunch that some of the gravel was wet, leaks in the plumbing or overflow from the creeks. We pulled up in between the decaying cabins, and I spotted the one where I used to live. Ahead of me was the empty pool, with a tarp spread across it. Pepper was out of the car before I could open the door. "Leave your headlights on." I saw him skipping ahead of me around the edges of the pool to the "entertainment complex" on the far side of the pool.

I stepped out of my car and into Dede's headlights. She cut hers, then cut her engine, then was standing beside me. Pepper felt along the portals of the door of the entertainment complex and skipped a bit on his short legs when he found a key. "Come on. Come on." From the sparse light on the opposite side of my headlights, I could see that Dede's hair had assumed its usual limp hang down the length of her face. Her mascara had been blown or dried away so that it caked in the newly forming wrinkles on her face. Pepper yelled back at us in a gleeful, high-pitched tone. "Be careful of that goddamn pool. Be just like it for one of us to fall in it and break a neck. Be its last revenge." I reached back into my Crown Vic and cut my headlights.

Dede and I joined Pepper in the doorway. Pepper bounced up and down on the balls of his feet, then reached inside and flipped the light switch. The large light fixture in the center of the room lit up. Pepper's uncle still paid for the electricity. "Goddamn, ain't it great!" Pepper practically jumped into the room. Dede and I followed. We saw the door to the kitchen, the long bar to our right, the pool table and Foosball table to our left, the table and chairs in between. Somewhere, floating in a dark corner, was probably Ignacio's ghost—my other roommate at Cleburne Hot Springs Resort. Pepper raced around the room, turning on all the lights. He went through the swinging door into the kitchen and came out, saying, "The refrigerator still works." He looked around. "Oven doesn't, though, no gas. So no heat." As soon as he said that, I shivered just a bit. An October desert night. It could get a bit chilly. "But you could still eat here. I got an electric hot plate." I looked at Dede, then she at me, then both of us at Pepper. Our dark dress clothes were streaked with the salt left from evaporated sweat and coated with dust.

"Pepper, let's get out of here. We both have to go."

"No," Pepper answered, and looked down at his own dirty shirt and slacks. "Let's take a bath."

I looked at Dede. She smiled. "A short one," she said.

We pulled the ice chest of beer out of the trunk of my Crown Vic and went into the main cabin, Pepper's old cabin, the one with its own private bath. Another cabin had two communal bathtubs. We all sipped a beer. And then Pepper looked anxiously at us as he turned the wheel-like valve to the opened-mouth pipe. We heard gurgling; then hot water gushed out of the pipe, filling the air with steam as it filled the rectangular pool-size tub with water. Pepper had the lights out and candles lit and placed around the tub before we could say anything. In the candlelight his eyes sparkled like the dots of light in the hot water, like the reflections in his diamond stud earring. He chugged his beer, peeled off his clothes, grabbed another beer, and jumped into the water, splashing me and Dede. "Come on. I said we were gonna take a bath. It's a cool night, and we got hot water."

Dede smiled at me and then looked at Pepper. "Come on. You still ain't got that little-girl modesty, do you? You never would take a bath with me." Dede beamed. Pepper looked at me. "And I don't know what you and Dolph might of done while he was staying here and I was playing tennis with crooked CEOs and learning about embezzlement instead of drug smuggling. Come on. Get a beer."

Dede reached behind her and unzipped her dress. She let it fall down her shoulders to her waist, then shook her hips to make her dress fall in a bundle around her ankles. She stepped out of her heels and her dress at the same time. Dede's body was hard; all angles, almost no breasts—just symmetrical bulges. She had converted hers from the body of a soft, flowering girl at her most attractive to the body of a woman prepared for being shot at. If she stayed behind a desk, she would develop some softness, gentleness, curves, titties. I felt embarrassed because I was now the fat one. Pepper and Dede watched as this softening and bulging middle-aged man slipped out of his dirty suit. I looked at the scar on my stomach, the one I got when the backpacker shot me. It looked like it was still a suture keeping my expanding stomach from ripping open my skin.

I eased into the water. Dede scooted beside me, and I put an arm around her. And she pulled Pepper to her other side. I caught a glint of light making trajectories across the room and noticed that it was caused by Pepper's diamond stud earring—all that was physically left of the old Pepper, the one who would call whores over in Ojinaga and they'd drive over in their big, ancient, beat-up American cars and then jump into the bathtub with us. Like old times, he was drinking beer. I looked at Dede. "Have you heard about any other women getting stopped with those licenses?"

Dede looked at me and scoffed, "Dolph, you're at sector headquarters. Check around."

"I'll check."

"Of course you will. Oh, Dolph, I'll never be as good an agent or agent-in-charge as you. But that doesn't bother me. Because I'll never be as concerned about it. It's my job. For you it's something else."

"You're goddamn right, it's something else. Dolph wants to be a saint."

"Somebody is luring young women to the country, then, no doubt, abusing them in some way."

"Imagine, poor young Mexican girls being abused," Pepper said.

"Dolph's just concerned," Dede said, and looked at Pepper.

Pepper took a sip from his beer and smiled at the night and the steam and the trajectories of light across the candle-made shadows. "Remember what happened the last time you got concerned?"

I pushed my back against the side of the tub. Pepper had a right to say such things to me. "Dolph didn't know how it would all turn out," Dede defended me. She always defended me, not just when others questioned me, but when I questioned myself— especially then.

Pepper wasn't going to let the point go. "That's my point. You can't tell what you find out."

"This time maybe nobody will be hurt," Dede said, growing irritated. And I was growing irritated too, for Pepper was spoiling this nostalgia.

"I ain't worried about somebody else. I'm talking about Dolph." Pepper swished away from his edge of the tub to see me. He pointed his beer bottle toward me. "Remember the bad shape you were in last time. You lost that woman, put me in jail, made Fuentes shoot himself, so you blamed yourself and your hand started shaking the bourbon out of your glass. You stopped drinking and starting taking antidepressant pills and had to take time off and go see your momma. You're fine at being a cop, Dolph. But investigating gets to you."

I felt like the water around me was beginning to boil. Dede swished to look at me. Way down deep inside me, the same something that made my hand shake the bourbon out of my glass told me Pepper was right. "So if I am so goddamn bad at investigation . . ."

Pepper stopped me. "You're good at it. It just upsets you."

"So why do you want me to start my own private investigator firm with you?"

"'Cause you wouldn't have the Border Patrol, the U.S. Department of Justice, and the welfare of all society counting on you. It'd just be for money. You wouldn't have to worry about any morality. Hell, the only morality would be to solve the case. Find the truth, even if it's ugly or not really the truth."

"Give me a beer, Pepper."

"I learned some things about all of us while I was in prison, thinking," Pepper said as he reached into his ice chest and brought out a beer for me and another for Dede. He handed us our beers, and he started to mumble. "It ain't an evil world, just an unpredictable one. And all we can do is try to be ready—for when we fuck up. We can try avoiding fucking up, but we will fuck up." It was as though the new Pepper and the old Pepper were thrashing around in the water. He looked directly at me. I could tell he was advising himself but addressing me. "You know, Dolph, you shouldn't let the past haunt you. You especially try to avoid fucking up, and because of it, your fuckups hurt you all the more."

And I addressed him but advised myself, "How can you help but let the past haunt you? It's not your decision. It's the past's choice."

Pepper's smile came back. "Well, I guess you just got to get used to being haunted or fucking up." He was through his morose mood and thus felt content to drink.

We all drank two more beers apiece while we let the warm water wash away the knots in our bodies and minds. After about half an hour, he said, "Well, I can see that I'm the odd man out."

"Wait, Pepper," I said.

"We can spend the night. I'll stay in your old cabin."

"I've got work in the morning," Dede said.

"So you got to get up a little earlier. Always sleep with you government employees. If the two of you'd go into business with me and become private investigators, you could set your own hours." Pepper slid his wet legs into his suit slacks, bundled his other clothes, and, dripping, stepped out of the door into the cooling night.

I looked over at Dede. "I've got to get to work, too."

"I guess I'm spending the night."

"I guess I am, too."

We had no towels, so we dried with my dirty shirt. We hopped into the bed and shivered, so we wrapped our arms around each other and pulled the sheet and the old blanket over us.

Dede curled toward me and shivered, and I felt her hard body against mine, her cool thighs against the sides of mine. She could, she had, turned back into a young woman with me, and I wondered if she could do that with anyone else, like Pooter.

"Do you know about Sister Quinn?"

"Everybody along El Camino del Rio knows about her. And

they know that you took her to the hospital and that you paid a part of her bills. Dolph, you can never leave this area. I'm glad you're here. I mean now. Here."

"I would have thought you would spend the night with that Pooter guy."

"He comes and he goes. Sometimes he stays with me, sometimes with Sister Quinn. I think she's hexed him."

"And now you're in bed with me?"

"He's only a visitor, Dolph." She kissed me, and I returned it.

"It feels good to be in bed with you, Dolph." She rested her head in the soft part of my shoulder. "Green on green."

"I wear a white shirt now." Dede bounced her head on my shoulder. "Ouch, Dede."

"Same thing. We're both Border Patrol. We know some things." Dede and I weren't in love with each other. It wasn't like we were dating. And we weren't really using each other. We had become, maybe, a comfort to each other. And in this desert, you need some comfort or you became just a part of the landscape, like a rock, a lizard, a puma.

* * *

I made it to work late, in my dirty funeral shirt, tie, and jacket. And I let Pepper take my car back to Alpine. I went into my office and began opening letters, going over my e-mail, answering what I could, putting a spin on the press releases, the questions, the news copy, and making sure that everything looked agreeable. I didn't lie; I wasn't immoral; I just left out certain facts and maybe reinterpreted others. I knew the value of interpretation and audience. So I was valuable.

I was lucky—I had a window next to my office. And from it, I could look down 67 and see the Marfa Art Institute's property. Tiny Marfa actually had an artists' colony. Artists liked the light and the solitude in the restored World War II armory, so the art institute was the only thriving business in Marfa. Sometimes, for lunch, I liked to wander down the highway and take a walk through the art institute. The artists stared at me, though. Just as parochial as any of the residents, they kept to themselves and distrusted outsiders, especially the Border Patrol. So they stared at this creature, who, they reasoned, could never understand them, and thus, though artists, they refused to understand anything around them.

I was catching up from my work by avoiding my coworkers when Billy Sosa came into the room. The Marfa sector chief, Billy Sosa, as they said, bled green. With green blood, he no longer needed to worry about his Mexican blood and American citizenship. Promoted like me, though, he hardly ever wore green but a uniform similar to mine and other southwestern lawmen: white shirt, tie, big belt buckle, boots, white hat, and a badge. Sometimes, though, when he appeared on TV, he wore his dress greens. He hiked his hip and rested it on my desk.

"You know, there was a guy used to work here looked just like you."

"I had business."

"I thought your business was the Border Patrol."

I spun around from my computer and looked at him. "My Special Task Force business."

"Damn, Dolph," he said, and pulled his hat lower on his forehead. "You're an assistant chief patrol agent. Not many people get to that level. Come back and join us."

"Well, the task force doesn't just answer to the Border Patrol."

"Goddamn, Dolph. You sound like those fucking Feebies. Never a straight answer."

"Jesus, Billy. I'm doing my job."

"I know. Unless you couldn't detect it, I was trying to be serious. Hell, why don't you come back to work for us? We shouldn't be doing this covert spy shit. It ain't the Border Patrol. Come back to work with us."

I leaned back in my chair. I was lucky. I had a cushy ride until retirement. I could almost name my own hours. I had plenty of sick leave. "Hell, I do the Border Patrol's PR most of the time. That's the hard part. Thinking of how to put something delicately so the politically correct people won't come down on us. The Special Task Force work is mainly cush. I just forward mail. Introduce people. It's easy."

"Yeah, but it makes me nervous not knowing what's going on

in my own house." Billy stood up. "But that's my personal preference. Officially the Border Patrol is behind you."

"I know. I wrote the official Border Patrol position."

"Shit, Dolph," Billy said, and left.

Even though I came in late, my mother picked me up early in her year-old Lexus so I could get back to the Alpine courthouse. Dorothy McFarland worked in the vital statistics office—births, deaths, marriages, and divorces. I walked in, waited in her line, and asked for her. She met me at the window, and I recognized her. She had worked with me before. She had always been pleasant and had gone out of her way to help me, but I also remembered her as being jittery. Her name had escaped me. More proof that I was losing it. "Aren't you Dolph Martinez with the Border Patrol?" she asked me.

"I'm honored that you remember me, Ms. McFarland. I'd like to ask you something, though."

She smiled and gestured with her hand toward the files. "I've got the answers."

I showed her the notarized form. "Who asked you for that?"

She stared at the form, then tried to keep her gaze on me and a smile on her face. But first her smile drooped; then she raised a trembling hand to her neck, spread out her fingers, and dropped her eyes. "Dorothy, this is not an investigation," I said. "It's just a question."

She slowly lifted her eyes to see me. I met them, and we held our gazes for just a moment until she again dropped her eyes. Steel gray hair, horn-rimmed glasses on a chain, a high collar, Dorothy looked like your sweet grandmother, but this area could make even your sweet grandmother do strange crimes. "Oh, my," came from between her lips.

I cocked my wrist to look at my watch. "Dorothy, do you get off for lunch?" She nodded without looking at me. "Why don't you let the United States government buy you lunch? And we'll have a civilized conversation about this." She nodded again.

So I took her to lunch. We drove to a little Mexican restaurant south of the tracks. It didn't have a name yet, just a sign saying "Mexican" food. She waited in her seat for me to open her door, and as I let her out I watched her walk ahead of me. She was a small woman in an oversized, formless dress, so that she had no form, no curves. In the restaurant, her big glass of iced tea was in front of her, and she slowly raised a taco toward her mouth, but her hands started to shake, so shredded lettuce fell out of her taco. Her glasses frames came to a swirling point at the corners where the arms connected to the lenses, and a gold chain around her neck connected to each arm of the glasses. Though it wasn't cold, she kept a sweater over her shoulders. Her face showed creases in the thick makeup she wore, and her hair was an unnatural-looking silver-blue, and right above her ear, where her hair should have met her head, was a tiny gap or fold.

It was a wig. Why, I asked myself, would anyone, especially an older lady, wear a gray wig? The sweater, the glasses, the thick makeup, the baggy dress, together with the wig, hid her femininity, as though Dorothy McFarland were trying to look old.

After she ate, she folded her hands and rested them in her lap. "Dorothy, I'd like a little explanation in payment for the lunch."

Again she dropped her eyes and raised her outstretched hand to her throat. But she kept her smile. It too was fake. "I'd like to retire, but I just can't. I don't mean to complain, but I don't have the money."

"And so you got some money for signing the form."

She dropped her head. When she pulled it up again, she had several tears in her eyes. "Years ago, an eternity ago. After my kids left home, my husband, well, well, well." She pulled her purse into her lap, poised her hands above it, and then dug into it. She brought out a handkerchief and dabbed at her eyes. "Well, my husband just left. We divorced. I got the house and the debts. So I got a job at a bank in Fort Stockton. Oh, Fort Stockton was where I was from. Then I heard about this job, so I moved to Alpine. Even went back to using my maiden name. Now I've gone back to my married name. I've been here, let me see, two years. This job, this town is all I have, Mr. Martinez. He paid me a hundred dollars."

"Who is 'he'?"

She dropped her head. "I don't remember his name." It was

almost endearing that she was trying to protect the guy, who was probably Lyle Blackwell.

"What did he look like?"

She touched her face with her fingers. "Medium height, medium build."

"Just one more question. What was your maiden name?"

"I don't want to remember that, that time. And I don't want anyone to know about that time." She lowered her head. "This is a new life for me. I'm born again." She pushed her plate away from her and looked at me with wide eyes. "Am I in trouble?"

"Not with me." I handed her my card. "Call me if you remember anything. Please."

She dropped her head again and nodded. Then she adjusted her glasses and reached up to her cheek and dabbed at the down-turned peak where the wig came down beside her ear. She managed to smile. "I shall never do something like that again, Mr. Martinez."

I dropped her off at the courthouse, and I watched her shuffle back into it. She turned and waved good-bye.

I didn't want to look into this whole affair any further. Dorothy McFarland was hiding something, but it was probably some burning secret that I need not know. As Sister Quinn said, "Mercy should trump justice." As Pepper said, there's this thing inside of me that wanted to know the answer, that made me investigate things that might surprise me and set my hands to shaking. So I fooled myself into being content by telling myself that Lyle Blackwood was guilty, that he concocted the scheme, that no one else need question poor Dorothy McFarland even if she was hiding something, that the case was closed. Justice had triumphed. Evil had been foiled. Let it go, Dolph! But then the Parrs came into my Marfa office.

PART II

THE BATTLE OF CLEBURNE HOT SPRINGS

FIVE

Jerri Johnson had found my e-mail address through a supposedly secure government list of federal employees, and so she contacted me about Lyle Blackwell. I wasn't used to getting such direct requests from the public, so I was evasive. She telephoned and said that she would be in the area and wanted to meet me. I didn't know that she would bring her husband, Joe Parr. They wandered into the sector headquarters and met Billy first. He took them into the lunchroom and had coffee with them. It wasn't until midafternoon that Billy knocked on my door and escorted them into my office.

They were dressed almost the same, she in sunglasses, jeans, boots, and a starched white shirt, he in sunglasses, khakis, boots, and a starched white shirt. She wore a turquoise necklace; he had no tie on, but his shirt was buttoned to the top, the way Pepper and some of the cowboys around here wore theirs. I never understood this habit. Why tighten a noose around your neck when you don't need a tie? When the Parrs walked in, my collar button was unfastened and my tie was loosened. I straightened the tie but didn't have time to get my collar buttoned. Usually, if we have visitors, the receptionist will call us out. But the Parrs, led by Billy, just walked on back to my office. "Mr. Martinez," Jerri Johnson said, pulled her sunglasses off, and stuck her hand out toward me.

I reached across my messy desk to shake this short, compact, muscular woman's hand. "I'm Jerri Johnson, and this is my husband, Joe Parr." I shook the tall cowboy's hand. He was at least twenty years older than she.

"Have a seat," I said, and motioned toward the chair in front of my desk. Jerri shrugged her shoulder to let the straps of a heavy purse slide down her arm. Adroitly she grabbed the straps before the purse hit the ground and lowered it down beside her. I motioned toward the other chair in front of me, but Joe Parr took a chair against the wall. He sat down and crossed one long, thin leg over his knee to let it dangle, the way a woman crosses her legs. Then with his forefinger he pushed the underside of his brim to scoot his white Stetson farther back on his head.

"This is my wife's business, not mine. I'm retired from law enforcement," he said more to Jerri than to me. She smiled back at him. His eyes rolled to the top of their sockets as he stared at the underside of his brim. He took off his hat and rested it, crown down, in his lap, and I saw his silver hair freshly trimmed so that no part of it touched the top of his ears or the back of his collar. He raised his hand in front of his face to grab each temple of his sunglasses. He pulled them off, folded the arms, stuffed them into his shirt pocket—all with one hand. "I called, remember?" Jerri Johnson said, and I remembered checking my computer calendar to see that she had scheduled an appointment. I remembered that she had come all the way from San Antonio, and I remembered that she worked for some private detective firm, maybe her own. I focused on her. Her blond hair was cut short. She crossed her legs the way a man would. Might as well take advantage of having jeans on, I figured she figured. With her natural tan, the uneven kind that makes wrinkles and spots, she looked as though she could have been a Border Patrol Agent. He was more pink complected. She for a moment reminded me of an older Dede.

"Coffee? Coke?" I said, and swung my head between them. They both shook their heads, and I sat down.

"Mr. Martinez, as I said in my previous call, I'm a private detective. I have a client in a little difficulty, and you could help him out."

"I'll tell you what I can."

Jerri uncrossed her legs and leaned toward me. On first glance, you couldn't say that Jerri Johnson was a stunning woman. It wasn't until you saw her eyes that sparkled and begged at the same time that you thought she could be attractive. They were a deep blue, and the blue deepness seemed to have no bottom. "My client."

Joe Parr harrumphed from his seat against the wall. Jerri turned to look at him, scowled, then smiled. "Joe."

"Well, hell, tell him the truth. A man in his position can smell subterfuge." Joe smiled at me. "Of course, he knows what I mean instead of subterfuge."

"Okay, okay." Jerri turned to look at me. "Palo Fuentes is my friend." She turned to look at Joe. "Is that better, Joe?"

"Fine, honey," he said, and smiled first at her, then at me.

Then something way back in my mind clicked. "You're *the* Joe Parr, aren't you?" Joe nodded. "You're that Texas Ranger who arrested Bud Harrelson and shot it out with Fred Carrasco. You were even hanging around at that Fort Davis Republic of Texas silliness."

"That's right. And you're the Border Patrol agent who tracked down Vincent Fuentes and busted his own best friend."

"That's right."

"And I talked to you once when those soldiers shot that poor Mexican boy." He slumped in his chair. "But I'm retired now. I was retired then when those soldiers shot that boy, but the DPS just asked me to help out and ask a few questions."

"I hear that Rangers never really retire. You can still help with cases. You can still shoot somebody."

Parr squirmed and looked at his wife. "Like I said, I was help-ing with those cases. I'm not on this one."

I turned to look back at Jerri Johnson. I felt a little embarrassed. Jerri let her smile spread back across her face. "Palo Fuentes was arrested. He's out on bail now. The reason that he was arrested is that a Lyle Blackwell named him as an accomplice in an illegal-alien-smuggling operation. Blackwell lied." Parr harrumphed. And Jerri frowned and looked at him. "I'm telling the story, Joe. Please."

"Sorry, honey," Joe said, and looked at me and said in a confidential tone, "We're not sure how much is a lie."

"Palo is this old, sick man. He'll die in prison," Jerri said as though to defend Palo to me and Joe Parr. She faced her husband and pounded the arm of her chair with her forefinger to emphasize. "What we do know is that Lyle Blackwell plea-bargained to save his ass. And he gave them Palo."

"Ms. Johnson," I said softly. "Your husband knows the story. Maybe you ought to explain it to me." She turned to me and almost began to giggle. "Sorry," she said, then she turned to Joe Parr. "Sorry, Joe."

Joe Parr sat up straight in his chair and leaned. "The point is that Lyle Blackwell was set up. He was arrested just so he would talk." Then Parr pulled his head up, realized that he was stealing his wife's performance, looked at her, then crossed his legs. "You got something to read in here?"

Jerri was now pressing her hands against the front of my desk. Her voice almost sounded desperate. "And you were the one who picked up Lyle Blackwell."

"But we ain't accusing you of being in on this," Parr interrupted. "That would be too easy."

Jerri dropped her head, looked again at her husband. She pressed her hands against the side of my desk and leaned closer to it. "Why don't you ask Lyle Blackwell?" I asked.

Jerri waited for Joe to respond, and when he didn't, she said, "Because he's dead. Found hanged in the Bexar County jail." I had relaxed because I was starting to enjoy the Parrs, but I tensed because I didn't want to push further into what I was already involved in.

"Smells, don't it?" Parr asked.

And just as quickly Jerri added, "Somebody set up Lyle just so he'd give up Palo." Jerri looked at me with those inquisitive, attractive, pleading eyes and said, not in an accusative way, but almost as Sister Quinn would have said, "And you helped." I looked up at her and let my eyes drop to her turquoise necklace.

I leaned back in my office chair and breathed in. I was scared. I didn't want to go where they were pulling. Jerri scooted toward me until she was standing across from my desk. "We need your help."

"You want to know who sent me after Lyle."

"We want you to help us rescue Palo. It would help if you could bust whoever set him up. But short of that we need information," Jerri said.

"In other words, you want names and crimes so Palo can plea-bargain his way out of prison."

From the opposite wall came Parr's voice. "We've done our homework. We know about your 'Special Task Force.' Looks like somebody in it is playing double."

When this all started, I thought I was in control. "Why did you come to me? How do you know it's not me? How do you know I'll help? Set up my own people?"

"'Cause you got a reputation, too, Dolph," Joe Parr said. "Busted a dope- and gun-smuggling ring. The last man to see Vincent Fuentes alive. And you can smooth things over."

Jerri took over. "We figured you weren't the type of detective to let this go."

I made myself think and plan. I eased up out of my swiveling and rocking office chair. "I'm sorry. I'll do what I can. I'll make some calls."

Smiling, showing me her eyes, Jerri said, "We kinda thought that I would drive Joe back to the Midland airport so he could get back to San Antonio to take care of the rest of our business and then that I'd drive back and you could help me find the right people to talk to."

"Well, that's my wife's idea," Joe said. "Mine was that I'd come back and help you."

"Joe, you're seventy years old."

"Not quite, another couple of months yet." Jerri tsked, and Joe said, "Well, honey, it's no job for a woman alone." Jerri's eyes suddenly became intense as she glared at her husband. Joe ducked the glare.

"Just a girl, right?" She looked at me. "I hope that's not your attitude, Mr. Martinez."

"I'll help, but I'm not working with either one of you. I'll find out what I can. But I can't take you along with me. It's against policy. It's . . . it's . . . I won't."

Joe stood and walked toward my desk. "Dolph, look, that

goddamned ol' bandit Palo doesn't deserve much help. I don't know what to think of the old bastard. But he's been screwed, and my wife, well, she likes the old thief."

Jerri said, "And Palo is Vincent Fuentes's father." I looked at her while she begged me with those eyes. "So you see, you see, Dolph? See why you have to help us?" In my shiny, freshly painted, air-conditioned sector headquarters office, with these two seemingly mismatched people in front of me, I saw Vincent Fuentes standing in the grass and canebrakes next to the Rio Grande and pressing a little .22 to his head. He had smiled at me, that goddamn smile that hid something, that revealed just a little of his secret twisted plans, that mocked you because he knew more than you did. I got the feeling that Joe and Jerri were here because Fuentes was trying to get even with me.

"Okay, okay," I said. Then I gathered my thoughts, pulled open my desk drawer, and brought out a copy of the notarized form that I had found on Lyle Blackwell. I held it out toward them. Joe nodded at it, and Jerri took the form. She grimaced. "You know what that form probably means, don't you?" Joe got curious and looked over her shoulder at the form.

"It's an old trick," Jerri said. "Sell some chica pobrecita this form, and she thinks she has American citizenship. She gets here, and she's doing slave labor in a chicken-processing plant or a pig farm or selling her body."

"Is Palo involved in that?"

They both looked at me. After a long moment, Jerri said, "No." Jerri handed the form back to me and shook my hand, and then Joe stepped up and shook my hand. "We thought we'd spend the night," Joe said. "So why don't you let us buy you a nice meal? You know of a decent motel where Jerri could stay?"

"There's only one decent hotel in Marfa since the Paisano closed down. And the Thunderbird isn't that decent." I almost felt like these two were family. "I know of this great bed-and-breakfast, and tonight they're having dinner, too; it's over in Alpine. And I'll be there for dinner. I'll let you know if I can help tonight. I need to think." I gave them the address of my Alpine home.

When Jerri and Joe left, I tried to cool down. They might have rehearsed this whole interview—good cop and bad cop. Perhaps they were congratulating each other on how they had reeled me in. I wondered why I felt the need to invite them to my unfinished bed-and-breakfast. Pepper would be happy. They'd spread the word to San Antonio; we'd get more business. Maybe I wanted to spy on them. Maybe it would just be fun to have some people over.

I tried for several hours to figure out what I should do. Around the end of my shift, my thoughts just making me more confused, I called Trujillo. Before he could even say "Hola," I began cussing. "Look, if you got me involved in some of your corrupt Mexican political horseshit, I'll goddamn shoot you myself."

"Good to hear from you," Trujillo said in his purring sort of voice. He was as smart as Fuentes and just as slippery.

"Goddamn private detectives were just in here because that Lyle Blackwell you had me deliver spilled his guts and got a friend of theirs arrested."

"Accidents happen."

I pounded on my desk with my fist. "Don't give me any fucking platitudes. How much did you fucking know?"

"No more than you. I got my 'request' from an American on your side of the border."

"Who?"

"Let me make some phone calls."

"Now?"

"I'm sure you didn't divulge everything. I'm sure you didn't give them my name. Calm yourself. Who were these private detectives?"

"Get this, they're representing Vincent Fuentes's father, some Palo Fuentes."

"Their names," Trujillo said curtly.

"Jerri Johnson and Joe Parr."

"Will they be in Alpine tomorrow night?"

"She will."

"Make a reservation for three at the Reata, and tell Pepper I especially like his quail. And don't mention my name to Jerri Johnson."

"You know her? You know him? What the hell is going on?"

"You'll know."

"Well, you want to give me some kind of a clue? A little pilón here for a cuñado?"

"You might see some sparks fly at dinner. Jerri Johnson was Fuentes's lover, and Joe Parr hit me with his fist in the San Antonio police station after he tried to arrest me and Vincent Fuentes." He started laughing as he hung up. "See you tomorrow, cuñado."

Even after he hung up, I could hear him laughing, and then the Parrs and Fuentes joined it. Without any planning, though, almost like the way Sister Quinn said she could sense someone's pain or trouble in the desert air, I felt like they needed to play some gigantic joke on me.

* * *

I drove across the flatlands on 67 between Marfa and Alpine. This was the home of the Marfa Lights, the eerie, crisscrossing lights that you could see in front of you some nights, and the ruins of the mansion for *Giant*. Depending on who you talked to out here, the Marfa Lights were the natural reflections from the mountains, changing atmospheric pressure, deserted space aliens, or witches. And everyone out here had a piece of the false front mansion from *Giant,* and several women claimed to have had James Dean's child. To my left, coming over the mountains, were a few dark clouds spilling light rain into the Davis Mountains. Way out in the flatlands were a few pronghorns smelling the rain and trying to outrun that smell. Behind them were several slow-moving mule deer. In another month, they'd all be rutting, the scent of what they had to do making them frenzied and obsessed, and the hunters from Houston, Dallas, and San Antonio would be out in the flats sniping at them.

I almost pulled off at the Railroad Crossing, a bar with good foreign beer, settled right along the old Southern Pacific tracks. For the last several years, people like Charlie, my mother's boyfriend, had been trying to "discover" Alpine. So we had a bar that served foreign beer, a decent bookstore, and a Swiss-style bakery that made fancy pastries and cinnamon rolls.

I waved to the police as I drove past the police station and pulled into my driveway. A new Suburban was pulled off to the side between our carport and Pepper's tennis court. My mother was running to the car. She had dust all over her, and her knuckles were bleeding. "Dolph, what are you thinking? We're not ready for guests yet. And here Charlie and I are in the middle of laying Mexican tile, which is incredibly cheap if you are willing to haul in from Ojinaga like Pepper did, and in walks this pleasing lady and her attractive husband to say that they have a room for the night. God, Dolph."

"Mom, are they here?"

"They're resting in a room, but Pepper, bless his heart, is going to bring over some lamb chops from Reata, a new recipe he's been working on."

"Mom, he's going to steal lamb chops from Reata?"

"But what are we going to do? You promised them dinner. They expect dinner."

I walked into the kitchen to see Charlie sucking in air. He nodded at me. "Be careful, careful," my mother said. "We've got the tile laid out." They had the markers stuck into the floor; they had the centerpieces of tile set. They had a couple of cracked or cut pieces piled up.

"You two have been trying to do this?"

Charlie nodded.

"You two shouldn't be doing this."

My mother said, "Well, of course, we have to. Who do you think is going to do it?"

"You could hire someone."

"Why, when we could do it ourselves?"

"But you're too . . ." I stopped before I said "old."

"Maybe, if you'd quit the Border Patrol and become a working partner, then *we* wouldn't have to do all the work."

"Have you been talking about me to Pepper?"

My mother showed up to dinner in a high camp outfit: jeans, red belt, red boots, her hair up in a red bow. Charlie wore a fringed buckskin jacket and a string tie. The Parrs wore the same clothes they wore to my office. The perfect host, my mother made a salad, warmed the lamb chops, carrots and broccoli, and new potatoes that Pepper brought over, and served, in porcelain bowls, the white mousse that Pepper also stole from Reata. Over coffee and brandy, my mother flirted with Joe Parr and left Charlie to Jerri. "He certainly is a handsome man," she said to me as I helped her clear the table.

For a while Jerri and Joe sat on the porch with me and drank a few beers. The mountain showers had left a clean feel in the air that drifted down to us. Ahead of us tiny sparks of houses and the Sul Ross campus dotted the mountain. The police station was quiet. I told them that I would help them.

So with business out of the way, these two pleasant people and I spoke about pleasurable places. For me, I said, this place was the best. The only place close was the beach at Boca Chica, across from Brownsville, on a late summer night, where the humid gulf air seemed to caress your face. And Joe Parr said he could feel that same gulf breeze bring the smell of his neighbors' freshly cut lawn mixed with the odors of honeysuckle and chlorine from their swimming pool. This was the house he shared with his first wife, the one who died. Jerri wasn't upset, but she said she remembered the beach at Puerto Peñasco in Sonora, Mexico, where she spent a summer with Vincent and Palo Fuentes. "Those two corrupt villains," Joe Parr said, and thank God she laughed.

They turned in for the night, and I sat in the dark and envied them for finding and keeping each other. And then Pepper pulled up. He sat out on the porch with me and absorbed the air from the mountains and drank his two-beer limit with me. Our conversation turned to the women we had lost: his three wives and my El Paso girlfriend who married a fellow lawyer and Ariel Alves. Then we discovered a flaw in our bed-and-breakfast. The beds squeaked. From down the hall, from the last bedroom, the one under construction, came the squeaking of my mother and Charlie's bed. And from one of the bedrooms upstairs came the squeaking of Jerri and Joe's bed. Pepper and I looked sadly at each other. And Pepper had another beer.

I woke to the sound of banging, but it wasn't the bed, but Pepper bouncing a tennis ball off the ply board base on one side of his tennis court. I struggled to get on a sweatshirt, shorts, and jogging shoes. Pepper was at my door before I could open it.

We ran east, toward the breaking line of light, and after a mile, just enough to get to the edge of town, I had to start walking. I kept recalling my conversation with Fuentes before he shot himself.

"Come on, sissy boy," Pepper said as he jogged in place in front of me. I don't know if he had been to bed the whole night. The new Pepper, the one out of prison, functioned on energy without rest. Feeling every bit my age, I walked back for breakfast with my mother, Charlie, Jerri, and old Joe Parr. I had gotten too soft in Alpine. And I wanted to blame Fuentes for making me need softness and for sending Jerri Johnson and Joe Parr to summon me.

SIX

As I left for work, Jerri backed out of our driveway. She was on her way to the Midland airport to drop Joe Parr off for a flight back to San Antonio. He'd do what he could there while she helped me. As I drove off, I saw the old ranger lean across the front seat of the Suburban to kiss his wife on the cheek. At my office, I phoned Colonel Henri Trujillo and invited him to have dinner with Jerri and me.

Colonel Henri Trujillo, comandante at the Ojinaga army garrison, made an entrance into Reata. It was theater, or melodrama. He wore a white linen dinner jacket. He held a cigarette holder in his right hand, sticking out from between his forefinger and middle finger. As he customarily did, he let his right hand plop backward over his wrist. His black hair was slicked back with mousse, and his pencil-thin mustache was trimmed and too black. He had been dying his hair since it started turning gray the last couple of years, and now it looked as though he was spreading black eyeliner through his mustache.

A waiter was beside him, asking him to please put out the cigarette. There was no smoking in this part of the dining room, but he smiled and patted the young waiter's shoulder with his left hand. "It'll be all right. My cigarette will soon be out."

"But please, sir," the waiter said. Trujillo raised the cigarette holder to his lips, inhaled deeply, pulled the cigarette out of the holder, and then handed the still lit cigarette to the waiter. The waiter, in jeans and dress shirt and tie, hurried away with the cigarette. People looked up, but in the faint light of the restaurant, they couldn't make out the details of what was going on.

In Mexico those who dared called him a maricón. I didn't know if his effeminacy was fake or not; I never knew if he liked boys or girls. But I knew, as Vincent Fuentes must have known, that his manner fooled people into underestimating him. Because he was small, maybe he affected that posture to fool the enemies of Mexico and thus gave himself a slight advantage over them. If this was all an act, I suppose, he had been doing it for so long that it had become a part of him. At any rate, he was good at what he did. And though I had first detested him for it, I now felt a little sorry for him because of what he had sacrificed for the Mexican government.

He spotted us and moved toward our table, and I saw Jerri tense up. She had on a sundress, but because it was cooler than she had thought, she had a jean jacket draped over her shoulders. It wasn't inappropriate dress for Reata. Several high-toned restaurants had cropped up in the area because of the tourists. Reata had some good wine, a slightly exotic menu (more than chicken-fried steak and tacos—Pepper had really learned to cook well in prison), and exotic prices. But the locals, like tourists, weren't about to put on a coat and tie to eat. So the waiters wore dress shirts and ties with jeans, and most of the crowd wore jeans and boots—all but Trujillo.

As he came to the table, he smiled at Jerri, and she ducked his gaze. He sat down, looked around, and motioned a waiter over. "Wine," he said. "Let me buy a bottle of wine for my two friends."

"You little son of bitch," Jerri mumbled.

"Jerri Johnson, you are mistaken about me, about that whole nasty affair."

"You turd. You little turd."

Trujillo pointed to the wine list. "The merlot. We'll have that." He lowered the wine list and said, "Have you ordered? The quail. You know I love the quail. Pepper is preparing the quail?"

Jerri's cheeks were flushed. One corner of her lip curled into a sneer and showed the wrinkles in her upper lip. She brushed at the dove wing that her short blond hair made on one side of her head. The deep blue of her eyes no longer begged but revealed loathing.

Trujillo reached across the table for her hand, but she pulled it away from him. "Jerri, Jerri . . . Jerri. What happened was not what I wanted."

She recoiled, jumping straight to her feet and knocking her chair over behind her. Its hollow slap on the tile floor echoed through the dining room. People turned to look. Her voice got higher and louder. "Quit your condescension. I should have guessed. I should have known. It's not enough to get Vincent. You have to come after Palo. You set him up. You little bastard. Pinche puto."

More people looked. I turned around in my seat and saw Pepper coming out of the kitchen door. He had my back. The teenage maître d' was suddenly beside Jerri. "Ma'am, ma'am. Please. Could I help? Maybe, you know, you'd like another table." She looked around for guidance. Pepper was soon at her side, picked up her chair, and guided her into it. He smiled, then leaned over Trujillo and whispered, "Shut the fuck up." Then, smiling, he walked back to the kitchen.

I realized that I was the only one standing, so I sat down, and Jerri looked at me. She placed her hand over my wrist and talked. "Dolph, don't you know who this is? Don't you know what he is? He double-crossed Fuentes—and me. Joe nearly killed him. Ask him about the police station in San Antonio. Ask him about a poor pelado named Angel Martínez. Henri Trujillo killed him. You can't trust him. He's absolutely a bastard." I squinted in the soft light to see her face, but I couldn't see the details of it, only a soft glow. But her eyes were deep blue and begging again. Hell, maybe it was my eyes not focusing well enough.

Trujillo hung his head. "Dolph, explain to her."

They both looked at me. "He's my contact. He's a part of my Special Task Force."

"Then your task force sucks."

"Dolph, tell her what I said when we bagged Fuentes's

body." Jerri's eyes shot toward him. There was a quiver on her lip. I didn't answer. Trujillo motioned with his hand for me to say something. When I didn't, he said, "I miss him. I never wanted him harmed."

"You beat him with a Saltillo telephone book. You tortured him. You lying son of a bitch."

"I am a Mexican. At that time I worked for the ministry of defense of Coahuila. Later I accompanied Vincent Fuentes on American tours. I was a spy for Mexico. He was the double agent. As you well know, he played you against me, against Angel, against everybody. He was only for himself. And then he crossed me and a drug dealer and sealed his doom."

"Yeah, and I bet you were real cozy with the drug dealer."

"Explain to her, Dolph."

But I had spent several years forgetting all about the complexities and the alliances and double crosses of the little iceberg tip of the plot I discovered. Pepper went to prison; Fuentes killed himself; Sister Quinn got crazier; Ariel Alves left me; I started taking antidepressants. And we were just the "little people." "It's the border, Jerri. It's just the border."

A smiling teenager was suddenly at our table, telling us the specials for the night. I motioned for the waitress to leave us alone, but she said, "Huh, sir?" and went on. Pepper soon walked out, put his hands on her shoulders, and led her away. It was too dark. The dim lights were supposed to make the room intimate, romantic, cozy. But suddenly this stylish darkness seemed to hide everything. Instead of revealing who we all were in harsh light, like the desert does, it clouded our intentions in a romantic glow.

"Dolph, how can I trust him? Don't you see? It's impossible. I'm convinced. I know that he did this to get even with Palo." She dropped her head and stared at the table. I started to speak, not really knowing what I would say, but she interrupted me. "How can I trust you, Dolph?" I was suddenly glad that Joe Parr was back at their home in San Antonio. Had he been here, there might have been gunfire. "Maybe we better forget the whole deal. I can't trust you." I felt glad. She would leave. She would do the investigating and find out why Lyle Blackwell was dead and why

Fuentes's father was going to jail. I would be out of it. No risk of finding out what I didn't want to know. Pepper had warned me.

"Jerri Johnson. Jerri." Trujillo spoke up. "Like it or not, this time we are on the same side. And we are helping the same people." He didn't sound affected. He didn't have any effeminacy in his voice. His hand didn't flop back on his wrist. "I am here because I'd like, after all that has happened, to help Palo. As Dolph said, this is the border. And Dolph and I are a part of a team that does things in a border style. You've been cheated, hurt, double-crossed. So has Palo. But so have Dolph and I and our little organization. We can make it all right."

"So how do I even begin to trust you?" Jerri grabbed the lapels of the jean jacket, curled her shoulders, and pulled the jacket around her.

I answered for him. "Faith. Grace. Mercy. Not forgetfulness or forgiveness, but awareness." Sister Quinn had incoherently uttered those same words at me as I shook Trujillo's hand while several Ojinaga policemen and soldiers bagged Fuentes's body. I had watched while they loaded the body onto a helicopter, and I had watched the helicopter lift up and swirl dust, and I had heard Sister Quinn's words mix with the whir of the helicopter's rotors as it began its flight across American airspace to Ojinaga. I repeated those words. "Faith. Grace. Mercy." As Sister Quinn said, they should always trump justice.

Trujillo looked at me and nodded. "Bueno, mi amigo." Then he turned to look at Jerri. "The man who requested that I capture Lyle Blackwell was Leland Carter." Jerri seemed to relax. "There, you have a name. There, I gave you the place to start."

Jerri remained staring at Trujillo. She squirmed in her seat, then looked at me. She asked out loud, "Who is Leland Carter?" But her eyes asked me to help her somehow trust Trujillo.

I knew that the muscles in my face sagged. I squirmed in my chair. "A deputy sheriff for Brewster County. Shit." The sheriff of Brewster County was a part of my Special Task Force and the war on drugs. Leland would know about it.

"So what's the deal?" Jerri asked.

"Someone on this side of the border, once again, is the corrupt person. Not a Mexican," Trujillo said. "As I have said, as I told you and your Joe Parr, I am not the corrupt one. I just do the dirty business. Same as you."

Trujillo gingerly reached toward Jerri. His fingertips settled just on top of hers, and Jerri looked at his fingers on top of hers, looked at him, looked back at the fingers, then slid her hand away from him. "Jerri, you have the luxury here. You are a private investigator. You are bound to money or your own desires. You let the money, you let your allegiance determine right, wrong, good, bad. I have a government to answer to and for. I, like Dolph, am bound to things outside of me. I have to consider a wider good. Vincent, at the end of his life, never considered a wider good."

"Horseshit," Jerri said to him, and met his gaze. He dropped his eyes to the table, and she tried to bore a hole through him with her deep blue eyes.

The teenage waitress was suddenly back at our table and asking if we had made up our minds. "I'm not too hungry," Jerri said.

Neither was I, so I stood up to escort her to the door. "Their drinks are on me," Trujillo said. "And bring the merlot, bring the wine. And I'll have the quail; tell Pepper those cute little birds are for me. He knows how I like them."

"We'll be in touch," I told Trujillo.

⋆

It was a very short drive, like all drives in Alpine, back to our house. I told myself that I shouldn't feel too bad because I had probably saved well upward of a hundred bucks on dinner.

Jerri and I didn't say much, but we found ourselves sitting on my front porch with a couple of microwave dinners and some iced-down beers. She pulled the jean jacket tightly around her shoulders and stabbed at her reheated meat loaf. "It's pretty here," she said, and looked up at the sky as she chewed. "You can see the stars. San Antonio is too big now. You can't see the stars. Even on the outskirts. Joe and I live on the outskirts. We have deer coming into our backyard and nibbling on our plants."

I looked into my tray of Salisbury steak and macaroni and wished, for a second, that I was back at Reata, drinking wine and eating Pepper's rich food with Trujillo. "People here would love to be in a mall in San Antonio. They don't mind asphalt, parking lots, and crowded freeways."

Jerri set her pasteboard carton full of its nuked grease and gravy down on the porch. "Dolph, from what I know, from what I've seen, how do I trust you if you work with Henri Trujillo?"

"I used to say that if you eat with the devil, you better use a long spoon. Now I don't know but that every meal is with the devil. You just got to outtrick him. It's a matter of favors. I do this and this, like picking up Lyle Blackwell, and then when I need something, I call Trujillo, he calls somebody in Mexico, and some badass drug dealer is busted. It's the border."

"I don't have to play that game," Jerri said, without looking at me.

"You have any other options?"

"I could make a few phone calls and start over."

"Well, maybe you can't bring yourself to trust me, but I was the guy who Fuentes chose to trust. Course, I let him down. I wouldn't walk with him across the river and arrest him in the U.S. But he still thought I was his last best chance. I see that now."

"I was once Fuentes's last best chance, too. You think I could trust Vincent Fuentes? You see, I knew him through several of his stages. And he was so full of shit that . . . that if you pressed him, your finger would sink into him like he was dough." She, I decided, could have kept up with Pepper in her disgusting metaphors. "So I know about trusting when you shouldn't."

"Sister Quinn calls that faith."

Jerri wrung her hands together. "For me it wasn't faith, but love." Jerri pulled her eyes from her hands to look at me. "With Fuentes I risked faith, I risked a lot, for love, or the possibility of love."

"So why Joe Parr?" I didn't really want to ask the question, and I raised a beer to my lips to take a long swallow and hide my face.

Jerri straightened in her chair and crossed her arms over her chest. She looked as though she was disappointed in me. "I'm not sure I need to explain that to you."

"No offense." I lowered my beer bottle and stared at my toes. "Of course it's none of my business; I'm not busting your chops; I'm just really, genuinely interested. I mean, you have to have faith in Joe Parr, right?" She didn't speak.

I felt Jerri staring at me, so I raised my head to look at her head-on. She cocked her head as though sizing me up, and before she smiled, her eyes got deep, so that I could see into them—even in the faint light from our naked porch light bulb. "I learned to love Joe Parr. But I loved Fuentes from the first, even though I didn't know it. And I've still got just this sort of an itch for him." She chuckled to herself. "And the son of a bitch is dead."

I stared back down at my toes because I didn't want her looking into my eyes and seeing clear through into me, maybe seeing what I couldn't figure out for myself. I thought about Ariel Alves living way off in Maryland or wherever it was she went to get away from me and El Camino del Rio. And Dede's face stuck itself in the middle of my mind. I raised my head to look at Jerri, and some beam of sight and dim light from the one bulb fixed our gazes, locked them. "Let me do this. Maybe, I'm thinking, just maybe, if I can help Palo, then I can make up for what I didn't do for Vincent."

Jerri broke the fixed gaze by chuckling. "Be careful, Dolph Martinez. Helping Fuenteses can get you confused and in trouble. I should know."

"So there's you and Joe Parr, and you and Fuentes, and you and Palo? Sounds pretty complex to me. Byzantine, even."

"This from the man who's partners with Trujillo." Jerri smiled, her eyes lit up. "Why, Dolph Martinez, I bet sometime in your life, you wanted to be something other than what you are. I bet you had promise. I bet you were your momma's 'pretty boy,' her golden child."

"I ain't done bad."

"Well, I once had promise too. And Vincent Fuentes encouraged it. He was my teacher before he was my lover. And Palo as much takes care of me as I take care of him. And Joe Parr has found some degree of wisdom." Jerri stood and stuck out her hand. "Okay, you have a deal, then. But we're partners. I go along." I shook her hand, and she said, "Good night." And left me alone.

I sipped beers and waited until Pepper came walking up the steps of the front porch. He reached into the ice chest and pulled open the first beer for this setting. "Trujillo got a little drunk. I escorted his ass out."

"He gets carried away."

"Where's he get that kind of money? He must have dropped two hundred dollars drinking that high-dollar wine and eating (I don't mind if I say so, thank you) my goddamn good-as-shit quail." Pepper sipped his beer. He no longer simultaneously guzzled and spit out tobacco juice.

"He's got family money."

Pepper let out a giggle. "Don't we all. Goddamn, Dolph. You, me, him. We got money. We even try to piss it away, and still we do all right. So why ain't we happy and getting laid?" Pepper started chuckling at himself. I looked up at the mass of stars, streaks of white, and thought that maybe happiness was in a city like San Antonio where I couldn't see the stars. "You know, you cock your head and squint just right and that Jerri Johnson, despite her age, ain't bad looking."

"Hell, she's our age, Pepper."

"Yeah, but we look our age, and I started out ugly. But you're a 'pretty boy.' You still got some hope. Maybe." My mother called me pretty boy. Mexican ladies would call their bright, good-looking, promising sons "pretty boy." Fuentes told me that he, like me, was called a "pretty boy." Then he shot himself.

"I'm gonna help her, Pepper."

"Oh, shit." Pepper took a long gulp of his beer. "What is it with you and these blond women? Has it got something to do with the way your momma raised you or something?"

"It has to do with my job."

"Bullshit. It has to do with you. You could just coast in your job. Hell, you work for the government. Now, if we had our own agency . . ." Pepper squinted in the dark to see me.

"Now who's got the fantasies?"

Pepper stared down at his jogging shoes. He smelled like vinegar and grease. Even in the dim light, with my bad eyes, I could see the tiny red burns on his hands and forearms. Since he had been cooking at Reata, he burned himself a lot. "So you gonna play cowboy?"

"You gonna go along for the ride there, cowpoke?"

Pepper tipped his beer at me. "I got your back." After his second beer Pepper went inside to clean the kitchen, make plans in his head, jot down a menu, whatever it was that kept him from sleeping. And I stared up at the stars and then at the dark shapes of the mountains and wondered if I would miss them if I ever moved away.

SEVEN

While I was at work at the Marfa headquarters the next day, I got an agent who knew her way around a computer to look up the state records on Leland Carter. He had bought a new truck. Next, with a phone call, a wink, and a few promises, I got a credit check on Carter and found that he had paid off one card but had starting charging on two others. A local dealer told me that he had paid cash for his new truck.

Meanwhile Jerri went to the Brewster County courthouse and looked for Leland's name. She met Dorothy McFarland and told her she was a private detective. Dorothy McFarland, no doubt a bit scared, helped Jerri. Jerri found out that Leland had bought some property next to the land that he rented, the land where he and his wife and two kids lived, and that he had tried to tap into some water and electrical lines that the county owned. She noticed, too, that Dorothy seemed a bit nervous.

I called the Fort Stockton sheriff and asked if he could locate any county records on a Dorothy McFarland. Then I described her. Two hours later, he called back and said that he had found nothing. She said that she had changed back to her married name; no crime there. Then I called banks, described Dorothy, and asked if anyone remembered her working as a teller. No one recalled her.

People knew Pepper, and he had a knack for getting people to talk as they listened to him, so he spent a morning driving around town and asking questions. He talked to contractors and building suppliers and found that Leland was building some great tin barn on his property.

That night I called Dorothy McFarland and asked her if she could remember any more about the notarized forms. "We have a new lead. I think a name would help."

After several long seconds, I heard a sob. "I'm afraid, Mr. Martinez."

"Call me Dolph. And there's nothing to be afraid of." She sobbed again, it seemed to me for effect.

I waited several seconds. I was becoming impatient with her demeanor. "I believe it was a Leland Carter who asked me to sign those forms for a Mr. Lyle Blackwell. He was a deputy sheriff. He worked for the law. I thought that I was helping out. How could it have been wrong if a lawman asked me?"

"I'm not after you, Dorothy." She had just confirmed Trujillo. And I was getting better at my job: pressuring "a little old lady."

Several moments passed along with several sobs, more drama—maybe she liked the drama. "Well, thank you, Dolph. But oh, my, my. Is he in trouble? Did I get the poor man in trouble?"

"No, Dorothy, no. Don't worry." I waited for her to say something. "Are you sure you can't tell me anything more?"

I pictured her raising her hand to her throat, her eyes darting away from me. "I don't know what else I could tell you, Dolph." This investigation wasn't about this poor woman's woes, so I let her go.

The next day I dropped Pepper and a horse off at a fence adjacent to Leland's property. The horse and the key to several gates belonged to Pepper's uncle. As Pepper led the skittish horse out of the trailer, its hooves clattering, I told him, "Don't do anything stupid."

"I'm sneaking around in pastures that I don't own looking for some kind of a building. And you're telling me don't do anything stupid. You're a little late with your advice."

Pepper got the reins in one hand, stuck a foot in the stirrup, and was up on the twirling horse in one easy motion. "You know this horse is special trained," Pepper said from up above me. "He ain't scared of cattle guards. He'll jump or cross 'em."

"Be careful."

"Ah, Dolph, we could be doing this for a living. This is what I'm talking about. This is what we're good at."

"I am getting paid for it."

"But I'm not."

"I've got a fund I'm keeping for you."

"Well, hell," Pepper said, and touched his spurs to the horse's flanks. The mare jerked and kicked one leg, then she trotted quickly up the slight incline and hit the gravel road, but Pepper jerked the reins, and she settled into an easy trot, Pepper's shoulders and head bobbing with the mare's gait. He rode into the big red ball of the sun, and I had to squint to watch him. Like a Comanche, Pepper was short, bowlegged, ruddy complected, and rather clumsy looking, but like a Comanche, he was a beautiful man on a horse.

I got into my car, drove to my house, picked up Jerri, and drove to the Alpine McDonald's. It was the only McDonald's in the Big Bend area. After my years in Presidio, a hardship station in the border, I thought of malls, McDonald's, and 7-Elevens as a part of American normalcy. After living in Presidio for all those years, I came to like the sameness, the cleanness, the antiseptic quality that you could count on in a McDonald's.

The city cops and county deputies gathered there for 10 A.M. coffee. Jerri and I walked in and spotted Leland Carter sitting in the plastic McDonald's chairs with three city cops. It would have been a good time to commit a crime in Alpine. We approached them, and I tipped my cowboy hat to them. "Leland, could we talk to you for a second?"

"Sure, pull up," he said, then stopped to look at the plastic-and-steel chairs bolted to the floor.

"A little privacy, huh?"

Leland smiled at his fellow police officers, said, "Fellas, excuse me," and pushed himself up. He walked beside Jerri toward another table. I followed them. From behind, Jerri's butt seemed to be spreading, but the way her pants fit her, her trim waist, the outline of a muscled back that I could see press against her shirt showed that she fought that spread, she fought her age. Jerri seemed the type of woman who struggled against a lot, not just her body but her past, her temper, her indignation, her sense of injustice. Fuentes must have been attracted to that; he must have hurt her enough to make her the way she was.

Leland sat down, Jerri sat across from him, and I sat next to her. Leland was in his early thirties. He had flunked out of Sul Ross twice, tried his hand at being a mechanic and then an insurance salesman, married one of the most beautiful women in town and quickly had two kids; then, in a career move, he had gone up to Midland College to get a two-year law enforcement certification. As a deputy sheriff in Brewster County he made about the same money as a janitor at Sul Ross, and in fact, he was always looking for odd jobs and extra money. He took off his cowboy hat, laid it crown down on the table, and ran his fingers through his hair. He was a rugged-looking western sort of guy. The blond hair on his head and the downy fine blond hair on his arms next to his tanned face made him look golden but dirty.

"Leland, this is Jerri Johnson. She looked me up because Lyle Blackwell named a client of hers in his testimony. She must be good because she traced Lyle to me, and then I told her about Trujillo, and Trujillo told her he had heard from you." The handle of my pistol caught on the edge of the plastic back of my chair, so I reached behind me to straighten out the .357 magnum. The government now provided us with the automatic Berettas, but I still preferred the knockdown power of the magnum.

"Sort of a daisy chain," Leland said.

I forced a giggle, and Jerri looked at me. Her blond hair was neatly cut; I noticed just a trace of perfume. She had replaced her jeans with a pair of khakis. She had replaced her boots with a pair of black tennis shoes. She wore a denim shirt and her turquoise necklace. "Well, I told her you were on the up-and-up. But she wants to ask you a few questions anyway." Jerri's eyes darted at me and then back at Leland.

Leland looked at her. "Miss Johnson, you gonna like this. The daisy chain goes on. The sheriff over in Terrell County wanted Lyle."

"And the sheriff here, Weldon Phillips, didn't know about this?" Jerri asked.

Leland caught his smile before it dropped. He looked at Jerri and then at me. "Sure, he did."

Jerri reached into her pocket and pulled out a copy of the notarized marriage form. Leland raised his Styrofoam cup of coffee to his face and sipped it instead of looking at Jerri. "Do you know anything about this?"

Leland looked at me. "I found one just like it on Lyle. But I couldn't figure out where he got it. Jerri here must have found another one." Leland reached for the form and gently held it. I couldn't tell if I saw a slight tremble in his hand, but Jerri pushed forward, toward him, and grinned.

"No. I don't know what this is." Leland handed it back to Jerri.

"Well, Mr. Carter, do you know that Lyle Blackwell is dead? He was killed in the Bexar County jail."

"I didn't know about poor ol' Lyle."

Jerri straightened again and grinned. Her eyes looked deep and smiled more brightly than her mouth. "So you knew Lyle?"

"No. No. I just meant poor guy, you know."

"Yeah," I said. "You know what he meant, Jerri. I can vouch for Leland."

Jerri just barely raised one eyebrow toward me. Then she turned her attention toward Leland. "What do you think happened? Who do you think ordered Lyle killed?"

And I interrupted her again. "As a lawman, Leland. You know, you're a trained lawman. Jerri wants your opinion." Leland smiled at me. Jerri's eyes seemed to flash at me.

"Accidents happen. That's what I meant. Poor ol' Lyle must have pissed off some bad people there in jail."

"Yeah, you can't tell in a big city jail like San Antonio," I said.

Jerri looked at me and made herself grin. "Agent Martinez. Please, let him answer."

"Sure."

Leland giggled. "Yeah, Dolph, let me do the interview, huh?"

A teenager pushing a mop bucket and spreading water with a foul-smelling mop passed by us. "Look, Miss Johnson. I'm a small-town deputy sheriff. I do what I'm told. I don't know if Lyle Blackwell was in some sort of witness protection program that screwed up, was a drug dealer, or what. I got a call. I called Trujillo. I don't know what happened after that."

"Hell, Leland, I picked him up. Jerri questioned me too."

"It's all routine," Jerri said.

Then we heard a beeper. "Excuse me," Leland said, and hurried to find a phone.

When he got up, Jerri glanced my way. "Could you explain to me what you're trying to do?"

The city cops and the deputies looked over their shoulders or over the rims of their coffee cups at us. I stared down at my coffee cup to keep from meeting their gazes. I whispered, "So what do you know?"

Jerri looked toward the gathered cops, then back at me. She smiled with both her mouth and her eyes. "He's lying."

"Call that Terrell County sheriff tomorrow. If he won't talk, tell me."

Jerri stared straight ahead out toward the McDonald's arches. "So what are you doing? You didn't answer my question."

I stared at my coffee. "If we keep on with this, some local people are going to get hurt, and I'm probably going to be the one to hurt them. I've got to live here. You don't. It's a small town. Are you sure Palo is worth it?"

"We both seem to be asking and not answering. But yes, Palo is worth it."

Before we could go on, Leland came back to the table. "Dolph, what you been doing?"

"What?"

"Sheriff Phillips has got Pepper over on my property and is about to arrest him." I hung my head. Leland kept on. "Dolph, what you been doing? What's going on? You screwing me?"

* * *

On the way out to Leland's place, I didn't talk to Jerri. Ahead of me, off in the distance, was Leland with his siren and flashers going. I held back to think and to look at Jerri. She looked at me as though begging for some response.

"So what did you do?"

I didn't answer but kept watching the road. "So what's up, Dolph? Goddamn it, I thought I could trust you. What the hell is going on? You all but take Leland Carter's side in that McDonald's, and meantime you send Pepper out scouting around. What's up?"

"Nothing." I couldn't allow myself to be sucked into this. I needed distance. I needed discretion. I didn't need anyone distrusting me.

"Goddamn it, Dolph. You told me that I could trust you. I did. Am I going to regret this? Are you going to screw it all up because you've 'got to live here'? If you and your flaky people can't handle this, then tell me now so I can get some other help."

We turned off 67 a couple of miles out of town, crossed a cattle guard, and then bounced over a gravel road. We passed a decrepit mobile home and saw Leland's beautiful wife, an ex–Miss Brewster County, step out the door of the trailer with a small child balanced on her hip. She stood on the metal steps and watched. She was barefoot. Her hair dangled in strands over her face. She had an idiot's simple smile on her face, as though she was trying to figure out just how she got from a Miss Texas contest in San Antonio to this trailer, this property, with her husband and now two other law enforcement agents bouncing over the ranch road past her. An older kid, maybe ten years old, squirted out from the door behind her and ran through the rough grass in the front yard to the side of the ranch road. Jerri didn't seem to notice Leland's wife, but I wondered if she had the queasy feeling in her stomach that I got when, because of my job, I saw into other people's futures. Vincent Fuentes, because of all his twists and deceits, must at some point have felt that knot, that hot liquid. Trujillo must have felt it. Did they get past it? Did it just fade? And look at them, what they became. Not all knowledge is good or powerful. Forgetfulness may not be powerful, but it can be a blessing.

The bouncing of my car and Jerri's voice brought me back.

"Dolph, Dolph. Are you listening?" I looked across the seat to Jerri's intense blue eyes. They were an almost unnatural blue, deeper than other blue eyes. "Are you okay?" she asked, and tentatively reached for me and rested her fingertips on the top of my right forearm. My left wrist was flopped over the wheel of my car. I could feel it trembling.

I choked on the dust coming in through the windows and swirling around in my car. "I should have been a lawyer like my mother wanted, or I should have sold slacks and suits to newly, nearly well-off Chicanos in my mother's old department store. I should have just stayed a regular agent, squatting in the brush, tracking signs and chasing wets."

Jerri patted my forearm, pulled her hand away. "Relax. It's started."

"I always get this way when I plunge toward the shit that I know is gonna happen but I can't control."

We followed Leland through another gate, over a cattle guard, some mesquite scratching my Crown Vic's paint job. The sun was high, no shadows, and we dropped down the side of a ravine into a small valley. In the middle of this slight depression was a gleaming aluminum barn. In front of it were several people. One, I could tell from his silhouette, was Pepper. His hands were behind his back. Sheriff Weldon Phillips had handcuffed him. I punched on the gas and pulled up in front of the barn.

When I opened the door and stepped out, the reflection from the barn nearly blinded me. "Weldon, what are you doing with Pepper?" As I talked, a Mexican stepped from around the corner of the building. With one hand, he held the reins to Pepper's horse. He cradled a shotgun in his other arm.

"That's Esteban," Leland said as he walked up to us. I eyed Esteban. He had close-set dark eyes perched just above his nose, which had a slight twist to it. He let himself smile, and I saw that he was missing one tooth. The gap in his teeth, the broken nose were probably the results of bar fights. I wanted to know what the other guys looked like.

Jerri, Leland, and Esteban formed a half circle around Pepper and Weldon. Pepper had several drops of sweat on his forehead.

"Tell 'em, Dolph. Tell 'em. This is a goddamn, sorry ass country when a man can't take a ride on his pony."

"Not on other people's property," Leland said.

"So this is your property?" Jerri asked. She jerked her head toward the barn. "And what is that?"

Pepper answered. "It's a goddamn airport for E.T.'s landing strip. You can't see it from the road, but from up above, from the top of that rim"—Pepper jerked his chin because his hands were cuffed—"it blinds you. So I just had to come down and look at this damn Disneyland." I imagined Pepper, made tall from sitting on top of his horse, spotting this silver eyesore, then leading his horse down the slope, around the century plants and yucca. I envied him for that sight, that discovery. Pepper could still peer into the distance and see details, not just a haze.

"But what were you doing here on my property?" Leland asked.

"Riding my horse on Fred Curtsinger's property with his permission."

"But this is my property."

"My horse likes to jump across cattle guards. And he doesn't know where your property begins."

"You should know."

"You ain't got a fence."

Weldon said, "Wow," and loosened his tie. He pushed his hat to the back of his head with his forefinger and dug at the dirt with the pointed toe of his boot. "Let's start with some introductions." He turned to Jerri. "Who are you?"

"I'm a private investigator, and I—"

Weldon interrupted her. "Shit. She with you, Dolph?"

Jerri stepped in front of him. "You can talk to me."

Pepper giggled. "I'm helping her," I said.

"Helping her try to accuse me of something, Weldon," Leland said.

"Shit," Weldon said. "Oh, shit."

I loosened my collar. I hefted my holster to balance my pistol. Had it not been regulation, I would have left my pistol at home. Some days, after walking or driving around, my hip ached from the extra weight. I wrote reports, asked questions; I no longer needed to shoot or defend anybody. Not that I was any good at it in the first place. "I need an introduction, now. Who is Esteban?"

"I hire him to help me around here."

"To do what?" Pepper said. "Pull up behind me with a goddamn sawed-off shotgun and threaten to shoot me?" Then Pepper turned to Jerri. "Jerri, so I ride up to Disneyland here and decide to take a look 'cause I've never seen nothing like that Taj Mahal, and so I lean against it to take a look in the window, and suddenly this goddamn alarm goes off, and then this ugly son of a bitch comes out of it with this illegal goddamn weapon here. And Weldon here arrests me."

"Goddamn it, Pepper," Weldon said. "You're not arrested yet. But if I do, you've violated parole." He kicked at the dirt. "Jesus, it would've all been simpler if he shot you." Weldon had voters to face. People knew Pepper and wouldn't want to see him go back to prison. He looked at me. "Dolph?"

Jerri squared away in front of him. "If I were you, I'd investigate some other areas."

I reached out to grab her arm. "Jerri, Weldon's busy." I squeezed her arm, felt the knot of muscle in it. She again looked at me with flashing eyes. "Weldon, I think Pepper's learned his lesson. And he is in my custody, and I'd be a little embarrassed if he broke parole. Just take his horse away. Fine him."

Weldon looked up. "For what?"

"For riding his horse on private property."

"Dolph, I'm a little hazy about this private property issue," Pepper said.

"Shut up, Pepper," I said.

Weldon grabbed his hat with one hand and took it off and pulled his forearm across his forehead. A slight breeze picked up the loose ends of his tie and blew them across his chest. I noticed that my tie ends were raising with the wind also. Weldon's eyes stopped on Leland. "Leland, why are you living in that old trailer out by the road, yet you're building state-of-the-art barns and hiring thugs to guard your property?"

Leland took a step back. Weldon looked at me, asking me to let him in on what I knew. "You got no right to ask, Weldon. But

I got nothing to hide. My in-laws gave me some money. You can ask my wife." Jerri and I both knew that if we asked the former Miss Brewster County, she would no more know what Leland was talking about than the Terrell County sheriff.

"Turn around, Pepper," Weldon said. Pepper smiled at Leland and then at Esteban as he turned, and Weldon took off the cuffs. "Dolph, get all your friends out of here. Esteban, I want to talk to you."

"What about my horse?"

"Well, get it the hell out of here too."

Pepper smiled. "How about if I keep it there in Leland's barn until I can get my trailer?"

"Get out of here, Pepper," Weldon said.

Pepper rode his horse to Leland's mobile home. Always a sucker for kids, he swung Leland's ten-year-old up into the saddle and took him for a short ride. Then Jerri and I drove him to his Bronco and horse trailer. I sent Jerri back to our house in my car, and Pepper and I drove back to Leland's place. On the way back Pepper said to me, "That's no barn. From what I can see, it's a motel or warehouse. It's got several bunks, a bathroom, and shelves for storing stuff. As a former drug dealer and gunrunner, I figure he hides illegal people or goods in that building. And Dolph, be careful of that Esteban. He's ignorant, but he's a bad fucker, real border trash."

When we got back to Leland's, Leland's boy was still in the saddle and shooting at imaginary bad guys or Indians with his finger. Pepper gave him another ride, and then as we loaded the horse into the trailer, Leland's wife came to the door of the trailer and looked out at us, and then Leland came out and looked out at us. As I walked toward the cab, Leland yelled at me, "Dolph, don't let 'em do this to me."

Inside the cab of the truck, Pepper said, "Fuck him."

* * *

To relieve my mother of cooking, I had dinner with Jerri at a steak house. And then, as though she just sensed our habits and molded herself so that she would fit nicely, she sat on the big front porch and had a beer with me. As the mountains to the east and north became dark shapes that broke the orange and purple streaks of the sun, she twirled her beer can in her hands and rested her elbows on her knees, sort of the way a man would. "So tell me what went on today in our *interview* with Leland Carter. What were you doing, shucksing and good ol' boying?"

"Well, you know he's guilty now, don't you?"

"So does he." The streaks of the sunset dipped below the mountains, and we were in the quiet, star-dotted darkness that Jerri admired the night before.

"I've become a public relations man. I don't lie so much as reinterpret. No different for criminals. If you give people a way out, they usually tell you more. You listen close; most just want to tell you something. The details. You got to pick out the details from the big picture. Same as in the desert, when you're tracking the signs."

Jerri smiled at me. "You were right back there in the car. You should have been a lawyer. You sound like Vincent Fuentes."

"And what was he like?"

"Confused, but charming. He got lost in his delusions. But at one time he was clearheaded and brilliant."

"And what is Joe Parr like?"

"Not like you. He's a Ranger. The best defense is a good offense. Ride into the middle of them and shoot first."

I looked down at my beer. "I mean is he a good husband?"

Jerri smiled and pulled her elbows off her knees. "Why, Dolph, I think you mean, 'Is he a good lover?'"

I couldn't look at her, so I stared at the toe of my boot. "No, not really that. It just seems like you and him have something I been looking for most of my life. Pepper keeps looking and fucking it up. My mother, well, my mother has spells of wanting what the two of you seem to have. What is it? How do you get it?"

"You're still young enough. Joe is seventy."

"Are you still young enough?"

Jerri's grin went away. She straightened and leaned back in her chair as though to put distance between her and me. We both knew that I had pushed this all too far. "Maybe you just have to get lucky, or have good timing, or make God love you. I can't tell you what you want to know."

"Tomorrow we're going to go on a tour. Talk to some of my friends. Maybe we ought to take your Suburban. And I might need some more money."

"Your friends always take money." Jerri smiled again and relaxed.

"You pay for information."

"You can get a warrant."

"Not yet; we don't have enough on him. We don't know who all is involved. We don't know how much he'll fight back. We don't know how much damage we'll do or to whom. Not yet. Palo doesn't have enough information yet."

"You're a good investigator, aren't you? You can't stand not to know, but on the other hand, you don't want to know."

"Just trying to do my job."

"Yeah, sure." Jerri straightened up and breathed in the night air. "I think I'll get some sleep."

Not long after she went upstairs to her bedroom with its open window and breeze ruffling the curtains, my mother joined me. She had a glass of wine and sipped at it in her dainty fashion. "That Pergo is just too expensive. Tile. We'll go with Saltillo tile."

"Whatever, Mom."

My mother pulled her head back to look at me. "You and that Jerri lady make an attractive pair."

"Mom. She's married."

"I think maybe her husband and I could make an attractive pair." My mother used even her hand with the wineglass in it to talk. Sitting still, she still seemed to move.

"What about Charlie? I thought maybe he was going to become my new daddy."

"Charlie's a fine man. But there just seems to be so much more dignity in Joe Parr. And in his wife." She kept her legs together, in a more feminine posture than Jerri. "So have you decided how long you're going to stay?"

"Are you running me off?"

"You and Pepper seem to work well together, and as you said, Charlie is a fine man."

My mother raised the wineglass to her lips, and she looked

at me over the top of her glass. She brought the glass down and patted the bun her hair was pulled into. She never took her eyes away from me. "Oh, Dolph, thank you for bringing me here. Presidio was so dusty, hot, and just dirty. But there's a cleanness here." She now looked up at the sky. "I feel good here."

I guessed that this was my mother's way of saying that she was planning on staying quite a while.

EIGHT

You never called Socorro directly. He didn't have a phone, and if he did, he probably wouldn't have answered it. You called a friend of his or one of the other squatters. And if the friends felt like it, if they trusted you, if Socorro trusted them, then they might tell you where he was. A friend like Sylvia Walker, who worked at the Terlingua General Store—a faux general store, designed to look like Tommy Lawler's genuine general store in Lajitas. It wasn't crumbling, dusty, and smelly like Tommy's century-old store but well scrubbed, and it sold a variety of items—even books—to the tourists who came down to visit Big Bend or the new state-owned wildlife area on the other side of Lajitas.

Walter Bean, a Houston businessman, had the same sort of fantasies about a desert resort as Pepper, so he built his fantasy around Tommy's store. So Tommy's authentic store was surrounded by a faux-western hotel, a row of motels, a nine-hole golf course, a small-plane landing field, a restaurant, a bar, and various curio, souvenir, and camera shops. The Terlingua General Store was surrounded by the Terlingua ruins. An old mercury and silver mining town, Terlingua went bust in the 1940s. But people like Socorro started squatting in the old adobes, and eventually some moneyed people from outside the area opened an upscale restaurant and then the Terlingua General Store. The adobes were repaired, whitewashed, air-conditioned. If they left them alone, the newcomers got along with the desert rats like Socorro, who just burrowed into the desert to escape the sun. The population listed out in front of the town was forty-five, but that figure didn't account for the Socorros living in the ruins, the deserted trailers, the shacks out on the back roads. They wouldn't let themselves be counted.

For "a living" Socorro gave horseback tours and riding lessons over in Lajitas. I couldn't imagine him having the patience to guide some ten-year-old up onto a horse. He didn't have a car registered with the state or any proof of insurance, but when something went on, he'd drive up in an old van. Like a perverse Sister Quinn, he'd show up at gatherings and make himself a nuisance. I had this feeling that, though I regularly paid him for information, I'd one day arrest him or shoot him.

So Jerri and I descended out from the comfort of the Davis Mountain range, over the south rim, down 118, through the squat, cracked-dome mountains dotted with yucca and ocotillo reaching up toward the sky as though begging for a little moisture. In her Suburban we curved around the rock formations that kept the county busy dynamiting or sometimes closed the road when boulders rolled down onto it and cracked the asphalt. Again, as I drove through these not *bad* but *mean* lands, I got itchy, spooky, waiting for the Indian, Mexican, Catholic prayers and curses that lived in the rocks to make me crazy again. But I was also calmed by being in a Suburban again. It was like the SUVs I drove in the Border Patrol along our drags, down El Camino del Rio, up into the mountains or rugged backcountry as far as four-wheel drive could go and then a little farther.

Jerri must have thought that I was in a trance because I didn't say much of anything until we pulled into Terlingua. She spoke first. "Oh my God," she said. "I haven't seen anything like this outside of Mexico. It's poverty."

"Some of it's fake poverty. A couple of teachers at the new high school here live in these shacks."

Jerri laughed. "If they're living on teachers' pay, then it's poverty." I looked across at her into the deep blue of her eyes and saw them sparkle as she laughed at her own joke.

Old mining equipment was scattered around. The steel was rust colored, but it wasn't the rust that comes with humidity but from wind and sand and heat sandpapering top layers of paint or coating. The adobe ruins, made with the brittle alkali dirt of the desert, collapsed in on themselves, disintegrated, or blew away. The small valley and hillside where the adobes had sprouted seemed to be breathing, and the adobes clung to them as the hills heaved for breath. But the old school was still intact, and the company headquarters that housed the Terlingua General Store and restaurant was shiny, new, and clean. And there was literally something new in the air. I could taste and see it in the distance and in the way a haze hung between the slopes and me. The maquiladoras, the Mexican factories and power plants in Juárez, Chihuahua City, Piedras Negras, and all the way down to Matamoros, were belching out their pollution into the easterly winds that brought it to Big Bend.

Jerri walked ahead of me, and I watched the sway of her body. No feminine high head, out-turned wrists, or short delicate steps. Like a man, Jerri cocked her head to one side, took long strides, and swung her arms. And one shoulder knotted even under her shirt and strained against the straps of her heavy purse. She again had on khakis, a fresh denim shirt, hiking boots, silver earrings, and her turquoise necklace. She added a wide-brimmed straw hat, probably Joe Parr's suggestion. She didn't wear a uniform, but she had the same color, texture, and material for three changes of clothes. Probably the most expensive things she owned were her shoes. A private eye to the heart.

I felt easy walking behind her because I had left my gun stashed under the seat. Right now, for this job, I was officially off duty. I wore jeans, boots, a pocket T-shirt, and my short-brimmed Stetson. We had each packed an overnight bag.

She stepped onto the porch of the store and let some air out of her lips. I did the same. The October sun was hot—not like the July sun that just pushed down on you while it cooked you, hoping to dry you out while it crushed you into dust—but once you stepped into that priceless desert gold—shade—you were actually cooled. You relaxed and blew a little air through your pursed lips. Jerri pulled the sleeves of her denim shirt down to her wrists. The big, bald man came out of the door of the general store and smiled at me. Pooter stuck out his hand and said, "Dolph Martinez?"

"Dr. Pooter Elam, right?"

Pooter chuckled and laughed. "That Ph.D. just makes you a bigger target."

I shook his hand. "Have you seen Socorro?"

"He was here yesterday evening. But I haven't seen him." Pooter giggled to himself. "Just as well. When I'm around him, I get the feeling he just might bite me."

"Yeah, I get that same feeling."

"You know where he is?" Jerri asked.

"Sylvia might." And Jerri and I ducked into the cool inside of the Terlingua General Store. Sylvia, wearing shorts that showed off a length of her chunky thigh and dangling a sandal from her up-turned foot, sat on a high stool behind the counter and looked inside a book. Jerri got to her first, and Sylvia looked up. She smiled at Jerri. "Can I help you?" Then she saw me, and her smile dropped. She pulled off her half-frame glasses and cocked her head to look at me. "Dolph Martinez, right?"

"Hello, Sylvia," I said, and stuck out my hand. "Nice to meet you again." And she stuck out her hand. I grabbed her hand, and with a man's strong grip, she shook my hand.

Jerri glanced at me, pulled off her straw hat, and then stepped to one side. "I'll look around."

I turned back to Sylvia. "Where's Socorro?"

"Why?" She straightened her head, and I noticed that her jaw dropped so that her mouth was agape. She laid her book down and stood up. "He said something about you looking for him."

"I'd just like to talk to him."

"What would you like to say to him?"

"It's private."

She wiggled while she stuck her toes into her sandal. "You know, he's mentioned something about you."

I heard a clanging and saw Pooter come in through the door.

He smiled broadly, and I looked at Sylvia to see her frown at him. His smile disappeared, and he walked back through the doors.

"You sound just like Socorro said you would." I could see her thinking, the furrowed brow, the jaws knotting. She was considering whether she should cooperate with the law or defend her new boyfriend. "He's told me about you. I don't know that I should talk to you." I felt sorry for her because she wasn't bright enough or experienced enough with people like Socorro to see that he was using her.

I smiled. "So how long have you been dating Socorro?"

Again she said as a question or plea, "He's not involved with anything illegal."

"What has Socorro told you?"

She cocked her head again. "He told me you coerce him for information. But you don't look like a bad guy." She turned and looked around at who was listening.

"There's usually a couple of bills with some lesser presidents attached to the information that he tells me. Courtesy of the United States Department of Immigration and Naturalization. Did he tell you about that part?"

"Didn't you sneak up behind him, hit him, and threaten him to get information about Ignacio and Pepper Cleburne, and then you used that information to send them to jail?"

I was wanting to sneak up on him again, plant a shoulder in the small of his back, and bang his head against the side of a van. "I've also written letters of recommendation for him and served as a character witness when the Brewster County sheriff wanted to arrest him."

"I can tell about people, you know. Like Socorro, for instance, he ain't much to look at, maybe, but he's got a good soul." I looked around; Jerri was listening. She looked like she was about to laugh.

"Do you know where he is?"

"No."

"Sylvia, look, he would want you to tell me. I pay him for information. If I find him, he'll make some money."

Sylvia hung her head to consider. She shook her head and said reluctantly, "All he said was something about a job. He said he was going to this convenience store over by Redford, to see this guy named Eduardo Suárez." She looked up at me. "Are you sure you're gonna give him money? I mean, he said not to tell you." I grew worried that perhaps Socorro was using her to tell me.

"Sylvia. This is none of my business, but why are you hanging out with Socorro?"

Sylvia stared at the floor, then looked at me with her mouth agape. "I came out here and opened a massage, colonics, and sandwich shop. I hired Socorro to help out." She smiled at me, and I didn't laugh. "When my shop closed down, Socorro found me this job. So he's not what I'm used to, but he's all that's available around here." She smiled again, and I knew, as Socorro must have known, that she would soon leave the area.

"You've been an enormous help."

I walked away but couldn't help sneaking a glance over my shoulder at Sylvia. She had sunk back onto her stool, dangled her sandal over her toe, returned to her book, but had caught my glance and so waved good-bye.

Outside, Pooter came up to me, and Jerri walked out behind me and pulled her hat on and cinched up its leather thong strap. "She's not real perceptive when it comes to Socorro," Pooter said.

"She doesn't sound too perceptive about much," Jerri said, and went through some contortions to stick her thumb up under the strap of her purse, then hefted it off her shoulder to let it gently down to the ground.

Then I asked Pooter, "Just how exactly did you get mixed up with Socorro?"

"We were kinda both dating the same woman at the same time, Joan Phelan. She and I go way back. My best college buddy, the third wishbone quarterback for UT, married her years ago. A while back, he drove his car through a guardrail out on I-10 between Ozona and Sonora. Some said he did it on purpose. Some people said he did it because of her. I think he did it because she had given him a big dose of hope, like they could make it all over again, like his life wasn't so bad, and full of euphoria, he just lost control of his car." He stopped his story and looked at us, and I could tell, as I could from Sister Quinn's dreamy looks, that he was smiling to himself. He tilted his head to let his dreamy thoughts roll to one side, then started again. "Joan got in trouble, political problems." He stopped again and looked at us again, this time as though to beg us not to force him into details. "She ran away. This area was far away from everywhere. When I found some time off, I came down to see her and she was dating Socorro." He looked at me and said cautiously, "And I started seeing Dede Pate." Pooter and Sylvia weren't very good at hiding their pasts, not like Socorro or Dorothy McFarland. Pepper and I couldn't hide ours at all. Sister Quinn didn't have a past. This place had made her. It was the only place she could have existed, and then I hoped that it wasn't true of me and Pepper and Dede.

Jerri stared at him. I stepped off the porch. Jerri asked him, "So what happened to her?"

"She, Socorro, Sister Quinn, and I tried to save this old man. When he died, Joan just lost interest in this place. It scared her."

"Not you?" Jerri asked.

"I like it here. I learn a lot."

As Jerri stepped down, Pooter asked, "Do you think you could give me a ride?"

"Where?" I turned to ask.

"Somewhere close to Presidio. I want to meet Dede."

"Sorry. You'd have to sign a release form."

"Oh, hell, Dolph," Jerri said. "We're in my car. Some extra company, huh?" She flipped the keys to me. "You drive." Looking into her eyes, you'd think you were looking through clear, blue-tinted spring water. You couldn't see a bottom, just the deepness.

"Wait, I'll get my bag," Pooter said, and dashed into the store and came out with a gym bag.

When he left, Jerri looked at me and wrinkled her nose, like a girl. "*Dr.* Pooter?"

"He just got a Ph.D. in philosophy, from what I hear."

Jerri looked back at him and smiled at him, then me. "You do collect them out here. No wonder Fuentes ended up here." Again she smiled at me more with her eyes than her mouth.

So with Pooter in the back of Jerri's Suburban, we cruised to

Lajitas, asked for Socorro at Tommy Lawler's general store, fed a beer to Clay Henry—Tommy's beer-drinking goat—then asked for Socorro in the shops, corrals, and restaurant. No one would say anything.

We drove past Lajitas and hit El Camino del Rio, an engineering marvel, the prettiest road in the state, also the roughest; one of the patrol areas for the Presidio station. As I itched some more from the memories created by this area, Jerri leaned back and talked to Pooter. "So you're a philosopher? What is your dissertation on?"

"Whiteheadean process philosophy."

"You know, Vincent Fuentes," Jerri said, and turned to look at me, "once told me about that. He knew everything, had studied everything."

"Lucky man. I don't know much."

"So, uh, as a philosopher, what do you do? I mean, I studied English, writing, and art and became a private investigator."

"Nothing so interesting. I'm a bartender."

"You don't want to teach philosophy?"

"I don't like teaching, just learning. I'm taking a couple of physics courses. And I like to come down here. I learn a lot here, especially from Sister Quinn." I cocked my head to look at his face in my rearview mirror. He looked serious.

Jerri glanced at me and squinted. "Who's this Sister Quinn?"

"You'll find out," I said to Jerri.

Jerri leaned across the backseat to look at Pooter. "What do you want? Surely you want something."

"Joan's husband, Bailey Waller, the guy I told you about who went off I-10, he was a star; I was a lineman. I was a simple, dumb, West Texas boy, a lineman. Slow, dumb, no star, ugly. So I put in my eligibility at college, I got a job selling cars, then I got Bailey a job. He hit bottom over Joan. Then he just drove over that bridge. I *wanted* to know if he committed suicide, as some people whispered, or not."

"I bet it was suicide," I interrupted.

"Dolph," Jerri said.

From my rearview mirror, I saw Pooter smile. "I wanted to

be smart. So I re-enrolled at UT, just started all over, and got a Ph.D. in philosophy."

"So did you get smart?" I asked.

"I don't feel a whole lot smarter. But life seems easier."

Jerri smiled. "Well, I think Dede is a lucky girl, whoever she is."

I glanced at Jerri, then back to the road. I could see why Dede liked Pooter. She was hungry for information, but she got it from other people, not from schools, or orders, or even experience. She was always hungry for a teacher. I glanced at Pooter in my rearview mirror again. He sat in the backseat, a UT baseball cap protecting his bald head from the sun, his hands folded in his lap, smiling almost innocently—this dumb West Texas boy, far away from the rest of West Texas, far away from Austin, and he was the picture of contentment. No wonder he liked Sister Quinn.

"Where's your car?" I asked him.

"I rode the train out this trip. Amtrak. It's great, no road to get in the way. The landscape looks more like it must have before we started paving things. Then I hitched a ride here."

After we curled around mountains on the roads that seemed to be hung from cliffs and then got into flatter land, just east of Redford, I pulled the car off the road and walked, not toward the canebrakes and salt cedar lining the river, but across the road and up a slight rise. I dodged the lechuguilla, felt the tug of muscle and sinew as my ankles rolled in the loose rock until I got to the top of the rise. I squatted down and squinted out over the desert. I looked for the details, not the big picture that the tourists see, not the false panorama created by a windshield. Feeling my eyelids pull tight, feeling an ache in the back of my thigh, I looked for the trail of smoke behind a car, the puff of dust. I looked for something that I could see as a sign. After a certain distance, my sight grew fuzzy.

And then Jerri was squatting beside me. I turned to look at her. Soon, puffing and dripping sweat, Pooter lumbered up beside her. "Dolph, what the hell are you doing?" Jerri asked. Pooter pulled his UT cap off his head and swabbed at the sweat on his forehead with the sleeve of his shirt.

"High pointing. From a slight elevation, you can see the whole desert. And if you know how to look, you can interpret what's happening. This was my favorite part of being an agent. When I was up here and looking, I felt a little power."

Pooter squinted into the desert, then Jerri turned up the brim of her floppy straw hat and squinted. "What am I looking for?"

"A puff. Something that doesn't fit. Something that's too distinct."

Pooter seemed in a trance, as though the view had sucked him in. Jerri turned to look at me. She smiled like she thought I was crazy, then her smiled dropped. "What are you really doing, Dolph?" I looked into her deep blue eyes that matched her turquoise. "You're not just reliving old times."

"I can't see as well anymore. The distance gets fuzzy. I can't spot the details. The eye doctor says that I'll soon need bifocals."

"So?"

"So I can't see as well. I can't high point like I used to. I wouldn't be as good out here as I once was."

Pooter said, "I don't see too well, either. And I wouldn't dare to play football again."

Jerri raised herself. "If you noticed my eyes, I have this deep tint of blue. It's from the contacts." I looked up at Jerri. "And I dye my hair. It's not the blond it used to be, but it hides the gray. And if Joe didn't talk me out of it, I'd get liposuction." She dusted the dirt off her knees. "We get old, Dolph." And I looked into the false, artificial deepness of her contact lenses. Then I looked out at the desert and saw a fuzzy line in the distance. Several buttes and a polluted sky met. "You're not bad looking for a man your age, you know."

Jerri walked down the slope, but just for a moment longer, Pooter and I eyed the expanse and the details. "I see what you mean," he said.

We walked back to the car and drove through the flattened land that Indians, Spaniards, Mexicans, and now Texans had used to grow corn, cantaloupes, onions, and beans. I pulled off the road and followed the gravel road through the Alamendarizes' fields, then scratched Jerri's paint against the mesquite and creosote lining the road, then parked in the makeshift parking lot next to

Sister Quinn's templo. Sister Quinn was at a card table, having lunch. She had her dirty white tennis hat squashed down over her red curls, and her sweat had pasted them to her forehead. She had waxed paper unfolded from sliced lunch meats, a loaf of home-made Mexican bread, tomatoes, a jar of pickles, two bags of potato chips, and a six-pack of beer. She looked up nonchalantly and said, "Lunch is ready."

We closed our doors in unison, got out of the Suburban, and walked to her. She used her weak arms to push herself up from her chair and then took a couple of steps toward us. Pooter hugged her, then I did. She seemed to have lost more weight. I introduced her to Jerri. Someone had probably brought the food over. Leave it to Sister Quinn to turn lunch into a ceremony. Any hungry kid, bum, or wet who could get to Sister Quinn's templo, if he could endure her preaching, would have a beer and a sandwich. Feeling the growls in our bellies, the three of us stacked mounds of meat, tomatoes, and pickles between the thick slices of bread. Sister Quinn nibbled. Between bites I asked, "Have you seen Socorro?"

"No," Sister Quinn said. "I wish he were here, though."

"Come on, Barbara," I said as I chewed. "You're allowed to not like someone."

She laughed and sniffed at the air. "Can you smell that, Dolph?" Pooter smelled. Jerri looked at me from behind her sandwich and from under the brim of her hat, pleading not to have her pawing the ground and smelling. "Can you smell winter coming? And soon, the Alamendarizes will start plowing to plant their onions."

"I'd like to be here for that," Pooter said, and pulled the UT cap lower onto his head.

Jerri, with her fake-blue eyes, asked me what was going on. She didn't know that Barbara Quinn was trying to suck up every detail, every change of temperature, every smell of this little piece of earth before she died. Since this might very well be her last winter in this shack-church, I was surprised we didn't find her crawling around trying to feel, taste, and memorize each rock.

After we finished the beers, I asked Sister Quinn if I could talk to her privately. This of course meant that she opened the padlock to her templo, walked in, knelt at the altar, and looked up at the painting of the Virgin. The Virgin looked down. From the back of the templo, out from the old photograph, Pedrito Jaramillo, with his cataract-covered eyes, stared at our backs. This was our ceremony, the one we had created for our exchange of information. It started when I began questioning her about the wets she smuggled in, her so-called political refugees. This was the site where she would whip herself to try to approximate the misery most of the world felt. And to spread that misery, she had the then-young Azul whip her with an ocotillo branch. And then, because of her weird logic, the night, and my need to find Vincent Fuentes, my former lover Ariel whipped Sister Quinn and me. A contest to see who could take the most misery-craziness, a shame that I dared not tell anyone, even the psychologist I saw after the whole ugly incident. But I had won. Sister Quinn told me where Vincent Fuentes was hiding out, and thus she became my informer. The macabre, twisted, scary incident sent Ariel packing for a saner place and a saner lover. "I miss Azul," Sister Quinn said.

She knew what to say to torment me, to stir up my regrets, to confuse me, to remind me that I was still half Mexican, the half that belonged to my father, a drunk who died in an irrigation ditch after an all-night bender. Sister Quinn wanted me to help Vincent Fuentes when I found him. Instead he ended up with a bullet in his head and a local legend surrounding his death. The sales of his book went up. And Sister Quinn, like all the others in this stretch of desert, wanted to see the boys who killed Azul prosecuted. She didn't have a TV set, but Gilbert Mendoza drove her to his house and showed her videotape of me on the national news, talking the U.S. government around and through the incident. I heard that Gilbert cussed me and that his wife and Sister Quinn cried.

Several small shafts of sunlight full of motes, chunks of desert, bored through the holes in the templo and spotlighted points of it, including Sister Quinn's ocotillo-scarred back. "Remember those notarized forms that I asked about?" I saw her nod. Because of her concern for human suffering, Sister Quinn had become a sucker for melodrama, so I used it to get her to tell me what I wanted to know. "Barbara, they're selling those girls into white slavery. They'll get them to Houston or Dallas or San Antonio and make them prostitutes." I didn't lie too much.

Barbara nodded again as though the action was a part of her prayer. She grunted as she tried to straighten up and break the gazes of Mary and Pedrito that were locked on her. She couldn't get up. I stepped to her, grabbed her arm, and pulled her up. "Luna. The Luna brothers. They're twins. A woman stayed here. She said she was offered one of the *contracts* by one of the Lunas."

The woman who stayed was no doubt a wet. Part of our deal, our truce, our trust was that I no longer busted her for helping wets cross—as long as they didn't have drugs or guns. "Do you know them? Who they are?"

"No. But I heard that they're really mean, broncos. Especially Reynaldo. He's been in a mental ward and has a record. They look alike, but Esteban is missing a tooth."

"Esteban, with a missing tooth? I've seen him."

"Be careful of them." Sister Quinn and I both knew what she meant. They were poor desperate men. They saw others get rich with drugs or other smuggled goods. So they joined the smuggling business. They probably knew that they weren't smart enough to get really rich, to rival the big cartels, so they would figure to make up in ruthlessness what they lacked in intelligence. There were dozens of Lunas in the area, and I hoped that Leland Carter would supply them with a little intelligence.

Sister Quinn exhaled and sat down on a bench. She sucked in for some air. "Are you all right?"

"Yes, Dolph," she said, and held her open palm to her chest. "But now I want to ask you for a favor. I have a little business to settle." Tit for tat, barter, as usual. "Dolph, when I die—" But I interrupted her by turning away. "Now, Dolph. We have to talk about it. It's coming." I turned to her, and she smiled until I smiled. "When I die, I want you to execute my will."

"Oh no, why me?"

"Who else?" Then she clapped, her fingers straight up, the way a child claps, and she giggled. "Of course, I don't have much to leave." She laughed some more; then she opened one palm and tapped it with the finger from her right hand as she listed the points of her will. "Everything is in the cupboard above the sink. I have a list in there of things I want you to do. But briefly, I have very few relatives, so just write my brother. His address is on the list. I have a small savings account in Presidio. Distribute that money locally. I'm sure you'll do so wisely."

"Oh, Barbara, why not just leave the money to Jesse Guzmán for St. Margaret Mary's?"

"That will be fine with me if you decide to do that."

"Aw, Jesus, Barbara."

"Now I want you to take over my templo."

"What?"

"Just keep it standing for a while. Maybe drive down and check on it. Maybe pick up Dede and have a picnic. Bring people out. Just for a while. Then just let it fall down."

"You know that this isn't your land. The Alamendarizes just tolerate you."

"Well, then, they can tolerate my templo for a while after I'm gone. The keys are in my cupboard too." She stopped tapping her finger into her palm and looked at me with soft eyes. "And Dolph, I would so much like to die here if at all possible. Not in some hospital. I can take the pain. And, if at all possible, I'd like to die with someone nearby."

"I'll do my best," I said.

I helped her stand, and then I helped her to the open door, and as we neared it, I reached into my pocket for my wallet. I unfolded a hundred-dollar bill and put it in the collection box by the door. Since she had been excommunicated, federal money, payoff money, helped keep Sister Quinn's templo open. Her church and my state were all mixed up. And now, I supposed, when she died, my state salary would go in part to keep her church standing.

We walked through the door of her chapel and into the sweet, slightly polluted October desert air to a sweating Pooter and a wryly smiling Jerri. "Don't any of your friends own phones?" Jerri asked.

NINE

We parked the Suburban right down 170 from the crumbling convenience store just outside Presidio's city limits. "Now, see if you can find Eduardo Suárez, and then show him the notarized forms and just try to see his reaction."

"Dolph, I've done this before," Jerri said as she opened the door to the Suburban and jerked her shoulder so that her purse cleared the seat. She pushed the brim of her hat up to see me better. "Don't treat me like a *girl*."

"So this is real cop work?" Pooter asked, smiling. "It's kind of exciting. Can I go along?"

"No, I didn't want to bring you along, remember?"

"Relax, Dolph," Jerri said.

"Maybe I ought to go in too?"

Jerri grimaced. "Look, we decided. Someone might recognize you. That's why we didn't bring your car. I'm a tourist. Then if I find Eduardo, I'll tell him who I am."

"Yeah, but a woman alone in a bar like this . . ."

"See. See. I'm not just a *girl*, Dolph."

"So I'll go with you," Pooter said.

"No!" Jerri and I said in unison.

She cocked her head, leaned forward, set her shoulder against the weight of the purse, swung her left arm to the rhythm of her gait, and slightly swayed her hips as she marched toward the convenience store. "What's in that purse?" Pooter asked.

"I don't know."

"She looks kind of like John Wayne marching up to duke it out with the bad guys," Pooter said. Though I was doing work that I usually did alone, I was beginning to enjoy Jerri and Pooter's company.

Pooter and I waited. He sipped a soda, and I checked my watch, and the Suburban filled with Pooter's odor. I looked at the backseat. The windows were down, but it was still hot, and he was drenched with sweat.

Pooter and I both snapped to when Jerri came from the store smiling, her heavy purse bounding off her hip. I saw a man come up from behind her and run toward her. I lay across the seat, cussed, dug, and fumbled under the passenger seat and came up with my holstered pistol. As I jerked the handle of the driver's door, then pushed it open with my knee, Pooter opened his door and hit the ground running. I unsnapped the leather thong around the hammer and had my .357 out of the holster. Pooter ran with ease yet deliberateness. His palms were no longer turned back but clenched in fists, his fat turned into taught muscles; as the muscles in his neck bulged, he lowered his bald head and pumped his feet and arms in exact rhythm, the old pulling guard. I could barely catch him. He would be a good man to back you up.

Before the man could grab her, showing some sort of training, Jerri got her left forearm against his and thrust the heel of her right palm at the man's nose. She caught him in the forehead, stunning him, but he was able to grab her purse and cut the strap with a knife. But with her right hand, she grabbed the other strap of her purse, pulled it away from him, and circled it above her head like she was twirling a lariat. And then, with lipstick, credit cards, and nail files spilling out, she planted the purse along the man's head and sent him reeling. She pulled her hat off and spun it like a Frisbee into the man's face.

"Back away," I yelled as I passed Pooter.

The man staggered back from Jerri, holding his face. Heaving the purse, jerking it, grunting from its weight, she again circled the purse around her head, aiming for the man's knees. But this time the remaining strap gave way and the purse slid across the gravel in the convenience store parking lot. The purse snatcher turned his back and started to run. Jerri started after him. I wished that I had jogged more with Pepper. I just barely kept ahead of Pooter.

The purse snatcher ran behind the convenience store and then churned his legs down the long slope of a dry wash. He let himself drop to his butt and slid, trying to push himself out of the way of the prickly pear, the mesquite, and the creosote. I saw Jerri do the same. She skidded on her butt, yelling just a bit when she hit a big rock. I went down the bank after her but tried to stay on my feet. As I churned my feet, I looked behind me and saw Pooter, wiser than us, slowly picking his way around the big rocks and the cacti. "Go the hell back," I yelled at Pooter.

The thief slid to the bottom of the slope and started running down the wash toward a barbed wire fence that stretched across it. If he could clear the barbed wire, he had a shot at making it to the canebrakes next to the river; then he could hide or cross it. With my feet working as fast as I could move them, sometimes jumping, I made it to the end of the slope, winded from my effort. I pulled my gun, leveled it, and started to yell. Panic, disappointment, and disgust blew up inside my head. I had all but forgotten Spanish. Working from the Marfa headquarters for so long, I had no reason to speak it. Squinting to help me think, rolling my tongue around in my mouth to loosen it up, I tried to remember the Border Patrol mantra. "Stop! Para! Arriba las manos." It came out. The man didn't stop. I fired one shot in the air. The man stopped. "Shoot him, shoot him," Jerri yelled, and ran up to him. The man slowly turned around to face us.

I held my gun on him and inched closer to him as both Jerri and I studied his face. I smiled at him, and he let his lips part. He had all of his teeth. His nose had never been broken.

"Vete de aquí," I said.

Jerri turned to look at me. "What? You want him to go? What?"

The man looked at me, then he smiled. "Vete," I yelled again, and motioned with the gun. His smile turned to a quizzical look, and he took one step back, then another. He had a long face with an ugly scar on it, and now he probably had a broken cheek. Pooter was now right behind me.

"What are you doing?" Jerri demanded.

I jerked my head and motioned with the gun. The man smiled as he figured out that I meant it, that he wouldn't get shot in the back. The robber turned and ran for the barbed wire fence, flattened on his back, and crawled under it. I watched him as he made it to the canebrakes and burrowed into them.

"What did you let him go for?" Jerri yelled at me.

"He saw a gringa with a heavy purse. He's just some pelado too desperate not to take a chance."

"He just wanted some money, right?" Pooter asked.

"Are you all right?" I asked.

"I think so," she said, and bent to look at a tear in the knee of her pants. I knelt beside her and felt her knee. She tugged on her pants leg so that it rose up just a bit, and I noticed that, taped to her ankle, was a dainty little .22. "Why didn't you pull that?"

"You seemed to be doing fine with your big gun." She giggled. Then I noticed that the seat of her khakis was shredded. This middle-aged woman wore thong bikini panties—and her butt was scratched and bruised.

Pooter stared at her butt too. "You're not going to be able to sit down," he said with more sympathy than I could have mustered. I was trying not to laugh.

We all caught our breaths, then Jerri straightened and brushed her hair off her forehead. At the top of the slope, looking down at us, were three patrons from the bar. One of them held up Jerri's purse and smiled. "He's Eduardo," Jerri said. "He wouldn't say anything. He's guilty as hell, though. Palo's now got him and Leland to trade." Jerri looked up at him and smiled and waved. He smiled and waved and strained to hold up the purse.

As we made our way up the hill, Jerri winced against the pain in her butt. Pooter asked, "What's in the purse?"

"A brick. Another one of my own little tricks."

Eduardo politely handed her purse to her and helped the three of us pick up its scattered contents and her crushed straw hat from the parking lot. I recognized one of the men with him—a farmworker for the Alamendarizes.

Back at the Suburban, Jerri gingerly tried to sit down but winced again. I tried to stifle my laugh. "You better get something on your knee and your behind."

Jerri giggled. "I was scared to death, but then I got excited. If I could have gotten to my gun, I'd have shot him, Dolph," she said. Then she unzipped her khakis and slid them off. Pooter and I both tried to turn our heads, but we stared. She wadded them up and put them beneath her feet. "Well, these are ruined." She stuck her right leg in the air and tore the tape from around her tiny .22. Both Pooter and I winced as we heard the tape tear. Jerri giggled. "Sometimes it's good to be a girl. No man would shave his legs just to hide a little gun like this. No man would carry a little gun like this. One of the advantages of being a woman. And believe me, I take all the advantages I can get." She folded her thick, short muscular legs under her butt and got ready for the drive into Presidio. Pooter dug into his bag, pulled out a towel, and handed it to her. "Why, thank you, Pooter," she said sweetly to him.

Jerri folded the towel over her lap. "I didn't really want you to shoot him. But something about a crazy middle-aged lady screaming and threatening to shoot makes a bad guy nervous. And sometimes if he's nervous enough, he'll talk to you a lot more."

"So what did you find out?" I asked.

Jerri smiled, and her lip just barely quivered from the pain in her butt. "He didn't know anything about the form. Said it must have been forged." Jerri smiled as though giving a show. She turned around to look at Pooter, but then she turned to face me. "He's guilty as shit."

We stopped at Dede's house, which had a forked gravel road running around it. Presidio had no zoning laws, no real city plan. People built houses, and the bulldozers that made streets followed them. The man who Dede rented from had built the house at the end of a block, but when the city decided to lengthen the street, the driver of the bulldozer cleared the street around both sides of the house. It really didn't matter. There wasn't much traffic anyway, and no one had a lawn.

When we pulled up, Jerri, with Pooter's towel around her, followed Pooter and me into the house. When Dede saw us, she kissed Pooter, then me, then shook Jerri's hand. While Dede and Jerri went into the bathroom so Dede could swab and bandage Jerri's butt, I called Trujillo and asked him about the Lunas. He didn't recognize the name, but he said that he would find out what he could. Jerri came out in a pair of baggy sweatpants that she borrowed from Dede. I noticed a bulge on the outside edge of her right calf. She had taped her gun back in place.

Dede grilled hamburgers for us while the sun was still up, and we sat in her backyard (Jerri again with her legs folded under her), drank beer while we watched the sun set behind the Chinatis, and felt the sudden refreshing surge as the sun sank behind the mountains. Suddenly we were cool and the world was better. "Dolph," Dede said to me as she smiled at Pooter and put her hand over his, "whatever became of Pat Coomer?"

Pat was sort of my partner when I was at the Presidio station. A long, lanky, red-haired Irish guy from Louisiana, he went native by marrying a local woman with three kids. "After Nogales, then San Diego, he got transferred to the Canadian border, somewhere in New York." And Dede and I both laughed as we thought about Pat and his Mexican wife and kids in snow and ice.

As I sipped my beer, I smiled as I watched Dede hold Pooter's hand and nodded to her, hoping to tell her that I was indeed happy if what I saw with her and Pooter was real, or good, or at least amusing. We felt the night, the company, the stars beaming down on us and the first tipsy feeling from a few too many beers. It was late, and Jerri and I decided to stay at the one motel in town, the Three Palms Inn. As we left, I looked in the rearview mirror as Dede waved to us with one hand and held Pooter's hand with the other, his palm turned back, forcing her hand to twist forward. He dwarfed her, and he pulled off his UT cap with his free hand and waved good-bye to us. I chuckled to imagine their lovemaking.

The Three Palms was the only motel in town in the only

organized part of town—where 67 joined 170, the two paved roads. Down from the Border Patrol station it offered some of the appearances of America—fifties architecture, a dining room, a gaudy sign, and the prefab-looking units of a motel. We pulled in. I checked Jerri into a room and then got myself another. I helped Jerri carry her suitcase up to her room, and I waited outside her door as she said, "Good night, Dolph," and closed the door in my face. I went back down the steps from her second-floor room, twirling the keys to her Suburban on my finger. I wanted to retrieve my toilet kit and the small suitcase I had brought with me.

When I opened the door, some force from behind me slammed my face into the padded seat, and I dropped the keys and reached behind me. I squirmed and twisted to get square with my mugger, but two sets of hands grabbed me, on either arm, and jerked me out of the Suburban. I caught a glimpse of two men in ski masks; I even saw the sweat streaming out from under the masks. Unable to resist, I let them throw me over the hood of the car. I strained and pushed against the pressure of a hand on the side of my face. On the other side of my face I could feel the still hot hood of the Suburban and brim of my Stetson bent under my head. Then I felt a sharp point just above my ear. "You ask too many questions, Dolph Martinez."

"Can I ask one more?"

"Fuck you."

"Who the hell are you, and what do you want?"

I tried to raise up, but I felt the pressure from the point, and I let it push my face back down onto the hood of the Suburban. This time I twisted my head out from under my hat and saw my bent-brim hat lying next to my face. "You need to stop asking so many questions. Your case is over."

"What case?"

I felt the point of the knife press into the side of my head, and I felt like it broke the skin, for I thought that I felt my warm blood running down my neck. "I bet your name is Luna," I said, and I felt my head lifted, then slammed into the hood of the car. I looked, but all I could see was the blue metal of the hood. I fought against the memory of the backpacker who put several nine-millimeter bullets into my gut. I anticipated the wasp stings of the nine-millimeter bullets.

"Look, vato, one little push and your brain is fucked. So don't be fucking with me. Palo is going to jail. Let him. Tell this woman to go back to San Antonio and forget about this."

"What woman?" If I could stay alive, I was determined to get as much information as possible. If I was to stay alive, I had to remember to bargain and not threaten. If I was to stay alive, I couldn't let fright or anger or instinct maybe make me stumble into another bullet, another scar, more years of replay and nightmares.

I felt myself being lifted again, and I felt my head being slammed into the car, but I got some more information for my blackened eye. "Don't play shit with me. We don't know what she wants to know. What she's after. But no more. Tell her to go home." They weren't too sure about Jerri Johnson.

"Well, let's go talk to her. Sounds like your argument is with her, not with me."

I felt the point of the knife start to burn. I was sure I felt a trickle of blood running down behind my ear and down my neck. "Right now, motherfucker, right now, you're dead. Say something, motherfucker, say something, and you're dead." I kept silent. "Now you don't talk so big, Mr. Border Patrol motherfucker. Come down here starting shit. What's your squeeze Jerri Johnson gonna say when she meets la verga mi compadre? He gonna put it to her, huh." I jerked up and twisted, and just as suddenly, both pairs of arms pushed me down onto the hood of Jerri's truck. "Maybe you don't know who you fucking with? Who you think that baboso at the store was? You think that was just an accident? You the big policía, and you don't know shit. You let him go. You think he was an accident?" I squirmed and pulled and felt anger make a perhaps fatal surge rush through my blood and muscle. "It's going to get ugly for Jerri, you don't cut this shit out."

"Let me see your face, Luna." And I felt the knife pushing against my skin, and just as quickly, I felt the release of the pressure.

I heard a slam as the man with the knife plopped against the side of the Suburban and crushed my hat beneath him. "That's enough," the other man said.

"What are you fucking doing?" The smaller man was up in a minute, squared off with the knife pointed at the bigger man. He couldn't see well because his ski mask was twisted to one side.

"I'm here to scare him, not to puncture anybody's brain or rape some woman."

"Shut up, pendejo."

"Ease up," I heard. The man with the knife lunged for the other man. I twisted and got a knee up between somebody's legs, and the man with the knife gasped, stepped back, breathed heavily, and stared at me and his former partner.

"You fucked yourself, man," he said in a sputtering way to his friend. I wished that I had worn my gun, then was relieved that I hadn't so that no one could have grabbed it from me. I debated jumping toward the door, opening it, then fishing around for it.

"Nobody's fucked yet. We warned him. That's it. Now let's go."

"You're both fucked." The man with the knife stepped away, then ran.

I pulled my fist behind my ear, ready to coldcock the other guy, but just as I was about to push my fist through the air, the man pulled off his ski mask. I saw the thick, scraggly mustache hanging over his lip. I noticed the ponytail now. "Socorro!" I yelled. "What the fuck do you think you're doing?"

"Making a little extra cash." Socorro relaxed because he realized that I wouldn't hit him now. His whole body seemed to slump. His eyes had a sad weariness in them, as though begging me not to give him any more shit.

"Hell, I came down here to pay you to inform on those guys. What the hell are you thinking?" I reached behind my ear to dab at my wound.

"We were gonna scare you."

"Who?"

"Now I can't tell you."

"What do you fucking mean, you can't tell me? I already know who—alls I need you for is to confirm."

"Why do you think I can't tell you? I been working for this guy, picking up some extra cash, man. And here you come stumble-fucking around with that goddamn lady private detective."

"Tell me something. You made any money by signing some notarized form to marry some poor pelada?" Socorro dropped his head to keep from looking at me and from answering my question. I looked at the blood on my fingertips. My wound wasn't serious.

"I'm telling you, Dolph. Lay the fuck off," he muttered toward his shoes.

"Holy shit. And you been telling Sylvia Walker that I was some kind of strong-armed hoodlum cop."

"Ease up on my honey, fucker. Who just saved your life?"

"He wasn't gonna do anything."

"You don't know him. It was getting spooky. You didn't see his eyes."

"Whose eyes?"

"Fuck you, I ain't telling you."

"Two hundred dollars for a name. Anybody's name."

"You think I'm crazy?"

Then I remembered Jerri. "How many guys with you?"

"Fuck you."

"Goddamn, Socorro, is one of your crazy-ass lunatics fucking with Jerri Johnson?"

"Oh, fuck!"

"You gotta gun?"

"No."

"What the fuck is wrong with you? You come here threatening to kill me, and you ain't got a gun."

"We weren't gonna kill you. That's why I came along. That's why I told them we could scare you off. Hell, Dolph, you stupid bastard, I was thinking of you. If you would have played scared and told him you were scared, maybe if you'd have shaken a little, we'd be on our way. I'd have five hundred fucking dollars plus the money you're offering me to tell on the bastards, and everybody would be happy, but you gotta be a smart-ass and piss him off and fuck everything up so I can't tell you shit. Fuck, fuck, fuck." He jumped up and down.

I got in his face. "So I'm supposed to know it's you playing both sides of the fucking law when some bastard whose breath smells like he just ate some bad chili pokes a fucking switchblade in my ear? What are you thinking? What the fuck you want me to do?"

"So we both didn't plan ahead. But don't rub my fucking nose in it. Goddamn, Dolph, you piss me the fuck off. All you fucking federal cop people got this burr up your ass just 'cause poor people like me exist."

I dammed the blood flowing too fast through my veins. "Okay, okay, okay, I apologize. Now help me go rescue Jerri."

"Shit, shit, shit. So I suppose you're not gonna give me shit unless I spill my guts."

"You got that right."

"Fuck, so that means I don't make shit. I got the same right as the next guy to make a living."

I reached into the Suburban, fumbled around for my belt and holster, and pulled it out like it was a snake. As I buckled it on, Socorro kept bitching. "Just like Vietnam, the military, the fucking establishment, industry, etc., the officers, the boss, the CEO, corporate fucking America doesn't give a shit about the likes of me."

I turned to Socorro and thought about shooting him or hitting him over the head with my pistol. "Okay, okay, I'll give you a hundred to check on Jerri. I just feel comfortable with a little backup." Then I added, "Even if he's an incompetent fucker who didn't even bring a gun."

"I don't own a gun."

"Well, excuse me, but I'm Border Patrol, and I've been gut shot and nearly died, so I just feel better with someone backing me up." I spotted my Stetson on the ground, picked it up, and tried to reshape it.

"Let's go, then. I got your back."

Our boot heels clicked on the metal stairwell as we climbed up to Jerri's room. When we got to her door, I turned to Socorro and whispered, "I've only seen this done in movies, but we're gonna both plant our shoulders into that door and bust it off of its lock." Socorro nodded, and then I held up one finger, another, and then a third, and we both pushed our shoulders into the door. I heard splintering wood and then a few grunts. I fumbled with my gun and got it raised just in time to see Jerri pointing her dainty .22 at me. A man against the wall started scooting toward the door. Socorro was on the ground under my feet and trying to push himself up. My Stetson was on top of him.

"Jesus, Dolph," Jerri said. "Knock." She swung her gun toward the man sliding down the wall and kept it on him. "Where you going, vato?" I swung my gun toward him too and looked out the corner of one eye at Socorro.

"You all right?"

Socorro grunted, put his hand up to his face, and stared down at his boots. I stepped closer to the man pressing himself against the wall. He had an indentation from his hat around his thick mop of tangled hair. I recognized the dark, close-set eyes and the nose with the twist. I smiled, and he smiled back. He was missing a tooth. Esteban, Leland Carter's thug. He was sweating, and his eyes darted back and forth between us.

"I was just about to shoot this guy when you two came busting in here," Jerri said as she eased herself onto the bed. Still in Dede's sweatpants, Jerri sat crossed-legged, then wriggled to fold her legs underneath her. Esteban's smile went away. He looked at Jerri, then at Socorro, and the look in his eyes changed from a threat to a plea. Socorro backed into one corner of the room and shut up. "I was going to shoot him just to make him think twice about hiding in a woman's room." I looked at Jerri. "He came up behind me and grabbed me. You remember him?"

"Esteban," I said. "And I bet his last name is Luna." Esteban dropped his head.

"That's a start, but I want to know why he was here."

"He and his twin brother wanted to scare us. Reynaldo jumped me out in the parking lot, but Socorro here helped me out."

"Goddamn it, Dolph," Socorro said, and slid along the wall.

"It's getting complicated, Dolph," Jerri said.

I was tired of holding up my gun, so I let my arm drop to my side. "How do you feel, Esteban? You just got your ass kicked by a little lady." I bent over to pick up my Stetson. When I put the bent, crushed thing on my head, I knew that I looked stupid, so I took it off and put it crown down on the dresser. I would have liked to put my gun down.

"I'd still like to shoot him." Esteban pressed his back to the wall.

I walked to the phone and dialed the home phone of Raul Flores, the Presidio County deputy sheriff assigned to Presidio.

As I told Raul to come pick up Esteban, Jerri said, "What are you doing?"

I interrupted my comments with Raul to say, "Getting him out of our way."

"Let's shoot him." Jerri lowered her gun so that it was pointed toward his crotch.

"Esteban," I said, but Esteban wouldn't look away from Jerri.

"How about a warning shot in a knee?" Jerri asked.

"Esteban," I said, and this time he did look at me. "How many people are you working with?"

"No hablo inglés," Esteban said.

I saw Socorro shake his head. I said, "You spoke English the other day to my friend Pepper." Esteban hung his head.

"Let's shoot him for lying."

"Who hired you?" Esteban just shook his head, telling himself to hold out. "Let me try a guess. Leland Carter?" Esteban turned to look at me. "Did Leland Carter hire you to do this?" Esteban smiled. "What about your brother? Is he running this?" Esteban jerked his head toward Jerri. "Now, you know I've got Socorro here, who I'm gonna ask," I said, and jerked my thumb toward Socorro.

Esteban looked at Socorro, but Socorro hung his head and muttered, "Shit."

Esteban looked at me. "Okay, okay, Leland Carter. That's all I'm saying, man."

Jerri kept her dainty gun on him until Raul Flores came puffing in, pulling his gun belt to lift up his gut and looking around the room at everybody's face. After he handcuffed Esteban, I took Raul by the arm and escorted him to the bathroom. "Qué pasó, Dolph?"

"Raul, look, book this guy for whatever, take him to the

county jail in Marfa, and have Abe Rincón question him. Find out as much as you can." Raul was nodding, but I could tell my information was rattling around in his head. "Now, look, Raul, I'm going to call Abe and tell him how you helped me on this." Abe Rincón was a good man, the sheriff of Presidio County. He cooperated with the Border Patrol and with my task force. We went way back together.

Raul's eyes brightened. "Cuñados?"

"Cuñados, family, Raul. But look, tell Abe to scare him. Threaten him with something. Attempted rape. And see if he agrees to testify against anybody."

Raul turned away from me, but I pulled him back around. "He's not a citizen of this country. And try to get a steep bail on him. Keep him locked up as long as you can. And see who bails him out." Raul was nodding. I held up a finger. "You got it, Raul?" He nodded. Raul and I go way back too.

We walked back into the motel room. Esteban seemed to be begging us all with his eyes. He looked like a deer caught in the glare of an oncoming car—just like the wets I had picked up for most of my career in the Border Patrol.

"I still have a few questions," Jerri said.

"I've got the answers."

"What about him?" Raul said, and motioned toward Socorro and pulled Esteban up.

I looked at Socorro, who raised his head. He didn't get the placid, trapped-in-the-headlights look that Esteban got. He looked defiant, threatening. He was the ex-something—vet, con, drug dealer, deserter—with a chip on his shoulder and a grudge against any authority. He was also a member of my team. Socorro and I go way back. "He's with me," I said.

"What?" Esteban said. "What, what? You going to let him go? You not going to take that lying fucker in?" Raul pulled him out the door.

When I closed the door behind them, Socorro looked at Jerri. She rolled to her side. "So is this the guy we've been looking for?"

"Shake hands with Jerri Johnson." Socorro stuck out his hand like he was reaching for a rattler. I looked into my own hand. I had been squeezing my heavy pistol for so long that I had gotten used to the heft of it. I put it down on the dresser next to my hat.

"Aren't you gonna thank me?" I asked Socorro as he let go of Jerri's hand.

"I figure we're even." He slouched toward the door.

"Wait a minute. You know the score on this." Socorro surprisingly stopped to let me taunt him. I turned to Jerri. "What do we have now?" She caught the wink in my voice if not my eye.

"We know just about this whole deal between the Lunas and Leland Carter," Jerri said.

"You can get caught up in this, you know," I said to Socorro.

"Not if you leave me out," Socorro said, and looked me in the eye.

"You're asking me to lie."

"You're used to it."

"But I know too," Jerri said. "Tell us what you know without my having to bring in police."

Socorro pressed his flat hand against the bottom half of his face and pushed his mustache up. He looked at Jerri but then turned to speak to me. "You got to be fucking kidding. These are mean fuckers, and I ain't in too good a position right now. So you're asking me just to sell my own ass down the river." He turned to Jerri. "And as for you, Miss Cop, FBI, Narc, or whatever the fuck you are, you can go fuck yourself."

I reached out to grab his arm as he was trying to leave the room, and he cocked his hand back like he would nail me. I smiled, expecting to have a tooth or my nose broken. Socorro and I had been threatening each other for several years, and the realization of the absolute futility of beating the shit out of each other and the results—him unable to afford medical expenses, me unable to afford too many more wounds—kept us from finally throwing punches.

"You ought to apologize to Ms. Johnson. You've always been a little rude to women, and you ought to really think about who could do you the most harm."

"I know who can do me the most harm." He turned his back to me and walked through the motel door.

"Nice fella," Jerri said. "Have y'all been friends long?" I sat down in the chair and sucked in for some air. Jerri stared at me.

"We're staying together."

"I can take care of myself." Jerri smiled, and even if contacts made her look as she did, her deep, pretty eyes seemed to flash just for me.

"Maybe I want you to protect me."

"Okay, Dolph, we'll save me and the U.S. government some money. We'll split the room."

I went back out to her Suburban and retrieved my bag. Then we both moved to my room and reported the broken lock to the motel management. As I explained what I thought I knew and what I had planned, Jerri smiled at me, then said, "You ain't no slouch, are you?" Jerri took a shower while I watched TV over a very poor cable connection. She came out of the shower with her hair slicked back, pajamas on. She was clean, fresh, older looking, limping. Without her contacts, her eyes didn't look like deep blue pools. Instead her eyes shifted, lazily, like a cat's. They were dull but wary, knowing, tough. She caught me watching her. "Your turn."

During my shower I scrubbed at the slight puncture Reynaldo had made in my head and rubbed my bruises. Clean, feeling fresher and relaxed, I put on a clean pair of jeans and rested in the chair. Jerri turned off the light, and I could hear the rustle as she pulled the sheet and bedspread over herself. "Dolph, take off your jeans and come slide into this bed."

"Yes, ma'am."

I slid under the covers on the side of the bed next to the open window. I felt the cool breeze from the north coming in, and I felt the barest brush from the hair on Jerri's arms on the other side of me. For a few moments she tossed and turned, then she rolled onto her stomach. "I have some antiseptic and some lotion in my bag in the bathroom. Would you mind putting a bit of each across my wide ol' butt?"

"At your service."

Jerri clicked on the light. She looked down at the blood-speckled pillow sheet under me. "Dolph, you're bleeding. Bring my whole first aid kit out here."

I went into the bathroom, came out with the antiseptic and some Band-Aids and gauze. I felt Jerri's breath on my face as she leaned over me to rub antiseptic on my slight wound and put a Band-Aid on it. Her breath was sweet but heavy.

She smiled, rolled away from me, lowered her pajama bottoms, and pulled the sheet up to the edge of the two healthy scoops of her butt. As I sat down on the bed, I saw the blue and yellow bruises, the scrapes, and the one long cut. She must have been hurting all afternoon, but she had swallowed her groans and complaints. She let out a slight whimper as I gingerly touched the raw spots. She had been hurt far worse than I had been.

TEN

I had never seen Leland Carter smoke, but as he sat in front of me, he dabbed his lit cigarette at the ashtray in front of him. "Goddamn it, Dolph. You've got to give me some room here. I mean we got to stick together."

I crossed my arms and looked at the lunch crowd at the Thunderbird restaurant. The ranchers and various county or federal workers were stuffing chicken-fried steaks, hamburgers, or burritos into their faces and watching Leland and me—or so it seemed to me, the heads ducking and raising just above the chewed top of a burger. People talked, word got out. I didn't want anyone to know what had happened—yet. "I'm not in on this. I know what she's thinking. Right, Dolph? I mean why else would she be asking me?"

"Well, I can tell you this much, Leland. Jerri Johnson is suspicious. But she's a private detective. There's nothing legal she can do."

"Lyle Blackwell just died. That's all." He held his cigarette over the ashtray far too long. He wasn't accustomed to smoking.

"Well, all she wants is some information for this friend of hers who is in jail."

"Look, that's Palo's problem." I could see him squeeze the filter tip of his cigarette. As far as I knew, no one had said a thing to him about Palo. I looked around the place to see who might have noticed his screwup. He had proven himself to be just some dumb, out-of-luck local guy whose only real attribute as a cop was a sort of dim-witted persistence. I didn't see how he could be the one running this, and my thoughts shifted to Reynaldo Luna.

He had called me in the morning and asked for a meeting. He chose the Thunderbird because it was in Marfa down from sector headquarters. I stuck my forefinger between my collar and neck to loosen my tie. My waist, my neck, all of me was expanding. I looked down at my half-eaten burger. There was the partial culprit for my expansion, but I had left half of it. I talked while looking at my soggy burger. "Leland, you better get a lawyer. You better not talk to me."

"But Dolph. Not to talk to you, man? Come on. You could fix this. You're the man. You know I'm not guilty." He leaned toward me, over his plate with its enchilada sauce. He slanted his head as though to interrupt my concentration on my soggy burger. "This is us, man. We're locals. I'm the victim here."

I pulled my head up to look at him, and my eyes darted to the hand with the cigarette in it. It twitched. "I'm federal, Leland. I'm not local. I've been here a long time, but that doesn't mean anything to my job." But because I had been here a long time, I felt that I ought to help him. "It's just accusations now. The lawyers and DAs in San Antonio are working on it. If you're innocent . . ."

The table shook from Leland's vibrating hand, but he stopped his quiver as soon as he started it. "Of course I'm innocent." He looked at me. "And don't give me that shit about I'll be let go because I'm innocent. Hell, just the rumor could ruin me, cost me my job. Weldon would fire me for the sake of the office. Dolph, please."

"And just what would you want me to do?"

"Stop it."

"How?"

"Just stop it."

Leland reached out and grabbed the bill. "I've got to get going. Thanks for the lunch." Leland grumbled, stood, and turned from me. I rose up out of my chair so I wouldn't have to raise my voice. "How's Esteban doing?"

He looked at me like I was a rattler. He slowly moved to one side, and in the pulse of blood that ran through one prominent vein on the side of his forehead, I could see the convulsion of thought and confusion blocking his speech. "He was just a guy I hired."

"I hear he's already out on bail. Where did his bail money come from? Who paid it?"

Even as we spoke, Jerri was talking to the bail bondsman and people at the Presidio County courthouse, trying to find out who bailed Esteban out. Abe Rincón verified what she had heard. A well-dressed Mexican lawyer had showed up and started flashing money around in the courthouse. Right now, we could arrest some people, Leland included, but we didn't have anything that would stick. We needed, Palo needed, more. Jerri had felt that with a subpoena or pressure, Socorro would talk. I didn't believe he would. Besides, I didn't want to harm my "business" relation with Socorro. And I wanted to leave Sister Quinn out of it.

Leland looked at me; the vein bulged. He leaned past me to crush his cigarette out in the ashtray. He straightened up. When he spoke, his voice was firm. He almost sounded like a policeman. "Esteban is out. He's mad. Stop this." He turned his back to me and picked his cowboy hat from the hat rack. As he opened the door, I held his eyes on me with my stare. I then smiled, and he averted his eyes. His last statement sounded like a threat.

* * *

That night, my mother, as usual, orchestrated the serving of Pepper's venison roast and the conversation. She pushed Charlie into talking about the TV shows that he had produced and then pushed Jerri into talking about her past—until she stumbled over Vincent Fuentes and looked at me with half of a new potato bulging in the side of her cheek. When Jerri came to dinner, she had lowered herself gently into the seat and then, as she ate and talked, she leaned to one side. She didn't let the indignity of her scraped, cut, and bruised butt keep her from being a professional or a lady. Her eyes again were deep and sky blue, and I found myself not caring if the look was artificial.

After dinner I sat on the front porch, and Jerri, having sat during dinner, leaned against a column. There was no sunset for us to watch. While we had been in Presidio, daylight savings time ended for the year, and so the sun set during our dinner conversation and left us with a rapidly cooling night. "There's the tracks, and on the other side is the old Mexican side of town," Jerri said.

"It used to be the Mexican side of town. But now yuppies are moving in because they like the adobe."

"There's a beautiful old church. I'd like to see it. I'll take a drive through that part of town tomorrow. Joe and I, we're lucky. We like the same things. We like Mexicans, Mexican stuff; we couldn't live in a city that didn't have a lot of Mexicans."

She swiveled on her toes to look up at the sky.

"You talked about Fuentes, but what about Joe Parr? How did you meet him?"

"Fuentes again. Fuentes had come back to this country after being in prison in Mexico. He had changed. And Joe Parr suspected him of smuggling guns. Joe was right, but not in all ways. But love, or a love that was over, foolishness, pride made me help Fuentes. And some poor Mexican carpenter was killed, by your friend Trujillo. That was Angel Martínez. And Ranger Joe Parr, like John Wayne or Clint Eastwood riding to the rescue, busted everybody. Including me."

I looked at her, beaming now with a smile. "I barely beat the rap. I could have done some time. But I'm happy with what I did. I did what I had to. Joe did what he had to. So we *grew* in love." She seemed almost to be talking to herself. Then in the dim light she turned her gaze toward me. "Talk of Fuentes bothers you. And I think you're jealous of Joe."

All I could do was gaze out at the darkness and mutter, "No, don't be foolish."

"I knew the moment I saw Fuentes that I could settle with him and for him. I just knew that I could be so totally satisfied with him that I could spend what rest of my life I had trying to fully understand and appreciate him. But he got crazy." Jerri leaned over to look at my face. I tried looking away, but those eyes caught me, and I stared into her face. "And I resented him for so many years, but now, this late, I kind of appreciate him, not for him, Dolph. But for the feeling that he gave me. That feeling of being sure, of knowing, is a luxury. The rest of the time, mostly, in regard to lovers, hell, in regard to human beings, we're just confused." She leaned again to catch me in her gaze, and I thought that I would soon be crying and admitting all to her. "For the other good graces in our lives, like the Joe Parrs, for example, like the Palos, we have to work. And God, Dolph, Joe and I have made ourselves dear to each other by the work we've put in. We've made each other someone whom each of us can settle with or for. And Palo, you just get used to Palo."

I became as nervous as Leland Carter, and I found myself reaching up toward her cheek. She didn't move, so I pulled the back of my finger down the length of her cheek. The touch wasn't sexual, wasn't loving, it was, I think she sensed, just a deeply needed touch of another human being. I, the guy who gave the Border Patrol a positive spin, who made the official words, couldn't come up with sufficient words, or maybe I was just scared and nervous, and so, instead of risking the wrong word, I changed the subject. "You did a good job. Throughout this you've really done well. You're a good detective."

Jerri smiled with her mouth and eyes, and I thought, no, I hoped, no, I prayed, that she knew what I couldn't bring myself to put into some sort of words. She said, "We've got him by the balls, don't we?" I nodded.

She reached up and patted my cheek. "You deserve because you want so hard. But . . ." She didn't have to tell me that we don't get what we deserve. She pulled her hand away from my face. "Well, excuse me, Dolph. I'm going to go call my husband."

As she stepped toward the door, I said, "I sure like the way those contacts make your eyes look."

Jerri left, and my mother came out and drank a beer with me. My mother sipped at a beer. Just tiny quick movements of her hand to tilt the bottle back and let just a little carbonation tingle in her mouth. She could take an hour to drink a beer. "Too bad that Jerri is married."

"Okay, Mom. I'll ask, 'Why, Mother?'"

"You know why I said that. She'd be a good woman for you."
I squirmed worse than Leland Carter. "You both have similar
interests. You have the same attitudes. I'll bet she was just like you
growing up."

"And how was that?" I looked at the dark shape of the mountains, a little lighter than the sky but growing darker.

"Independent." I turned to look at my mother and squinted
into the darkness to make out the shape of my mother, legs that
you could see were firm, slender, a short, tight, round halo of hair,
thin arms making long shadows. "Maybe contrary would be a better word. But you had to see for yourself. You had to find out. You
could never take someone's word for it. Just like her, I suspect."

"Just like you, I suspect." She giggled, and I noticed that her
voice was changing. It broke sometimes, sounded hoarse or raspy.
"Or like my father."

She stopped her giggle. She still couldn't joke about Miguel
Martínez. "I didn't say 'obstinate.'" I never knew that my name
should have had an accent in the i until I had to learn Spanish for
the Border Patrol. Anglos never bothered with them. "You're
going to lead us into an argument, Dolph."

"Okay, no more about my father. But why are you so concerned about my romantic life?"

"Because you are so concerned about mine."

I turned to see her better in the dark. "Come on."

"Oh, come on yourself, Dolph."

I smiled to myself. "Maybe we're all alike. You, me, and my
father. We have problems in the romance department."

"I thought that you weren't going to mention your father."

"Well, after you, he didn't do too good in romance either."

"He was a drunk."

"What's our excuse?"

My mother stood up and stomped her foot, and I could hear
it echo the length of the porch. We both looked down to try to
spot the wooden slat that needed to be replaced. "You were a
pretty boy, Dolph."

"So what's happened?"

"And I'll bet that Jerri was the pretty, gifted little girl."

"So what happened?"

"Our bodies betray us. And if we could only realize just how precious certain moments were, we would all be more careful."

I squinted in the dark to try to get a view of her while she stood in front of me.

"Mom, have we failed—and succeeded in the same ways?" But a phone call interrupted her, so I didn't get an answer. I answered the phone. The call confirmed Leland's threat.

ELEVEN

Socorro met us at the emergency room of Big Bend Regional Hospital, the only hospital for the entire area. He stared at his boots and spread out his hand and pulled it over the lower half of his face to smooth his mustache over his lips and cheeks. He lifted his eyes to look at me. He held my gaze with his eyes, and for a moment I thought one or the other of us would just start flailing at the other, and then we'd be in the ear-biting, eye-gouging fight we'd been avoiding for several years. After a few moments I said, "I ain't gonna hit you. Don't hit me."

"Then don't give me no shoulds or shouldn't ofs or any of your brand of preaching."

I nodded, and he started his story. "I just dropped by and found her lying there, breathing heavy. She said to leave her, to let her die. But I ran to my old van, and I drove to the closest house, and I dialed the 9 1 1 they just put in, and I drove back, and she was smelling bad. She shit her pants. Lying in her own shit, unable to move, and she wants to stay. And I ain't about to clean the crazy bitch up, but I wait until an ambulance gets there, and she fights them, won't let them take her, so they have to drug her, and then I drive with her up here. And so I call you. You, mother-fucker. I come up with her, and I call you, and I fuck myself."

I broke the stare and stormed passed him and through the sliding doors that opened for me. "She's in intensive care," I heard Socorro say from behind me.

I whirled around. "So what happened?"

I stepped back as Socorro stepped forward, and the doors opened for him. He paused, and the doors shut. He stepped back from me, and the doors opened. I moved out of his way, and we moved next to a wall. "He beat her, Dolph. The motherfucker beat her. Kidney punched her, man. She's bruised all the fuck over."

I dropped my head. "Who's he?"

"Who the fuck do you think he is?"

"Did he know about her liver?"

"I don't know."

"Did you know about her liver?"

"Everybody along El Camino del Rio knows about her liver."

I pulled a finger up in front of his face. "So I'm gonna assume that Reynaldo Luna did it, and I'm gonna remember that you helped him jump my ass."

"Then you better goddamn remember that I helped you, motherfucker. You got no right threatening me. You know what I done for you and now for her. Huh? Huh?"

"Don't go anywhere. Wait here."

I left him to run down the hall, looking for the ICU. I found a nurses' desk that overlooked a glass-walled row of beds. In one of the beds, in the dark, the only patient in ICU, with her head turned to the side, was Sister Quinn.

A woman in surgical pajamas caught me before I could open the door and push into the room. I looked at the name tag. DR. HELEN RAMÍREZ was on it. "Are you Dolph Martinez?"

"Yes."

"She's been asking about you."

"You wait here," I said to Dr. Ramírez, and turned from her while she said, "Wait." But I went through the door, felt it swish behind me, and felt Dr. Ramírez come in behind me. Sister Quinn rolled her head toward me, and her eyes smiled. I looked at the IVs on either side of her and knew one was morphine or Demerol. "Barbara?" I asked.

"You're not supposed to be in here," Dr. Ramírez whispered behind me.

I stepped closer to the bed and nearly jumped out of my boots when I heard the bed creak and its gears grind as its front slowly rose and the small reading lamp highlighted Sister Quinn's ashen face. "Dolph, Dolph. Oh, Dolph. Take me home."

I slowly approached her bed and bent over to look in her eyes. They were yellow. Her breath was stale. "Don't let me die here," she said. "Take me home."

Home for Sister Quinn was in New Jersey, I think. Like me, deep down, in her marrow, her home wasn't in this part of the world. Like me, she had to adapt too much. She wasn't like the locals. It was a force of will. And then, as with me, the desert just took her over. Some said it made her a saint. Some, like me, thought it made her crazy. Her goddamn templo, the goddamn place that made her mind all fuzzy, that got her excommunicated, that gave her dreams or visions or wishes of flying or goddamn actually made her fly wasn't her *home*. But without a doubt, her templo was where she wanted to die.

I gingerly reached out with my left hand, and she reached out with her hand, but the IV restrained it. I turned to look at Dr. Helen Ramírez. I could barely see her in the dark. "We've got to talk."

"Yes, we do," Ramírez said.

Outside in the hallway I leaned my back against the wall and felt my back begin to slide, so I squared my shoulders and prepared to square off with Dr. Ramírez. "What kind of shape is she in?"

"Why didn't she take any treatment for her liver?"

"That's a long story."

Dr. Ramírez pulled her glasses off and rubbed at her nose. "This has been a long night. I have time."

"I bet she doesn't."

Dr. Ramírez shook her head. "She's got two busted ribs, some internal bleeding, some bruises. But in addition to the damage from the hepatitis . . . well . . . her liver is gone."

"How long can she last?"

"The night."

"Then let me drive her home."

"The ride could kill her."

"Look, I'm in the Border Patrol. I've got a little medical training. I have police authority up to fifty miles from the border. Just give me the morphine or whatever; I'll make her comfortable."

Ramírez chuckled. "Border Patrol, huh? The best thing for her would be heroin." I smiled back. "I can't let you take her out of here. I don't have the authority."

"Then give me authority. I'll take all responsibility."

"I'll have to make some calls. We have a portable medicating unit. We could let you borrow that."

I nodded. "Do it. Please." Dr. Ramírez put on her glasses and looked at me. I guess she could see that if she had refused, I would have pushed the bed out and then on to Redford. "I'll be back to pick her up."

I left Dr. Ramírez uttering, "But, but, but," and walked down the hall toward Socorro. This was a little place, not much bigger than a clinic. It was the only hospital for the whole Big Bend tip of Texas but probably had fewer than twenty-five thousand permanent residents to treat. No killings, no stabbings, no sickness this night. Socorro sat on the floor with his back pressed against the wall. He stood when he saw me, ready to duke it out.

"I'm going to take her back."

"What? After I busted my ass to get her here? She'll die there. Fuck, I shoulda just left her."

"She wants to die there. That's the point."

"Shit." He raised his flat palm to the lower half of his face and pulled his mustache toward his cheek. "Shit, piss, fuck fire." He turned away from me, placed his forehead against the wall, and gently banged it. Then he banged it harder.

"You want to help?"

He stopped banging his head and closed his eyes to think. "No, no, I watched Arnie Patton die with her doing her voodoo shit. It spooked me. I don't want to see that again. You got it on your own."

"You know she trusted you."

He gently banged his head on the wall. "Let up on me, Dolph."

"What do they know?"

"'They' know everything." He increased the banging, then stopped. "The Lunas are small-time marijuana and cocaine runners. Just the two of them, really. But that dumb son of a bitch Leland Carter came up with this mail-order-bride scheme. Hell, he worked with you. He knew me. So he contacts me. I got married a couple of times, and then he got me to go with him to Chihuahua City, and I met Reynaldo Luna, the bad one of the twins, not like that fuckup Esteban. They were Leland's partners, so they were suddenly my partners too. And now look at Sister Quinn." He turned to look at me. "And now look at me."

"How does Palo Fuentes fit into this?"

"I don't know everything here. I'm not sure of the details of what I told you. I had to piece it together myself."

"Let me arrest you or stay here in a motel. Don't go back where they can find you."

Socorro shook his head. "No, no. I'm going back to spend a night with my honey. Maybe then I'll come back up."

"Will you testify?"

He hesitated, looked around, then looked at me. "They fucked up a poor ol' lady like Sister Quinn. My honey likes her. Hell, she's a crazy bitch, but everybody likes her. Yeah, I'll fucking testify."

I stuck out my hand. He stared at it, then hesitantly reached out to shake it. "Thanks. Be careful." He nodded and left me again.

.₊*

My mother, Charlie, Jerri, Pepper, and I sat around the long, wooden authentic nineteenth-century reproduction table in our kitchen. In the middle of the table were three candles; it was all the light we wanted. I told them the situation. My mother squeezed Charlie's hand as she read my face. She had a look of sympathy and of understanding but not of approval. Lately she had given up judging me. Jerri just shook her head at what I advised her to do: go home. Pepper nodded, agreeing with me. Charlie sat passive and stoic.

I asked to borrow Pepper's Bronco to haul Sister Quinn back to Redford. "You ain't going by yourself, though," Pepper said. "Like I promised, I got your back."

"You can use mine," Jerri said. "And who knows, two cars might come in handy. Pepper can follow us." We all looked at Jerri in the dark kitchen. We could see the shadows from the candles darken the indentations and wrinkles in her face. She brushed the short bangs off her forehead. "I can see this is serious to you, Dolph. I helped cause it. So I want to help."

"But—" Pepper said.

Jerri interrupted. "I ain't just some *girl*. Right, Dolph? Don't pull any West Texas, cowboy little-lady shit on me, Pepper Cleburne. You know better."

"Yahoo. Ride 'em, cowgirl," Pepper said.

Pepper disappeared and came back with an arsenal in his arms: a twelve-gauge shotgun, a .30–30 Winchester, and a .30–06 bolt-action deer rifle. I looked at him. "Hunting rifles. They're all I've got." Then he pulled an old Colt pistol out from the back of his pants. "And this is a souvenir. My grandfather's. He supposedly shot a bandit with it." Pepper winked. We packed suitcases, loaded them, and drove to the hospital.

Jerri and I pulled into the emergency-room entrance, and Dr. Ramírez met us at the door. Pepper pulled in behind us. Several attendants pushed Sister Quinn out in a hospital gurney and scooted a portable drug dispenser alongside of her. The two attendants, Pepper, and I hefted the gurney over Jerri's open tailgate. We rolled the gurney farther in over the folded-down backseat. "I don't know. I don't know," Helen Ramírez said, frowning. "Thank you," I said to her. Then she explained to me which dials to turn to increase the drugs flowing into Sister Quinn.

Jerri drove, and I sat in the back. Sister Quinn, on her back, stared up at the ceiling of the Suburban. She rolled her eyes to look out either side window of the Suburban. Finally she let her eyes settle on me. With the drugs swimming in her blood and into her brain and blocking sense as well as feelings, she took a while to recognize me. "Thank you, Dolph," she said. I looked away from her and out the back windshield to see Pepper's headlights making two beams of light that came together on Jerri's rear windshield to make a golden, protective halo around Sister Quinn and me. Then I shifted my eyes to see Jerri's back. I patted Sister Quinn's hand.

When we pulled up to Sister Quinn's templo, the three of us nearly dropped her as we slid her out the back of Jerri's Suburban. Even as we were pulling her out, Sister Quinn's eyes focused directly above her, and she whispered, "The stars, let me look at the stars. Wait." So we set the gurney down and looked at the stars while Pepper fiddled with the key to her shack and Jerri and I pulled the drug-dispensing machine out. "No," I shouted at him. "Her templo. Open the templo. Let's take her in there." Pepper walked back up to me, shaking his head.

We tried rolling the gurney over the rocks and gravel but almost tipped it over, so with Pepper in front, me in back, and Jerri trying to guide the drug dispenser over the rocks, we carried Sister Quinn into her templo. We set the gurney down between the stares of the Virgin Mary and Pedrito Jaramillo. I looked at Jerri and said, "Help me push some of these benches aside." Jerri and I pushed the benches aside to clear a space in the middle of the templo. I went into her shack and came out with several sheets and a blanket and some candles.

I spread one sheet out and then made a pallet in the middle of it. We unbuckled and unstrapped and pulled Sister Quinn from the gurney onto the pallet. Jerri scooted the drug dispenser close to the sheet. I put a candle at each corner of the spread-out sheet and lit it. The candles would scare the evil spirit in Sister Quinn's body. He wouldn't cross by the candles, so he'd stay at the borders of the sheet. After a while we would pull the sheet out from under her and burn it, and with it, the evil spirit would burn. The mal curando would be broken. This is what Sister Quinn did for Lupe Rodríguez when she was dying of cancer.

Jerri scooted off to a dark corner of the templo. Pepper shook his head. I lit the larger candles under the painting of the Virgin and under the photo of Pedrito. Pepper's, Jerri's, and my shadow grew thin and stretched up the sides of the templo and onto the ceiling. The flickering light made dark, dull colors dance in the contours of our faces, and I reached into my pocket and brought out the vial of silver and blue metallic liquid. I had gone to my bedroom, gotten it out of the dresser by my bed, and slipped it into my pocket before we left my house. It was the vial Sister

Quinn had pressed into my hands when she found me gut shot and dying. I bent over her and pressed it into the palm of her hand. She felt it for a moment, and when she realized what it was and that I had given it to her, she said softly, "Oh, Dolph," and clutched the vial.

Pepper walked up to me and whispered, "I ain't sticking around for the voodoo shit. I got your back. I'm gonna plant myself out by the road and make sure nobody sneaks up on you. You do what you got to do."

And as soon as Pepper got through the door, Jerri was at my side. "I heard about this in San Antonio. Does she believe it?"

"No, but she likes it," I said.

"Dolph, oh, Dolph. Dolph," Sister Quinn said as she looked around and realized where she was. "Dolph, you brought me here. Dolph, you're my savior now. Dolph, come hold me."

Jerri scooted away. "No, no. You too. Please. Young lady, sit by me, touch me. Let me feel you. Touch me." I squatted, then sat beside her and stroked her forearm. My fingers jerked back as I touched the tube on the underside of her forearm. Sister Quinn sensed my jerk. "Don't worry. Don't worry, Dolph." Then Sister Quinn raised her head to look at Jerri. "Come. Please come."

Jerri inched to the pallet and sat on the other side of Sister Quinn. I unbuckled my gun belt and laid it beside the sheet. I stretched out and made myself lie alongside Sister Quinn. The light from the candles caught the profile of her nose, the yellow tint of her skin, the hollows under her cheeks, and I remembered the puffy, fat woman's cheeks when I first met her and the way ripples of her flesh used to shake when she laughed.

She screamed. "It hurts. It's pain, Dolph." I reached for the dial on the drug dispenser, but Sister Quinn said, "No, no. The pain is bringing my senses back. I want my sense, and the pain."

She screamed again. And then Jerri screamed, "Give her more drugs." But I wrapped my arms around her and held on to her. She screamed and started to sweat, foul, drug-filled wetness. She became so slippery with her awful sweat that I thought she would slip out of my arms. She screamed.

"Goddamn it, Dolph," Jerri screamed. "Don't let her suffer."

"No, no, no," Sister Quinn uttered through the pain, and tapped her head into the soft spot of my shoulder.

I looked from Sister Quinn's contorted face to Jerri's angry face, then back, then back again. Light danced on both their faces. Jerri kept her stare on me. Sister Quinn jerked her head from me, to Jerri, to the Virgin, to Pedrito Jaramillo. "She wants to suffer," I said to Jerri, but looked at Sister Quinn. "That's the point." For a moment, Sister Quinn was able to keep her eyes on me. They smiled.

Jerri stopped her argument and held on to Sister Quinn's other side. Sister Quinn screamed, thrashed, and then passed out. Jerri and I looked across Sister Quinn's chest, held our gazes, but said nothing. Jerri was asking, but both of us knew that my answer might spoil Sister Quinn's struggle with the demon inside her. I lost track of time, laid my head on Sister Quinn's chest, and got lost between sleep and consciousness. I felt Sister Quinn's chest rumble and saw her eyes jerk between Jerri and me.

"Dolph, the pain's gone away. It was pure. There was only the pain. I could see the great pain of the world. I felt myself an owl, and I perched on the tombstone of Lupe Rodríguez, and she told me how to be dead." The demon had left her body and, scared of the candles, he crouched somewhere beside me, Jerri, and Sister Quinn.

Jerri looked at me, and I tried to tell her that these were not Sister Quinn's delusions but her actual thoughts. I didn't need to. Sister Quinn turned toward Jerri. "Don't be scared. I'm not crazy." She giggled. "Not too crazy." She reached up and touched Jerri's cheek. "Don't worry, kind lady." She turned her head back to me. "Thank you, Dolph." She smiled at me. "My feet hurt, not as bad as a while ago when my whole body hurt, but they ache. Could you rub my feet?"

Before I could move, Jerri was kneeling by Sister Quinn's feet and massaging them. Sister Quinn had tears in her eyes. "Dolph, I was wrong about so much, but I know some things now. You can blow out those candles. The demon has already left. I saw him walk out the door. He wasn't scared of the candles." Jerri blew out the two candles at Sister Quinn's feet, and I blew out the candles near Sister Quinn's head.

"The pain helped. I can endure it. It's no longer a problem. It's not the candles or the vials or the pictures or a crucifix. It is faith, Dolph."

I nodded and saw her blink against my tears that had fallen in her face. "No, you don't understand. Not faith in God. Faith in humanity. Faith in you, Dolph, and that sweet lady rubbing my feet." She reached for my cheek and the tubes in her arm trailed across her body, and she wiped at the tears on my cheek. She then rubbed my tears on her cheeks. "See, see. You're crying for me. Justice isn't a problem. It's easy. Mercy and grace are hard." She swallowed in a big, difficult gulp and laid her head back, and I thought she had passed out. And Jerri leaned forward to see. But she was just resting. "I am dying, and what I most want is for some human touch, some human comfort, and here you are crying and holding me and that lady is rubbing my feet. It's finally not God who gives us grace. It's each other. We can't save ourselves, but we can save someone else. And you've given it to me. You've saved me, Dolph, and you've gone a long way toward saving yourself. I'm so happy for you, Dolph."

I could see the colors draining from her face, could feel her hand growing clammy, could feel that demon or this desert or this human condition she was talking about pulling her life out from her. I heard a rustling as the tubes in her arms scraped across the top of her chest, and she pressed the vial back into my hand. Jerri was crying. Sister Quinn smiled. "Dolph, I wanted to be buried out there with Ignacio and Azul. But they'd make a shrine of it. An old dead shrine. So burn me. And let the wind take my ashes into Mexico or wherever. It'll be like I'm an owl flying through the night."

I squeezed her, and then Jerri lay down beside her, and then she just stopped breathing. Jerri held her hand in front of Sister Quinn's mouth and then checked for her pulse, but I didn't need to.

I pushed myself up and walked from her templo into her shack. I held my arms out in front of me and sniffed at the odor of Sister Quinn, felt its damp chill now spreading across my body, looked at its stains across the front of my white shirt. I slowly unbuttoned the shirt, and then I slid out of my T-shirt. I pulled off one boot, then the other, and fell into her queen-size bed. I stared for a while at the dark, then I heard a rumbling and saw Jerri's short form feeling its way through the dark. I saw her slide out of her sweatshirt, felt the mattress depress as she climbed into the bed. "Hold me, just for a little while. Give me some of that grace." I laid one arm across the bed, and she rested her head on my shoulder. We felt each other breathing. We smelled Sister Quinn, her sweat and sickness soaked into our clothes and rising up from her compressed mattress. "Now let me go," Jerri said. "So we don't go too far, and so we can get some sleep." Reluctantly I pulled my arm out from underneath her and rolled away from her. But I couldn't go to sleep, and I could feel Jerri tossing and turning.

* * *

At sunrise, I pushed myself up out of the bed and rolled over to look at Jerri. Sometime, just before dawn, she, like me, must have drifted off to sleep. I folded the sheet off of me, slipped my arms into the sleeves of my awful-smelling shirt, and walked outside. Pepper came walking up with his Winchester cradled in his arm. To his left, the sun was a bright orange bulb lighting El Camino del Rio for its first day without Sister Quinn in a long time.

As he got closer, I could see his bulging eyes, the bags under them. He had been up all night, covering my back. "Did you get any sleep?" I asked.

"Did you?" Pepper looked at the ground, toed the dirt, then looked at me. "I suppose she's dead."

"Yeah, and she wants to be cremated. We better start getting together some wood."

"So how in the hell are we going to get enough wood?"

We pulled at brush and found what decent wood we could until Gilbert Mendoza pulled up in his old pickup. He approached with his hat in his hands, like a peon, a posture the proud man resented and guarded against his whole life and now resorted to in the face of Sister Quinn's death. He asked about Sister Quinn. When we told him, he drove back to his place and returned with a chain saw. His oldest boy, Azul's older brother, went into the canebrakes and salt cedar and cut some poles. By this time Jerri was up, and she helped us gather wood for the funeral pyre.

Gilbert, Pepper, Jerri, and I went into the templo half expecting to see Sister Quinn come back to life, but instead, we folded the sheet over her, twisted the edges, and with me and Pepper at either end and Gilbert and Jerri pushing up on a sagging middle, we carried our make-do coffin to the funeral pyre. And we threw it onto the wood.

An old van drove up, and Socorro, Sylvia Walker, and Pooter came out. A Presidio County sheriff's car pulled up, and Raul Flores walked out, pulling his gun belt up to push his belly into a respectable position. A church bus from St. Margaret Mary's, the new prefab Catholic Church in Presidio, pulled up, and Father Jesse Guzmán walked out of it in his full clerical garb. Dede drove up in a Border Patrol Suburban. The Alamendarizes showed up. Maybe she had turned into an owl and had flown to the houses of all the inhabitants of this awful area and told them she was dead. Maybe they just heard her last gasp in the air. Or maybe God, a Catholic God or some god of the old Jemezes that lived in the area before the Spaniards arrived, went door-to-door, knocking on them and telling the folks that Sister Quinn was dead.

Raul asked me what I meant to do. I told him that I was going to cremate her, and he said that county ordinances forbade that sort of thing. He cited death certificates, forms, funeral directors, laws. Father Jesse Guzmán led him away from me and whispered to him that all would be okay.

We started the fire with some gasoline, and Father Guzmán tried to say some words as we watched the sheet ignite, but no one seemed to pay attention, so he slipped into a mass. He had actually brought wine and wafers. The men removed their hats and watched. The women held their hair in place against a stiff east wind. The smoke from the fire came up in swirls, got so high, then got picked up by the wind. I imagined that in Presidio and Ojinaga, people were getting up and smelling or seeing this smoke and saying, "Sister Quinn has died." And they would cross themselves, just as some of the mourners at the pyre side did.

For the hours the pyre took to burn, we all watched, Raul and

Jesse Guzmán included. Dede held Pooter's hand, and then he swung his arm around her. Pepper squatted and held his gun stock down, barrel up as he watched the blaze and told Raul that he had permits for all of his rifles. Gilbert Mendoza kept one arm around his wife and another around his oldest son. They all cried. Socorro and Sylvia hugged. I stood next to Jerri.

I was the first to break away from the hypnotic fire. I just started walking toward the river. From behind me I heard Socorro yelling at me. "Dolph, so what's the plan? We gonna fuck with them?"

"You going to testify?"

"I'll roast his ass."

"Can I count on you?"

"Fucking A."

"Stick close to me, then."

"I'm going back with Pooter and the old lady."

"Be careful."

I left Socorro and walked into Sister Quinn's shack. I opened the kitchen cupboard, and in between the plates and cups was a sheet of notebook paper with two keys on top of it. Sure enough, with a looping, little-girl scrawl, Sister Quinn had written out her will. As she had told me, I was the executor. One key I knew was to the padlock on the templo and the other was to the padlock on her door. When we left, and I padlocked those doors, it would be the first time they had been locked in years. Sister Quinn didn't wish to lock anyone out of her house or church while she was alive. I grabbed the keys in a fist, shoved them in my pocket, and stepped out of the shack into the glaring sunlight. I saw Jerri, and she cocked her head to smile at me.

I turned away from her and walked down the slope toward the Rio Grande, past the mesquite, into the canebrakes and salt cedars, upwind, away from Sister Quinn's ashes, until I was surrounded by the cane and could smell the dirty river. I was angry, but I had to subdue it. The last time I was this angry, Pepper went to jail, Sister Quinn was excommunicated, and Fuentes blew his brains out. And I couldn't be careless; my carelessness, my lack of paranoia had killed Sister Quinn. I pushed through the cane until I came to the river, and I looked at the two gleaming aluminum-and-tin hovels on the other side of the river and the mountains rising back beyond it. I screamed at the river, the mountains, this desert for what it made me know. And I screamed at myself because what I knew hadn't made me better, hadn't taught me anything.

When my lungs were out of air and my throat felt seared, I turned, and in the stark desert light that made figures distinct, no haze, no softness, I saw Jerri Johnson stepping out from the salt cedars and looking at me. "Are you all right?" she asked.

I walked up to her and dug into my pants pocket. I pulled out Sister Quinn's keys and the vial that Sister Quinn and I had exchanged. "She left me in charge of her templo." I held my open palm in front of her so she could see them. Then I picked the vial out of my palm and handed it to Jerri. She took it and looked at me. "It's yours," I said.

"But she gave it to you."

"She was crazy. And obstinate. Always was. I don't want anything from her. Use it for a charm on a bracelet, a necklace. Throw it away. I don't care. Just get it away from me. The spell is broken. The demon is gone."

Jerri stuffed the vial into her shirt pocket. "I'll save it in case you change your mind." Then she grabbed my hand and pulled me back into the cane and salt cedars to join the other mourners.

TWELVE

By noon the funeral pyre was burned out. Even the coals had cooled. Gilbert Mendoza was the first to scoop some of the ashes with their chunks of wood and bone into a pot. All I had was a plastic milk jug. With a pocketknife, I cut out a wider opening and scooped what I could into it. Pooter just grabbed a handful of ashes. Pepper steered clear of this. Gilbert, Pooter, and I promised to spread the ashes on the ground and in the air wherever we were at six o'clock that evening. That way Sister Quinn's remains would be spread farther over the area. We watched as the mourners pulled up the road through the Alamendarizes' onion field; then we loaded the drug-dispensing machine and the gurney into Jerri's Suburban. As we were getting in, Pooter came up to me. "I know she left this place to you, but do you mind if I kind of watch over it for while? Just take care of it."

I didn't think that it would be safe for him at Sister Quinn's place. "Stay with Dede. Let her bring you out once in a while."

"I'll be okay here." Pooter stuck out his hand. "Thank you for honoring her, Dolph, for helping her die."

I shook his hand and walked to Dede, who looked at me with swollen eyes. "Watch out for him, Dede. Protect him."

"Oh, Dolph," Dede groaned. "I know how hurt you must be.

Just go away. Take some time off." I smiled at her, then turned away to climb into Jerri's Suburban.

Jerri's head nodded as she tried to steer her Suburban, and Pepper crossed the center stripe and then veered back in his Bronco, so we pulled into the Three Palms Inn and ate lunch. We gorged. We ate two bowls of chips and all of our tortillas before the food arrived, and then, when we had finished our meals, we rolled our flour tortillas and soaked up chili and pushed rice onto our forks, and then Pepper suggested a bath and a nap at Cleburne Hot Springs Resort.

Jerri accepted, but I had an uneasy feeling about the whole idea. We had a crazy man chasing us. We didn't know where he was. But then Pepper pointed out that Reynaldo Luna didn't know where we were either and that he couldn't possibly know that we would be at Cleburne Hot Springs. "Pepper, my mother's still in Alpine," I finally said. "I've got to get her out of trouble."

"Hell, Dolph, they don't want her; they want you. She's probably in less trouble as long as you're not around. Besides, she's got Charlie to watch over things."

All I could say was, "Shit, Pepper. Charlie?"

"Hell, why don't you bring the two of them down to Cleburne Hot Springs? Nobody knows we're there. Nobody knows where it is. That's why it was a failure as a resort. That's why it's a great hideout."

I always got scared when Pepper started making sense, but I gave in to him—again. In my one concession I phoned Dede at the Border Patrol station in Presidio and told her where I would be and then told her to telephone my mother. Then Jerri, Pepper, and I caravanned to Cleburne Hot Springs Resort.

The water seemed to massage my shoulders and neck, and for the first time in days, since I had last been in this tub, I felt myself relax. All my muscles just turned to putty. If I let my head hit the water, I felt like I might just let myself go to sleep and not mind the drowning. Jerri's head bobbed up above the hot water, her chin dipping into it. Tired, sore, she squatted and bounced on the balls of her feet to keep her breasts below the waterline. Pepper spread his arms out along the edge of the tub and laid back his head along the lip. He had opened the windows and let sunshine stream into the main cabin. Spots of light, reflecting off his diamond stud earring, darted across the room.

Pepper snapped to and pulled himself out of the tub. A short, naked middle-aged man with a taut body and no modesty, he waddled to the bed and threw himself in it. He grabbed the bedspread and sheets and twisted until he had a cocoon around him. Pepper, who slept so little, would treasure sleep whenever it came to him. Jerri and I stared at each other long enough for Pepper to start snoring. Then she pulled herself up out of the tub and gathered her stinking old clothes under her arms. I pulled myself out too, and we caught ourselves looking at each other. Two more short, naked, middle-aged people unable to take our eyes off our bodies, noting the fight between flab and muscle, between creamy smoothness and the wrinkles and speckles of too much southwestern sun. Of the three of us, I had grown the softest.

Modesty between Jerri and me had left the night before. Pepper had never had any modesty. But these weren't clinical or lecherous looks. It was more like we both wanted to freeze time by remembering exactly the look, feel, smell of the last surreal day. I broke the spell and grabbed a towel and wrapped it around me. Jerri did likewise. I picked up the master key on the bed stand by that snoring lump in the bed, and then I grabbed my suitcase. Jerri grabbed her suitcase and followed me out of the cabin. Barefooted, we picked our way across the gravel and weeds to the other cabins. I opened the door to my old cabin. Before I even set my suitcase down, I was falling toward the bed. I woke once when I heard Jerri's slight snore and felt her breath on my neck.

I woke again at six and dressed. In clean clothes that felt good against my clean body and smelled fresh, I retrieved the plastic milk jug with my share of Sister Quinn's ashes. I walked out to the gate to Cleburne Hot Springs, walked down the road, then turned into the desert. With rocks rolling beneath my feet, I climbed what I judged to be the highest elevation I could find. I could see the orange and purple spreading across the tops of the hills and the darkening arroyos. I shook the plastic jug with its enlarged mouth to spread the ashes.

It was all but dark when I got back, and I found Jerri and Pepper in the kitchen/entertainment complex. Pepper warmed some canned chili for dinner, but we didn't eat much. We were still bloated from lunch. For a couple of hours Pepper and Jerri played pool while we talked about what we knew and what we should do. Restless and worried, we decided that we'd hide out another day and then go back to Alpine. Then we heard a car honk at the front gate, and the three of us reached for our guns. Pepper peeked out from the front window of the kitchen, turned to us, and said, "It's a Border Patrol truck." It honked some more and stopped just in front of the entertainment complex and the empty pool. The headlights went out, and Dede stepped out of the driver's side.

I was out of the door first. I ran to meet her. She hugged me and said, "Thank God, you're all right." Pooter got out from the other side of the front seat. Dede turned to look at them and then to me. "Socorro's dead."

Pooter was drained of color. His eyes were open but seemed incapable of sight, so Dede walked to him and guided him as if he were blind. "Be careful of that empty pool," Pepper shouted, and held the door open to the kitchen. Pooter heard Pepper, shook his head, looked at Dede, and no doubt felt embarrassed about depending on her. Under control now, he walked toward Pepper's kitchen.

"Pooter called me," Dede said as she adjusted the holster on her hip. "I picked him up as he was running down 170. When we got back to Sister Quinn's place, Socorro was lying out in front. He'd been practically gutted."

We followed Pooter inside, and Pepper pulled a chair back from the table for him to sit down. He sat down, and Pepper laid a bowl of canned chili in front of him, the only offering he had. Pooter just stared at the chili like he had forgotten how to use a fork. Jerri said, "Somebody ought to try to tell the story."

Dede started. "The killer must have been following them or something."

Pooter took a bite of Pepper's canned chili, and it revived him. He looked around. "He was drunk," Pooter said. He tried to smile.

Pepper appeared with another bottle. This was a dusty liquor bottle with a label for gin. But it wasn't gin. "This is sotol," he said as he poured a bit into a glass. "A sip will hurt at first, but it's better than a tranquilizer. Might even make you feel good."

Pooter waved off the sotol. "He was drunk. He pulled up to Sister Quinn's and started banging on the door. I let him in. Then he started pulling stuff out: the bed, her table, chairs. He said he was going to sell the stuff. Get what money he could from 'the crazy bitch.'"

Dede looked at me, and Pooter continued. "I wouldn't let him. I pushed him outside. Then I hit him. Put him down. And I locked the door on him." He breathed in for some air. "Then he yelled through the door. He had gone to the place where the guy tried to steal Ms. Jerri's purse."

"He's talking about Eduardo Suárez's bar," I said to Dede.

"But I didn't let him in. No way, not if he was gonna steal everything that belonged to Sister Quinn. I'd have beat the shit out of him first." He looked at the small glass of sotol, grabbed it, raised it to his lips, and gulped it down without a grimace. "He said that he'd threatened everybody in the place. He said he'd kick my ass," Pooter said, and turned to look at me. "And he said he would kick your ass, Dolph."

"He always says that," I said. "He's my informer. He's on my payroll. He was working both sides, Pooter, and Sister Quinn got killed by his former accomplices. That's why he was drinking."

"Then he starts screaming, and I realize he's getting hurt. So I pulled open the door and find him pressing his guts in while this man in a ski mask stares down at him. The man with the ski mask takes a swipe at me and starts running. I chase after him, as fast as I can. I run until I think my heart is going to jump out of my chest. And when he jumps in an old pickup and takes off, I keep running. I know I should have gone back to help Socorro, but I keep running because I'm thinking that I need help. Arnie Patton wasn't bleeding. There was nothing to do. But Sister Quinn's magic wouldn't have worked with a bleeding Socorro. So I ran, and ran, until I flagged someone down, and they drove me to that—that Eduardo Suárez place. Two guys stared at me when I walked in, but I stared back. I dared them to come at me with a knife, a gun. I'd have killed them both. I called Dede. Then I started running back."

Pooter looked at Pepper, then at the empty glass. Pepper poured another shot into the glass. Pooter downed it. "Like Bailey Waller used to say, sometimes you just got to get drunk, son." Pooter held up his hand. "A big ol' dumb lineman. With lineman's hands. I could have torn him apart if I just could have caught the son of a bitch." Pooter rubbed one of his big ol' lineman hands over his shining dome.

I looked at Dede. She explained, "Weldon Phillips has the Brewster County Sheriff's Department investigating. I've got several agents driving the back roads, checking up and down 170, stopping anybody who remotely looks suspicious."

"Who knows we're here?" I asked.

"Just me."

I looked at Jerri. "I'm going to call Joe," she said. And my eyes held on her until she turned away from me.

"I'll have agents up and down this road all night," Dede said. "For what he's worth, Raul Flores is out looking around."

Dede scooted around behind Pooter and rubbed his shoulders, and he let his head fall. I looked around at the room and the people, and I then said to myself as well as to anyone who would listen, "My mother." Keep your head, Dolph, I said to myself. Think. Trujillo was in more trouble than my mother, and he was closer.

I looked around me. Jerri was talking on the telephone to her husband. Dede had Pooter's head in her hands. Pepper was loading a .30–30. I felt very much alone.

I stepped outside and dialed my house on my cell phone. Thank God, my mother was at home.

"Mom, look, go to Charlie's."

"He's over here."

"Well, then make him stay the night."

"He usually does."

"Well, sleep with him."

"Well, Dolph."

"No, I mean literally, stay in the same bedroom, and get a revolver out of my room. It's in a drawer, and get Pepper's shotgun. The one in his room."

I heard her gasp. "What's wrong, Dolph? We're not going to have some shoot-out, are we?" She almost sounded excited.

"Be careful tonight. Don't go outside. Lock the house. Don't be afraid to shoot, and if you hear or see anything, scream across the street for the police."

Then I tried to call Trujillo at his home. I heard the annoying static that the Mexicans can't get out of their phone lines, and then I heard a buzz like the phone was busy. I dialed the army garrison headquarters and asked for him. With my tongue tripping over the newly strange Spanish words, I asked some officer to try to find him; I tried to explain the busy signal to him. They would send some soldiers out. Walking along the edge of the empty pool, I remembered Ignacio, who used to sit by the edge and throw rocks into it.

I looked to the other side of the courtyard and saw Pepper come out of the main cabin. He sat down in front of it and cradled his Winchester in his lap. I walked over to him, and he calmly nodded. I said, "I guess I got you in a bucketful of shit."

"Well, it won't be the first time. Of course, usually I do well enough getting myself into a bucketful of shit."

"No matter what happens, I won't let them revoke your parole."

Pepper chuckled. "In the shit that we're in, my parole don't seem so important."

"Can I borrow your Bronco?"

Pepper threw me the keys. "Try to keep it in one piece."

"When I come back, I'll honk twice, wait, and then honk twice more. Tell Dede to do the same. Open fire on anybody who doesn't."

"I can hold 'em off," he said. As I started to turn, Pepper said, "You know what I'm really starting to miss?"

"What's that?"

"Those whores who used to come across from Ojinaga and bathe with us." Pepper looked at the toes of his boots. "And once this is over, I'd like to drink a whole bunch of beers, dip some snuff, and have a tug or two on that sotol."

"When it's over, I'll join you," I said.

I turned away from Pepper when he stiffened to look at two

figures emerge from his kitchen/entertainment complex. By their shapes, I could tell that it was Dede and Pooter. "Round them all up, Dolph," Pepper said. "I'll take first watch."

I walked to catch Dede and Pooter. They stopped by Dede's Border Patrol truck, circled their arms around each other, and kissed. I looked to my left to see Jerri leaning against the entrance to the kitchen complex and looking across the empty pool at the two of them kissing. Pooter then stepped back from Dede and walked away from her. He reached into the backseat, pulled out a coffee can, and walked to the edge of the courtyard. I saw his dark, thick shape start shaking the coffee can. I got up to Dede. "What the hell is he doing?"

Even in the dark I could see her smiling at Pooter. "He didn't have time to spread Sister Quinn's ashes back at six o'clock." I looked at Dede. Her smile, the one for Pooter, made me want to kiss her. She didn't look at me. She just kept staring at him. "He's big and strong, and he'll rely on that. It'll get him hurt if he stays here and tries to help. He's not short like us." She looked at me. "He wouldn't survive a real fight. Get him out, Dolph. I can't make him go."

Suddenly I felt a lump of trust, admiration, and fondness for Dede. And in that way that you both want and wish but know that your need can't be quenched, I wished that I could have felt more for her than I did, and I wanted her to feel more than she did for someone better than Pooter. "Do you love him?"

"I care for him. If ever I was to finally love somebody . . . it'd be you, Dolph." She turned her smile on for me, and I smiled too but backed away from her—once again. Then I let business into my head. "Dede, get some agents to Terlingua and get Sylvia Walker out of the area. Get her to El Paso, Midland, just get her out of here." Dede nodded.

I walked to my old cabin to get my gun. I stepped into the dark and didn't bother turning on the light. As I buckled on my holster, Jerri stepped into the dark cabin. I couldn't see her eyes in the dark, but I looked for them anyway. She had put her contacts in, and I wanted to see the deep blue of them. "I thought I'd better move to a different cabin," she said.

I nodded. "We ought to all stay in the kitchen, not get separated."

Jerri stepped toward me, threw her arms around me, and gave me the long hard kiss on the mouth that we had both been waiting for.

* * *

Trujillo's house was surrounded by a six-foot-high and one-foot-thick rock wall with broken glass embedded in the cement on the top of that wall. The house used to belong to a real bronco, a drug dealer, but he got busted, the police confiscated the house, and Trujillo wound up living in it. I knocked on the front door but got no reply. So I walked along the wall until I came to an old tarp thrown over the top. I shone my flashlight along the tarp and spotted a smear of blood. I put my hands on the top of the wall and felt the jagged glass through the tarp; I pulled and dug my toes into the side of the wall. I got a hip over the wall, then pushed myself over it. I landed loudly in Trujillo's courtyard. I raced to the back door and peeked in. A light came from somewhere in the house. I slowly stepped in and inched through the kitchen. I wished I had a gun.

Because I didn't want to explain to any Ojinaga police that I was allowed to carry a gun on the other side of the river and thus risk being held up for hours if not days, I had left my guns with a customs agent on the international bridge in Presidio. Now all I had was a flashlight. I planted my feet as softly as I could but knew that I could be heard. I chanced it. "Henri Trujillo. Dónde está?"

"Aquí," I heard.

"Dónde?"

I got to the dining room, still dark, and slid past the chairs and table toward a light in the living room. Staying in the shadows, I stepped into the living room. Across the room lay Henri Trujillo, and he slowly raised his left hand. He could barely hold on to the pistol. "Henri. It's me. Dolph," I said, and stepped out of the shadows. He smiled and let his head fall back against the wall. "Look at this place. How am I going to get my blood out of my carpet?" I looked around and saw swaths of blood on the

| 152 |

beige Berber carpet. In the middle of the floor was the ripped-out telephone. Beside him was a bottle of Patrón tequila. "Good to see you, Dolph."

"Well, I ain't letting you out of my sight now." I stepped toward him. "What's wrong?"

"I'm losing blood." He held up his right hand. Where his little and ring fingers should have been were two bleeding stubs.

"Jesus, Henri." I grabbed the phone cord, pulled my pocketknife out, cut the cord, then put a tourniquet around the base of his two fingers. It didn't help much. "You wouldn't think fingers would hurt so much." He giggled. "I can feel them hurting even though they're not connected to my hand anymore. They're somewhere in this room. I had them a while ago, but I dropped them when you came in. I thought you might be coming back to finish me."

"Goddamn, you're a mess. Why'd you start drinking? Why didn't you go somewhere?"

"Because of a little secret." He held his eyes on me, asking me not to ask about this secret. "And because it hurts and because my own blood scares me." His eyes held on me for a while. "I think that I passed out for a little while." He put the gun down and, clumsily, picked up the tequila bottle with his left hand and took a drink. His face was pale and beaded with sweat. "It would have really been silly to bleed to death because of two little fingers. Thank you for rescuing me."

"Reynaldo Luna, right?" He nodded. "So you can identify him?" He nodded. I looked around for a towel to bandage his hand. "Good. You can testify. You know he killed Socorro—and Sister Quinn."

Trujillo closed his eyes. He started to chuckle. "I saw Vincent Fuentes with a bullet through his head. Huh, I've seen worse. But the sight of my own blood . . . bothers me."

I ran down the hall and into the bathroom and got several towels and returned to find him feeling around on the floor—with both of his hands. "Here." I started wrapping the towels around his hand, but he felt along the wall with his left hand. "They were here."

I let his hand go and saw his blood immediately stain the towels. "Here, here," he mumbled. He reached with his left hand, grabbed once, then again. He held his left fist out toward me and opened it, palm up, to show me his two fingers. "I want to keep them. Make a necklace out of them, to remind me."

"Well, maybe somebody can graft them back on. Maybe we ought to put them on ice." I jumped up and ran to the kitchen and pulled ice out of the refrigerator. Trujillo yelled to me, "Oh, forget it. I'm kind of getting used to this shorter style."

I came back in with a plastic baggie and plastic tub full of ice. "Give me the fingers." He held out his hand. I held mine under his, and he dropped the fingers into my palm. I shivered, then put the fingers in the baggie, then put several ice cubes into it.

"I had just got off work. So I had some drinks, nice wine. Okay, okay, I had too much. A little steam let off. And I showed a little indiscretion. He came up behind me, and I stuck out my hand." He raised his bandaged right hand. The towel had more blood staining it. "He had a big knife, nearly a machete. I pushed myself into him, pinned him against the wall, but he twisted, hacked at my hand, and got these two fingers. But I got to this." He held up his left hand with his pistol now in it. "But you ever try to shoot with no fingers to hold the butt? You ever try to shoot left-handed? I got one shot off, and he ran. I just sat down. Then I got up for the bottle." He picked up the bottle and took a sip. "Thought I needed a drink. Then I guess I fainted, passed out. And you started yelling."

"Can you stand up?"

"Mexico, huh? I shoot and no one pays it any mind." He chuckled. He tried to stand, but his legs were wobbly. His white pants and light blue shirt were stained with blood. I scooped him up like he was a woman or a little girl and carried him to the front door. "I'll testify. But in a Mexican trial. I want him to go to jail in Mexico—where he can be killed in prison." I set him down. He wobbled but then got his footing.

"In America, he'll get the death sentence."

"Huh, in America, you sentence everybody to death and nobody is ever executed. In Mexico we don't sentence anybody to execution, but they have a habit of dying in prison. I say Mexico."

"His crimes are in America."

"Not this one." He held up his mutilated right hand.

"We'll discuss it later." I ran into his bedroom, turned on a light, and looked into his closet. You could see what he spent his money on. One suit after the other, hung according to color, lined the closet. Then the uniforms started. They were all small, like they belonged to a boy. Beneath them were ordered pairs of little shoes. I saw a pair of tennis shoes and grabbed them. I saw slacks and knit shirts and grabbed them. Next I went to his dresser and opened a drawer to pull out a couple of cotton T-shirts and some silk boxer shorts.

I was on my way out, about to turn off the light, when I saw a foot. I walked to the other side of the bed. Nearly rolled under the bed was a naked body. I inched toward it. With my foot I rolled the body over toward me. And a naked young boy tried to stare out of bulging dead eyes. His tongue hung out of the side of his mouth. His face was pale blue. A lamp cord was wrapped around his throat.

The light went out, and I nearly jumped through the bedroom window. From the light coming in through the bedroom door, I saw Trujillo leaning against the door frame. "My little secret."

"How old is he?"

"Not old enough."

Trujillo stepped toward me. "What you heard is my official story. You asked why didn't I call, why I didn't go out. How could I explain him?"

"Did you hire him?"

"He comes over sometimes."

"What's his name?"

"I don't want to say."

"God, Henri. Jesus, what were you thinking?"

"What you thought when you used to hire the whores to come up to see you and Pepper." I looked at him. "Yeah, I know about that." He started to tremble. "So now you know what really happened. He came home with me. And he went into the bedroom to wait for me, and I went into the kitchen to make some drinks. I heard a rumble. I ran toward the bedroom. And Reynaldo met me. Dress him, Dolph. Dress him. Don't leave him like this."

I inched closer to the body, reached out, and nearly pulled my hand back when I touched the cold skin. I pulled him by the shoulders until he was in the middle of the floor. Suddenly the light was on again, and Trujillo was beside me, and we both stuffed the young boy back into his clothes. Trujillo wasn't much help dressing his whore or lover, whichever, and he got blood on the dead boy's clothes.

When we got the boy dressed, neither of us could look at the other. I stepped outside with him, and he fumbled with his keys while he tried to lock the door. I locked it for him. Then we ran to Pepper's Bronco. Trujillo wobbled, but he was able to run.

I took him to a clinic where a nurse and medical student trimmed, sewed, and patched his two stumps and shot him full of drugs. He met me in the lobby, smiling and holding up his bandaged hand. In his other hand he held a glass jar. In it, his two amputated fingers floated in alcohol. The nurse wanted him to stay or check into a hospital. But he refused to go, and I wanted him with me. The young medical student gave us some pills for pain, and I thought that if he really began to hurt, we could hook him up to the drug-dispensing machine from Alpine.

From the clinic he called the army garrison to report what had happened. I had to dial for him. As he talked in crisp, rolling Spanish, which I couldn't fully translate, he showed no emotion. He said, "Niño," when he referred to the boy. When he hung up, he turned to me and said, "I spent all that time thinking about what to do. This could mean my career. No pension. Dishonorable discharge, as Americans say. My family disgraced. The best thing, the only thing, is say no more than is necessary . . . and to kill Reynaldo Luna."

THIRTEEN

On the way back to Cleburne Hot Springs Resort, I opened up the windows to let the wind whistle through the front seat. The wind in my face kept me awake, and together with the drugs, it must have made Trujillo talk. He twirled the jar in front of his face to look at the two tips of his fingers floating in the alcohol. I didn't want to look at him or listen to him. "Vincent, Henri, Dolph, our names tell on us. You don't even spell your last name correctly. You leave off the accent. You Americanize it. Just like you, Dolph. Just like Vincent and Henri."

"My name is my father's revenge against my mother and her family. My worthless father named me Adolph, not Dolph."

"You called Vincent Fuentes's father, old Palo, worthless. Now you said your father was worthless. Vincent's worthless father, your worthless father, my worthless PRI father wanted us to be aristocratic, 'European,' not Mexican."

"My mother raised me."

"See, see. Education, refinement, anything to keep us away from the lower classes, from the mestizos. Because of our parents we aspire to be Creole. And look at us now. We deal with the worst classes. Criminals, drug dealers. We arrest mestizos. Revenge on our parents, on Mexico. Little Henri, little Vincent, and little Dolph—

Mexicans, even though we tried so hard not to be. Pobrecitos. Dolphito, Henrito, Vincentito."

He held up his bottle and looked again at his floating fingers. "I wish I would have held up my left hand."

"You can't think that fast or that far ahead."

I could feel him leering at me. "But you try, Dolph. And you fail just as bad as I do."

He was quiet, and I felt the air swishing by me, giving me a slight chill that kept me awake, and I wished that he would just shut up, even if his talking helped keep me awake. "I was supposed to protect the muchacho in my room. Yeah, I paid him, but that is what he was. But he was going to quit. I was going to watch out for him. We talked about it. Now another peon, a mestizo, a Mexican, un lilo is dead . . . because I couldn't think far enough ahead. But nobody cares. Mexico is safe."

"Would you just shut up for a while?" I finally said.

When I got him back to Cleburne Hot Springs, I honked twice, waited, then honked again. Then I drove into the compound and saw, in my headlights, Pepper pushing himself up from the front steps of the kitchen. He cradled the Winchester and opened the side door to let Trujillo out. Trujillo held out his bandaged hand and showed Pepper his pickled fingers.

Dede had gone. Pooter was drinking coffee in the kitchen; Jerri was asleep in my cabin. I told Pepper to wake Jerri and get everybody to the kitchen. I walked in, said hello to Pooter, and waited for them all to get there. When Jerri walked in, she looked over at Trujillo and said, "Now I've got to stay with you?" And Trujillo showed her his two dismembered fingers as though they were a war trophy, a talisman.

"Pooter, get ready. I'm getting you out of here," I said.

"I'm not afraid to stay," Pooter said, and rubbed his bald head.

"Well, I'm afraid of having you stay. Besides, I got something else for you to do."

"I'm staying."

"Don't be a big, dumb lineman. I've got something else for you to do. And it's what you're good at."

I didn't wait to see what he said, but I turned my attention to Jerri. "Jerri, be nice to Trujillo. Don't hurt him while I'm gone."

"Joe's coming," Jerri said. "He can help."

"Tell him not to. I don't want anybody else to watch out for."

"Dolph, Joe Parr can take care of himself. He can take care of all of us." She squared off in front of me. "I wouldn't dare leave him out."

I nodded and got busy. I folded Pepper's backseat down and moved the drug-dispensing machine and the gurney to Pepper's Bronco. Pooter got in the front seat and pulled his UT baseball cap lower down on his forehead. I got in the driver's seat and left Pepper, Jerri, and Trujillo standing in front of the empty pool. I hoped that Jerri wouldn't kill Trujillo.

Nearing Presidio, I looked out of my side window to see the first slim line of light outlining the Chinatis. I shifted my eyes from the road to the mountains in the distance. As I rounded a curve, I purposefully slowed down to check out a drag. For miles, the Border Patrol or state maintenance workers would drag a tire or a piece of chain-link fence behind a truck. So at this first light, particularly at this bend, you can stare down a drag, and footsteps in the sand nearly glisten for you. Surely, I thought, I could still find footprints in a drag. The sun cleared the mountains, the sand in the drag grew bright, and I spotted several footprints. The tracks looked fresh; the wets would be wandering toward San Antonio Pass. I almost pulled off the road, and I found myself reaching for the radio that wasn't there, to report that some wets had crossed. I reasoned to myself that if I could still spot tracks in the sand, then maybe I was good enough, smart enough, observant enough to keep everybody safe. No little muchacho under my bed.

Pooter pulled himself awake and pushed his cap farther back on his head. He had been riding with his head bobbing in the passenger's seat.

Pooter blinked as the sun pulled higher and made the rocks and cacti glisten in the intense light. He looked at the streaks of light in the sky, at the landscape, at the moving shadows of the ledges and mountains. "It's beautiful out here."

"But it can kill you."

Pooter smiled at me. "As it should be. The thing that is out of place is the thing that can appreciate the beauty—humanity. But who knows, maybe some animals can 'appreciate' it in some rudimentary way."

"You don't seem to be too shook up."

"I think the sight of him lying there and bleeding was the worst part." And I began to think that maybe I ought to keep him around.

"Okay, then, Pooter, look. I want you to do something. You say you're good at looking out for people. Well, I want you to watch out for my mother. I'm gonna put you in a car with her and this Charlie guy, and I want you to drive them out of here. Go to Midland and get a flight somewhere. Go back to Austin, just get them the hell out."

"I could stay, you know. I could do something."

I stared at him. "No, you do what you're good at. You watch over them."

"And you watch over Dede and the others." The way he said it sounded like a question, like he was accusing me of letting them down, of letting Sister Quinn down. Then he looked at me. "Why were they killed, Dolph? What's going on?"

"'Cause I fucked up. Now don't fuck up with watching my mother."

* * *

I had the door to Pepper's Bronco open before I was fully stopped, and I was running toward my house with the yellow police crime-scene tape stretched across the front porch. "Hi, Dolph," a cop said as I raced up the steps.

"What the hell?" The cop jerked a thumb toward the front door. Squinting, I saw a chunk missing from the wall and then a jagged hole in the door.

"That boyfriend of your momma's like to got him. Nearly nailed the burglar with the shotgun."

I slipped under the tape and went in the front door. "Hey, Dolph," the cop yelled. "Don't touch nothing. We're trying to get fingerprints."

I raced down the hall and slid to a stop in the kitchen. My mother and Charlie were having coffee and orange juice. "Hey, Dolph," Charlie said. "You should of seen it. I heard something, got up, saw this burglar creeping down the hall. I let him have it."

"With Pepper's shotgun, right?"

My mother hugged him. "You should have seen him, Dolph. He was marvelous. Just gunned him down."

"You did?"

"The first shot went over his head. The second through the door."

"Did you hit him?"

Charlie bounced in his seat. "If I just would have held a little steadier. You know used to I shot skeet. More of a distance man myself."

I looked toward the living room. "Did the police find anything?"

Charlie shook his head. "They're dusting for fingerprints, but it looks like the burglar wore gloves."

I lowered myself into a chair. "You want some coffee?" Charlie asked.

"We've got company."

My mother jumped up. "Well, Dolph. I'll try to get something for breakfast."

"No, no breakfast. Go get packed. Y'all are leaving."

"Well, Dolph. You're being rude again," my mother said, and sipped from her cup of coffee. Charlie was still puffing out his chest.

"I don't have time. You two are going to have to help me with this. I have a friend out in the car. He's rattled because he saw a . . . a . . . a friend of mine get murdered. I want you two to drive him out of here. Anywhere but here. I want you two to watch over him." I looked up at Charlie. "Can you handle it, Charlie?"

Charlie winked and beamed at my mother, then he looked back at me. "I'll load the guns."

Charlie left and came back with several suitcases. My mother tried to limit herself, but she loaded her Lexus with suitcases and paper bags full of snacks. I gave Pooter my cell phone number, my home phone, and the number at Cleburne Resort. I told him that I'd tell him when it was safe to come back. I kissed my mother and waved good-bye as they pulled down the street, past the police barricade, like an elderly couple and their grown kid going on vacation.

* * *

After I got Pooter, my mother, and Charlie out of the way, I called Dorothy McFarland at the courthouse. She sounded glad to hear me. "Listen, Dolph, I just feel terrible about signing those papers. But I don't make much here, and Leland was just so sure . . . and insistent."

"Well, don't worry about it for now."

"Oh, Dolph, I'm not going to go to jail, am I?"

"No, no, but meet me."

"Oh, Dolph, I can't just take off work."

"Meet me, Dorothy. This is not a choice."

I explained to Dorothy how to get to one of my favorite places in the area. North toward Fort Davis is a tiny stream that cuts through someone's horse farm, then flows under the road. The road gains a little elevation, so there are some trees beside it, and the state put up a concrete picnic table under one of the trees. So, with my Crown Vic on the side of the road, I sat at the table watching shiny-coated horses jump across that stream and prance in the pasture and waited for Dorothy McFarland.

She pulled up in a proper car, a Buick Century, an old lady's car. She drove slowly with both hands on the wheel and stopped well before she got to the picnic table. She pulled her sweater around her shoulders with one hand and held her purse with the other. The breeze caught in the folds of her oversized dress and billowed it out. She lowered herself onto the concrete slab across from me, took off her horn-rimmed glasses, and let them dangle from the gold chain. They bounced for a moment on her chest, and I noticed that she did have a chest, full breasts that her dress couldn't hide today. She dropped her eyes. And I stood and looked back at the direction she had come to see if she had been followed.

"Dorothy, look at me. I'm desperate. Look at me."

She raised her eyes and her head. She said without a stutter, firmly, "What do you want?"

I started to tell her, but I noticed the sun's reflection off her thick makeup and gray wig. Unable to resist, I reached toward her face, and she slowly pulled away from my touch. But I leaned farther toward her, and she held still, so that I ran the back of my finger over the thick makeup on her cheek. I sat down and looked at the flesh-colored smear with the reflecting silver sparkles on the back of my browner finger. "Why the makeup? Why the wig?"

Dorothy leaned back, away from me, but she didn't drop her gaze. She set her purse on the slab between us. She said, "I don't believe a lady's toiletries and refinements are a gentleman's business." I wondered if she thought that anyone in this area talked like that.

"What can you tell me, Dorothy?" She said nothing. "What is your maiden name?"

"That part of my life is over. I told you that." She looked down at the concrete top of the table.

"What do you know about Leland Carter?" She didn't answer. "What's between the two of you?" She reached into her purse and kept her hand in it.

"Should I get a lawyer?" She removed her hand from her purse and remembered her act and looked off at the horses. In the distance, you could see the shadow of a cloud moving over the long pasture.

"Have you ever met a Reynaldo or Esteban Luna?" Again she put her hand on her purse.

"Leland Carter is a friend, a very special one. And whatever you think of him is not true. As for the Lunas, I don't know them."

I placed an elbow on the table, leaned toward her, planted my elbow on the table, and pointed my finger at her. She put her hand into her purse and pulled it to her chest with her other hand. Her hand started to come out of the purse as if pulling something out of it. "Leland Carter and the Lunas are killing friends of mine, and they're going to try to kill me. Now, if you know them at all, you tell them that I contacted you. If you don't know them, if they truly are strangers, then you take some time off and get out of town. If they see me talking to you, they could come after you."

Dorothy's shoulders fell forward as she relaxed and pushed

the purse away from her and back onto the table. She pulled her empty hand out of it. "Thank you for thinking of my safety, Dolph. But I'm sure that I'm not in any danger."

I smiled. "Just the same, get out of town for a while."

"Bye, Dolph," she said. She stood and turned around to look at the horses. "This is a beautiful spot." She walked with an unusually sprightly step for an older lady.

* * *

After I talked to Dorothy, I was tempted to go into my bedroom and get some more sleep, but I pushed the dreariness to the back of my mind and took a shower, and got dressed in a white shirt, tie, slacks, and boots, and strapped my holster on—like I was going to work. I got ammunition and food. I went into Pepper's room and yanked some of his clothes off hangers, then I went into Jerri's room and rounded up some of her clothes. I loaded everything into my Crown Vic, and I parked and locked Pepper's Bronco with the gurney and drug-dispensing machine still in it. I'd wait to return them. I drove away in my own car. It felt good to be behind a familiar wheel.

Driving toward Marfa, I stared at Leland Carter's cutoff as I approached. I fingered the butt of my gun in its holster, then turned down the gravel road. I pulled off the road and drove to the edge of a slight drop. Checking around, I pulled my binoculars out of the glove compartment and stepped out of my car and walked to the edge. From this height I had a good view of his trailer. His pickup wasn't around. He was probably on duty. I half hoped that he would pull up and the shouting, the shooting, the beating would begin. I hadn't fared too well in gunfights. I lost my first one, and Sister Quinn had to rescue me. In later tight spots, when guns were around, a terrible anticipation of wasp stings knotted my stomach. If I could get past the anticipation, I figured I could take another shoot-out.

The door to Leland's trailer opened, and his young son ran out of the door and began shooting imaginary bad guys in the front yard. His wife leaned on the railing next to the trailer. She looked around, reached in her pocket, and pulled out a pack of cigarettes. Safe, with no one watching, she thought she'd sneak a smoke. With the binoculars on her I watched her exhale as though she were exhaling from her tired life.

Both she and her rancher daddy must have assumed a great future for the ex–Miss Brewster County. Maybe a degree from Sul Ross, modeling in Dallas, a career, but somewhere along the way she got sidetracked by Leland Carter, who must have had his share of West Texas charm. So she ended up married and pregnant and poor.

She looked back into the door she had left open, muttered something to herself, then ducked back in. She came back out with the infant balanced on her hip. She took another drag on her cigarette. She couldn't even find a few moments of solitude to enjoy the vice she had to hide from her husband.

And I knew what my mother must have felt and what my grandfather, ol' Charles Beeson, must have felt when Miguel Martinez, who must have had some charm to coax Sandra Beeson away from her bright future, turned out to be worthless. And I knew Miguel's people's disappointment when his Anglo wife and pretty half-Anglo boy left him. And I knew his disgust with himself and with the world he was stuck in, and I knew his resulting surrender to booze, panhandling, and resignation. And I knew why Pepper's hand started shaking the bourbon out of his glass when a wife left him because of fading West Texas charm—just like the way my hand shook my bourbon out of my glass when the Chicana lawyer in El Paso left me and I volunteered to transfer to Presidio and when Ariel Alves left me because I was obsessed with my job and the area.

Who knows, maybe Leland Carter got involved in his mail-order-bride business because it offered him the money that would turn his family's life into the potential life they had once believed in—just as Pepper started running guns and then drugs to repair a leaky swimming pool, which would turn Cleburne Hot Springs into another Lajitas and thus fulfill the potential he and his family and wives believed he had.

And then Sister Quinn began preaching. Buzzing around in my head were her crazy sermons. Grace trumps justice, she said.

Mercy, compassion, grace, she said. Dead, she was still pestering me. I didn't want a shoot-out with anybody.

I walked back to my car and drove on toward Marfa. In Marfa, I chased Sister Quinn out of my head to deal with the real world: my job. I pulled into the sector headquarters and walked straight into Billy Sosa's office. "Where you been, Dolph?" Billy said, stood, and walked up to me. "You ought to be accruing all the sick leave you can toward retirement."

I sat down in the chair across from his desk. Billy bent over in front of me. "God, you look terrible. You been on some kind of bender or something?"

"I've been up for a while," I told Billy.

"I guess this involves that curandera you're fond of?"

I looked at Billy. I needed help, orders, official rules. I started rambling to him, then picked up the pieces and tried again to fit the details together. I finally got the story out. Billy offered to call the Feebies, but I didn't want the FBI in on this. I didn't want any more of my Special Task Force involved. I wanted the Border Patrol to help me. I wanted my old chief patrol officer at the Presidio station, R.C. Kobel, to tell me what to do, even to scold me. The story about R.C. was that in the old days, when we used horses a lot more, he was patrolling on horseback around Marfa, just as Pepper had cut across Leland's field, and got in between two feuding ranchers. One, thinking his rival had come for him, shot at R.C. Kobel, but his horse raised his head and took the bullet for R.C., who got off two shots before the horse hit the ground. Both shots hit the rancher and killed him. It was R.C.'s favorite horse. The second shot, he said, was for the horse. I took his place. Now, in his place, was Dede Pate.

So I left feeling as though Billy Sosa and the Border Patrol couldn't advise me or help me—only Dede could. But the Texas Rangers rode to the rescue—in an ancient Lincoln Continental. For when I got back to Cleburne Hot Springs Resort, Joe Parr's Continental was parked in front. And Joe Parr was commanding the kitchen. One mob, one Ranger.

FOURTEEN

Pepper had shot over Joe Parr's head when he pulled up, and Joe started cussing and screaming. Then when they led him inside, Joe Parr threatened to kill Trujillo. The little pissant was hiding out with his wife.

Trujillo didn't help matters. Still on painkillers, sipping Pepper's sotol, he taunted Joe Parr, saying, "Ringes, ringes," the Mexican derogatory term for the Texas Rangers. But Jerri and Pepper calmed them both down. I was glad I had missed the introductions.

It wasn't comforting that Joe Parr found us so easily. We were hiding out, and after a phone call from his wife, he'd driven all night and found a forgotten, abandoned place. But Joe Parr was a famous Texas Ranger; he'd tracked down criminals. Still, it wouldn't be long before Leland Carter and the Luna brothers figured out where we were.

We were all sleepy, and Trujillo was drunk. Pepper was especially spooky, sort of jumpy; after all, he'd stayed up two nights guarding first me, then the rest of us. Jerri and I had stayed up watching Sister Quinn die, then spent the previous night worrying about Pooter. Trujillo had had his fingers cut off and had nearly bled to death while he drank tequila and stared at his stumps and thought about his dead lover. Joe had driven all night. But none of us could relax until we knew what to do.

Trujillo had a glass full of sotol. Since he had gotten to Pepper's, he had wrapped his bandaged hand in plastic and taken a shower. He wore the clothes that I had grabbed for him: brown tropical wool slacks and a satiny bright lavender shirt. "Who dresses you?" I asked him when I first walked in.

"Apparently, you do," he said. His left hand trembled as he raised the glass to his lips, and he spilled some of the sotol. His eyes were glassy. He rambled. He would be worthless until the drugs wore off and he sobered up.

Pepper rubbed his hand over his head to feel the fuzz of his short hair. He took his diamond earring out as if to guard it, as if to get rid of even more weight, to become slicker, to stay ready. Prison had made him coil tighter when trouble was around; if he had to strike, he was quicker and deadlier. And since his prison term, he had come to distrust his own plans, opinions, tactics, and strategies. Look at what he had done to himself. Now he'd let someone else design the plan; then he'd follow it exactly and ask no questions. Or maybe he distrusted all plans or strategies, knew they'd all eventually fail, and just no longer wanted to take the responsibility for the screwups. At any rate, he could help.

Jerri glanced at me from time to time while she hovered around Joe Parr, like she was afraid to get too far away, like she wanted to protect him yet be protected by him. I kind of felt the same way since he had come in the door. He was tall and sinewy, and his white hat made him look taller. He wore a starched white shirt and crisp, creased khakis. He had on a tie, a wide one with a map of Texas on it. It was a Texas Ranger uniform; all he needed was the badge. The Ranger who directed the assault against those crazy Republic of Texas outlaws in Fort Davis, the ones who wanted to secede from the union so they wouldn't have to pay income or sales tax, wore an outfit like Joe Parr's. Once a Ranger, always a Ranger. Like a Ranger, Joe would want to set the terms, negotiate within those terms, then attack—just like that Ranger captain from Midland when he and the national guard stormed the Republic of Texas crazies. It was a good plan, but it scared me.

"So who's the honcho here? Dolph, you in charge?" Joe looked at me, but he cocked his head back and forth to get the right view through his bifocals.

Trujillo lifted his eyes. "I have the highest rank." Joe scowled at him, and Trujillo smiled at him and Jerri. Trujillo stuck his left hand into his shirt pocket and brought out his pack of cigarettes. He reached into his slacks pocket and brought out his cigarette holder. We all watched as he tried to get the cigarette into the holder with just one hand. After a minute Pepper stepped up to him and put the cigarette in the holder. Jerri lit the cigarette with a kitchen match once Trujillo got the cigarette holder in his mouth. He looked at me, waiting for me to tell him that he was disgusting or immoral or degraded. But I didn't know what to tell him. I wasn't about to tell anyone in the room that my partner, a member of my Special Task Force, had the body of a naked boy in his bedroom.

"I guess I'm in charge," I said.

"Well, what do you want to do?" Joe asked.

"I haven't had a whole lot of time to think about anything other than saving my ass and trying to protect everybody else."

"Excuse me for saying so, but it looks like you've lost some people there, Dolph."

"Why, Joe," Jerri said. "That's no fair."

"Honey?" Joe said to her, and pushed the underside of his white Stetson's brim with his forefinger to position the hat farther back on his head.

"He's protected me, and Pepper, and Pooter, and his mother."

Trujillo held up his hand. "I could take care of myself until I lost my fingers. Now, though, he's protecting me too."

Parr looked around at all of us, muttered, "Sorry," took his hat off, and put it crown down on the table. And I could see the circle of indentation that his hat had made in his silver mane of hair. "What I meant is that you need to forget about the losses. You can't help them. You can never see everything." I didn't want to see Sister Quinn as a loss, or Socorro, or Fuentes. But loss was the term in my business's language.

"So there's my theory. We keep anybody else from getting

hurt. That's most important." I studied all of their faces for just a moment or two. Sister Quinn begin whispering to me again about responsibility to the poor and the dispossessed. I wanted to yell at her nagging psychosomatic voice to shut the fuck up. I was tired of responsibility and of protecting people. "But you're right, Joe. I fucked up. I got some people killed. So you got any suggestions?"

Jerri stepped toward me and reached out. I looked at her outstretched hand, as did Joe. My hand almost automatically reached for hers, but I fought against that need with my knowledge. We all knew too much.

Jerri pulled her arm back to herself, and Joe wrapped his arm around her, and she circled her arms around him. Joe said, "I'm a Ranger. We ride into the middle of them. Attack them before they can attack us. So we go right after these Luna boys."

"We don't know where they are," I said.

"Then we go after Leland Carter."

"Fucking A," Pepper said.

Joe stepped away from Jerri and toward me. He spread his large palm across the front of his face, grabbed the corner of his glasses between his thumb and middle finger, and pulled them off. "Jerri tells me he has this tin barn or some such shit. I say we go bust into it and see what's inside."

"It'll set off an alarm," I said.

"You're goddamn right," Pepper said.

"No more alarms," Trujillo mumbled.

Joe came back, "So we set off an alarm. So he comes running. With or without the Luna boys with him, he's ours." He waved his glasses as he talked.

I looked around at all of them, waiting for them to say something. "What about Palo?" Jerri asked.

"Honey, that old bird can take care of himself. We're in deeper shit than him right now."

"But Joe, the more evidence we can get, the better."

"And if we go in without a warrant, nothing will hold up in court," I said.

"Chingaderes. Warrants," Trujillo said.

"And if we do get a warrant and don't find anything, then we'll hurt our case against him," I added.

"And Palo's chances," Jerri said. I wanted to think that she was taking my side because of me, because she wanted to, not because of Palo.

"Dolph," Joe said, then swung his head toward his wife, "Jerri, honey," then swung his head back to me. He stuffed his glasses into his pocket. Talk to her, convince her, not me, I wanted to say to him. "You said this was about saving our asses. This isn't about legality or Palo's defense strategy. It's about us getting out of this alive."

"Fucking A," Pepper said. He looked at me. "They're mean sons of bitches, real broncos, which means they're fuckups. Otherwise Pooter wouldn't have caught what I'm guessing is the real fuckup, Esteban, and Reynaldo would have killed Trujillo. And because they're fuckups, they're not going to pay attention to the law. And that makes 'em dangerous." He looked at me to emphasize his next point. "I been to prison. You didn't send me there. My fucked-up partners did. I know about dangerous fuckups."

"So they wouldn't be so dangerous if I was dead," Trujillo said, and took a drag on his cigarette. Noticing Trujillo's newfound fatalistic humor and drunken rambling, Jerri and I were sure that Vincent Fuentes's ghost, spirit, or residual attitude had taken him over.

"You got Esteban and Reynaldo accounted for here. Well, who broke into my place?" I asked.

"The guy who attacked me at Eduardo Suárez's," Jerri said.

"Or maybe Eduardo," Pepper said.

"Or maybe Leland Carter himself," Joe said.

"Maybe Santa Claus or the Virgin Mary," Trujillo said.

"He's right," Joe said reluctantly. "We don't know how many of them there are. We don't know how many to look for."

"Just like with the Comanches," Pepper said.

Joe looked at Pepper. "Just like that ol' Ranger Jack Hays charging into the midst of them. But what else we gonna do? Somebody got something better?" Joe said, and held up his hands. I felt everyone look at me.

"Okay, okay," I said, just thinking that I wanted someone else to take the burden of a decision and a fuckup away from me.

"Dolph?" Jerri asked. "Do you have any ideas? I'm agreeing with Joe unless you have something better."

My mind started working. I stared at each one of them. "Or we piss 'em off. We talk to Leland Carter. If we can't find him, we go to his barn. He'll be scared to bring in Sheriff Weldon Phillips this time. Besides, we can probably just drive to the Alpine McDonald's and walk up to him. It should be me since I'm a federal officer . . . and you since you're a Texas Ranger." I looked at Joe. "We'll scare him or piss him off, and we should show him that we're now willing to break the law." I was really thinking that if we were going to charge into their midst, it should be with as few of us as possible. I thought that I could do it. And Joe Parr, despite Pepper's cool and willingness, seemed to be the best backup. Besides, I had done enough harm to Pepper. And though she didn't need protecting, though she could have protected me, I wanted to save Jerri Johnson.

"Go, Dolph!" Trujillo yelled as though giving a cheer.

"Yeah, go, Dolph," Pepper chimed in.

"So he'll have to come after us or send the Lunas after us. And eventually they'll figure out that we're here."

"Whoa," Pepper said.

Joe Parr smiled. "And we've got good ground here. We go up there, we're fighting over open country, a cavalry attack. But here we've got woods. We can pick 'em off."

"Pepper goes into town and buys motion detectors and barbed wire. And we string up some flares. Dede plants some sensors by the front gate, and anytime they go off, she calls to see who it is. And we'll play Border Patrol and Indians right here." I looked to Pepper. "It's your place. Can we shoot it up?"

Pepper smiled. "Well, hell. If we're gonna play Alamo on my property, can I be John Wayne?"

Joe Parr stuck out his hand. I shook it. "Good plan there, Dolph. You could be a Ranger." Jerri smiled. "So tomorrow you and me go visit this Leland Carter fella. And Jerri and Pepper and that drunk pissant over there prepare the defenses for the

Alamo." He reached into his shirt pocket and pulled out his glasses and put them back on. Then he grabbed his hat and put it back on his head.

Trujillo looked up. "I get confused. If this is the Alamo, are we the Mexicans or the Texans?"

"You can be Laurence Harvey," Pepper said.

Pepper said that he would take the first watch, so he grabbed his deer rifle and stomped outside. Joe sat down in one of Pepper's wooden chairs, and a little air escaped from his mouth. He slumped over, then unbuttoned his collar and loosened his tie and became a tired old man, no longer a Ranger. Jerri stepped up behind him and massaged his shoulders, and he smiled and placed one of his hands over hers as she kneaded the soft part of his shoulder. She smiled and looked down at the top of his silver head. Joe groaned a little, curled forward in his chair, and tugged at one of his boots until he got it off. Then Jerri walked around in front of him and placed a palm over the top of his boot and the other hand around the heel and yanked off the other boot. And as he massaged one socked foot with the sole of his other, Jerri kissed his wrinkled forehead.

Since we had decided to stay together in the kitchen/entertainment complex, Jerri and Joe, after a while of massaging, moved off to one corner for some sleep. I turned off the lights and flicked on a lamp by the bar, and I sat down next to Trujillo. I poured myself a shot of sotol. I had to choke its flame down to my stomach. I thought about my army: old Joe Parr, Trujillo with his missing fingers, Pepper out defending us with a deer rifle, and fat, paunchy me. Hell, Jerri was probably the best man among us.

In the dim light, I looked at Trujillo. He seemed to have had the blood drained out of him, and his pale face seemed to be trying to absorb color from the scarce light. Trujillo slapped my back with his good hand. "Do you see it? Do you? Vincent Fuentes was right."

I looked at him as I poured myself another shot. I just wanted this knot of tension, thought, and knowledge to go away for a while so I could get some sleep. "Fuentes was crazy."

"Sister Quinn was crazy too, but still you listened to her."

"Not by choice."

"He gave up on being a priest, or rather Catholicism gave up on him. He gave up on intellect, on academics. He found politics and became a proud Mexican, then he learned to both hate and love Mexicans for what they could be but always fucked up. For their attitudes that condemned them but made them what they were."

"And how's that different from Americans?"

"And then there's the border. And that's where you and I are, and where he was." He reached for the bottle. "But Fuentes went farther."

"I don't think you need any more."

"I need a lot." He poured himself another drink and downed it. "I'll be fired, disgraced. I gave my life to Mexico. I did horrible things for Mexico, and then because of an indiscretion—" He stopped and looked around the room. "Because of a sweet little boy, Mexico will desert me. And then I'll be where Fuentes was. And I, because I'm smarter than he was, know what comes next."

Now he had my interest. "What?"

"Nothing. Nothing outside of self. That was his point. The glory of selfishness. It is the same thing that ol' Palo believes. It is what you are going to do—save your ass. Nothing matters except trying to see that you see another day."

"You're full of shit. That's not what he believed. That's not what Sister Quinn was about." I surprised myself by defending them. "How much you going to drink?"

He started to giggle. "When we are concerned only with the holiness of our own blood, ours alone, then extravagance isn't extravagant. We want to, we should indulge." He rested his chopped-up hand on the table. "Pobrecito," he said to himself, for himself. "And you know the worst, I miss my fingers more than mi pobrecito, mi hijo."

"Shut up. I'm tired. Don't make me think."

"Dolph, you're just a little behind me, and I'm just a little behind Fuentes. Catch up."

⁎⁎⁎

Dede Pate and some of the other agents did the hard work: burying sensors, setting up some flares, spreading a tarp over Pepper's empty pool. All while Joe Parr and I headed for my job in Joe's car. When he got ready to go, Joe had said that we should take his car, and he opened his trunk to show me why. He could have armed a small Central American army. He had a sawed-off shotgun, several automatic pistols, an automatic rifle, a flak jacket, boxes of ammunition. "Up front I've got a fingerprinting kit and a laptop computer that uses satellites to tell you where you are. Some of it's standard Ranger issue. Some of it some friends loaned me."

"You must have some kind of friends."

He drove with his wrist draped over the steering wheel and his body angled into the car. If he had straightened up, the crown of his Stetson would have bumped the roof. He wore his sunglasses; his bifocals were stuffed in his shirt pocket. Somehow his clothes stayed freshly starched. "You know it's pretty out here, but I never liked this part of Texas much."

"You gotta get used to it."

"I guess I got used to trees and buildings. It's too open out here. . . . 'Course I guess you can see 'em trying to sneak up on you. But still, San Antonio is for me. The Rangers are mostly a rural police force anymore. But I ended up helping urban cops in San Antonio. You ever been there?"

"Maybe three, four times, total."

"I like downtown, though Jerri and me now live in some goddamn yuppie suburb that's kind of in the country. But like I was saying, I like downtown. I like to sit in Military or Alamo Plaza. It's like I can feel ghosts there. It's like ol' Rip Ford, Teddy Roosevelt, those old merchants and businessmen like Groos and Steves, all the old Rangers and Confederates are there with me." He stopped, looked over at me, and said, "I guess you're thinking I'm crazy."

"Out here I can practically feel the rocks. And hell, I had to listen to my friend Sister Quinn with all her talk about spirits, so I guess I don't consider seeing ghosts crazy."

"Hell, I used to think my ex-wife was talking to me. The dead don't die." He looked ahead off into the country. "I don't think that I could feel the landscape like you say. Probably 'cause the landscape has all changed in San Antonio. But I can feel the people. I guess what I mean is I can feel all the history in San

Antonio." He looked at me. "I'm not bitching. I'm glad I can feel history."

I looked out at the rough, mean country, the ocotillos, whose withered arms seemed to be begging the sun for water. "We're planning on shooting somebody and getting shot at. Doesn't it scare you?"

Through some movement of his ears or nose, he made his sunglasses slide toward the tip of his nose and looked over the top of the frames at me. "I guess I'm scared right now. But when the shooting starts, if you're good at what you do, if you're prepared for it, you don't notice it, you just do it. You do the best you can. What you should. That's what I meant about your losses. You got to accept them. You're gonna lose some." I thought he was going to run off the road. Before he did, he pushed his glasses to their proper place on his nose and looked back at the road. "I tell you what scares me. A friend of mine, an FBI agent, the fella that encouraged me to chase Jerri down, his name was Ollie Nordmarken, died two years ago. He was an old fart like me and his heart just stopped working. He knew he was gonna die, saw himself dying, just shriveling up, turning into something he wasn't, and then died. It was the way my first wife died. It's the way old folks die. That scares me."

I could hear a slight waver in his voice. "This car started out as my wife's. I mean my first wife's. I'm still not used to calling Jerri my wife. But now I like to drive this old car. I've made some changes in it." He turned his head to smile at me. "I can't bear to get rid of it."

"Now that you're retired, do you miss your job?"

"This sounds like an interview." He looked ahead and smiled.

"Part of my job is to write promotional copy. I could use some quotes from a famous Texas Ranger. But mostly I'm interested for me. I'm thinking about retiring sometime soon."

"Truth be told, I was encouraged to retire. You see, I hit that little pissant friend of yours, and he was a Mexican official of some sort. You should of seen it, though. It was in the San Antonio police station. And a lot of cops were looking on, and most of 'em didn't like me, and most of them were thinking I was just some limp dick ol' man. And there's Jerri, and she's screaming for me to bust his ass. And I did. He ever tell you about that?"

"No. Just about Fuentes."

Parr exhaled some air between his lips. "Another crazy-ass Mexican. What makes them spout all this half-cocked political bullshit?"

"Maybe it's the water."

"Well, ol' Palo is a thief, a criminal, but he's the best of the bunch. At least in the sense that he takes care of his own and seems to keep a level head. He's not mean like Trujillo. Of course, I wouldn't trust the old bastard. Look at all the trouble he's caused just trying to keep his sorry ass out of jail."

"Your retirement, though. You enjoying it?"

"I miss playing cowboy. But retirement's given me more time to spend with Jerri. Of course, she's pretty busy. It's what I should have done for Melba." His voice caught on her name. "She wanted me to retire. I should have. It would have helped her die. We had no kids. No real relatives close by. It was just me and her. I should have taken better care of her." He hesitated, tried to say something, caught himself, thought, then said, "I mean to not let it happen with Jerri. I'm getting the most out of my life with her."

I turned away from him and looked at the road. What I had wanted to know about was his marriage to Jerri. They cared for each other, had a certain kind of love. But they each had a memory of an old lover floating around like a ghost through their consciousness. Joe would never love Jerri like or as much as his Melba. And Jerri, bless her, was content with that.

We came up from Shafter, passed the Marfa Art Institute, and pulled into the sector headquarters. Joe hung around with me at the headquarters, met Billy Sosa, and generally was treated like a visiting dignitary. Then we drove to Alpine to look for Leland Carter. He wasn't hard to find. We pulled into McDonald's and saw him at a plastic table with Weldon Phillips and another deputy.

With Joe Parr behind me, I walked up to the table and nodded at Weldon while I said, "Leland, could we have a word with you?" Weldon swung his head between Leland and me as if he

| 177 |

wanted an answer, as if he were angry at being left out of this Special Task Force investigation. Leland pushed himself up from his hamburger and hung his head. He wouldn't look at Weldon. Behind me, Joe Parr tipped his hat at Weldon, smiled, and adjusted his tie, and I saw the map of Texas swing across his chest. It occurred to me that, dressed for administrative duty—white shirt, tie, slacks, Stetson—I must look like a short, pudgy version of Joe.

Parr turned and Leland folded his hamburger in its wrapper and started after Parr. "What's this, Dolph?" Weldon asked me. "What's this you got up your ass about Leland?"

"It's about to come to a head."

"And you can't tell me?" The other deputy excused himself and left his drink and hamburger.

"Soon." I followed Parr to a table by the large window overlooking the parking lot, and I glanced over my shoulder at Weldon. Left by himself, he cussed silently. I could see the words form on his lips.

Parr sat down across from Leland and straightened out his tie. I sat next to Leland. Leland set his hamburger in front of him and stared at it. "Leland, this is Texas Ranger Joe Parr." I motioned to Parr. "I've brought in some extra help. I've got some bad news."

"Can I see a badge?" Leland asked. A peculiar Texas law made it a felony to display a Texas Ranger badge, but you could buy a laminated facsimile. Joe Parr, retired, pulled out a leather case and showed a badge. Leland didn't look closely.

"The Texas Rangers are in on this, Leland." Leland hung his head.

"Why do you want to fuck with me, Dolph? I asked you nice." He looked at Joe, and Joe smiled at him.

"Leland, my back's to the wall. Reynaldo Luna is killing friends of mine, and I mean to stop him. I also aim to stop this mail-order-bride smuggling scheme. So I'm counting on you telling me about Reynaldo, or I call a federal judge and get a search warrant for that tin barn of yours. But first I thought I'd give you a chance to explain yourself in front of the Texas Rangers." I motioned to Joe again.

"I got nothing to say. I think I need a lawyer." He rose, but

I grabbed his arm. As I did, I saw Weldon looking on, so I nod-ded to him.

"Now, I could go over there and talk to Weldon, but I haven't and I won't. What I want instead is information. So I was hoping you'd tell me how to sneak up on Reynaldo and his bad guys."

"I've got no control. You don't understand. I got nothing to do with this killing."

"I understand that my life is in danger. I also understand that I'm going to have to get a search warrant and a warrant out for your arrest. And Ranger Parr here is just recording everything."

"The fucking Texas Rangers? You brought in the Texas Rangers? Jesus, Dolph. It's simple. No need for the Texas Rangers."

"Why don't you tell me how simple it is?"

Leland hung his head. He dug into his shirt pocket and brought out a pack of cigarettes. He shook the pack, and a ciga-rette popped out. He raised the whole pack to his mouth and pulled the cigarette out with his lips. "You want too much, Dolph. I better get my lawyer."

"This place is no smoking," Joe said, and Leland looked around, pulled the cigarette out of his mouth, and crushed it.

I started again. "I've got several witnesses to the whole story. They're willing to testify. I've got other people willing to testify. Whoever isn't talking to me is going to talk to a federal court with mandatory sentencing laws."

Leland shifted his eyes between me and Parr. "Damn it, Dolph. You're trying to scare me. I don't see what you have."

Joe Parr leaned toward Leland and whispered, "Now I know I look like a scrawny old man without enough ass in his jeans to do anything." Leland turned toward Joe Parr to hear him. And Joe Parr circled his hand around the back of Leland's neck and pulled it just a bit. Leland grew rigid and pushed against Joe's grip. Joe tightened his grip and gave a slight twist to Leland's neck. Leland looked around for help. "I'm a Ranger, and I got contacts, but that does-n't matter. You threatened my wife. You tried to intimidate her. Now, she can take care of herself, which she has already done. But I ain't got mine. Warrant or no warrant, I'm coming after you, and I'm gonna start by busting down that steel barn of yours to see what I

can find in it. Then I'm gonna skin that Luna fella. Now, listen—"
And Joe Parr stopped to look at Leland. "Are you listening?" Leland
nodded. "I'll kill you if I have to."

Leland pushed against Joe's grip, and Joe held tight, smiled,
then released his grip.

I grabbed a napkin, wrote a cell phone number on it, and
passed it to Leland. "You can call me at this number. I'm down
at Pepper's old resort. I want a confession and some information
by tomorrow."

"I'm not that patient," Joe Parr said. "I'm gonna drive by your
trailer home and talk to your wife."

"No, no. Leave her out of this." Leland panicked.

Joe Parr got up and tipped his hat to Leland, turned away
from him, and headed for the front door. Weldon now was gawk-
ing at us. I got up, turned my back to Weldon. I caught up with
Joe Parr while the mommas and their kids munched on their hamburgers and sneaked glances at us.

When we climbed into Joe's Lincoln, I asked, "Jesus, Joe, you
think you scared him enough?"

"Hell, I scared myself." Joe started the car. "Seventy goddamn
years old, and I'm playing hard-dick cowboy shit."

"Well, you scared me too," I said as we pulled away from
the Alpine McDonald's. "I guess you really could charge into the
Comanches with old Jack Hays."

Parr's eyes darted toward me, then back toward the road.
"Why, thank you, Dolph," he said.

FIFTEEN

The red dot on the sensor's receptor went off, and we knew that one just like it was blinking in the Presidio station. I was on the phone to Dede at home, and she started making calls. With his boots on and his automatic rifle slung around his shoulder, Joe Parr was at one of the windows of the kitchen and sighting through his infrared binoculars at the open space between the two rows of cabins on either side of the kitchen. Jerri was beside him, holding the shotgun. Pepper was at the other window and sighted through the scope of his deer rifle and leaned his .30–30 Winchester and his shotgun on either side of him. I holstered my pistol and picked up my own automatic rifle and joined Pepper, my binoculars hung from my neck. "Yahoo," Pepper said.

I looked at his guns. "Pepper, why don't you use just one gun? Things get going, you could knock one of those over and shoot one of us."

"I got your back," was all he said. Trujillo came up behind me with his pistol in his left hand. "Just stand back," I said to him.

"I can shoot. I just can't hit anything."

Joe Parr turned to face Jerri. "Honey, here, you put this on." He had put his binoculars down and was trying to get her into the bulletproof vest.

"No, Joe, you."

"We don't have time to argue," he said, and dressed her in his vest and helmet.

All we heard was the rustle of Jerri sliding her arms into the vest and the ticks of a clock on the back wall. "I guess I don't need to tell you that if you got an automatic weapon, put down a field of fire, and if you got a single fire, find you a target," Joe said.

"It ain't like *The Alamo*," Pepper said. "It's more like *Rio Bravo*. Y'all seen that one?"

I felt a little familiarity, memories of squatting in the dark waiting for wets. But then the realization that there would be shooting chased the comfort of familiarity and replaced it with a stronger memory. I felt a coppery taste in my mouth because I anticipated the wasp stings from nine-millimeter bullets. Once the metal enters your body, you even taste it. I waited for the real bullets to end the awful anticipation of bullets in flesh. It occurred to me that I had never shot anyone—just been shot and shot at. Taking bullets and getting shot at was what I was good at.

And I looked around me and saw the reasons that we all were here. Curiosity, faith, a favor to a friend, some notion about justice, a job, our mutual past fuckups. Some little accidents, some simple trait and we do *x* and then *y* and things get complex, and we're playing a comic version of the Alamo.

I heard Fuentes laughing. Before he had shot himself, he talked to me. He believed in neither fate nor accident nor God nor evil nor destiny nor meaninglessness but some conspiratorial combination that sent us doing the thing that we most had to do, and this thing was probably absurd. The way we got there made sense, but the result was stupid. I clenched my teeth, begging something to start so I could get Fuentes's laugh out of my head.

Then Pepper's motion-detecting lights lit up the row of cabins, and we saw three men freeze like pronghorns caught in headlights. They turned to face us, eyes begging, just as deer seem to beg before you mow them down in your car. In the light, I saw a face with a missing tooth and a broken nose: Esteban. Another man had a long face with an ugly scar and a misplaced cheek: the thug Jerri hit. Then I focused on the man who must be Reynaldo.

It was the first that I had seen of his face. He was clearly the brother of Esteban. His nose was straight; he had all of his teeth, no bar fights. His face was more angular; he was almost handsome. My training took over. A Border Patrol agent always shouts a warning and does not fire unless his, a fellow agent's, or a wet's life is in danger. I tried to choke the mantra, but, "Párense! Arriba los manos!" came out of my mouth. And momentarily, before they started to fire, Joe Parr and Pepper looked at me.

Joe Parr let loose with his field of fire; Pepper began rapidly cocking his rifle; Jerri squirmed for a view; Trujillo just trilled an, "*Ayiii*"; dust kicked up in front of the three men as they tried to shoot out the lights shining on them. Their bullets tore chunks of wood and mortar from Pepper's cabins. They shot out all the lights but one that was behind a cabin. Then blood spurted out of a hole in Broken Cheek's chest. In the glow of the remaining light, I saw Esteban come running toward the kitchen. Pepper sighted in on him, and Jerri got off a shot, but they must have missed. He hit the tarp over the swimming pool and sank as it gave way beneath him. His head fell beneath our eye level. And we all looked away from him, squinting to see by the one beam of light far behind the wounded men. Broken Cheek was lying in front of us, shooting at the kitchen. We saw Reynaldo's back as he ran to his right, out of our line of sight.

The rock that Pepper's uncle used to construct half of his front wall protected us from bullets. But bullets punctured the lumber that made up the rest of the wall. We crouched and took turns rising, briefly, to get a shot out of a window. "Shit, look at this damage," I heard Pepper say. "Hell, why didn't we bring a bazooka?"

Then other holes appeared along the sides of the kitchen/ entertainment complex. "They're circling us!" Joe Parr yelled. "Dolph, you should be good at tracking and hiding in the dark. How about me and you get to the back door and try to circle around ourselves?"

I crouched and started to duckwalk toward the kitchen. Trujillo was immediately in my vacated spot and shooting with his left hand, just wasting his ammunition. I looked back over my shoulder and saw Jerri tug on Joe Parr's arm. She kissed him.

Joe and I crawled through the kitchen and stopped at the back door, and soon Trujillo was behind us. "I thought I better stand guard over this door. I can't hit anything unless it's right in front of me."

"Okay, okay, okay," Joe said. "I'll go out first. Then you follow." He flung open the door and stepped to one side, breathed in, then ran out the door. I followed him. He turned to the right, and I turned to the left. My feet rolled in the gravel, and I was afraid that I would slip. Again I cussed myself for not running more with Pepper. I heard some shots from Parr's side of the kitchen/entertainment complex. I slowed and started to walk. I saw a figure. I crouched, shouldered my rifle, and waited. Training was putting my life in danger, but it had chased the anticipation of wasp stings away. Hell, I should have panicked and shot. But I rose and said, "Párense!"

The man turned his face toward me, and from what I could see in the moonlight, I realized that I didn't recognize him. My finger started to squeeze the trigger, but the man turned from me and started running through the lechuguilla. He'd be stinging from the cactus cutting him, and eventually he'd hit barbed wire. I stepped up. He had thrown down his gun. I touched the hot barrel, then kept walking forward. So much for Reynaldo's broncos.

I heard more shooting from Parr's side of the building and slowly rounded the corner of the building. Esteban was pulling himself out of the pool. He must have broken an ankle because he fell once he planted his foot. I raised my rifle to my shoulder, thought, tried to squeeze the trigger, and my teeth clenched.

I swiveled, saw Broken Cheek, his rifle raised, and I fell as he and Esteban fired. Suddenly I was looking up and saw stars. Then they began to spin. I heard a blast from Jerri's shotgun and rolled and crawled until I was on my belly and looking at the front door to the kitchen. The door was open, and Jerri, in her body armor, was out it and got the second round off from her shotgun. Esteban, just out of the pool, looked at a spray of blood and bone coming out of his chest. He fell face forward and then Jerri dove for the ground. Then Pepper came out the kitchen door, and I tried to shoulder my rifle, but when the butt hit my shoulder, I felt a searing rod plunge from my shoulder into my neck.

Broken Cheek raised up to fire. Jerri fired. From around the corner, Joe Parr came walking straight and tall and firing. Pepper, short legs churning, working the lever of his rifle, was shooting and trying to get to me. Then he crumpled, rolled, dropped his rifle, and held his knee. My neck didn't work, so I had to twist my whole body to see Broken Cheek writhe as bullets from Mr. and Mrs. Parr entered him.

I twisted back to see Jerri slowly rise. She looked at me and took off her helmet. "Oh, Dolph," I saw her lips form but not say. I tried again to twist and see. I saw stars, the one streak of light, and then Joe stepping cautiously toward Esteban. Shifting more, I saw Pepper roll and scoot on his butt as he held his knee and screamed, "Shit, shit." I heard sirens, saw flares, headlights, and spotlights. The place lit up. The Border Patrol to the rescue. I felt the barrel of my gun. Another shoot-out and I hadn't gotten off a shot.

I stared at the stars, and then Jerri's face was between me and the stars, and I tried to memorize her deep blue eyes. She leaned beside me and stroked the side of my face with the back of her forefinger. Bits of light caught off the tears or sweat on her cheeks. "Should I rub your feet?" she asked, and smiled as I laughed, then grinned.

I rolled and raised myself to look around. I couldn't move my neck. Several agents were carrying Pepper in a stretcher, and then my hand was in Jerri's, and she was saying, "All this over Palo. He's not worth it."

Joe Parr walked up behind her, looked at my hand in hers, and said, "What's the damage?" I tried to raise my head to see him standing above me, but I could only hold my neck in one position.

I tried to answer Joe Parr, but before I could, I used my breath to wince from another hot rod in my shoulder, and I squeezed Jerri's hand way too tight. I twisted as Dede eased her hug on me. "Dolph, Dolph, Dolph," she said. She was crying.

SIXTEEN

While in the hospital, I dictated a letter to Sister Quinn's brother. My mother tapped the letter out on the notebook computer that she had bought for Beeson's Bed and Breakfast. When she got the brother's reply, my mother brought the letter back to the hospital and read it to me. He asked if he needed to come down for anything. We wrote back and told him no, all was being taking care of.

When I got back to work after the battle and my arm healed a bit, I didn't mind running my Special Task Force, but I didn't have the stomach to write the press releases or speeches. What I probably did best made me ashamed of myself. Had the Border Patrol demoted me, sent me back to patrolling, where I could squat in the desert and look for wets, I probably would have been happier. Hell, it should have assigned me back to the Presidio station, where I could work for Dede. But I had gone too soft. My distance vision was getting worse; I had an appointment with an optometrist. Sitting still, I had gained another inch around my belly. And I'd probably have wet my pants if anybody pointed a gun at me. I had disability pay, a lump of retirement money. I was still young enough to do something else. My mother urged me to exploit my talents and become something better. I talked with investors, bought my own computer to keep track of my stocks and bonds, counted and recounted my money, then I retired.

Back when Pepper, Dede, and I soaked in his tub, Pepper was right about morality in private investigation—his point about solving the case being the only morality, the purity of working for money instead of justice. And Trujillo was right in his defense of himself to Jerri, about the burden of working for a government. In private investigating there is only one imperative. That is to spot the details, every one, to see what is out of place, what doesn't fit, or what does fit. After that, the investigator-for-hire's job is over, no apprehension, no arrests. He doesn't correct the problem. He gives the facts to someone else, and that person interprets them, puts them together, and makes the case or defends the client. The lawyers, the cops, the spurned husbands put the details together and look at the big picture, see the landscape, the horizon.

As a Border Patrol agent I had failed to observe closely enough and had gotten people hurt (and I hadn't done too well with my private life either). But if I were a private investigator, I wouldn't have as many people depending on me. Private investigating would better accommodate my failures. There was no U.S. government giving you a mission and a principle; there was no Sister Quinn whispering in your ear about grace and mercy.

So my mother managed my retirement party, and Pepper catered it. She wanted all the agents to wear their uniforms, but no one did. Border Patrol agents work in green; they don't celebrate in it. But somehow my mother did con Billy Sosa into lending her pennants, flags, badges, newspaper articles, artifacts, and documents—anything locked away and forgotten at sector headquarters. So the bottom floor of Beeson Bed-and-Breakfast was covered with Border Patrol regalia. In a large frame, covered with glass, were newspapers articles about me: getting gut shot, shooting it out with smugglers crossing the Rio Grande, busting Pepper, tracking down Fuentes, winning the battle of Cleburne Hot Springs.

My mother stayed in motion and charmed everyone as only she could. It was as if it were her party. I stayed in the background, sipped beer with my one good arm, and didn't say much. I was still learning to do things left-handed. Eventually I would heal;

I had had far worse wounds. The bullet made a small wound at the top of my shoulder, cleanly broke my collarbone, and ripped up some muscle and tissue when it exited out the back of my shoulder. I didn't want a party.

With some help from my mother, Charlie, and a waitress from Reata, Pepper had cooked venison stew and quail. He limped around on his crutches and, like me, stayed out of the way and watched in case Reynaldo Luna crashed the party.

Beeson Bed-and-Breakfast was complete. The carriage house was an exact replica of its original self. In the old mansion, the rooms upstairs and down had late-nineteenth-century carved and polished wood over the arched doorways. The huge stuffed head of a longhorn looked over the dining room. My mother knew how to decorate in a style that would attract the tourists. They came, as Pepper had hoped, and so he and I had a second income.

Dorothy McFarland sat in a corner of the large dining room. She folded her hands in her lap and smiled but didn't speak, guarding her secrets. I offered her a beer, and she accepted and rested the can of beer in her lap. She smiled at me, and after a few minutes, she thanked me and said that she had to get home. I'm not sure that I could forgive her for signing a paper that indirectly led to the deaths of so many people, but I refused to hold anything against her. I had pardoned her in my mind.

Steady ol' Pooter, a lineman, the guy you don't notice, who makes the holes for the stars, talked about Socorro and Sister Quinn instead of himself and gave all the credit for stopping the band of women smugglers to me. Dede trailed behind Pooter, looking sad eyed. I got the impression that they just fizzled on each other.

Joe Parr was quick to tell the story of what was becoming known as the battle of Cleburne Hot Springs. He praised everybody involved, especially me. The way he told the story, I was the real hero. At great risk to myself I had exposed myself to the broken cheek man and to Esteban, who was stuck in the pool. And by taking the shot, I had allowed Jerri, Pepper, and him to nail Esteban and the broken cheek man. In a way Joe was returning my favor, for in my report, in the press releases that I wrote, I mentioned the Border Patrol and Joe Parr, the ex–Texas Ranger. The

San Antonio Express-News carried the story, and Joe got an interview with the *Midland Reporter-Telegram* and a San Antonio TV station. My headlines helped stretch Joe Parr's already sizable legend. And with the shoot-out, Pepper had finally made his family's failed property famous. Along both sides of the river, the locals had a new source for their corridos.

Jerri stayed close to Joe. But late in the evening with everyone drunk, we ended up in the kitchen and stared at each other over the rims of our glasses. "You know, the last time I saw Vincent Fuentes, his right arm was in a cast because he got shot in the shoulder. He'd jumped in front of a bullet to protect me and got his shoulder mangled."

I rocked my arm back and forth in the sling. "I wish it wasn't my right arm."

"I wish it wasn't any arm, Dolph."

"Maybe, sometime, we could visit again. Maybe you, or you and Joe, could come out again."

We tried to talk around what we really wanted to say. But then Jerri summed up what we both felt. "I should feel dirty or ashamed for what we could have done. But I don't. There's just too many rules, shoulds and shouldn'ts. It's just so hard not to hurt somebody. Sometimes I pay attention to what we should do. Sometimes I don't. This time I did better."

"That's why I quit."

"You mean you're quitting the Border Patrol, or you mean you're going to quit trying to figure shoulds and shouldn'ts?"

"I mean all my bad habits."

We were all good detectives, so Joe Parr probably suspected the way I had come to feel about his wife. Still he said nothing, showed nothing. He had a graciousness that matched my mother's.

As the party ended, couples drifted to their rooms. My mother and Charlie went to their master bedroom. Jerri and Joe went to their guest room. Pooter followed Dede into her room, for what I suspected was a long talk. Pepper and I, once again, were left out on my front porch, two aging, crippled men, me in my sling, Pepper in his cast and crutches. Pepper lowered himself into his chair and kept his leg with its thigh-high cast sticking out in front of him. He drank his second beer, still on guard, still covering my back. "You gonna sleep tonight, or are you going to stand guard?"

Pepper sipped his beer. "I'll take the first shift."

"You can relax, Pepper. Just take it easy. No more Border Patrol. No more resorts. We run a bed-and-breakfast now."

"And a private detective agency. Look, Jerri can put in a good word for us and get us licenses. Hell, we got to. We owe it to the community. Who wouldn't want to hire the heroes of the battle of Cleburne Hot Springs?"

The old Pepper sometimes surfaced. But I figured that I owed both the old entrepreneur Pepper and the new cautious Pepper a little cooperation. "I could still rely on all my old contacts. I think that's a good idea, Pepper."

"Holy good goddamn. You mean you actually think I had a good idea? You're not going to try to argue me out of it?"

"It's not just your idea."

Pepper chuckled. "Huh, maybe I better rethink this. Just how good are two middle-aged, crippled men gonna do? Hell, I'm an ex-con, and you're an ex–Border Patrol agent that's been shot all to shit. Hell, every time you get close to somebody with a gun, you get shot. We ain't nothing like Marlowe or Spencer or Tom Selleck."

Pepper had a new knee and a plate and a screw above and below it. He had to go to Midland to an orthopedic specialist to piece his leg back together. I got out relatively easy. I bled a lot and broke my collarbone. I was mostly healed, but after having my arm bound for several months, I could only keep it out of a sling for an hour at a time. Pepper and I both went to therapy at the Big Bend Regional Hospital to get our body parts to work properly again.

"A nice winter night," Pepper said. "Better air than that desert air coming off the Rio Grande. We done good to leave behind Cleburne Hot Springs. Now if we could either find us some good women or learn to be content without 'em. If it weren't for that patch between their legs, there'd be a bounty on 'em."

The board that considered Pepper's parole didn't want to send a hero of the battle of Cleburne Hot Springs off to prison or add years onto his parole, but they were troubled by his owning several weapons and firing them: "a violation of his conditions of parole." But Pepper, his lawyer, his parole agent, and I all argued that he owned the hunting rifles before his crime, so board members dismissed him with his one year. All of us appeared before an inquiry, but no one seriously considered indicting us. Leland Carter was awaiting trial, the grand jury had indicted him, and Weldon Phillips had put him on leave without pay. He couldn't afford a good lawyer, and I had heard that Miss Brewster County had moved herself and the kids out of his trailer and into her daddy's ranch house. Luckily for Leland all his confederates were dead or disappeared. No one mentioned Dorothy McFarland.

Esteban, the man with the broken cheek who had attacked Jerri, and the man who threw down his gun and ran away from me were dead. Three days after the battle a Border Patrol Agent spotted circling buzzards; he drove in their direction and found the man who ran from me.

When Joe Parr was circling on his side of Pepper's kitchen, he spotted Reynaldo, fired, and missed. Then when Dede pulled up with her Border Patrol cavalry, Reynaldo Luna disappeared into the desert. Customs and Border Patrol couldn't find him. DEA agents couldn't find him. On this side of the border the official assumption was that he died out in the desert but that no buzzard had led a Border Patrol agent to his carcass. Trujillo, Pepper, and I believed, though, that Reynaldo had made it to Ruidosa, then across the river to one of the ejidos. We were scared that he was still alive.

Trujillo had friends in high places. So even though the newspapers reported that the boy was found dead in his house, Trujillo was given a temporary leave without pay. He returned to work, but his job became torture because of the soldiers' and citizens' rumors and smirks about the little maricón. If he could find Reynaldo, Trujillo thought he could stop the whispers and rumors. So he went to his sources and asked questions and phoned me when he found out something. But Trujillo made me nervous; perhaps he reminded me of Vincent Fuentes. I didn't want him around. I didn't invite him to my mother's retirement party for me.

The locals made Sister Quinn's templo into a shrine. They

stacked flowers and photos of sick loved ones around the templo. They said that in death, as in life, Sister Quinn supposedly could heal them. I felt guilty, but I simply gave all of Barbara's savings, $2,000, to Jesse Guzmán at St. Margaret Mary's and asked him to help the poor. He had said, "Bless you, Dolph." I had dropped in at the templo once, looked around, picked up some trash with my one good arm, and then made a copy of the keys, gave them to Gilbert Mendoza, and paid him to keep the place up, but I kept the originals on my key chain. A few times Pooter drove out, stayed a night or two at Beeson's Bed-and-Breakfast, then drove down to spend several nights in the templo, communing with Sister Quinn and having her dreams. After a while, Pooter stopped coming, and I stopped hearing from Gilbert Mendoza.

Pepper pushed himself up, leaned on his crutches, and swung himself into the house. "I think I'm going to get some sleep tonight. You take the first watch."

I looked up at the sky and then heard a hooting. Over in a dead tree on the edge of the police station was the dark shape of an owl. Sister Quinn did more than watch me. I heard her whisper to me. "Dolph, Dolph. Forget about justice. Grace, mercy, forgiveness." Maybe her whisper was why I quit the Border Patrol. Then I heard Fuentes laughing. Then a second laugh joined him, and it took me a while to recognize it. It was my father. Fuentes, the lover who wouldn't leave Jerri's memory, the priest who further twisted Sister Quinn's fragile sanity, the gunrunner who caused me to bust Pepper, was laughing at the twists and turns of a good joke. My father was laughing because, without la migra, despite my mother's upbringing, I was now just another Mexican.

PART III

GRACE AND JUSTICE

SEVENTEEN

Joe Parr knew that the history of San Antonio was forever connected to the river. So he requested in his will that his ashes be spread over the river, which was now mostly a canal, and that a tombstone be put up beside his wife of thirty-five years, Melba. Jerri obliged both wishes.

At the funeral service a rented Methodist preacher who never knew Joe stumbled through a eulogy. Afterward, several friends gathered along the banks of the river. We walked past the southernmost stretch of the river, past the HEB Grocery home office in the old armory complex, and nearly to the old Pioneer flour mill. There, on the edge of pavement, where the cement stopped and the river became choked with trees and weeds, Jerri uncapped the urn, shook it, and let the gentle breeze blow Joe Parr's ashes to the other side of the river.

The old ladies—the widows who had been Melba's friends and neighbors in the exclusive Alamo Heights section of San Antonio and who had hoped they might land Joe Parr, only to lose him to Jerri—thought it disgusting to place a tombstone over an empty grave. But the tombstone was for Melba. The ashes sprinkled over the river were for Joe. Jerri got Joe's money and perhaps the best years of his life. Like Sister Quinn, he wanted to become a part of the landscape, and here in San Antonio that landscape was brick, glass, steel, and manicured plants—no wilderness. Joe probably wanted his ashes to choke some tourist along the river walk.

Jerri endured the funeral, the arrangements, the wreaths, the visits from old Texas Rangers, and the call from the governor without a tear—as far as I could tell. Then she went down to the river walk and the edge of the river with me; the commander of Company D of the Texas Rangers, Captain Jack Dean; Pepper, because he was with me; Pooter, because he had shown up; her son from her first marriage, J. J., an engineer in San Antonio; and a cleaning lady from the Bexar County Courthouse, where Joe kept an office. And she shook the urn with all of her might as we watched.

The cleaning lady cried. "He's joined the other ol' Rangers," Captain Jack Dean said solemnly. Pepper looked at Jack Dean and said, "Shit. He's been cheated." Jerri, as she had at the funeral, kept all tears out of her eyes, made deep blue by her contacts. J. J. tentatively wrapped an arm around his mother. It was June, and I pulled my glasses off and wiped the sweat out of my face. Pepper, Pooter, and I, unused to suits, squirmed inside our jackets and tugged at our collars to give us some room to breathe. Jerri was dressed in a beige suit. It was a hot day in summer, and she wasn't about to let tradition make her swelter in a black dress.

I wished that Sister Quinn had been here. I wished that she could have handled the eulogy instead of the hired preacher. She would have rambled an incoherent mix of Christianity, superstition, politics, and her own weird notions, but she would have stumbled across a phrase or two that might have summed up how we felt. And she might have said something that got at how Joe really was. I walked to Jerri and reached for her with both my hands. She took mine in hers and asked me to come by "the house" for dinner. Then Pepper shook her hand, and she invited him too.

When Jerri called me to tell me that Joe Parr had been gunned down, Sister Quinn began to haunt me. She wasn't some ghost that might be exorcised but just a whisper that echoed through my head. I had never thought or wished Joe Parr dead, but Sister Quinn made me think that some wind blew my unthought thought into

Reynaldo Luna's ear to get trapped in his head. And Fuentes's laughter became some chorus behind Sister Quinn's whisper and told me just what Reynaldo was thinking. He could appease his itch for revenge and my unwished longing by gunning down Joe Parr.

When they married, Joe Parr and Jerri Johnson moved out of Joe's old house in Alamo Heights. Joe left that house to thirty years of memory and looked forward to creating new memories with Jerri in a ranch-style house way out in the farthest northwest suburbs of San Antonio. On the morning of his death, he had stepped out in his front yard in his underwear, as was his habit—no close neighbors to see—to retrieve his morning newspaper. An old car pulled up into the driveway, and the driver stepped out and put several shots into Joe's chest. Because the assassin used a silencer, Jerri didn't hear the shots. But wondering where Joe was, she stepped out of the front door and saw tire marks and a crumpled Joe. She got to him in time to squeeze his hand and to look into his eyes to see them smile. Then he died, still holding her hand. I don't know if she cried then.

The FBI had no hard evidence. The police could only make guesses. The old car was found burned to a smoldering steel lump. A retired lady had seen the car enter the suburb. There wasn't much to go on, but everyone knew who did it, the supposed dead man, Reynaldo Luna.

After we spread the ashes across the river, we walked down the river walk. Captain Jack Dean hugged Jerri and kissed her on the cheek. Pooter shook her hand and offered condolences. After a few words to me and Pepper, J. J., the son, went back to a car. Pepper took off his suit jacket and looked at me. "We going back?"

"Take a walk with me, Dolph," Jerri said. "I'll get you back to your hotel." I reached into my pocket, pulled out my keys, and handed them to Pepper.

"I think maybe I'll drive around a little. Look at the sites. Have me a drink. How often does a country boy get to come to the big city?" I nodded, and Pepper limped away on his cane. I turned to face Jerri. She was slipping out of her jacket.

"Take your coat and tie off, and let's walk."

I tugged until I loosened my tie and slipped it from around my neck, and then I shrugged my shoulders out of my jacket. My chest and back were spotted with sweat, and I felt just a momentary chill as a breeze came down the river. I stuffed my tie into my coat pocket, then draped the coat over my arm. Jerri slipped her arm around my other arm. Arm in arm, each with a jacket over our free arms, we walked down the river walk, back toward concrete and tourists. I pulled my head back on my neck to look through the bottom part of my glasses at Jerri. Then I turned my attention to the tamed, man-made scenery.

The humidity seemed to surround me. I felt as though the plants and trees along the river were breathing and sucking in my air. Blossoming flowers seemed to erupt in natural but obscene-looking patterns, not at all like the tiny desert flowers. Cypress and pecan trees provided shade. It almost scared me. From a land where things were outlined clearly in bright sunshine, I felt like shade was a touchable thing, as if my hand couldn't get through it. Below street level, surrounded by tall buildings and breathing trees and plants, walking into and out of shade, I felt confined, claustrophobic, but the steady pressure of Jerri's arm on mine kept me from bolting.

"What we just did was illegal. But it was what Joe wanted." I looked over at her. She smiled to herself and wouldn't look at me. A drop of sweat ran down one lens of my glasses and spoiled my vision. "Joe liked it down here, despite the commercialism and the tourists. He cussed them both. We met down here. He was trying to bust Fuentes, and I was trying to help him. Joe courted me to get information." She stopped, turned, and looked at me. "He went to bed with me. Maybe to get information. Maybe because he just couldn't keep from it. I know I couldn't keep myself away from this charming ol' cowboy." She started walking and pulling me after her. I realized why I was there. I was the person she wanted to listen to her. "Joe Parr could have busted me. He could have seen me prosecuted. But he didn't. And months later, after I lost my anger at him because I was even angrier at Fuentes, he came walking into Palo's big backyard, where Palo and I used to sit, and, like a boy, asked me if I'd have dinner with him. We got married within the year."

Jerri's hand slid down my arm until she held my hand. She raised it. "My, you are sweating, Dolph."

"The humidity, the vegetation, it's all so steamy, so rich, so hot down here."

Jerri reached up and brushed some of the sweat off my forehead, then swished her fingers to get my sweat off her. She put her hand against the side of my face, then her other hand on the other side of my face, and she started to cry. Hot as it was, I circled my arms around her and stained her white blouse and beige suit with my own sweat.

After a moment the heat became too much for us, and she pushed me back. We walked to a bench in the shade, and she sat down. I put my middle finger and my thumb on either side of my glasses and pulled them off and slipped an arm of my glasses over the top button of my shirt to let my glasses dangle against my chest. Several tourists walked by. She started crying again. "Oh, Dolph. When I met Vincent, I knew, I just knew, that this was a man with whom or for whom I could settle. I was sure, and it all went sour. With Joe, I had to work. I had to make a place for him. Joe was steady. You could depend on him. I could have cheated on Vincent. It wouldn't have mattered, not to him or me, and it wouldn't have changed what I felt about him. I didn't dare cheat on Joe."

She turned her head away from me and looked across the river at a momma and a daddy pushing their baby in a stroller. "I never cheated on Joe. Until I spent a couple of days with you."

"But we never," I interrupted.

Jerri shushed me. "I wanted to. Don't you see? I had to keep myself from doing so. Because . . . because I got that feeling I got with Vincent." She squeezed my hand, and the plants and the buildings and the river gasped and sucked my air away. "And I feel so horrible now. Like I wanted this. Like Vincent and Palo somehow schemed to get him out of the way so I could have that feeling back, not with Vincent, but with you."

Now I felt tears mix with my sweat. I reached toward her. We froze looking at each other. The deep blue of her contacts pulled me toward her, but she moved farther away from me. Feeling each other's and the plants' breathing, sweating and crying on each other, we kept ourselves apart. Jerri whispered, "I feel too awful, Dolph. Nothing can come of this. Nothing. Nothing. Nothing."

I dropped my head and muttered, "Okay."

Jerri forced a smile and, as though on command, regained her strength and her composure. "Well, I'm glad to see the jinx didn't hold. You got shot and had a cast on your arm, just like Fuentes. But now I've seen you again. You're healed." We both forced a smile, then hers dropped as the gnawing grief reminded her of its control over her. "Too bad it took Joe's getting shot and killed to break the jinx."

* * *

Jerri and Joe's was a modest house, built with native limestone, which costs a fortune nowadays, with a tin roof and an old-fashioned rock barbecue pit. It had a study for Joe and a master bedroom that looked through large windows at an unfenced backyard. White-tailed does eased to the edge of the backyard to eat the grass. From the front yard, since the house was on the side of a hill, you could see the lights of San Antonio. It was a perfect house for Joe and Jerri. It was the type of house I would have wanted if I had found someone like Jerri, if I had found San Antonio instead of Alpine.

At the wake we drifted around the backyard with its faint smell of burning citronella candles and with its soft light from Chinese lanterns hung from the trees. We drank beer and ate barbecue prepared by Sam Ford, Jerri's enormously fat old ex-boss, the one that left her the investigating and bail-bonding agency.

J. J., Jerri's grown son, acted as host and made sure that everyone had enough to eat and drink. Pepper, balancing himself on his cane, seemed to sniff around the house because he too realized that it matched many of his fantasies. "Goddamn, Dolph," he said. "Ain't San Antonio nice. Hell, it's got trees, water, shade, Mexicans, and cold beer. And I bet it's got its share of cleaned-up women, not like those ol' raw West Texas hides. Hell, it's heaven." I tilted my head back and then forward to try to find the right section of my bifocals to look through in order to see Pepper.

Jerri made sure that Pepper and I didn't leave early to return to our hotel out on I-10. When most of the guests left, she asked me into the study. She shut the doors behind me, then went behind the desk. She turned on a single light. Pooter was standing in the shadows. He stepped up behind her. "Sit down, Dolph." I sat in a chair in front of the desk. She rolled her chair from around the desk to my side. She sat down. Pooter sat on the corner of the desk to look down at us. Jerri took my hand in both of hers. Her hand felt different than that afternoon. With the trees and shrubs around us at the river walk, we both felt overripe, about to explode, but here, in air-conditioning, we didn't sweat. We were cool and calm. "This was Joe's room. You can still feel him here. I mean the books, the paintings." I looked around. All the walls were lined with full bookshelves. "He was a voracious reader." The paintings were Frederic Remington prints or the bluebonnet paintings of local artists. "You can smell him in here." I turned to look at Jerri and stared into her deep blue eyes. She let my hand go, and it just dropped to my thigh. She rested her hands on her thighs. "When he died, he couldn't get out the words, but he told me who did this with his eyes."

"We all know who did this," I added. I pulled off my bifocals because I wasn't yet used to shifting my eyes behind the lenses. I could see fairly well up close.

"And the police don't have the evidence. The FBI know, but they can't find him, and they don't have enough on him."

"How do you know this?"

"Palo."

"Does he know everything?"

Jerri smiled, and she grabbed my hand again. "Nearly." I felt Pooter hovering behind me. I twisted to see his shiny bald head in the dimly lit study. Jerri continued. "Even if the FBI caught him, and then even if he went to court, I don't want to see Joe's reputation smeared or used. If he is going to go like he did, then I want him to be legend. I want the mystery, the suspicions that keep people guessing, to keep his memory alive. I want the conviction to come from supposition, not from the legal system."

I shifted my head between Jerri and Pooter. "You want him

to get away?" Jerri looked at me, but not like she had that afternoon. Her eyes were still deep blue, but her half-formed smile, the furrows in her face made them look less deep.

"I want him dead. But not by the system. I want him to die in Mexican fashion, in Fuentes's fashion, like Joe, knowing that his death has nothing to do with right, wrong, justice, lawyers, officials, or cops. I want him to know he's dying because of what he is, what he did, and because he fucked with Joe Parr." Jerri dropped her head, then pulled it up to gaze at me with those deep eyes—not to show me she could settle with and for me because I was like Fuentes, but to beg me and to heap a burden on me before she even said the words. "I want you to kill him, Dolph."

The Border Patrol Dolph Martinez stood up. "No, don't tell me any more. You do what you want. But leave me out. And for chrissakes don't tell me any more." She wouldn't look at me. "How can you say this? Especially now?" I looked around at Pooter. "Especially after this afternoon. Especially after knowing what you do of me."

"I misguessed, then, Dolph. I was wrong about you."

I started walking toward the door, but Pooter stepped in front of it and begged, "We trust you enough to ask."

"You're asking too much," I said to him and then to Jerri. "It's all too much."

"The law isn't going to work here, Dolph. Sit back down," Jerri said. I stared at her, and her eyes softened. "For what you think of me, for what I think of you, listen." She looked over at Pooter, then back at me. "We trust you that much."

The Dolph Martinez who was Sandra Beeson's little boy, who was the lover of the Chicana lawyer in El Paso and of the manager of the hotel in Lajitas, sat back down. I wondered which Dolph Martinez would accept guilt and loss of respect for just one night alone with Jerri Johnson. Jerri knelt in front of me and took my hand. "I'm not a part of the Special Task Force anymore. I'm retired. I have no authority."

"All the better. You still have the contacts. You can still make the phone calls, but you're not hampered by the legalities. You and Pepper want to start this investigation service, but you don't yet have a license. So you're not traceable there. You're the best man for the job. And so I want to hire you. Joe left some money. Consider this your first case."

I rubbed at my chin and dropped my head. I couldn't look at her. I had to maintain rationality. I had to not feel. Sister Quinn could talk her voodoo and beg me with her eyes so that I got in a whipping contest with her. Vincent Fuentes begged me and made me feel guilty for doing my job. Now Jerri was stirring emotion and logic up. She cooed, "Reynaldo Luna is crazy with rage. A lot of people are scared of him and want to see him dead. But they won't talk to the law. They can't risk telling what they know to the police. Eventually the FBI will arrest someone who can be convicted, but probably not Reynaldo." I felt her hand on my knee. "Which is where you come in. Don't you see?"

I looked not at Jerri but at Pooter. His bald head had a shine that made it look wet. "Why are you involved?"

"Because I admired Sister Quinn. And Socorro turned out to be an okay guy."

"So which one of your philosophies says it's okay to kill a guy?"

Pooter crossed his arms and smiled. "All of them." He leaned against the edge of the desk. "I believe in process philosophy. I just wanted to hurry the process along." Pooter chuckled. He looked like the Buddha.

"Justice, right?"

"You should have listened to Sister Quinn more carefully. You've gotten caught up in the Christian aspect."

"What do you think she was?"

"Wiser than the church."

"But she'd never do this."

"That's why we have to. I ran away from the last fight. That last one was personal, existential, mere survival. So's what Jerri's asking you—this has to do with what we are. This is a giant leap beyond legality or morality. It's just us, and I'm helping you with this one." I could see that Pooter, the big dumb lineman, could be mean.

"Johnny Blackwell," Jerri said, and we both turned to look down at her as she knelt in front of me. "He's Lyle's brother, and he lives here in San Antonio. Palo found the name. The only one Palo's told so far is me. He'll tell the FBI if you don't cooperate. Dolph, I can't do this, not given the situation. I've got the FBI asking me everything. So I can cover for you. But now I need you." She looked at Pooter, then looked at me, and her eyes grew soft and deeper than they ever had, and she smiled. "This is, in a way, like a love affair, Dolph. I am as sure and as certain that you won't hurt me as I am sure and certain that I could settle with and for you. This, for right now, is what I can give you instead of real love."

I hoped that my mouth didn't drop open as I swung my head between them and wondered if they had rehearsed this, if they had written down the lines and read them to each other. "Holy shit. Holy shit. Pepper's really gonna like this."

"If you can't find Reynaldo within a week, then the deal is off, because eventually the FBI will find out something. But I'll go to jail before I ever mention your involvement."

She stood up and kissed me on the cheek.

"I'll try," my mouth said before I knew what I had let it say. Pooter shook my hand. "I want Pepper to help—and Trujillo."

"Fine," Jerri said, and kissed me again, again on the cheek.

"So what makes us different from Vincent Fuentes?"

"Nothing," Jerri said to me without smiling. "He just let it get to him. Strength, Dolph."

I looked at Pooter. "What about Sister Quinn?"

"Strength, Dolph," he repeated.

"Don't you two spout one-word clichés to me. Jesus." We stared back and forth at each other until I backed to the door. Joe Parr was dead, so Fuentes was again charming, cajoling, and coercing Jerri. I left her, thinking I had both lost and gained respect for her. But in truth, what I was probably confused about was me, and if I let it bother me, Fuentes would start talking to me too.

Back in our hotel room, as I told Pepper about my conversation with Jerri, he rubbed his destroyed knee. I looked at the scars crisscrossing it. I had lied to him. I told him that Jerri wanted us to find Reynaldo, not kill him. "We've got our first case, Pepper."

Pepper stared at his knee. "Trujillo could help. But between us, what she no doubt wants to do, what we can do, is kill him."

Pepper smiled. I couldn't lie to him if I wanted to. "That's the whole story, ain't it?"

"That's the other part of the deal."

"What is it about you and these blondes? Is it some kinda Freudian shit with your momma or something?" I had sent him to prison, gotten his knee shot off, and now I was asking him to help me commit a murder. I could hear the wheels working in his head.

"Forget it," I said. "You can't risk something like this. You can't get in trouble with the law again."

"Yeah, but this is kind of like that wild itch to build me that pool and then build a resort. You gotta dream big. None of you federal guys ever liked the Feebies. Here's a chance to show them up. Besides that, it's just best off for everybody if Reynaldo Luna is dead."

"Pepper, be careful."

"I got your back."

It wasn't Pepper's snoring that kept me up that night. Sister Quinn kept scolding me. So I took a walk outside across the parking lot. Businesses were closed down, and only their burglar lights and the streetlights lit the street. Because I was a country boy from Big Bend and hardly ever saw streetlights, this scene was eerie, otherworldly, like I was stuck on the set of a bad sci-fi movie. I sat on a curb and just watched headlights on the freeway overpass. Finally Vincent Fuentes laughed and asked me what else I could do. He calmed me; I relaxed and went back to the motel for a few hours of sleep.

EIGHTEEN

Through the screen door, Pepper and I watched as Palo walked down the wooden floor of his long hall. With his cane tapping in between his softer footfalls, Palo looked like a limping, three-legged bird. Age was curling him over, so he had to pull his head up over to the back of his shoulders to see, making the old bird's head and shoulders look like a turtle's. "You Jerri's friend?" he asked.

"I'm Dolph Martinez"—I jerked my head around behind me—"and this is Pepper Cleburne." He unlatched the screen door and pushed it open, and I scooted out of his path as he inched out onto the front porch.

"Follow me," he said.

He tapped with his cane down the length of the wooden front porch, and I followed, and the tap of Pepper's cane followed me. Palo slid around the corner of a table and sat in a rickety lawn chair behind it. Four chairs surrounded the table, and he motioned for Pepper and me to sit down. I sat across from him, and Pepper sat to his right. "I thought we'd eat lunch out here."

"We don't need a lunch," Pepper said.

Palo held up his hand to silence Pepper. "It's Lili's chicken enchiladas. They're left over, but she puts them in the microwave for us." And like clockwork, a short Mexican lady appeared with a large tray and put a plate of enchiladas and a cold beer in front of us.

"Damn." Pepper looked at both of us, stared at his plate, grabbed a fork, and said, "Looks good." He dug in. Holding his mouth open against the heat of the enchiladas, he began chewing, then said, "These are good."

Palo smiled and, with a shaking hand, scooped some enchiladas for himself. I looked down at my plate, and the food looked fuzzy. I grabbed either side of my glasses, right where the arms begin, between my thumb and forefinger, and, like Joe Parr, pulled them off my face and stuffed them into my pocket so I could see the green and off-white swirls of white cheese, tortillas, green paste, and chicken. Pepper and I would have preferred to have been inside in the air-conditioning. Used to higher and drier Alpine, we sweated in the San Antonio humidity. It was noon, and the humidity was giving way to the dry heat moving in from the west. The mix of heat and humidity knotted my underwear under my jeans and made my jeans themselves knot between my legs. I squirmed. But the enchiladas were good and the beer cool. "I like to eat out here," Palo said. "It's cooler."

Pepper looked at him and cocked his head. "I have some air-conditioning inside my house," Palo added. "But I don't like it. Artificial, unnatural, and just too cold. So I leave my doors and windows open. Sometimes, though, it does get hot inside." Palo the purist, I thought. Probably the only person in Texas who could still exist without air-conditioning.

"Palo, thank you for the lunch, but who is this Johnny Blackwell?"

"I live in San Antonio because it's okay to be a mexicano in San Antonio. And Mexicans don't discuss business until after lunch." So we finished our enchiladas and then ate bowlfuls of Palo's favorite, Blue Bell Caramel Turtle ice cream.

"Jerri likes you, Dolph," Palo said. Palo leaned toward me and smiled. "I can tell. I know her better than old Joe Parr. He never paid attention. He should have. I'm surprised Jerri stayed with him. If my fool son would have stayed with her, she might have saved him from himself. He might have saved her from all the trouble she's had because of him." Palo tsked. He smiled. "I think when he was last here, he realized the mistake he made in losing Jerri Johnson."

I began to see what Jerri saw in the old villain. So did Pepper, who smiled at him and said, "I blame my upbringing for the women who left me."

Palo pointed at Pepper. "See, your friend knows what I mean." He wagged his finger. "A good woman can save us."

Pepper imitated him and wagged his finger. "Or destroy us."

"Then you didn't have the right one or a good one." Palo beamed at Pepper. I wondered what qualified Palo for his expertise.

"You make me wish I had Jerri Johnson plaguing my memory instead of my three ex-wives. Well, two, the middle one just don't count," Pepper said.

Palo leaned his elbow on the arm of his chair and pointed. "Family, loyalty is the only thing. I lost one of my huevos and got a knee blown off over Mexico. Then I said the only country I have is here." He waved his hand over his property. "You know, while Joe was trying to propose to Jerri, she was living here." He pounded his finger on the table. "So she is family. And for that . . ." He pounded the flat of his hand against the table and made Pepper jump. "I'm going to help you with Luna." He bent toward me, and I felt a bead of sweat run down my forehead. I took my eyes away from him to watch it splatter on the table. "Johnny Blackwell might talk to you. He knows somebody who may know where Reynaldo Luna is." Palo shifted his gaze back to Pepper. "Somebody should kill Reynaldo Luna." He fished in his pocket and pulled out a piece of notebook paper. In a looping cursive hand, careful but unsteady, he had written Johnny Blackwell's address and phone number.

Palo looked back at me. "We just want to find Reynaldo."

"Exactly," Palo said. I wasn't sure if Jerri had baited a hook with charm and promise and anticipation and then reeled me in, but I was sure that Palo meant to use me to do his dirty work. For an old criminal like him, it was the only way he could have gotten as old as he had. Palo banged the table again with the flat of his hand. "Okay, business is over. Time for a nap." He tried to push himself up, and Pepper did rise, but I reached over and put my hand on his chest and gently pushed him so that he lowered himself back into the chair. I was not going to let his manner push me.

"I need some more explanations."

"Johnny Blackwell says he knows."

"How do you know him?"

"I know him. What, look, don't you want this information? Jerri says to trust you, says you the man going to fix everything." Pepper looked at me too.

"I figure you and Leland Carter were partners, and then he got greedy and tried to set you up. So you had me and Joe and Jerri get even. You damn near got us all killed. And you did get Joe Parr and a couple of my friends dead. You're a detestable old man."

Palo hung his head, and Pepper looked at me like I was out of mind. "Dolph, let's go talk to Johnny Blackwell."

Palo looked at Pepper. "Look how he talks to me. Jerri says I can trust you?"

"I want some answers."

Palo smiled. "You're like Vincent. You think you have it all figured out. Like there is just one answer. And then when that answer is no good, you find another one to believe. You go through idea after idea." He pointed to his head. "Be smart." He dropped his finger away from his head. "I was a fool because I didn't listen to what I knew: 'Don't get greedy.'" He shrugged. "So Lyle Blackwell comes to me and asks me if I can put up some girls for him. I do. Then he asks if I know somebody might hire the girls. I do. Then he says do I want to help transport some girls. I should have told him to go fuck himself." Palo hit the table. "But greed. Johnny was working for somebody else." He swung his head between me and Pepper. "Not Lunas. He started working with them after he started working with me. Then somebody got greedy. This Luna, this guy who came in, this Mexican guy, the only Mexican guy, was greedy. He got all the smart ideas. He was going to get rid of me and Lyle."

"What about Leland Carter?"

"I don't know about him. But he ain't that smart." I could see that Palo was smart. He knew what he needed to and refused to know what might indict him, and he gave just enough information. I smiled at the old man and put out my hand. Still sitting, he shook my hand. "Greed causes all this."

"Thank you, Palo," I said. He looked me in the eye, and I reached into my pocket, grabbed my glasses, and stuck them on as though to repel his glare.

"You the one who killed Vincent?"

I tilted my head back, trying to find a better way to see him. "I didn't kill him. He shot himself in . . ."

Palo held up his hand to keep me from going on. "It don't matter. He got himself in that position. But you were the last one to see him alive?" His hand gave a slight tremble.

"Yes."

"And he was like, like what?"

"He was snorting cocaine and drinking tequila." Palo shut his eyes. "I think that he was all confused."

"That sounds like him."

"But he made a little bit of sense, and I was tempted to listen to him." I was also determined not to give away too much to Palo.

Palo nodded. "Then that's good. I like you. It's good that you saw him. I just wanted to know. Like you, I got to know."

I stood up. Pepper stood up. Then we both helped Palo as he tried to push himself up on his cane. He went into his large house for his nap.

∗ ∗ ∗

Pepper and I drove down Dolorosa from Palo's house. We crossed the bridge that separated San Antonio's west side from downtown, and suddenly we were back in the United States. The locals looked cleaner. The billboards were in English. Then we crossed under a freeway, still heading east. We gaped, we pointed. Country boys in the city. Then I turned north to follow a sign pointing toward the Alamo.

I drove down congested Alamo Street, looked at the tourists and the advertisements, and felt more like I was at Disneyland than at a historical site. After a couple of right turns, I found a parking lot. "What are we doing?" Pepper asked.

"We're going to look around. How often are we in San Antonio?"

"I thought we were on a mission."

"We'll look at the Alamo. It's a mission; it'll inspire you."

Pepper hesitated. "Hell, you want to be John Wayne, don't you?"

I had two degrees in history, and Texas history interested me the most, and now I was remembering Joe Parr's comments about downtown San Antonio. So I paid the three dollars for a parking space and wandered through the Alamo, Pepper limping after me. I was disappointed. So Pepper and I left the Alamo and wandered past the big new hotels and the shopping mall. "I like the way downtowns smell," Pepper said.

I was looking for some history. I wanted to feel or see some remnants of the treachery, the tragedies, the negotiations, the failures, and the defeats of Indians, Texians, and Mexicans that took place in this city. Like every good Texan, I had made pilgrimages to San Antonio before but hadn't stayed long enough. I wished that I could stay longer now.

I felt my sweat. I felt the chafing of my jeans on the inside of my crotch. I pulled my straw hat off and felt the streams of sweat run down my face. It wasn't my West Texas heat. It wasn't quite the humid heat of my Brownsville childhood. It was new, somehow almost pleasant.

I looked beside me at limping Pepper. To compensate for his knee, he had made himself strong everywhere else. He lifted more weights until he had to get larger shirt sizes. He still pounded a tennis ball against the plywood backboard, though he limped after the ball. With more therapy, more of his own initiative, the doctors said, he might eventually throw away his cane. It wasn't fair. My shoulder was fine. It was my eyes that bothered me.

San Antonio wasn't southern like Dallas or western like Fort Worth or Amarillo, certainly not modern like Houston. It wasn't really Mexican, for the Mexicans had come, been chased out, and come back. The old Spanish Creoles—the Navarros, Guerras, Seguíns, and De Zavalas, who saw themselves become Mexicans and then Texans—had kept some European civilization in the old village. The Germans and Americans made it a mercantile town.

So all sorts came here. Next to Galveston, it had the most civilization, excitement, and comfort that Texas had to offer back in the nineteenth century. It was a slight relief from that tough, flinty Texas landscape and character. So for years, the old Rangers, the ex-Confederates, the ex-soldiers, the rich Alpine ranchers retired here. At one time or another, they all had gathered on Alamo Plaza.

We walked down a short block, and I recognized the Menger Hotel. In front of me, I knew, was Alamo Plaza. So with Pepper limping after me, I crossed the narrow drive to the front of the Menger and sat on a bench. This was the area where the ex-Confederates, Rangers, ranchers, or businessmen met to sit and discuss their old times. Pepper sat on the opposite end of the bench. We sweated, watched the pigeons and the tourists snapping pictures of the front of the Alamo. I thought for a moment that I felt the old Ranger John S. Ford, progressive Mayor Maury Maverick, cattle baron Richard King, and Joe Parr gathered around me. None of us were young; we all knew our crimes, mistakes, and regrets; we all had secrets. It was as though Joe sat between Pepper and me, with the others looking on, and explained what went on here and how a proper Texan should act. And suddenly, joining us, was the specter of Vincent Fuentes. "Dolph," Pepper said, and pushed me. "Something wrong?"

"Show some reverence—Teddy Roosevelt probably sat right where you've got your ass parked."

Out in that vast geological exhibit, the Chihuahuan Desert, so indifferent to humans, I could feel the rocks. Here at this historical exhibit, because I knew some of the history—like Joe Parr did, like Pepper did—I could feel the people who had sat on this bench and watched what went on before them, from the old padres who, despite their arrogant Christianity, really wanted to help the Coahiltecans, just like Sister Quinn wanted to help the people along El Camino del Rio; to the old Rangers and Confederates, who, despite their arrogant chauvinism, really had the nerve to try to make their misguided dreams or ideals become reality, just like Joe Parr and Pepper did. I knew Pepper could feel this too.

When Ariel left me and I went into a nosedive, I stopped in

San Antonio and sat on this bench but didn't feel any of the ghosts. What I needed then was Brownsville, the ocean breezes from my youth, something remotely like a home. So I stayed with my mother. And on one warm night, we drove out to deserted Boca Chica, the beach at the mouth of the Rio Grande, the one without condos or development, the beach where the Union forces landed and then camped when John S. Rip Ford chased them out of Brownsville at the end of the Civil War.

We rolled up our pants legs and walked in the water, then sat on the beach and talked about love. I asked my mother about whatever prompted her to marry my father. I was truly the result of a mismatched pair of people. "I needed him at the time. I guess he was somehow what I wished for. But that's really no good. Because after a while, you come to realize that need isn't love."

"I'm not so sure but that they're the same."

My mother shrugged; she would never stay philosophical for too long. "When push came to shove, I guess I never really loved him. I tried, but . . . And the real shame is that I didn't know until after it was all over. You just don't know what staying with or leaving somebody, or some thing or place, is going to do to you until you do it."

I knew mostly what she meant then, more so now. We splashed in the water, and I asked if she had ever lost anyone or anything really important. "*My* father," she answered. She meant my grandfather, old Charles Beeson.

My mother would have fit with the old Texans who had gathered on this plaza. Like them, she knew her needs and wants but just didn't know where her desire would take her or what it would do to her. I felt like scooting down on the bench to give her some room to sit down.

"Pepper, are we doing right here? Let's just get the hell out of here and forget Jerri and Palo and the rest of them."

Pepper looked away from the pigeon he was watching. "Don't go confusing me with right and wrong, Dolph." He dropped his head. Like me, he was somewhere far away. "I've got a couple of degrees, just like you. So I'm not dumb. But I've never been able to figure out right and wrong."

"I don't mean right or wrong this time. I just mean that we can't know what we're gonna do to ourselves if we do this."

"How we gonna know what's gonna happen to us if we don't do it?"

"So you're gonna follow me through this with no consideration of what's right, of consequences, of yourself?"

"You asked me. I figured if you didn't need me, or if you figured I'd just be in the way, you wouldn't have asked me."

"So why am I doing this?"

"Because you're half-assed pussy whipped over Jerri Johnson. She may or may not give a shit about you. But you got to help her out."

I turned to him and grimaced. "She's a friend."

"Well, we've already established the difficulty of establishing right and wrong. So if I'm gonna risk my ass for you, I'd prefer it to be over your being pussy whipped than much of anything else. It's a terrible thing to be a male of the species, knowing that all of your important decisions are gonna be made by a pair of fuzzy little balls."

Most of the ghosts on this park bench seemed to agree with Pepper. Joe Parr was undecided. Vincent Fuentes, who had three degrees, who had courted Jerri Johnson in this very town, maybe on this very bench, thought it a swell philosophy.

* * *

Johnny Blackwell had a dilapidated fifties-style tract house deep on the South Side. Pepper and I arrived at his house in the blistering midafternoon heat. We sweated and sipped Cokes and found Johnny ass-up over the fender of a car in his front yard. Several other old junkers were in the front yard. He uncurled. His hands were covered in grease, and his arms were covered in obscene tattoos. We introduced ourselves, and he led us to a mesquite tree and some paltry shade. He squatted like the wets always did. Pepper braced himself on his cane and lowered himself. I just plopped my butt on the ground and, like Joe Parr did, pulled off my glasses. Johnny jerked as he talked and pushed his long blond hair out of his eyes. I could see the resemblance to Lyle.

"You ain't cops now, right?"

"We ain't," Pepper said.

"I ain't talking to no cops." He held a finger out as though to threaten both of us. He reminded me of Socorro, and I thought if he was like Socorro, then he might end up trying to push me around.

"Why aren't you talking to no cops?" I asked, and Pepper looked at me.

"If he's willing to talk, who cares if he don't like cops?" Pepper said to me.

I didn't comment or look at Pepper. I stared at Johnny. "Look, a friend of mine asks me to 'find' him a car. I do. Next day, I see it's burned crispy and the FB fucking I is examining it." He swiveled his head between us. "Well, the guy I know drinks a little and gets to talking and says what a bad vato it was used that car. And—" He pointed to his head with his forefinger. "I get to thinking. Maybe this bad fucker is the fucker who offed that old Ranger guy. But I ain't gonna tell nobody 'cause cops make me nervous."

Pepper, learning to be a detective, started smiling. "You stole that car. So you're scared of talking to cops."

I looked over at Pepper and wished that this weren't on-the-job training. "I didn't steal fucking nothing. I found that car in a junkyard and fixed it up." He jerked a little, and I remembered Lyle coming out of his coma kicking and thrashing at me with his boots, pissed and mean as hell, and I tensed up.

"We're not cops, so we can't do anything about it. Go on."

"Well, I done some business with Palo, and I hear Lyle narked on him, then Lyle got knocked off in the Bexar County jail. Fucking cops said it was just a fight. Bullshit, cops. See why I don't talk to cops? So anyway, then I get a call from Palo, and he tells me the guy shot the Ranger might be the guy got Lyle. Then he says, he knows a way to get that guy. And here you two guys are."

"So who's the guy?"

Johnny held up his hand. "Whoa, whoa, before I go narking on people, I want to know what's up. What are you fuckers? You look like a couple of dumpy old men. I mean what makes you bad if you ain't cops?" We didn't say anything. "Palo said some 'associates' of his were gonna come see me. You guys don't look like no 'associates' of Palo."

I looked at him square on. "One way or another, we mean to see the guy who killed your brother dead."

Johnny cocked his head. "You two?" Pepper suddenly reversed his cane and pushed the hook into Johnny's throat. Johnny started to choke, and then Pepper, bum knee and all, jumped up, got behind Johnny, wrapping the hook around his throat, and pulled until Johnny had his back pressed up against the mesquite.

Pepper smiled at me. I started: "Goddamn it, Pepper. You're not going to fuck up again, are you? He hasn't told us anything, and here you are pounding on his ass just like the last guy. What the fuck are you thinking?" Then I looked at Johnny.

Johnny, grabbing at the hooked part of the cane wrapped around his throat, choked out, "Get this crazy motherfucker away from me!" Pepper released pressure from the cane, and Johnny rubbed at his throat and asked, "Who are you fuckers?"

I hesitated, then said, "We're real, real good friends of Palo's. And we really don't like the guy who got Lyle killed."

Johnny looked at me, then Pepper, then rubbed his throat. "I ain't no badass or nothing. Just a working man." He looked at us again. "The guy's name is Israel Gonzales. The Starlight Club on Zarzamora." He smiled at me. "It's a tough club. You two old gringos better be careful."

I reached into my pocket, pulled out a wad of money, and handed Johnny a hundred-dollar bill. "Keep quiet."

I started to back away, and Pepper followed. When we got to the car, both of us were dripping sweat, me breathing heavy and Pepper smiling. "What in the shit?" I asked him.

"It worked, didn't it?"

"You've been watching too many movies."

"Dolph," Pepper said. "Catch." He tossed his cane to me. I caught it with one hand, and it nearly pulled me over.

"This thing must weigh thirty or forty pounds."

"The end has a piece of lead in it. It's better than lifting weights, and I figure I can get in one or two swipes before they get me down."

"What in the hell did you design a kung fu weapon like this for?"

"To be ready."

"For what?"

Pepper looked at me like I was stupid. "For this. Watching your back."

"But you just found out about 'this.'"

Pepper shrugged. "Sooner or later, there'd have been a 'this.'"

* * *

We drove way out Zarzamora, on the West Side—the bad part, the traditional Mexican side of town, the side of town that Palo, in part, controlled or knew about. We passed junk car lots, tortilla factories, and sweatshops until we found the Starlight Club. It sat back from the street and was sandwiched in between a deserted boarded-up building and an auto parts store. It used to be one of San Antonio's famed icehouses, but now the owner had walled up the place and stuck several air conditioners through the ply board. It was just beginning to grow dark. The hot West Texas part of the San Antonio day was changing into the humid night. To the west the evening was West Texas pink. From the southeast a gulf breeze was blowing across the hot asphalt. Suddenly there was just a taste of coolness in the air. The city streetlamps buzzed and then came on. As Pepper and I stepped out of my Crown Vic, the lights to the Starlight Club flickered on and made the small parking lot purple. Pepper sniffed, looked at the lights. "I like this," he said. "This is nice. I could do with some more of this."

My gringo friend and I stepped into the bar, and three heads turned to size us up: the bartender, a man pushing coins into a jukebox, and a man at the bar with his head slumped over a beer. A conjunto song with a fast accordion started.

Pepper and I sat on either side of the man, trying to keep his nose from bobbing in his beer. I put my head close to the bar and asked, "Are you Israel Gonzales?"

The bartender came up to me, and I saw that he held a sawed-off bat in his hand. I also saw Pepper tightly grip his cane. "Dónde está Israel Gonzales?"

"We speak English here, but we were wondering who you two are," the bartender answered for the drunk man.

"Is this Israel?" I asked. The drunk man slowly raised his head and tried to focus, but his head just wobbled.

"He ain't in too good a shape," the bartender said.

"We just want to ask a few questions," I said.

The bartender sized me up and then poked the man with the tip of the bat. The drinker shook himself. I held out my hand in front of him. "Israel, Johnny Blackwell said that he got a car for you."

"Johnny and I work together."

Pepper looked at the bartender and said, "It's private, okay? And get us a couple of beers. Your choice of the brand. Please." As the bartender turned from us and walked to the end of the bar, Israel watched as though his mother had abandoned him. I reached over and shook him.

"Who did you give the car to?"

He twisted his head in one way, then another, like a dog does when you stare at it. "You guys law?"

"We used to be," I said.

"Well, I ain't talking. I got nothing to say."

I turned to Pepper just as the bartender brought up a couple of cans of Budweiser and put one in front of each of us. "Can't you see he ain't in no shape to talk to you?"

"But we ain't got much time," Pepper said, and the bartender squeezed the end of his baseball bat.

"Get him a beer," I said. "Whatever he's drinking." Israel's eyes lit up, and the bartender left us.

"How does this guy do anything?" Pepper whispered to me.

"Israel, listen to me. We are not the law, but we want to know where Reynaldo Luna is."

"Reynaldo who?"

"The guy you gave the car to."

"I didn't give the car to nobody."

"Remember, the police found it. It was burned."

"Wasn't my car."

The bartender came back and set a beer in front of Israel. As Pepper paid him, he mumbled, "You guys shouldn't be coming to my bar and picking on my customers."

I reached into my back pocket, pulled out my billfold, and placed a fifty on the bar. I smiled at the bartender. "For your trouble, and for not giving us any trouble." The bartender hesitantly reached for the bill, grabbed it, then dropped it in the glass tip jar. He then reached back into the tip jar and positioned the fifty so that it was more prominently displayed. He walked to cash register at the end of the bar.

"Israel, Israel." I shook him. "I want to thank you for telling me that Reynaldo Luna is back in Mexico."

Israel pulled himself erect. "I didn't tell you shit."

"The FBI and the San Antonio police are really going to appreciate it. They'll probably be along in a day or two to confirm my story. They might even have to call you in to testify."

"I didn't say nothing to you old fuckers. I didn't say nothing to Johnny. What you fucking around about?"

I shook his hand. "I'll let everyone know about your help. You'll probably get some money from this." The bartender had put down his club. He leaned against the back of the bar, folded his hands, and smiled at us.

"Wait, wait. You telling me if I don't say nothing, you gonna tell everybody I did?" I smiled and nodded. "Why you want to chinga me like that, man?"

"So tell me something."

"So I tell you something, and you don't say nothing." I nodded again.

He turned away from me to think. I scooted closer to him and put my arm around him. His breath was stale and sour. "Reynaldo is crazy. And he's not going to like informers," I said.

"But I didn't tell you he was in Mexico. You guessed that."

"So now I'm guessing he's in Ojinaga." Israel froze. "Can you tell me more?"

"He'd kill me."

"He doesn't have to know if you tell me."

"He's somewhere around there, but I don't even know where that place is. It's in the country. He stayed with me, got the car, then drove another one away."

"What kind?"

"An old one. Ain't I helped you enough?"

"Who do I talk to now?"

Israel turned his back to me. "I ain't saying, ain't saying. Fuck you." The bartender started walking toward me. Israel began to mutter. "Reynaldo is crazy. I don't know how I got all mixed up with this. My boss should never got him involved. She's the crazy one."

I stiffened when I heard him, and Pepper stiffened as the bartender got near. "Look, you gave me the money, but you two guys are gonna chase my customers away."

"We were just leaving," I said.

"We were?" Pepper said, and eased his grip on his cane and his posture. I patted Israel on the back. "Thank you."

"Hey, you ain't gonna say shit?" He swiveled on his bar stool to yell at me when I turned my back to him, but I turned around to see him lean too far over, so that the bar stool fell out from underneath him. He caught himself on the bar just before he fell. I walked to him, straightened him out, and put a fifty in front of him. He smiled and ordered a beer.

I walked through the door first, and Pepper, from watching too many movies, stepped to one side and stared back at everyone. I had to wait for him.

Out in the dark, the gulf breeze blew against our faces. I stepped into the Crown Vic, and Pepper got in beside me.

"Damn, that was cool, Marlowe. I mean you played him like an old piano. Where did you learn that shit?" I looked over at Pepper. "Hey, and I think I'm getting better at this too."

I hit the wheel with my fist. I grabbed my straw hat by its brim and threw it like a Frisbee into the backseat. "Goddamn it. Goddamn it. I knew all the details. Why didn't I see it? I'm so goddamn good, huh? I never saw it. Run a Special Task Force and get fooled by old ladies."

"See what?"

"*She,* Pepper. *She.*"

"So his boss is a woman?" Pepper thought for a moment. "Oh, shit. Shit, Dorothy McFarland?"

I pounded the steering wheel some more. "Shit, Pepper. Shit. I had it all right in my hand. I had it in my fucking hand." I stopped beating my steering wheel and looked at Pepper. He let his head hang down. "I could have stopped all this. All these people didn't have to die."

"Don't start no shoulds or shouldn't ofs now, Dolph. I couldn't stand watching you."

I breathed in and looked at Pepper. "Pepper, I know shoulds and shouldn'ts can drive you crazy. But I'm thinking that just maybe, considering them is all we've got to preserve our souls."

Pepper considered. "You're starting to sound like Sister Quinn. And look at the trouble she caused herself and everybody else with all her shoulds and shouldn'ts. She's dead, Dolph."

NINETEEN

Before we left San Antonio, I had called Trujillo and told him to start looking on his side of the border for Reynaldo. Trujillo thanked me. With Trujillo looking, I needn't get involved in killing him. If he could find him, I was sure Trujillo would see Reynaldo dead. But I wanted to be close by.

On the way back to Alpine—with me driving, Pepper in the passenger's seat, Pooter sprawled across the backseat—we cruised down old Highway 90 and looked to our right and saw the hill country off at a distance. Coming the other way, east, we had looked at the hill country and felt relief, comfort at the sight of something other than thorn and rough rocks. Now when we drove west of Uvalde, the hill country just stopped. The land became cracked and rough. Just east of Del Rio it truly became West Texas. As we drove, Pooter, like a dog, kept his nose pressed against the backseat window to catch every change. And Pepper and I sighed, for we were leaving an adult Disneyland of tourist attractions, water, and greenness for all the different kinds of barrenness that are the Chihuahuan Desert.

U.S. 90 isn't like Interstate 10. It's mostly a forgotten old road that follows the Southern Pacific rail lines. It crosses the deep canyon at the juncture of the Pecos and the Rio Grande, and off to the right of the highway bridge is the old railroad bridge, the one that collapsed back in the 1880s and killed the Chinese and Mexican workers who constructed it. For a while it was the tallest land bridge in North America. Before I-10, 90 was the southern route west for cars and trains. Now, except from Hondo to San Antonio, the road is mostly deserted, and once you're past Del Rio, the country and the road become not just deserted, but desolate.

Pooter liked the desolation. He made me remember old images of patrolling when he started talking about how the land was so vastly indifferent to humans. He talked about our total miscomprehension of the world because our puny cultural memory is no match for the immensity of geologic time. Pepper must have gotten edgy too. He knew what Pooter was talking about, could keep up with him, for he too had studied some philosophy. But out of jealousy or memory or surliness, he was growling. So he interrupted the geology lesson. "*Pooter!* That can't be your real name. How did you get that name?"

Pooter pushed the tufts of wet hair just above his ears, thus pasting them to his dome head, and cleared his throat. "In high school and college I could fart on command. I could fart in different tones. I could make them sound different. I could press my big ol' lineman's cheeks against one of those steel examination tables they have in locker rooms, fart, and it would sound like a hand clap." His head shone in the sunlight coming into my Crown Vic.

"Could you still do it?" These were going to be my partners.

Pooter wanted to stop in Del Rio, but I kept driving. Then he wanted to stop at truly ugly and depressing Langtry to see Judge Roy Bean's old place. While Pooter looked at the impressive cactus garden and Pepper followed him, sipping a Coke and balancing himself on his heavy cane, I called Trujillo on my cell phone and asked if he had found anything about Reynaldo Luna, but he hadn't.

Once back in Alpine, I drove straight through town, with both Pooter and Pepper asking me what was up. "Pepper, you got my back, and Pooter, you're the muscle. I'm the investigator. I want to talk to Leland Carter."

"Don't you even want to take a bath or get a beer?" Pepper asked.

"We don't have a whole lot of time."

"Dolph, when you get the scent of something up your nose, you're hell. It leads to stress. And stress is really dangerous for a man your age."

"What do you want us to do?" Pooter asked.

"Wait in the car."

"What?" Pepper and Pooter said.

I pulled off of 67 and into Leland's gate and rounded the hill and pulled up to his trailer. Leland Carter had gotten lucky. Anyone who could have testified against him was dead. By the time we got a search warrant, he had cleaned up his metal barn and claimed it was just a barn. In the closing statement, his Chicano lawyer said that this whole case was yet another attempt by federal agencies to harass private citizens. When the trial was over, though, Weldon Phillips fired Leland. Whether he was found guilty or not, everyone in the area knew that he had done something, so they never would have tolerated him as a lawman. Then, since Leland had no job and since he owed most of the money he had made in the mail-order-bride business to lawyers, Leland's El Paso lawyer had filed a countersuit against the Border Patrol and Weldon Phillips, but that trial was still a long way off. In the meantime the El Paso lawyer's firm was negotiating for Leland in the divorce.

I stepped out of the driver's door and looked back in at the big man and the smaller one. "If something sounds funny, if you hear something, come running." I reached under the seat, got my pistol, and stuck it into my belt. As I walked to the trailer house, I adjusted my baseball cap. I was back in the clear, bright sunlight of West Texas. I was back in the high and dry pastureland of the Davis Mountains, the only real softness I had felt in a lot of years. I felt good, but I missed the promise of the humidity, the lush plants, and Jerri Johnson back in San Antonio.

I climbed the rickety metal stairs, knocked, stood back from the door, and fingered the butt of my pistol. "Who is it?" came a voice from inside.

"It's Dolph Martinez, Leland." Silence. "I know you don't

want to see me, but I want to talk to you. I promise, I don't mean you any harm."

"You said you didn't mean me no harm last time you saw me," Leland shouted.

"That was last time. You were committing a crime then."

"Go away."

"Come on, Leland. One way or the other, I'm gonna talk to you. Even if it's through this door."

"Okay, goddamn it. Door's open. But step lightly, 'cause I've got a gun."

"Ease up. I'm opening the door now."

I stepped into his trailer. It was a wreck. It smelled bad. The coffee table was piled high with pizza cartons, microwave dinner plates, and the leftovers from six-packs of beer. Leland sat in an old recliner with a bottle of tequila between his legs and a small pistol in his hand. A filled ashtray was on each arm of the recliner; another one had spilled onto the carpet. Leland had lost his police pistol and probably bought this one at some cheap gun shop. He wore a Sul Ross State University T-shirt, shorts, and sweat socks. A muted Texas Rangers baseball game was on the big-screen TV. Like Vincent Fuentes before he shot himself, Leland had crashed. He'd burn if he wasn't careful. "You're not taking this well, Leland," I said.

"Fuck you. I ought to shoot you, Dolph."

"Look, Leland, it could be worse." I stepped closer to him, reached up, grabbed my glasses, and stuck them in my pocket. There was no need to see distances in Leland's trailer.

"I got fired. This place is getting repossessed. I'm gonna have to declare bankruptcy. The finest-looking woman in this part of the world, the woman of my dreams, leaves me, and her daddy threatens to kill me. Just how in the fuck do you think it could be worse?" He stuck the bottle toward me.

I took the bottle, said, "You could be in prison," and took a gulp of the burning tequila. I looked over at the baseball game. "Who's ahead?" Leland clicked the remote, and the picture shriveled up. "My satellite disk won't move either. I can only get four stations. And besides, you didn't come over here to watch no baseball." Leland reached out and laid his pistol on the coffee table.

I handed the bottle back to him. He took it and sucked a mouthful out of the bottle. He grimaced as he swallowed. No, he wouldn't end up like Fuentes. He didn't have Fuentes's insight, an ironic sensibility that would nag him that he could have done better. First he'd swell up from eating bad food and drinking too much, then he'd start fights, and eventually Leland would get run out of town. He'd end up like my father, dead too early, probably from drinking too much. Thank God Pepper handled it all better. Thank God for me he did. I wondered what I'd do if faced with either of their plights. There was my father, who had given me some of his genes and meanness, and then there was Fuentes, who I was supposed to be like, and look how they handled their woes. I looked around and spotted a kitchen chair. I drug it up in front of Leland's recliner. "I'm looking for Reynaldo Luna."

"So am I," Leland said, and he looked up at me with swollen red eyes. "'Cause if I don't find him and kill him, he'll kill me."

"How do you know?"

"Because he called me and told me so."

"Do you have caller ID?" I started to stand.

"The idiot called me from Eduardo Suárez's place down outside Presidio. I could hear Eduardo laughing in the background. He said he was gonna kill me. He thinks I sided with you. I didn't do nothing. It was all decided without me. I was cut out. He was gunning for you, and all I could do was sit up here and wait. I was innocent." He was giving me his speech from his trial. With witnesses dead, Reynaldo became the villain and Leland the poor dupe.

"Hold on," I said. Leland wasn't innocent, but I had suspected him of being guiltier. "Do you think he means it?"

"Shit. He's a mean bastard. There were times I thought he'd just start shooting. He even scared Esteban, that poor simple brother of his. Poor dumb son of a bitch fell into an empty swimming pool. But Reynaldo . . ." Leland caught himself. He was telling me things that he shouldn't know.

"It's all right, Leland. You beat me in the trial. It doesn't matter what you say now. I'm not in the Border Patrol anymore."

"Yeah, but you know a lot of people."

"As far as I'm concerned, you've paid twice over for your crime. How do I find Reynaldo?"

Leland stood up and ran his hand through his hair. He'd aged. Tufts of his hair had just fallen out, leaving splotches of ugly skin all over his head. "You got to get him, then. And I mean kill him. You arrest him, he'll do time, get out, and kill you and me. You got to kill him. He's expecting you to."

"How do you know that?"

"He told me. He said he'd kill everybody." Leland set the bottle down and plopped into his chair. "He killed that Ranger, didn't he?"

"That's why I'm looking for him."

"I wish I could help you."

Leland leaned toward the coffee table and started rummaging through the garbage on it. I spotted the pack of cigarettes and grabbed them. I leaned closer to Leland and shook the pack of cigarettes so that a butt popped out of the end of the pack. "You mean you won't help me, or you don't know where he is?" Leland took the cigarette and felt around on himself for matches or a lighter. I spotted a book of matches amidst the junk on the coffee table, stuck my hand into the garbage once again, got the matches, and lit one for Leland. He held his face close to the match, puffed on the cigarette, and pulled it out of his mouth. He stared at me.

"He's in Mexico."

"I know that much."

"Close by, I'd say."

"Keep going."

"That's all I know."

I leaned away from him. "Could Dorothy McFarland tell me?" Leland dropped his eyes. I spoke to him as though he were a little boy. "Look at me, Leland."

He raised his eyes, then raised the cigarette to his lips. "I can't tell you nothing." He blew out some smoke.

"Well, then just shake your head yes or no." Leland sucked on the cigarette, looked at me, then nodded.

"Either Lyle Blackwell or Dorothy McFarland started this

little business, not you, right?" Leland kept his head still. In his trial he hadn't said a thing about Dorothy McFarland. "Come on, Leland." He nodded. "Dorothy, did?" Another nod. "So Lyle operated out of San Antonio. That's where they took the girls. That's why they contacted Palo Fuentes. He could help them. But she needed someone in Mexico to actually get them up here. That's where the Lunas came in. Am I close?" He nodded and blew smoke around his head. "And you were insurance? You provided the first stop across the border and a quick ride down 90." And I remembered our drive. "A deserted, older road to San Antonio. So you built that barn." Leland kept nodding, and I didn't know whether he was answering me or affirming his own knowledge of how he had fucked up. As Socorro had said, Leland was too dumb to pull off something like this. "But like Palo says, 'You get greedy, you fuck things up.'" I started nodding my own head. "So who decided that it would be real cute to get rid of Lyle and Palo?" He didn't nod. He blew smoke at me.

"That's what I'm saying. Reynaldo is crazy. He's the one."

But I felt my own mind working faster, and my indignation and past stupidity made me mad. "So you knew about my task force. You had worked with me. You recruited Socorro because you knew he was on the take. You got Trujillo's name and number from Weldon. You called Trujillo. He drugged Lyle. I picked him up. DPS boys picked him up on some old charge. And he's dead in Bexar County jail after he plea-bargains Palo's name." He stared straight ahead, not nodding, but sucking in on his cigarette.

"What about Dorothy McFarland?" He started shaking his head. "Who gave the orders?" He kept his head still and gazed at his sweat socks. One had a hole in it, and I could see his big toe. "Maybe you don't know. Maybe you got your orders from her. And you just did what you were told. Maybe you didn't recruit Socorro or Trujillo, not really. You just contacted them." I reached under his chin and pulled his head up. He looked like he was going to cry. "You know how I first got your name? You know who confirmed that you had called Trujillo? You know who narked on you?"

He sobbed. "She wouldn't do that."

"She was going to give you up when it looked like she might have to take the rap, when Jerri Johnson went down to the courthouse and it looked like we might connect her. Hell, she might be setting you up for Reynaldo."

"No, no, no." He took a drink from his tequila.

"Why not?"

"Because she's my mother."

"What?"

He stood up. "I was adopted. They were old, and my momma past childbearing. My daddy forbid me to look up my birth mother. My momma told me the reason he didn't want me looking her up was because he really fathered me by her. So when my daddy and then my momma died, I went down the courthouse and started looking through birth records. I met Dorothy. She helped me. She's my mother."

I stood up. "You saw that in the records?"

"She told me. Dorothy phoned me and told me she was my real mother. Confessed to the affair with my daddy. It was a scandal—she was just sixteen or something."

I sat down and put my head in my hands. I thought I'd cry. "Oh, shit, Leland. Oh, shit, shit, shit. You goof. You fuckup."

"Hey, you can get off my property if you're gonna cuss me."

"Let me guess. She got her facts from the county records, right? Real convenient."

"Yeah, it's where she works."

"Oh, Leland."

I stood up and patted Leland's shoulder. "Keep your doors locked. And if anything faintly suspicious happens, call me. Hell, for the next couple of days, call me and tell me where you're at, okay? I don't want anybody else who gives me information or helps me getting killed."

I reached into my pocket, pulled out my wallet, and gave Leland a hundred-dollar bill. I looked at his red, confused, sagging face. "She's a con, Leland. She researched you. She's not your mother."

Clinging to his faith, Leland said, "You don't know that she isn't. You don't know that."

Then I walked outside. Pooter and Pepper, my partners, were on either side of the door. Little glints of light caught on Pepper's diamond stud earring and on Pooter's bald head. Pepper held his .30–30 Winchester and his cane hooked around his arm, and Pooter held Pepper's shotgun. Thank God, I hadn't talked Pepper out of bringing his guns on the trip.

"Good goddamn," Pooter said, hefting the shotgun. "I haven't shot a gun since I was sixteen. I don't know if I could hit anything. Hell, I don't know if I could load it." But suddenly my partners looked a whole lot more reliable.

TWENTY

"You mean we ain't going home yet?" Pepper said from the backseat.

"No. We happen to be in a hurry."

"We've been playing cops and robbers long enough. Rockford went home once in a while to say hello to his daddy. You got a momma at home."

"Weren't you the one always complaining that all us public officials worried about was sleep?"

"Well, you ain't a public official no more. And Pooter and I ain't had much experience at this. Hell, what's it been, Pooter? How long we been Marlowe's assistants?"

"Seven-hour drive, a stop at Deputy Carter's house—I'd say eight and a half hours."

I turned to Pooter, and in the light from my dome lights, I saw the big man scratch his bald dome head. "You up for one more stop, Pooter?"

"It's kind of fun."

"Shit, shit, shit," Pepper said.

"By the way, you two guys did real good the last time. So I want you to do the same thing."

"Who we going to see now?"

"Dorothy McFarland."

"Holy shit, so you want us to shoot a little ol' lady. You afraid she might get the jump on you, Dolph? Why don't Pooter and me just rough her up for you? But why don't we wait until morning?"

"Don't make fun. She's gotten the jump on me once already. And I think she almost shot me."

Dorothy lived on one side of a duplex across the tracks in what used to be the Mexican side of town. We drove down her narrow street and disturbed a mangy black dog that chased us and barked. When I got out of the car, the dog braced itself, leaned back, and barked at me. Several lights came on, and a woman stepped out on her porch. I shooed the dog the best I could, but it left me alone to chase Pepper and Pooter as they got out of the car, Pooter trying to cradle the shotgun inconspicuously and Pepper fumbling his cane and his rifle. I let my fingers tap the butt of my pistol, pulled my baseball cap a little farther down on my head, pulled my glasses off and stuck them in my pocket, and knocked. Dorothy appeared in the lit doorway. She was wiping the sweat away from her face with a towel. "Why, Dolph." She smiled sweetly at me and opened the door. I stepped in. She looked at the pistol butt sticking above my belt.

She was dressed in workout tights, and she had a mat on the floor. In those tights, she was shapely; she had curves in the right places. Her dark hair, streaked with gray, was pulled behind. She had no makeup on, and I saw that her face, though lined, was attractive without the piled-on makeup. She looked ten or fifteen years younger without her courthouse disguise.

"I was working out. Excuse me. Can I help you?"

I looked around for a place to sit, spotted the sofa, and walked to it. It was a sleek, contemporary design, plaid colored, not what you'd expect from an elderly lady, no flowers. I sat down. Dorothy sat on the other side of me. I heard the dog bark, this time from the side of the house. "Dorothy, where is Reynaldo Luna?"

"Who is that?" She went into her old lady act and held her hand up to her throat. I wondered how she balanced the two different people she pretended to be; I wondered if Leland did the math, whether he saw the younger or the older Dorothy as his mother, and I wondered how I had been so stupid as to not see her act. Three friends were dead.

"Dorothy, I've talked to Johnny Blackwell, Israel Gonzales, and just now to Leland Carter. I know about you."

"Why, what did those men say?" I wanted to slap her.

"Reynaldo killed Joe Parr, and I'm thinking maybe you ordered him to. So now the FBI is looking for him. But I'm a step ahead of the FBI. I could give them your name, if Dorothy McFarland is your real name. And then they'd investigate, and I imagine they'll connect a past to you that you've tried to hide."

Dorothy stood up, spread her legs for balance—as if she were getting ready for a fight—and wiped at the sweat on her face with her towel. "I don't think that I should answer you."

"I'm going to find him." She started backing toward a bureau. "Stay where you are, Dorothy," I said calmly, and put my hand on the butt of my pistol. She held her chin up like she was proud, like she was taunting me. "How did you meet Luna? What is he to you? How old are you?"

She held her head higher, took two steps with her long graceful legs, and knelt in front of me. She leaned forward so that she was over my lap. She lifted her head up and purred, "I'm not put together badly for an old lady . . . am I?" She rubbed at my thigh with her forefinger. Then her hand moved toward the butt of my gun. I wiggled out from underneath her as if she were a rattler. I stood up. "I've got some money in that drawer. Open it and look. Take what you want."

"Just tell me where Reynaldo is."

"Reynaldo doesn't think I'm bad looking for a lady my age."

"We're not talking about your looks. Where's Reynaldo?"

"Ten years ago, he was my lover, for a while. But then, I've had lots of lovers." She curled up from the floor. She wasn't at all bad looking for a lady "her age." In this act, in this role, she wasn't much older than me. "Now we have a different relationship. So why do you think I would give him up?"

"Suit yourself, Dorothy."

I took two steps past her, but she grabbed my arm. "Okay,

then. Okay. But you're going to have to kill him. That's the deal. And you can never, never tell anyone what you know."

"Where is he?"

"I don't know."

"Come on. Stop acting."

"I really don't know. He called me and told me what he had done."

I grabbed her arm and shook her. Her arm became taut with muscle. She twisted it and broke my grip. "I told you I don't know. My caller ID shows he's at Eduardo Suárez's bar. But he doesn't stay there."

"Could you call him?"

"I could call Eduardo."

I stepped away from her because I was afraid she might lunge for my gun. "I might need you to do that."

"He stays in Mexico at this little place across the river, one of those ejido places, where a bunch of people just gather and try to make a living, but he moves around. He's got one, maybe two guys with him. But he doesn't trust them." I stared at her. She smiled and purred, "See, you can trust me."

"Okay, okay, I'll be back if I need you."

"What would you '*need*' me for?" she purred, and curled her shoulders.

"Why are you picking on Leland? Why did you drag him into this?"

"Because I could. I'm going to have a lot of money. I need a partner. Don't tell me that money doesn't interest you."

"Lyle Blackwell, Leland Carter, Palo Fuentes, Esteban Luna, Reynaldo Luna. Your partners aren't too lucky."

"You want to try your luck?"

"Did you order Reynaldo to kill Joe Parr? Sister Quinn? Socorro?"

She smiled at me. "There's no controlling him when he's in one of his moods." She dropped her eyes like a young girl. I thought that she might flutter her eyes.

"You broke into my house, too. Didn't you? It was you. You went in there ready to kill me, and you could have killed my mother. Or maybe you would have killed her had Charlie not shot at you."

"Dolph, where do you get these accusations, these fantasies of yours?"

Then more memories clicked on in my mind. "And the morning after, when I met you by the horses, you had a gun in your purse. And you almost shot me."

"Same as then, Dolph. You're desperate, and you're off track."

"I'll be in touch." I turned my back to her. As I walked toward the front door, I felt the anticipation of wasp stings in my belly, of the final teeth-clenching shot, of the hot sear of a breaking collarbone. I turned to face her. Dorothy McFarland had a gun on me and was about to squeeze the trigger. "No, Dorothy, think," I yelled.

"I'm gonna kill you, Dolph."

"Think, think, Dorothy. You can't afford it." I saw the hammer of the gun start to go back. A stupid college kid nearly killed me, an idiot who fell into an empty swimming pool shot me, and now a little ol' lady who was really some sort of vixen was going to kill me.

"Think, Dorothy," I heard from behind me. It was Pepper's voice. "'Cause if you kill him, I'm going to have to kill you." The door slowly opened. She had forgotten to lock it, and there, after listening at the door, just as they had done at Leland's, were Pepper and Pooter, stepping through the door. Pepper limped in, his Winchester leveled, his cane hooked around the crook that his right arm made. Pooter, now with his UT cap on to keep light from finding his bald head, stepped to one side of him and leveled the shotgun at Dorothy. "No way you can survive two blasts."

"Dorothy, neither one of us can afford any questioning. I'm no longer with the law. And if they question you, well, my partners here"—and I emphasized *partners*—"know the whole story." She slowly lowered her gun. The sweat on her face glistened. She shifted her weight to one side of her shapely body and smiled at all of us. "Of all the people in the world, of everybody involved in this, we're going to have to trust one another."

"Why, Dolph, dear, I trust you."

"But a lot of people you trusted are dead or broken, so I'm telling what I know to my partners, and Trujillo down in Ojinaga, and Jerri Johnson in San Antonio. So if I end up dead, one of them is going to get even."

"How could you say such a thing?"

"Good evening," I said, and tipped my baseball cap to her.

We all backed out of her place, Pepper limping and balancing his gun and cane, and the dog circled the three of us and barked. We loaded back up in my Crown Vic. We sat in the darkness for a while, the dog barking, and watched as she turned off all of her lights. We all realized that it wasn't Reynaldo we should be trying to kill. When I cranked the engine, Pepper said, "Can we go the fuck home so some choirboy or junior high girl don't shoot us, or we got to shoot him or her? I'm tired, I'm edgy, my hand was shaking in there, and Pooter was so scared, he was farting again. Thought he would give us away. So let's not do any more raping or pillaging tonight."

Pooter started laughing. "We sure kicked her ass, didn't we?"

* * *

When we got home, even Charlie hugged us. After my mother had kissed all of us, she welcomed Pooter and fussed at me for not telling her that I was bringing Pooter back. Then she told Pepper that we had a couple checked in, that she had made dinner on her own, that it was wonderful, and that she had some wrapped in the refrigerator. When my mother stopped talking, I went into the kitchen and called Trujillo.

I told him what I knew. He told me what he knew. Reynaldo was in an ejido across from Candelaria. But he drove some eight miles every night to go to a small grocery and bar to make telephone calls and to drink beer and brag. It was the place Dorothy McFarland had told me about. We would take him there, Trujillo insisted. We would kill him in Mexico, he insisted. He would die in Mexican fashion, and Mexican officials would discover his body, and he would be written off as another dead criminal. Trujillo would see to it. This time, I agreed with Trujillo. No Vincent Fuentes begging me to take him across the river to

America's legal system. No dark nightmares of a man's brains spraying out the side of his head.

Then I called Jerri and woke her up and told her the whole story. I told her to get here as soon as possible. I listened to her breathing on the other end of the line. "Do we want to do this, Jerri?"

"Yes, we do, Dolph," she said.

"What about me?"

"'You' is a question for much, much later. One thing at a time."

"I wish, I wish. Well, I just wish."

"Of course, you do," she said. "So do I. And I can't stop the wishing and the regretting. But you've got to make it stop. Look what it did to Vincent."

"Okay, I'll stop."

"I'll see you tomorrow."

When I hung up from Jerri, I walked out to the front porch and joined Pooter and Pepper. We hadn't eaten all day. "Y'all hungry?" We didn't eat my mother's leftovers. Instead, I drove to the McDonald's and bought ten small burgers and five fries.

My partners and I sat on the front porch with a six-pack of beer, and, paying no mind to calories or upset stomachs or the cardboard taste of the burgers, we gobbled them like they were Palo's chicken enchiladas. We sucked our fingers, licked the salt from the fries, fed our hunger and our renewed gratefulness for just being alive.

For all his bitching, Pepper wasn't tired. He talked over and around all the past three days. He told us the story that he knew and then went back over it all again. And he drank his two beers from the six-pack, then grabbed his cane and went back inside to bring out two more six-packs and a bottle of tequila. The old Pepper, the one who dreamed up a grand resort in the most deserted part of Texas, the one who would sit for hours with Ignacio and cuss the world and ex-wives and praise his friends, the one who could drink all night, had, at least for this night, made another appearance. His earring even caught a little light from the police station across the street and reflected bits of it, just like the old days. Maybe, over time, that Pepper would come back more and more and steal his soul back from the careful, prepared, disciplined, worried, two-beer-limit Pepper. I missed the old Pepper, and I was the one who destroyed him.

Pepper inspired Pooter, and he told us about his buddy, Bailey Waller, the third wishbone quarterback for the University of Texas. He told us how Bailey fell in love with Joan Phelan and how Bailey drove off a bridge on I-10 up around Sonora and how he, Pooter, didn't believe it was a suicide and how he would always take care of Joan because of his buddy, Bailey, and because he too loved her and fucked her for a while. "What about Socorro?" Pepper asked. "What did she see in that sorry bastard?"

"Something different. Somebody else to try. She was desperate to find somebody or something she could trust. All she has, really, is me. Socorro would have never lasted." For just a moment I felt sorry for Socorro, and then I felt sorry, and guilty too, for his death.

"But you're not getting none," Pepper said, and I looked at him to scold him for being so crude. Pepper turned to me. "What the hell, Dolph. Pooter admitted it himself."

"I'm just a big, dumb lineman. I could never be good enough for her. Just like Socorro. I don't hold it against anybody. It's the way society, culture, our looks, our potential works. I'm used to it." He rubbed his hand over his bald head to confirm his ugliness.

"I started out ugly, so I realized I had to charm them. Dolph, there, was a 'pretty boy' until a few years ago, but his age is catching him now." So Pepper poured us all a shot, and he said, "Here's to ugliness." We drank our tequila, and then Pepper toasted Pooter again for acts becoming a gentleman. Pooter, too, I think, even though I hadn't known him long, had stopped, for this night, being a Ph.D. in philosophy and became again that West Texas boy just delighted in feeling. "Ask Dolph about women," Pepper said. "There's a motherfucker can pick 'em. Had some of the best-looking pussy I ever seen, but the poor motherfucker, whether his fault or not, just watches them leave. But he does it with style. I don't watch 'em leave with as much style, so I've mostly given them up. So here's to Dolph." He turned his head, and light glinted from his diamond stud earring and from Pooter's head.

Across the way was the police station, and as we drank, we debated throwing some beer cans at Alpine's finest. And Pooter dropped his pants and mooned them, and then, when Pepper dared him, he grabbed the seat of his chair with both hands, one on either side of him, and let a fart that should have brought the Alpine police department running and looking for an explosion.

Later, my mother came out twice and shushed us, but we kept drinking. Then, in the cool of dryness and altitude, in the fullness of stars, I got back to business. "Pooter, you can't tell Dede about any of this."

"You know, that is one fine woman," Pepper said. "Pooter, you're a lucky man."

"You know what I'm asking. She's a Border Patrol agent. To know any of this, to know what we want to do, will compromise her. She shouldn't know."

Pooter looked at me over the top of his beer. "We haven't talked too much lately."

"You fool," Pepper said. "With both you guys always turning her down, why don't she come to her daddy?" And Pepper poked his thumb into his chest. We both looked at Pepper. "Okay, sorry, never mind. I forgot we're being sensitive now."

Pooter looked over at me. "I don't know that I will speak to her again." I felt indignant for a moment, for Dede's sake. I wanted to know why the hell not, why the hell he would mistreat her so, but he answered himself. "We had a thing, but we both knew it was temporary, a relief for a great need."

"Oh, shit," Pepper said. "Do I know about great need! Here's to great need." He took a long gulp of tequila and then chased it with a tug at his beer. "Here's to you, Pooter."

Pooter turned to me. "And Dede, she's too busy watching out for you and hoping for you."

I almost choked on my beer but caught myself. "Dede?"

"You ignorant, obstinate, foolish, hardheaded, soft-dicked son of a bitch," Pepper said. "What have I been telling you for years?"

We drank until we saw pink in the dark sky, and then we started drifting inside to find a bedroom. My mother was roaming around, and I followed her into the kitchen. She was making the morning coffee. "My God, Dolph. Have you been up all night?"

"I guess I have."

"Oh, Dolph, I worry about you. Can't you just give up this line of work that you're in?"

"Mom, Mom . . . was I a good son? Have I become a good man?"

She rustled around for coffee. "Oh, Dolph, you have always been my 'pretty boy.' You always will be."

I smiled and left her, and went to my bedroom wondering just how disappointed she had become in me since the time I had stopped being her "pretty boy."

TWENTY-ONE

We slept until noon. And then Jerri pulled up in her Suburban about one, and I called Trujillo and told him that we were ready. The next morning we took a change of clothes and loaded into Jerri's Suburban. We didn't want to risk being stopped by Mexican police for having guns, and besides, Trujillo would be responsible for helping us out and arming us on the Mexican side, so I tried to argue against taking any guns, but everyone was nervous about driving anywhere without some firepower. So we took an odd arsenal: my .357, Pepper with his Winchester .30–30 and Pooter with Pepper's shotgun, and Jerri with her ankle pistol. We'd have to leave them somewhere on the American side because I didn't want to let customs know that I was coming across or that I had so many guns.

Jerri was tired of driving, so I drove. With more power, more people to back me up, I drove by the courthouse, went to the county records, and asked for Dorothy McFarland. She hadn't come in. I then drove to her house. We all stepped out. The black dog circled us and barked. A neighbor stepped out. There was no car in the driveway. I knocked, but there was no answer. Pooter peered into a window. The place was a wreck. The neighbor, a Mexican lady, walked over to us. "She loaded up her car with all kinds of things this morning. And drove off. I ain't seen her since."

Pooter chuckled. "One of you Dolph?" the neighbor asked. When I told her who I was, she handed me an envelope. I opened it. In big, bold letters, written in red lipstick, was, *Fuck you, Dolph.* "There's our next case," Pepper said.

"No, no. It won't be anybody's case. She got away with it."

"Let's finish this case," Jerri said.

So I got in behind the steering wheel. Jerri got in beside me. And Pooter and Pepper got in the backseat. "Who do you suppose she really was?" Pooter asked as I drove away.

We dropped down below the south rim and saw the heat rise in swells from the asphalt, and even though we were in an air-conditioned car, we almost felt the heat push against it. We didn't talk. We stared at the ocotillos reaching for the sky.

As we passed the Border Patrol station, I was tempted to pull over and go in to see Dede and beg her to rescue me, like she had done before, from what I was doing. But instead I turned down 170, and Pepper asked where the hell we were going. "A practice run," I said. "You got your cane ready?" I was serious. I wanted some training for my team. And I knew how I was. I needed some practice. I needed to make myself crazy so I'd have the proper frame of mind for killing Reynaldo. I needed Sister Quinn to whip me. I needed to resurrect Vincent Fuentes's laugh.

At the edge of town and then past it, I pulled up to Eduardo Suárez's convenience store. "Okay, we're all going to walk up to the front porch. Then Jerri, you just keep a lookout and let me know if anyone is coming. Pooter, Pepper, and I will go in. Pepper, you just drop off to one side, then hand me that steel-tipped cane of yours. Pooter, when I give you a nod, grab Eduardo." I looked from one to the other. "Jerri, you still have that dainty gun taped to your leg?"

She smiled at me, and I looked into her deep blue contacts and she said, "Of course."

"If you hear anything, come running and open fire." As I looked at her, I flashed back to the shoot-out at Cleburne Hot Springs. If in no other way, I had taken Joe Parr's place as the commander of this army.

We stepped out of the Suburban in unison and immediately

felt the sun cook us. This sun that I ran away from sapped all the moisture from you. You would sweat, but soon you would have white streaks of your own salt striped across your clothes. I had forgotten about the immensity of heat. I had grown soft and fat in Alpine, and here I was back in the desert, about to commit one of several crimes.

Jerri positioned herself under the awning, in glorious shade, and Pooter, then Pepper, then I walked into the store. Pepper had his Winchester in his cocked arm. He handed me his cane and slid along the wall. Pooter and I walked up to the counter. The air-conditioning startled me. Eduardo smiled at me. "You back," he said. "How you doing, huh?" I saw his hand lying flat against the counter. I nodded at Pooter, and he, quick as a snake, grabbed the hand, then with his other hand, he pulled Eduardo over the counter. Eduardo twisted out from under Pooter, and using Pepper's cane like a spear, I jabbed him in the belly. Air swooshed out his lungs just as Pooter grabbed him and threw him against the wall. He slid down the wall, looking at me, while Pooter stood beside him with both hands backward on his wrists but doubled into fists. Pepper shouldered the rifle but pointed it away from us. Jerri looked in the door, then turned back around to check my back.

There was nothing in the confined space of Eduardo's store that I couldn't see without my glasses. So I spread my middle finger and thumb across them, lifted them off, and stuck one arm over the top button of my shirt. Then I swung the cane like it was a base-ball bat and knocked over a rack of junk food. I stepped on Fritos, Ding Dongs, and Twinkies, crushed them into the ground with my hiking boots. Eduardo jumped up, but Pooter caught him in a bear hug and squeezed until Eduardo turned blue and then coughed. Then I pointed the cane at Eduardo, dug into my pocket with my other hand, and pulled out the xeroxed marriage certificate. "You can get some more Twinkies. Notice I didn't break any beer. But I will next time. Hot beer on a desert summer day gets real messy. Then I'll bust your refrigeration, even worse for the desert. And you can't afford to have Raul Flores come out here. Not that he'd do anything anyway. Not that you can do anything because then you'd have to tell him why I'm visiting you. The only thing you can do is stop this shit." I shook the certificate at him, then wadded it up and threw it at him.

"Cabrón," he yelled at me. Pooter squeezed him harder, and he started to cough.

"You got it?"

Eduardo just stared at me. "Pooter, let him go." Pooter let him go, and he stepped toward me. I raised the cane. "You've seen what he can do. And I've got two people with guns." Pepper had his rifle shouldered and pointed at Eduardo. "So you better think real hard about getting even." Eduardo looked over his shoulder at Pooter, who smiled at him.

I started backing out the door with the cane raised. Pooter eased out the door, then I did. Pepper stepped out last, and I handed Pepper's cane back. As we recrossed the hot parking lot, checking our backs against an armed Eduardo, Pepper said, "Fucking Rambo."

Back in the car, I watched as Eduardo came to the door and stared at me with this shocked look on his face. I tipped the bill of my baseball cap. Pepper held on to his gun.

With all of them asking me what I was doing, I drove into Redford, then past it, then down the Alamendarizes' fields, the picked, stacked onions making the place smell like a hamburger, the cantaloupes adding rich ripeness to the air.

I pulled up in front of Sister Quinn's templo. Even in this remote part of the world, trash had found its way to walls and fences. And vagrants, wets, or teenagers had pried a board loose to sneak inside. Gilbert Mendoza wasn't keeping the place up very well.

I made my way to the door with flowers, tokens, silver-blue vials—like the one Sister Quinn gave me, which I had given to Jerri—and pictures of her and of sick loved ones pinned to the front door or stacked beneath it. I still had my keys to her padlocked doors, so I opened the templo door. I hesitantly stepped in, then the others did. Dust floated in the air and in the sunlight that crept through the widening holes in the roof and walls. Some of the wooden benches that she had used for pews had broken legs. On one wall was some graffiti: *Juan loves Priscilla* and *Fuck Terlingua*. A few beer bottles were scattered across the floor. I saw some condoms. Sister Quinn's shack had become a shrine and teenage hangout. I would have a talk with Gilbert Mendoza about the money I was sending him. We stashed our guns under the stares of the Virgin and Pedrito Jaramillo and hoped that no graffiti-writing teenagers would steal them. I let the others walk out first, and then I stepped out into the bright sun from the darkness of Sister Quinn's templo and locked it back up.

On the way back through Presidio, I again wanted to stop at the Border Patrol station and perhaps say good-bye to Dede, but we had an appointment with Trujillo.

* * *

Wearing a white linen suit that was too large for him, Trujillo met us on the other side of the bridge. He was embarrassed by the stubs on his right hand, so he shook our hands by offering us his left hand and limply touching our hands instead of shaking them. We crowded into his car and, always a gentleman, he took us out for lunch and a few beers. Because of his stubs, he was trying to teach himself to smoke using his left hand, so he barely kept his cigarette holder steady. Since we had time to kill before we drove out to kill Reynaldo, he took us on a tour of the army garrison. He let us go shopping. Pepper bought liquor to take back.

Then, as the sun was setting but the desert world still baking, not yet cooled, he pulled up alongside Jerri's Suburban. We climbed into it; Trujillo opened the trunk of his car and pulled out a pistol for each of us, a shotgun, and an automatic rifle. He also brought along several boxes of ammunition and a large bag bulging at the bottom.

We took Jerri's Suburban because we could all fit into it and because we were going over some rough roads. I drove again, squinting into the orange, pink, and purple sunset. We took a paved road as far as we could, then went down a rutted dirt road. After a few miles Trujillo asked me to pull over. When I did, he reached into a bag and pulled out a roll of duct tape, and Pooter got out to help him cover the license plates with the duct tape. As we drove on, the desert became dark and cooled just a bit. I was afraid that I was going to run off the road because I could barely distinguish it from the desert. Ocotillo and lechuguilla scratched the sides of car, and I hoped nothing would puncture a tire. Trujillo asked me to cut the lights. I cut them and drove slowly. When I rounded a curve, we saw a little shack that looked like Eduardo's store right next to the road. An old car was parked in front of it, a big early eighties Buick. "I think that's the car he'll be in," Trujillo said.

We all stared at the shack. Someone probably decided to open a place to sell beer, chips, tortillas, and maybe a whore or two to those farmers and pelados out here in the sticks so that they wouldn't have to drive or walk or ride all the way into Ojinaga. Trujillo reached into the jacket of his linen suit and brought out a small leather case. He snapped it open. Inside was a syringe and a small bottle. He held the bottle up, poked the needle of the syringe into it, and filled the syringe. "Okay, who's the boss?"

I looked in the backseat, where Jerri sat in between Pooter and Pepper. "Got your back," Pepper said, and smiled. Pooter just stared. Jerri caressed me with her eyes and her smile.

"We can turn back now. What we're going to do is going to haunt us for the rest of our lives," I said to them.

Trujillo said something like, "Phooey," as he gently put the syringe in his pocket. "American policemen have such moral luxury. You didn't worry about the people you brought to me or the people you picked up from me—like Lyle Blackwell."

I looked back at Jerri. "Jerri, please."

But Trujillo didn't let her answer. He started, and she shifted her attention from me to him. "Dolph, and especially you, dear Ms. Johnson, as you both well know, except for your information that he was back in Ojinaga, I could have found him myself. So I could do this myself. But he has hurt others than me. So you are here because of my graciousness. Please accept it."

Jerri looked back at me, and her face twisted as if she were in pain. "He killed Joe, your friend Sister Quinn, and Socorro." And as if to herself as well as me, she said, "Get over it, Dolph."

"Okay, okay." I hung my head. "He'll recognize all of us, right?" I had only heard his voice.

"I don't think he's ever seen me," Pepper said.

"Well, then you can't really recognize him. Probably none of us can really recognize him," I said.

"Hell, he's Esteban's twin, ain't he?" Pepper said. "How hard is it to recognize that son of a bitch?"

"I'll know him," Trujillo said.

"He killed Joe. I'll know him," Jerri said.

"Okay, he may have a guy with him." I felt myself becoming a Ranger. It didn't feel good. This was not what I was good at. I tracked the signs; I found people. I didn't plan their abduction and murder.

"Don't treat me like a girl, Dolph," Jerri said.

"Jerri, you and Pooter and me will sneak up to the car and see if anyone is in it. Henri, you and Pepper walk up to the place and check around beside it. Pepper, you're probably the best shot with a rifle, so you take the rifle, plop your ass down near the front door, and keep the area clear. . . . The rest of us go in. Trujillo points him out. Pooter circles him. Jerri walks up to him. She says, 'Hi.' He recognizes her. Pooter grabs him. Trujillo squirts him with the juice. I'll try to cover everybody."

"Showdown," Pepper said.

"You think that it'll all just work out that way?" Pooter asked.

"Anybody got a better plan?"

"You left out one thing," Trujillo said, and dug into his bag. He passed out rubber surgeon gloves to everybody. "It may be hard to pull a trigger, but wear these. Don't touch anything unless you have to."

Trujillo stepped out of the car. So Pooter and Jerri and I got out and crouched in the thorns. This was something I was used to. We got close to the car and peered into the closed windows. No one was in it. I waved my hand, and Trujillo and Pepper walked to the building. Trujillo kept his right hand in his jacket pocket, and Pepper limped on his cane and tried to juggle the semi-automatic. They checked on either side of the building; then each waved back to me. Pooter, Jerri, and I walked to the front porch of the building.

Once again I didn't need to see distance, so I pulled my glasses off and hooked them over the top button of my shirt. After I sucked in some air, I walked in and started for the bar. Pooter slid along the back wall, past a cigarette machine. Jerri and Trujillo were behind me. I bellied up to the bar. A dark man was at the other end, and a woman had her arms wrapped around the back of his head. She pecked little kisses at him. One man was behind the bar—a kid, really. Another man sat at a table by himself and sipped a beer. Trujillo nodded at him. Jerri started walking to him just as he looked up at her. But instead of looking at her, he stared at her rubber gloves. What was a short güera wearing surgical gloves doing in this bar? Then he looked at me.

He was indeed Esteban's twin. "Cabrón," he yelled, and reached under the table. Before he could draw the gun, Pooter had him in a bear hug, and he was trying to twist his wrist to shoot somebody. He squirmed, and Pooter lifted him right off the ground.

The woman screamed, and the man with her shoved her out of his way, but I had a pistol in his face before he could draw his, and I felt the awkward metal trigger through the rubber glove. Trujillo tried to draw a pistol but fumbled it and dropped it. So instead of holding a gun, he pulled out his badge and army ID in a wallet and flashed them around. Jerri had crouched, spun, and taken a bead on the bartender. With her other hand, she reached to her ankle and yanked loose the dainty pistol that she kept taped to her calf. She had gotten it past the customs officials. All of us sucked in for a breath. And the man who had shoved the woman out of the way and I locked our glances. Each daring the other. My eyes darted. The woman ran. Pepper, his cane falling beside him, was in the bar and swinging the rifle from one person to the next, and he stepped out of the way to let the woman run past him and down the dirt road. The bartender raised his hands above his head.

The henchman reached toward his belt. For once I squeezed the trigger. And after the slap of the shot, which echoed in my ear, the man looked at me with this dumb look, then crumpled as a red ooze came out of his chest and stained his shirt. "Now you're in it," Trujillo said. He held up his badge so the other two could see it. "Policía," he said.

The young bartender just shook his head, looking like the

scared deer that nibbled on Jerri's backyard grass. He came from around the bar and inched toward the door; then he ran through it. Reynaldo was kicking and screaming and cussing. Pooter's face turned purple as he squeezed, and we saw Reynaldo, likewise, turn purple. Trujillo walked slowly up to him, unsheathed the hypodermic, and plunged it into Reynaldo's thigh. Reynaldo tried to spit on him, but with Pooter's grip, he couldn't muster the strength or the saliva. His eyes rolled back, and he went limp. Pooter dropped him, stepped back, bent over, and said, "I thought I was going to have a heart attack."

"Goddamn, Dolph," Pepper said. "It's that Clint Eastwood one, where he faces these bounty hunters down in this bar."

Jerri had come prepared. We got a tarp out of her car and wrapped it around the dead man—the first man, to my knowledge, I had ever shot. Pooter and I carried him to Jerri's Suburban and tossed him in the back.

Trujillo didn't waste time. He went behind the bar and came back with a bucket of water. He splashed the water over the blood that had drained out of the dead man onto the wooden bar and floor. "Clean up the blood. We don't want to answer questions unless we have to." We all found what rags we could. Pepper found some Ajax, so we scrubbed, washed, then scrubbed and washed some more.

After washing the place down, we carried Reynaldo's limp, handcuffed body back to the Suburban and threw him in beside the bigger man. We turned out the lights and closed the door to the bar when we left.

We loaded up and pulled off our rubber gloves, as if we were ashamed of them, and gave them back to Trujillo, who stuffed them into his bag, but instead of turning back, Trujillo ordered us farther down the road. The land was rugged, and I was afraid that I might steer us into a ditch or an arroyo. I cussed us all. "Look, we're still legal. We take him back across and turn him in."

"You're no longer in the Border Patrol. You can't take him across," Trujillo said.

"So you take him in." Trujillo just turned and looked at me.

"Shit, one of y'all should have just shot him there at that bar," Pepper said from the backseat.

"That's not how we want it," Trujillo said. "We want an execution."

"That's fucking illegal," I said. "It's sick."

"It was our agreement," Jerri said from the backseat.

I drove until we started to see lights. Trujillo said, "The river is ahead. The lights are from some farmers, a little ejido. That's where he would have been staying." I drove a bit farther, and Trujillo ordered us to stop.

Pooter, Jerri, and I dragged Reynaldo back out of the car and into the desert, trying to pick our way through the rocks and cacti. Trujillo followed us and tried to smoke a cigarette. Pepper limped behind us on his cane. Our ankles rolled as the rocks tried to slide out from under us, and I was scared we might all roll down an embankment. We dropped Reynaldo in a cleared spot, and Trujillo bent over him and injected him with something else. After several moments he shook his head, came to, and started cussing us all. Trujillo kicked him. He stopped cussing. He was cleaner and more handsome than Esteban. His eyes weren't beady or perched right over his nose. He had all his teeth. His hair was coarse, curly, and knotted.

I looked up to see the stars. Anything white is easily spotted in the desert dark. It lights itself up. Reynaldo had on a white shirt. Trujillo bent in front of him, and Reynaldo twisted and rolled with the handcuffs holding his hands and arms behind him. Trujillo stepped right along with him. "You see all of us? You recognize us?" Reynaldo stopped twisting and rolling. This time Reynaldo did have enough saliva to spit.

Trujillo wiped the spittle off his face with his good hand, then went to his bag and pulled out something. He walked back to Reynaldo and held up a jar, and in the jar, floating in the alcohol, were the two withered ends of his fingers. He smiled, put the jar into his pocket, and raised his pistol with both hands.

"Wait," I yelled. "Think about what we're doing. This is an assassination. It's a crime. Fuentes never did anything like this." Jerri looked up at me. Trujillo shifted his head back and forth and let that creepy smile of his turn up one corner of his mouth. Pepper looked blank, like he had just been hit by a two-by-four. Pooter started stepping away.

"Fuck you, fuck you, fuck you," Luna said as though a mantra, his last rights, his replacement for a prayer.

"We become a part of all of it. We've reached total corruption," I said.

Jerri started shaking. "Just like Vincent."

"Yes, yes, yes," I said. "That should be the lesson of his life to us. He could have been a great man if it hadn't been for his corruption. Let's not be like him."

"We've always been like Vincent," Trujillo said. "We took him too lightly." He stepped toward me, crossed his hands, and rocked back and forth on his heels like Mussolini. I could see his meanness. "He is us. No different. No better. He was deluded, but he knew what he was doing. He had no options. Now we don't."

"Chinga tú, cabrón, maricón," Luna said, then shifted his gaze to Jerri. "Chinga tu panocha. Tu panocha stinks."

"He's daring us," Pepper said. "What you want me to do, Dolph?"

I shifted my head between them all and saw sympathy in Jerri's eyes and disdain in Trujillo's. Pepper's eyes showed confusion but absolute trust. Pooter turned his back to us and walked off into the desert. "What would Barbara Quinn say?" I said.

"What do you want me to do, Dolph?" Pepper said. "Give me an order."

"I'll give you an order. Shoot him," Trujillo said.

"Nobody here got the cojones. Maybe the bitch does," Reynaldo said.

I stepped up to Jerri, put my hands on her arms just beneath her shoulders, and cocked my head to try to see into her eyes. She raised her head to see, and one strand of her short blond hair fell over her forehead. "Jerri, Jerri, surely now you must see what we can lose here."

"What we can lose here is him," Trujillo said, and jerked his head toward Reynaldo.

"No cojones," Luna hissed.

"You got to respect his consistent meanness," Pepper said.

"Jerri, dear Jerri, this is perverse. It's cruel. Even Joe would know that." I peered close and saw Jerri's eyes water. "What we can lose here is our humanity. We may never get it back if we do this."

"Oh, Dolph, Dolph." She threw her arms around me and whispered, "You're right. You're right, but have we gone too far already?"

"No, we haven't. Not yet."

A pistol went off. I jerked just in time to see Luna's brains splattered across the rocks and lechuguilla. Jerri gasped. Trujillo jumped. Out at a distance Pooter shivered. I looked back toward Luna. His body convulsed, then stopped. We all inched toward him. Trujillo kicked him. He didn't move. "Para mi hijo," Trujillo said.

Pepper held up the smoking gun. "I know you had to debate, Dolph. But the time for debating is past. I did it. I'm guilty. You turn me in, you know what'll happen to me. I'm in for life or I get lethal injection. But the rest of you can beat it. I'll say so on the stand. You do what you have to, no hard feelings here. At least it's all done with now." I looked at Pepper. The confusion in his face was all gone, replaced solely by trust. And I tasted the bitterness of what I had done to him.

Trujillo reached to Pepper and took his pistol. "No one gets turned in. This is Mexico."

Jerri was beside me, her arm around me. "If Reynaldo had killed me, Dolph, wouldn't you have done what Pepper just did? Forget it, Dolph."

I looked around me. "Forget it?"

Joe Parr and Pepper were descendants of cowboys. They could take an action and live with the consequences. I was, in the end, like Vincent Fuentes—all the more dangerous because I was weak. I was the type of person Sister Quinn tried to protect. I was like the hungry wets I used to arrest. I turned to look at Jerri. She was stronger than me, but not as strong as Joe or Pepper. So I looked at Pooter, another weak person.

* * *

I got Reynaldo's blood smeared across my shirt when I helped Pooter and Jerri carry his body back to the Suburban. We put him beside his henchman, probably some poor, weak pelado who wasn't tough enough to yet be a bronco. Some guy hoping to make some easy money. I drove back up the road, past the bar.

After a few miles, Trujillo pointed, and I saw an orange spark off the road. Not much more than a trail led to the orange spark, but I followed it. The orange spark was a giant horno, big enough to roast a whole cow, and it was blazing brightly. We pulled up to it, and its light lit our faces and made us sweat as we stuffed first Reynaldo, then the henchman, and then the tarp into the fire. Trujillo had found some help, some conspirators besides us.

As we watched the blaze, Trujillo gathered all the guns, unloaded them, and then threw them and his bag in the blaze also. The Feebies would never find Reynaldo, and he would become a cold case and a blotch on their record. Case closed. Joe Parr was avenged. Justice was done.

Even if the scared witnesses who had heard or seen the shooting talked, the Mexican police or army would have a hard time extraditing three Americans. And Trujillo's position protected him. Someday, for some reason, some Mexican official might stumble on the bones and the melted guns. An investigation might even identify Reynaldo and the poor man I killed, but the Mexican authorities would know he was a criminal, and they'd interpret the discovery of his teeth and bones as a rival criminal's revenge. And then, if they felt like cooperating, they might tell the FBI.

And if he was never found (as he probably wouldn't be), and if the witnesses never talked (which they probably wouldn't), we had linked Joe Parr and Reynaldo (and maybe even Sister Quinn) and given them immortality in legend. Eventually the Feebies would have to figure out that Reynaldo killed Joe Parr. But they wouldn't find him. Not even the FBI could catch the crazy killer of the great Texas Ranger and the crazy nun. I could imagine the corridos. So silently, well into the night, we watched as the smoke from Reynaldo and the young henchman's bodies floated up and drifted north, toward the smoke and ashes from Sister Quinn and Joe Parr's funerals.

I asked Pepper to drive back the rest of the way. I was too tired, I said. So I sat in the back, next to Jerri, who was in between me and Pooter. After a while Jerri dug into her jeans pocket and pulled something out. She held it up in the scant light so that I could see it. Then she handed me the glass vial that Sister Quinn had given me when I was gut shot. "Maybe you should keep this. Remember, after we burned her, you gave it to me." I stuck it in my jeans pocket. Then, because I needed it, she held my hand; then she turned, looked at Pooter, and held his hand too.

Trujillo, always the gentleman, invited us to spend the night in his house. He shared some of his best wine with us. Pooter slept on a pallet in a living room, and I shared a bedroom with Pepper. He got the bed, and I got a pallet. Jerri had the room where Reynaldo had killed Trujillo's "boy." After everyone was asleep, I walked into Jerri's room. She folded back the sheet and the bedspread. Trujillo had gotten the bloodstains out. "Just hold me, Dolph. Just hold me." They found us asleep the next morning, still holding each other.

We picked up our guns, and on the way back to Alpine, Jerri now driving, me in the passenger seat, Pooter and Pepper in the backseat, just as we started the rise out of the Chihuahuan Desert and into the high, cooler, gentler pastures around Marfa and Alpine, I reached into my jeans pocket and felt Sister Quinn's vial. She started to whisper to me. She was disappointed in me. Then I heard Vincent Fuentes's laughter.

I was retired from a rough business. I had seen too much violence and border life. I was tired of fighting Indians and Mexicans. So like those scarred, wounded, shell-shocked Confederates, Rangers, and ranchers, this Mexican wanted some ease in Texas's oldest civilized city. Then again, San Antonio was presently caught in modern, shallow American culture; I could go there and become something like the majority of the population, not some maladjusted border desert rat. And Jerri was in San Antonio.

God can judge us. I don't care. But how are we to judge ourselves? Sister Quinn had said that in a Christian world, in a world worth living in, mercy should always trump justice. And if prayer is like this great want for things to be otherwise, for the world to be different from the way we know it has to be, I wished or prayed for grace and mercy—for Reynaldo, for me, for all of us. *San Antonio,* the words, sounded like a prayer. And Fuentes laughed.